CW00867903

Dory's Avengers

Dory's Avengers

Alison Jack

AES Publishing

Contents

Acknowledgements

My family and friends have given me tremendous encouragement from the moment I decided to write *Dory's Avengers*, and I would like to thank each and every one of them for their support.

Special thanks go to:

My partner Andy for walking mile after mile of South London's streets with me in search of the Unsponsored.

My friend Wanda for being my number one critic, naming the book and helping to keep my feet on the ground.

My enthusiastic 'communications manager' Bruce for spreading the word, taking the author photo and supplying me with much-needed IT training.

***

Proofreading by Julia Gibbs juliaproofreader@gmail.com

Cover art by James Willis of Spiffing Covers www.spiffingcovers.com

Author's Notes

Although the Lake District in Cumbria is a real place (and well worth a visit), the village of Blenthwaite is entirely a figment of my imagination.

***

The dull Olympic opening ceremony in *Dory's Avengers* bears no resemblance whatsoever to the spectacular show which heralded the London 2012 Games. Likewise, the lacklustre sponsored gymnasts in this publication are not in any way based on the magnificent Team GB gymnasts who make the nation proud.

Prologue

That evening, the fight between father and son was fearsome.

Going about her tasks in the kitchen of the grand old London townhouse, the cook found it impossible to ignore the alarming sounds from the rooms above. What *was* going on up there? Why was the boy screaming so relentlessly? What was that tone in his voice? Fear? Pain?

Both?

Knowing it was unwise to be too inquisitive, the cook hastily closed the kitchen door and turned up the radio, but the cheerful music was never going to be enough to drown out the crashes. Or that awful screaming.

The cook shivered involuntarily.

Without warning, feet pounded down the stairs followed by a shouted command: 'Mooreland, get that mess cleared up.' Then the front door slammed.

As Annie, the youngest of the housemaids, struggled through from the utility room, a huge basket of laundry in her hands, the kitchen door opened and the head of the household staff stood on the threshold.

'Girl,' he said sourly, 'go upstairs and clean His Lordship's office. You'll need a mop, scrubbing brush and hot water. And disinfectant.

'Yes, Mr Mooreland,' replied Annie, dumping the laundry basket in the middle of the floor and pulling a face at her boss's back. Resisting the urge to break into hysterical laughter, the cook instead tripped over the laundry.

'What's going on?' Mooreland swung round. 'You stupid child, can't you do anything right?' Watching Annie as she filled a bucket with hot water and detergent, Mooreland spoke again, his voice low and sinister.

'Whatever you may think you see and hear upstairs, girl, you will ignore. Understand? You will see nothing. You will hear nothing.'

'Yes, Mr Mooreland.'

'Now go.'

Winking briefly at the cook, Annie did as she was told. Reaching the master's office on the third floor, she looped the handle of the bucket over her arm and opened the door.

The sight that greeted her caused her to gag, stagger backwards and slop water on to the floor.

'Oh my God,' she murmured, casting wide, frightened eyes around the room. Screwing up her courage, knowing she'd be in deep trouble if she didn't get on with the task in hand, Annie mopped up the spilt water then moved into the room.

Half an hour later, her task was complete. Collecting her bucket, an unusually sombre Annie made for the door, tempted by the safety of the ground floor and the warm company of the cook. However, her youthful curiosity got the better of her and she lingered on the landing, gazing up the stairs to the darkened fourth floor and listening to the sounds drifting down. The sounds she was supposed to ignore.

What are they doing to that boy? she thought.

A figure loomed from the darkness above, descending towards her. Choking on a scream, only just remembering to keep hold of the bucket, Annie turned to flee.

Too late.

'Interested, little girl?' Slimy hands clamped on to Annie's arms and the unmistakable smell of blood filled her nostrils. 'Want to see upstairs?'

'N-n-no,' she stammered, despising her cowardice.

Her captor sniggered. Annie shuddered.

'Girl, have you finished yet?' yelled Mooreland, appearing from the lower floors. Never had Annie been so glad to see her miserable boss.

'Yes, Mr Mooreland. Just coming, Mr Mooreland.'

Mooreland glowered at the man holding Annie captive.

'Dyer, haven't you had enough... er... *fun* this evening?'

The man called Dyer sniggered again. Violence clearly amused him.

'Let the girl go.'

Inclining his head in deference to Mooreland's superiority within the household, Dyer did as he was told and crept back up the stairs, where the master's son was still yelling incoherently and pounding on his bedroom door. There was a sharp crack and a thud, the significance of which Annie didn't want to contemplate... then silence. Nothing to be heard but the ticking of the master's grandfather clock.

Annie fled. Down three flights of stairs she sprinted, running into the welcoming arms of the cook as she burst through the kitchen door.

'Glory, child, you look like you've seen a ghost.'

'Blood,' gasped Annie, 'everywhere.'

'Hush, Annie, you know the trouble loose tongues can cause.'

'But the boy's hurt, badly...'

'Hush!' Leaning closer, the cook whispered in Annie's ear, 'His Lordship's son is the strong one, you know that. He'll be right as rain tomorrow, you'll see.'

Nodding slightly, Annie allowed the cook to lead her to the table and make her a cup of strong, sweet tea.

Neither of them knew it then, but the cook couldn't have been more wrong. That evening a deep sadness descended on the grand old London townhouse. As the weeks turned into months, the months into years, it was as if the thirteen-year-old boy who'd once brightened its cavernous rooms with his energy and laughter had ceased to exist.

Part One – Louis

Chapter 1 – The Visitor

In Cumbria, the north-westernmost county of England, lies an area of outstanding natural beauty known as the Lake District National Park. Dry-stone walls border lanes and paths, deep lakes charm visitors with their timeless beauty, and lush green meadows sit between majestic fells. A retreat from the hustle and bustle of modern life, the Lake District is breathtaking at any time of the year, but on a warm midsummer's day, such as the day on which this story begins, there's simply nowhere to compare.

At the foot of arguably the most stunning of the fells, hidden by woodland affectionately known to the locals as 'Thwaite's Wood, sits the tiny village of Blenthwaite, a haven of peace and tranquillity. However, Blenthwaite born-and-bred Louis Trevelyan was feeling anything but peaceful and tranquil; in fact, he was feeling decidedly fed up. For the last couple of minutes (or was it hours? Louis was no longer sure) he had been balancing upside down on a pair of parallel bars, waiting for further instructions as his arm muscles increasingly screamed at him to give them a rest.

'Gideon,' he gasped, 'can I stop now?'

Silence from his companion.

'Gideon? Are you asleep?'

More silence. With a fluid movement, Louis righted himself and dropped gracefully to the floor before turning to the slightly built man in the wheelchair.

'*Gideon!*' he yelled.

'Who the bloody hell told you to get down?' roared Gideon, his eyes flying open.

'You did,' said Louis, launching into his warm down exercises without waiting for a prompt from his coach. 'You talk in your sleep.'

'Bollocks,' grumbled Gideon. 'And you were crap today.'

'How do you know? You were asleep.'

'Was not!'

Louis grinned at Gideon. 'You and I both know you were, but then it hardly matters. It's not like I'm ever going to make the Olympic team, is it? That's *your* claim to fame.'

Gideon wheeled his chair backwards and forwards restlessly, agitated by the reminder of his glorious past.

'You're damn good, Louis, so it does matter,' he snapped. 'I'd thank you to remember not all of us still have the gift of mobility.'

Long used to Gideon's strange moods, Louis handed his coach a bottle of water then settled on the studio's large window seat with one for himself, peering through tinted glasses into the street.

'Do you want to go for a walk, Gid? It's a gorgeous day out there, and I've got my sun block…'

'Three things, Trevelyan. One, no to your question. Two, never *ever* call me Gid again. Three, you're late.'

Louis's head snapped round and he squinted hopelessly at the clock above the door.

'It's nearly three, Louis.'

'Oh, crap!'

Grabbing a towel, Louis headed at a run to the studio's shower. By the time he emerged, the towel round his waist and his pure white hair soaking wet, there was no sign of his coach.

'I'll lock up *again*, shall I, Gid?' he said to the empty room. 'Shall I, Gid-Gid-Gid?'

Twenty minutes later, Louis arrived, breathless, opposite Blenthwaite Primary School's gates where Jenny, his six-year-old sister, was waiting patiently for him. Blonde and pretty, although not as fair as her brother, Jenny was immensely proud of the gap where her two front teeth used to be and the imminent arrival of 'grown up teeth', one of which was just starting to peek through her gum.

Squinting around to make sure Jenny hadn't been left alone, Louis was relieved to spot a petite woman waiting with her. Thinking vaguely that the woman didn't look much like Jenny's teacher, Karen Winter, Louis assumed she must be the Trevelyans' neighbour, Jane – with a completely different hairstyle. And a cracking figure – wow, her new fitness regime was certainly paying dividends. And without her daughter, Jenny's best friend, Alex.

No, that didn't make sense at all.

As Louis crossed the road and his erratically behaved eyes finally deigned to focus, the identity of the mystery woman penetrated the jumbled mess of his thoughts and he took a sharp breath. His pulse rate shooting into orbit, he found himself face to face not with Jane, nor Miss Winter, but the woman of his dreams, Abilene Farrell.

Abi Farrell. Olive skin, long, dark hair and warm brown eyes paying testament to her Italian ancestry. Slim figure, beautifully toned thanks to her love of sport. The fragrant, lovely Abi, smiling at Louis as she explained that she'd offered to wait with Jenny – Jane had to rush off, Sponsor paying a visit, really not a problem…

'Er, thanks, erm, Abi…'

Louis blushed frantically and attempted to hide beneath his huge hat. *Oh yeah, Lou*, he thought, *great look. Flustered albino in ancient sunhat pulls exotic Mediterranean beauty. Never going to happen!*

'Are you OK, Louis?' asked Abi kindly, laying a hand on Louis's arm and unwittingly reducing him to a gabbling wreck.

'Thank you, yes I am… thank you, Abi… sorry I'm late… Gideon… track of time… erm…'

'Really, it's not a problem. Jenny and I have been having a lovely chat, haven't we, Jen?'

'Yes,' replied the little girl. 'Miss Winter made us all draw a poster for the Sponsors' Fair on Saturday, and she said mine was the best. Abi liked it too.'

Jenny grabbed Abi's hands and jumped up and down with excitement, while the two young adults smiled at each other over her head. It was a rare moment of ease for Louis in Abi's company, and he silently thanked Jenny for breaking the tension.

'Well, thank you anyway, Abi. Say thank you to Abi, Jen.'

'Abi, come and have tea with us. Sarah won't mind,' said Jenny unexpectedly.

'I'd love to, Jenny, but I can't today,' said Abi, stroking the child's hair. 'My uncle Chris is picking me up soon and we're going to make some poorly animals better.' Looking at Louis and chuckling, she added, 'Or, in my case, attempt to learn how to make them better.'

Struck dumb by self-consciousness, Louis stared back at her without responding. Her smile fading, Abi sighed and turned her attention to what Jenny was saying.

'OK, Abi, see you another day. Will you be at the Sponsors' Fair?'

Abi frowned darkly and briefly; so briefly that had Louis not still been staring at her, he would have missed it.

'No, poppet, I won't be there, but we'll have tea together one day very soon, I promise. Bye, Louis. Take care.'

***

The evening was balmy. Slumped in a chair at his little sister's bedside, Louis fanned himself with the copy of *Wind in the Willows* he'd been reading to her as she'd fallen asleep. It was a good half hour since Jenny's eyes had closed and her breathing had deepened, but still Louis felt too lethargic to move, preferring to sit with his glasses perched on his head, attempting to stir the humid air with the paperback copy of the children's classic.

Jenny had been an unexpected addition to the family; a very welcome addition as far as Louis was concerned. His thoughts turning to his mother, Louis remembered his constant worries over her state of health during her pregnancy. For as long as he could remember, Nicola Trevelyan had passed her days in a tranquilliser-induced stupor, usually shutting herself away in her bedroom and only coming alive on the odd occasion that her husband returned home from his demanding job in London. Louis had been terrified that her unhealthy lifestyle would have a detrimental effect on the baby growing inside her, but to his immense relief, Jenny had been born perfectly healthy.

Smiling at the sleeping child beside him, Louis replaced the book on her bedside table, intending to perk himself up with a cool shower. Leaving the room, he closed the door gently behind him, crossed the landing to the bathroom…

… and froze.

Instead of the big, friendly bathroom with its freestanding bath and antique iron fireplace, in front of him was a room he'd never seen before. It wasn't an unpleasant room, but it wasn't the room he had been expecting, and Louis found that deeply troubling.

What the…?

Glancing over his shoulder, Louis saw that behind him, his family home was the same as ever, the spacious landing surrounding a handsome wooden staircase leading down to the ground floor, the large stained-glass window beyond gloriously backlit by the setting sun.

Glancing back, he was dismayed to find the unfamiliar room was still in the bathroom's place. Never renowned for his decisiveness, Louis stayed where he was, clinging on to the doorframe as if that were his last connection with reality, and staring at the scene in front of him.

Beautiful silk curtains framed two large sash windows. Deep, exotic rugs covered sanded and sealed floorboards on either side of a large four-poster bed, and the furniture in the room was clearly of the highest quality. All this impressed itself into the back of Louis's mind, but what really caught his attention was the young man lying on the bed. Tall and slim, he was sprawled on top of the quilt, eyes closed, forehead creased in a frown, and Louis took in light-brown shoulder-length hair framing a strikingly handsome face. As if he sensed he was no longer alone, the man opened his eyes and looked in amazement at Louis, but almost as soon as their eyes met, the scene faded and the Trevelyan family bathroom was back in its rightful place.

Ten minutes or so later, Sarah Lonsdale, the Trevelyans' long-term housekeeper and more of a mother to Louis and Jenny than Nicola could ever hope to be, climbed the stairs with a basket of laundry destined for the airing cupboard. As she reached the landing, though, she stopped in her tracks, surprised to find Louis clinging to the doorframe of the bathroom and staring into the darkened room.

'Louis?' she said, tucking the basket under one arm and laying her free hand on his shoulder. 'Are you feeling OK?'

'Sarah!' gasped Louis, jumping violently at her touch and finally letting go of the doorframe. 'Have you ever seen anything... er... weird in the bathroom?'

'Weird, love? What do you mean by weird?'

'Well, has it ever turned into a room that's not the bathroom? A posh room, with a bloke in it?'

Even as he spoke, Louis realised how ridiculous his words must sound to the down-to-earth Sarah, but her reaction wasn't the one he might have expected. Instead of teasing him gently and telling him not to be so silly, she asked him exactly what he'd seen, her expression serious.

'Well, the room was full of velvet and silk and, you know, posh stuff, and there was a bloke on the bed, looking seriously pissed off...'

Louis's voice trailed away as Sarah continued to gaze at him in concern.

'Sarah, what happened to me tonight?'

'I'm not sure, love, but I'm glad it's me you told. Sometimes it's wise to be a little cautious about who you trust. Now,' she continued, regaining her composure, 'how about you perk yourself up with a shower?'

Louis looked fearfully into the bathroom, which remained the familiar room he'd known since childhood.

'I'm not sure I'm up for spending too much time in the bathroom tonight, thanks, Sarah. I'll leave it until the morning.'

'OK, love. How about I put this washing away and check up on your mother, then we'll have a chat over some hot chocolate? I hear you saw Abi earlier…'

Sarah always knew exactly how to make Louis feel better, no matter what life decided to throw at him. By the time he went to bed, drowsy from the milky hot chocolate, he drifted into a sleep filled with dreams not of strange rooms and angry men, but of lying in sunlight that didn't burn his skin, running his fingers through Abi's sleek hair.

***

The next day promised to be gorgeous once again, and even Louis, who had reason to be wary of sunshine, felt his spirits rise at the glimmer around the edges of his curtains as he woke. Jenny and Sarah were singing happily as Jenny got ready for school in the bathroom, which was clearly still a bathroom, and the strange happenings of the previous evening seemed unreal in the light of a new day.

'Breakfast, Lou?' said Sarah cheerfully as he hammered down the stairs, kitbag in hand, twenty minutes later. 'I've no doubt that Gideon won't think to feed you.'

'Hardly,' said Louis with a laugh. 'He says I'm too fat as it is.'

Patting Louis's solid, muscular stomach, Sarah raised her eyebrows and shook her head.

'What is he like, eh?' she said. 'Bacon and fried bread it is, then.'

'I wish,' said Louis, thinking wistfully of a pile of bacon sandwiches smothered in brown sauce. 'But let's stick with the usual egg white omelette with salmon, shall we?'

'Coming up, my second favourite gymnast.'

'Second favourite? Who's your favourite, then?'

'Gideon, of course,' said Sarah with a wink.

Sticking his tongue out at her, Louis followed Sarah into the kitchen, noting with surprise that his mother was up, sitting at the table and sipping coffee.

'Oh! Hello, Mam.'

'Hello, dear,' said Nicola. 'How's the training?'

'Good thanks, Mam. How are you?'

'Oh, I'm fine. Is this for me, Sarah?'

'Yes, Mrs Trevelyan.'

Nicola looked vacuously at her plate of scrambled eggs as Louis offered to butter some toast for her.

'Or would you like some Happy Pops, Mammy?' said Jenny, offering her favourite cereal to her mother.

'Thank you, Genevieve, but I think they're for you.'

'Mammy! No one calls me Genevieve any more.'

'What do you like to be called then, my little peach?'

'Jenny, Mammy. I'm Jenny, everyone knows that.'

'And now I know too.'

'Time for school, Missy,' said Sarah, shunting Jenny upstairs to brush her teeth and leaving Louis to attempt conversation with his mother.

'So, how's the training, Louis?'

'As good as it was last time you asked, Mam,' replied Louis patiently. 'Why don't you come along and watch today?'

'I don't think so, darling. That Giddy bloke is always so cross.'

The idea of anyone calling Gideon 'Giddy' to his face was so funny that Louis couldn't help but laugh.

'OK,' he said impulsively, 'at least walk with us to Jenny's school. She'd love that so much.'

It was a high-spirited group that set off in the sunshine towards Blenthwaite's little primary school, Nicola having unexpectedly agreed to accompany her children on the short walk.

'Sun block?' yelled Jenny at her brother as they left the house.

'On.'

'Sunhat?'

'On.'

'Dark glasses?'

'On my nose.'

'Why do you need them?'

'Because of the sunlight – it burns my eyes!'

Curling his hands into claws, Louis let out a howl worthy of the most fearsome monster and raced off in pursuit of his delighted sister. By the time they returned to their mother's side a few moments later, the pursuer had become the pursued.

'Louis's a rubbish monster, I'm a much better monster,' yelled the child happily. 'I'm ever so much more scary. Sponsors' Fair this weekend, Mammy, will you be there? Daddy will!'

Full of energy, Jenny headed off once again at a run in the direction of Blenthwaite Primary, leaving Nicola wondering why her daughter's train of thought had jumped from monsters to Sponsors so readily.

***

'Work it, Louis!' yelled Gideon, fully alert today. 'Work it, hold that, hold *still*, boy! Good. Very good.'

'Enough?' Louis asked breathlessly, having 'worked it' for what seemed like decades. To his surprise, Gideon, in an unusually good mood, agreed.

'Yes, that'll do for today, Louis.'

'Will you wait here, or am I locking up again?'

'Questions, always too many questions. Stretch!'

Having fallen foul of Gideon's mood swings many times in the past, Louis wisely did as he was told and completed his warm down stretches in silence.

'Oh no, not you again,' he said in dismay, opening the shower door and finding the luxurious mystery room in its place.

'What?' Gideon yelled from behind him.

'Nothing,' Louis called hastily, looking over his shoulder to where all was normality before stepping into where all was not.

The view of the room was different this time. The bed was to his right, and sunlight was streaming in through the windows. Discovering to his surprise that he didn't need the protection of his dark glasses in this weird otherworld and his eyes functioned perfectly well for once,

Louis found his gaze drawn to the view outside. Tops of mature trees framed the uppermost storeys of a large and well-maintained red-brick house opposite, and cars that screamed 'top of the range' were being driven back and forth along the wide avenue down below – wherever the mysterious room was, it was obviously a very affluent area.

Looking around for the young man, Louis found him leaning against his bedpost, sharing the view of the street outside. The scene again faded as soon as they made eye contact, but Louis could have sworn the mystery man called his name before disappearing into the ether.

'Who *are* you?' he whispered uneasily.

Having showered, Louis found Gideon still in his favourite spot in the corner of the studio.

'What the bloody hell were you talking to yourself for? You going mad like your mother?'

Louis decided it would be futile to try and defend his mother's sanity. Instead, he made up his mind to confide in Gideon as he'd confided in Sarah the night before, his desire to make sense of his visions overriding his fear of looking a fool.

'Gideon, I keep seeing a room I don't know with a man I don't know in it.'

'That makes even less sense than most of your puerile utterings, Trevelyan. Stop gabbling or stop wasting my time.'

35

Undeterred by Gideon's rudeness, Louis told him everything, slowly and clearly, about the previous night's occurrence then the scene that had just played out in the shower. He had been expecting a number of reactions from Gideon – laughter, mockery, anger. What he hadn't expected was to be believed.

Grabbing Louis's shirt, Gideon pulled the young man close and said urgently, 'Don't you *ever* blab about this. Don't you tell a soul.'

Shocked, Louis found refuge in humour.

'Actually, Gideon, I was thinking of telling anyone who'll listen. Crazy albino has mysterious bathroom visitations…'

'Do not treat this lightly. Don't tell a soul. Trust no one. You haven't told anyone, have you?'

'Well…'

'Who, you bloody idiot? Who have you told?'

'Only Sarah, Gideon. If I can't trust her, who can I trust?'

Gideon regarded Louis steadily for a few moments before replying.

'You can trust Sarah. Be careful though, Louis. Do *not* go looking for the room or the man you have seen.'

'You believe me?' asked Louis, eyes wide.

'Yes, I believe you. If this man appeals to you again, ignore him. He's… it's too dangerous.'

'Do you know who he is then?'

'I am not going to discuss the matter further. Don't put yourself at risk, Louis, and do not talk about this idly.'

'Why? What's the worst that could happen?'

'What's the worst you can imagine?'

'I dunno… something bad happening to Jen, I guess.'

'So don't take the risk.'

'Gideon, are you trying to scare me?'

'Yes,' replied Gideon, 'and for your sake, I damn well hope I'm succeeding.'

Chapter 2 – Sponsors

The heatwave continued into the weekend, and the day of the Sponsors' Fair dawned gloriously warm and sunny. By the time Louis made his way down to Blenthwaite's White Lion Inn to offer help in setting up the fair, the temperature was already in the high twenties and the inn was a hive of activity, with stalls, tents and a large marquee set up around the meadow behind its walled garden.

'Morning, Louis,' called Dex Montfiore, his American accent still apparent despite two decades of running the ancient Lake District inn. 'How's it going?'

'Good thanks, Dex,' Louis replied with a warm smile, Dex being one of the rare people who always managed to put him at his ease. 'Is there anything I can do to help?'

'Absolutely,' said Dex, returning Louis's smile. 'All may look calm, but there's still loads to do. Second-hand books need to be displayed on that stall over there, we need tables and chairs setting up in the marquee for refreshments, the race track needs to be cordoned off for the kids' sports events later on…'

Chatting at a phenomenal rate, Dex thoughtfully led Louis out of the already harsh rays of the sun and into the marquee, where a number of folding tables and chairs were propped up against the side.

'We need these tables around the room, Louis, if that's OK. You sure? The big trestle table needs setting up over there, but be careful – it's a demon for trapping your fingers. Just yell if you need help. We're gonna have soft drinks, tea and cakes in here, and I think there'll be a "guess the weight of the cake" competition too, all proceeds going to the school...'

Dex was still talking as he went out into the sunshine to give instructions to the florists who had just arrived. Louis set to work on the smaller tables first, being heedful of Dex's warning about the large trestle table's finger-trapping tendencies, and local veterinary surgeon Christopher Farrell arrived right on cue when it was the only one left to tackle. Between them the two men got the table up and in place without losing any digits, then congratulated each other on a job well done.

'Do you know which is earmarked as the Pet Care tent, Louis?' Chris asked, looking out into the meadow.

'I don't, Chris, sorry,' replied Louis, 'I've not been here long myself. Wouldn't Georgie know?'

'She would, but she's had to go into Penrith to buy all the things Dex forgot. Ah, here's Al. He'll know.'

Flamboyant as ever, Dex's partner, Alan Santiago, entered the marquee, the ribbon around his sunhat exactly the same shade of pink as his shirt. Where Dex liked to keep his sexuality as *his* business, Alan wore his as a badge of honour, defying anyone even to hint at homophobia. No one was ever going to mistake Alan for a straight man, and that was exactly the way he liked it.

'Guys,' he said to Louis and Chris, 'this room looks fabulous! Who set out all these tables? You, Louis? Wow, you work fast. Now all we need is some colour. Oh fab, here's Georgie with the trimmings.'

Georgia Montfiore, Dex's younger sister, entered the marquee laden with a heap of tablecloths, napkins, bunting and balloons, which she dumped on the nearest table before grabbing Chris Farrell in a warm embrace.

'Get a room, you two,' said Alan absently, padding barefooted over to look at Georgie's purchases. 'Fab. May I?'

'Yes, dig in, Al,' said Georgie. 'Set everything out as you see fit, then I'll change it round so it looks nice.'

'Yeah, yeah,' Alan replied, affectionately cuffing the woman he regarded as a sister. 'We both know I'm the one with artistic flair.'

'Well, put your artistic flair to good use and blow up those balloons,' said Georgie. 'Artistically!'

Grinning at Georgie, arms still round her waist, Chris asked, 'Can you two stop bickering for a second and tell me where the Pet Care tent is?'

'It's the one over the far side there,' replied Alan, dark eyes gleaming with amusement as he pointed to a tent with 'Pet Care Advice and Best-Kept Pet Competition' clearly displayed over its entrance. 'I think love's made your fiancé blind, Georgia. Be a love, Chris, and ask the florist to pop in here on your way past, will you?'

'No problem, Al,' said Chris, dropping a kiss on Georgie's lips then turning to Louis with a knowing gleam in his eye. 'Do you fancy coming to suss out the vet tent with me, Lou? I'm hoping Abi might show up at some point.'

That was all the encouragement Louis needed.

Although the morning didn't bring an encounter with Abi, her uncle was extremely good company, and he and Louis passed an enjoyable and productive time together. Chris's enthusiasm for his chosen profession was contagious, and Louis found himself more interested in the world of animals than he could ever have believed possible. He stored up his newfound knowledge in his head, imagining scenes in which he, cool and calm, entertained Abi with a string of intelligent but witty animal care anecdotes. She would be so impressed that she'd fling herself into his arms, realising that she wanted to spend her life with him, have his babies, grow old in his embrace…

'Louis,' said Chris, amused, 'if you've finished hugging yourself, I could do with a hand moving this podium.'

Mortified that he'd been acting out his fantasies – in front of Abi's uncle too – Louis hastily did as Chris asked, then headed home at a run to hide his embarrassment from the world.

***

The meadow and school playing field were heaving with people awaiting the grand opening of the Sponsors' Fair by the time Louis returned to The White Lion Inn, accompanied by Sarah, a very excited Jenny and, unexpectedly, his mother Nicola. As Director of the Leisure and Fitness Sponsorship Group, Louis's father was the obvious choice to welcome the fairgoers to his home village, and almost as if his family's arrival was his cue to begin, he stepped up to the podium that Louis had helped to place earlier and switched on the microphone waiting there. Handsome and charismatic, Lysander Trevelyan had the crowd eating out of his hand before he'd even started to speak, and not for the first time Louis found himself wishing he could emulate his father's effortless charm and cool demeanour.

'Ladies and gentlemen,' said Lysander, his amplified voice booming around the meadow, 'good afternoon and welcome to the annual

Blenthwaite and District Sponsors' Fair. It is a pleasure to see so many of you here. The Sponsorship Scheme has benefitted all of us immeasurably, and today we gather to celebrate those benefits. What a wonderful day we have too – even the weather smiles upon the Sponsorship Scheme.

'I won't bore you any more with my ramblings. Without further ado, ladies and gentlemen, please would you give a warm Lake District welcome to none other than Lady Rosanna St Benedict!'

Lysander was himself a famous and powerful man, but that was nothing compared to the power wielded by the young woman who now took to the podium. While the crowd cheered as if their lives depended on it, the daughter of Earl Bassenford, founder of the Sponsorship Scheme which had controlled every aspect of British life for as long as Louis could remember, stood calm and composed as a couple of her attendants fussed around her, adjusting the microphone to perfection.

'Ladies and gentlemen,' Lady Rosanna said finally, tossing her sleek golden-brown hair over her shoulders and shooing her attendants away with one continuous flick of her hands, 'I would like to echo Lysander's words. It is indeed a pleasure to be with you to enjoy this splendid fair, and I will not keep you from the fun much longer. It merely remains for me to remind you of a few little rules and regulations.

'All those of you who are of age will have been given tickets entitling you to two alcoholic drinks. Please present your ticket at the bar when ordering – no valid ticket, no drink. If you do not wish to drink, please hand the tickets back to a steward. Do not under *any* circumstances give them to another individual. As you know, the Sponsorship Scheme condones responsible drinking, and anyone spoiling this beautiful day with drunkenness will be apprehended.

'The successful applicants chosen to enter the cycle race will have been informed by email during the last week. Please be at the starting line on the main street with your bike and all your cycling kit at two o'clock sharp. Anyone without the *full* Sponsor-endorsed safety kit will be disqualified, *no* exceptions. Sports Sponsorship and Lysander Trevelyan's Leisure and Fitness Group both condone safe cycling. For the benefit of us all, *anyone* practising sport unsafely will be relocated *immediately* to one of the excellent Health and Safety retraining centres provided by the Health Sponsorship Group.'

Louis, already bored by Lady Rosanna's speech, wondered idly what the Health Sponsorship Group would make of his gymnastic training sessions. Gideon's idea of Health and Safety was to rely on Louis having the good sense not to hurt himself rather than following any Sponsor-endorsed rules.

Lady Rosanna was still droning on, this time about the importance of washing one's hands after handling animals and threatening slackers with yet another enforced Health Group retraining course. Looking around him, Louis noticed that everyone else was gazing at her, hanging on her every word – if they too were bored, they certainly weren't showing it. Feigning similar interest, Louis let his mind drift off into a world where Abi held him close and told him she loved him, but to his frustration his mind drifted instead into an increasingly familiar room in a house God knows where.

The brown-haired young man was sitting at a desk in the corner of his room today.

'Who *are* you?' Louis asked silently.

'Look at me, Louis. Look at *her*.'

'Yes, but *who are you?* How do you know my name?'

'You've got to work it out. Think back…'

'You can stop being so interested now, Louis.' Alan Santiago's voice broke the spell and the mystery man disappeared abruptly. 'The speeches have finished, and the fun's just begun.'

Laughing, Alan walked off towards the pub, hand in hand with Dex. Finding himself conspicuously alone in the area that had been thronging with people minutes earlier, Louis was about to disappear into the anonymity of the crowd when he heard his father call his name.

'Louis, come here a moment.'

To Louis's dismay, Lysander was standing next to the podium with Lady Rosanna, beckoning to him. Looking around for an escape route and finding none, Louis reluctantly made his way over to join them.

'Lady Rosanna, I'd like to introduce you to my son,' Lysander said as Louis slouched up to them. 'Louis, this is Lady Rosanna St Benedict. It's amazing you two have never met before.'

Lady Rosanna regarded Louis's outstretched hand with disdain, as though touching it would violate her in some way. Embarrassed, Louis dropped his hand then started slightly as a voice echoed in his head.

'*Look at her!*'

Light-brown hair. Well-defined features. Good bone structure. Elegant poise. The resemblance was obvious and unmistakeable.

'Oh my God!' Louis exclaimed, hastily adding, 'It is such an honour to meet you,' when he saw his father's and Lady Rosanna's eyebrows shoot up in surprise.

'Likewise,' murmured Lady Rosanna unconvincingly before pacing off to join the party of Sponsors her father had chosen to accompany her to Blenthwaite.

'Don't overdo it, Louis,' said Lysander sharply. 'It sounded like you were taking the piss.'

As Lysander walked away from him, Louis's mind was working so furiously that he didn't even pause to wonder why he never seemed to do anything right in his father's eyes. There was no doubt about it, none whatsoever. Whoever the unhappy young man in the mysterious room was, he was clearly very closely related to Lady Rosanna St Benedict.

Still deep in thought, Louis wandered aimlessly around the various stalls and displays, stopping finally to watch a group of people participating in an energetic exercise class. 'Dance Your Way to Fitness. Endorsed by Sports Sponsorship and the Leisure and Fitness Group,' screamed the huge banner displayed behind the fitness coach, a hard-faced blonde woman who was putting her class through a gruelling warm-up.

'And step – two, three, four – kick and jog and turn – two, three, four – come on – two, three, four – and push – two, three, four…'

'Don't feel like joining in, Louis?' said a familiar voice at his side, and Louis turned in surprise to find that Gideon had wheeled himself over to watch the workout as well. 'If that's the warm-up, I'd hate to see what she puts them through later.'

'Come on now, no slacking,' shrieked the hard-faced instructor. 'Don't think I can't see you at the back – two, three, four – because I can – two, three, four – keep it going.'

'Let's move on,' said Gideon, 'or she'll have you joining in. Hell, she'll probably have *me* joining in!'

Smiling at Gideon's unusually good mood, Louis walked beside the older man's chair into the shaded pub garden, glad to get out of the fierce rays of the sun.

'Fancy a beer, Gideon?' he asked. 'You're allowed two, apparently.'

'I'm not allowed any, actually,' Gideon replied. 'But you go ahead.'

'Why ever not? Didn't you get one of these alcohol ration book things when you arrived?'

Louis waved the two tickets he'd been given. Gideon stared thoughtfully around for a while, and when he replied it was in a voice so quiet that Louis had to lower his head to make out the words.

'Got a bit drunk and disorderly a few months ago. Got a bit rowdy, bit out of hand, silly really.'

'How does that affect whether or not you can drink today?'

'Drinking ban,' whispered Gideon. 'You heard Lady Rosanna earlier – the Sponsors don't look favourably on those who drink irresponsibly, so I have an indefinite ban on drinking in public. Shame really, a cold lager would go down a treat right now.'

'Well, let me get you one out of my tickets,' said Louis, turning to go into the bar and stopping abruptly when Gideon grabbed his shirt.

'You lunatic! The place is crawling with Sponsors. If you're caught supplying an undesirable such as me with beer, you'll be in deep trouble. It's probably only the fact that your father's a member of Bassenford's inner circle that allows you to associate with me at all.'

Louis sat down on the table beside Gideon's chair. 'What do you mean, undesirable?' he asked.

'Shh!' whispered Gideon as Lady Rosanna's voice drifted from the inside of the pub. No longer calm and composed, the young woman was giving someone a very hard time indeed.

'What is this? What are you telling me? You *forgot?*'

An indistinct murmur came in reply before Lady Rosanna continued her rant.

'You cretins! You blithering idiots! How difficult can it be to take the vouchers from them as they buy their drinks? Don't tell me no one's had a beer, I can see plenty of people walking round with plastics full of the stuff. You know the rules we put in place: we need to know who's drinking and how much. How the *hell* can we do that if you don't take their tickets?'

Another murmur.

'No, do you hear me? No! There are children here today, this is a showpiece Sponsorship Scheme event. I will *not* have it associated with drunkenness and loutish behaviour. That's it, the bar's closed. What was Trevelyan thinking, *what was he thinking*, putting a couple of… of… your kind in charge? While we're on the subject, stop going round holding hands! There are children here – what kind of example does it set to them? Unnatural…'

The last word was louder as Lady Rosanna swept from the pub. Louis had the presence of mind to leap from his seat and grab the handles of Gideon's chair, hoping she would believe them to be approaching at that moment.

'I'm sorry, but due to a mix-up the bar's closed,' she said smoothly, her silky voice so unlike the screaming banshee she'd been a few minutes earlier.

'Um… wheelchair-friendly facilities,' stuttered Louis.

'Of course. Yes, they're inside, I believe. Oh, it's you, Liam. Do you know where I can find your father? I need a word with him.'

Without waiting for an answer, Lady Rosanna and her entourage marched off into the crowd.

'Well, *Liam*,' said Gideon, laughing, 'I think your old man is in for a hard time.'

Alan Santiago peered out from the pub. 'Has she gone?' he asked in a stage whisper, emerging into the garden to join Gideon and Louis. 'Did you hear her screaming?'

'Careful, Al,' said Dex, appearing at Alan's side and laying a hand on his arm. 'Walls have ears and all that jazz.'

'Best not touch me, darling,' Alan replied. 'It's unnatural, remember? Bloody woman!'

'They're not all bad,' said Louis.

'No, of course they're not,' said Alan, his ready smile lighting up his face. 'Especially the beautiful Abilene, eh, Louis? Come on, Dex, better go and mingle now we're no longer allowed to serve beer to our thirsty public.'

'Why did Dex tell Al to be quiet, Gideon?' Louis asked, blushing furiously as Alan and Dex walked away. 'He had every right to be angry, she was so rude to them.'

'Will you lower the volume, Louis!' snarled Gideon. 'I know you're not renowned for your observational skills, but surely even you've noticed that people as a rule do *not* criticise the Sponsors.'

'Why not?' asked Louis. 'This country practises free speech…'

'Does it? Does it really? Stop blushing, will you,' Gideon added, suddenly grumpy once more. 'Everyone knows you're head over heels in love with Abilene Farrell. Now, wheel me over there. I want to see what her brother's up to.'

Sighing, Louis wheeled Gideon in the direction he'd indicated. Cameron Farrell was at that moment engaged in demonstrating the fine art of keepy-uppy to a group of adoring children, all watching intently as the young man effortlessly bounced a football on his head. Eighteen years old with dark wavy hair and tanned skin, Cameron very much favoured his Italian maternal grandfather in looks, but his skill with a football was entirely courtesy of his midfield maestro father, the late Elliot Farrell.

'Gideon! Louis!' he said, passing the ball to an eager child and jogging over to join them. 'Enjoying the day?'

'It's all good so far,' replied Gideon lightly, laughing as he told Cameron about the gruelling exercise routine he and Louis had watched earlier.

'It's a wonder anyone sticks with those classes,' Louis added.

'I think they have to. Leisure and Fitness like the folk they sponsor to keep themselves in top condition,' replied Cameron, moving with Louis and Gideon in the direction of the Pet Care tent.

'Do they?' said Louis, wondering how he could be so unfamiliar with the Sponsorship Group headed by his own father.

'Well, yes. It wouldn't be a very good advert for the Fitness Group if its members were overweight. I thought you'd have known that, Louis.'

'Have you applied for Sponsorship yet, Cameron?' asked Gideon quietly.

'Not yet, Gideon. It seems I'm damned if I do, damned if I don't.'

'What do you mean?' asked Louis, more confused by the second.

'Well, I can't have a career in football without Sports Sponsorship, but the moment I apply Abi's going to skin me alive. Of course, after what happened to Dad…'

'Enough now, Cameron,' warned Gideon.

Louis's two companions suddenly became very interested in well-behaved large dogs competing for rosettes outside the Pet Care tent, and he frowned in frustration. He didn't care whether the Doberman would walk to heel better than the Husky; he wanted to know why Abi would skin her brother alive for applying for Sponsorship. In a flash, though, his frustration took a back seat as Abi herself exited the tent dressed in the shortest of denim shorts and a crop-top showing off her flat stomach.

My God, she's gorgeous, thought Louis wistfully.

'Ding dong, who is that?' said an unfamiliar voice beside him. 'I am so going to get to know that little lady better. Hello, what happened to you?' continued the cocky stranger, turning to look at Louis. 'Take a bath in bleach, did you?'

The stranger went on to introduce himself before Louis could react to his hurtful words. 'Max Barrington. Freelance journalist, covering this little fête for the Media Sponsorship Group.'

Louis regarded the stranger for a while before replying. Tall and slim with dark hair framing a strong-jawed face and sparkling green eyes full of self-confidence, Max was undoubtedly good-looking.

'Louis Trevelyan,' he said eventually, not even attempting to mask the dislike in his voice. However, if Max realised he hadn't made a friend of Louis, he didn't seem to care.

'Trevelyan – what, as in Lysander? So, who is the babe? I've just got to get up close and personal with her… Oh. My. God. Don't tell me you fancy her too. Bit out of your league, don't you think, Bleachy?'

At that moment a distraction appeared in the whirlwind forms of Louis's little sister, her best friend Alex and Alex's West Highland terrier Mackie.

'Louis, there you are!' exclaimed Jenny, grabbing him round the waist. 'You just missed Mackie, he was so good in the little dog behaviour class and got second prize. Alex, show Louis Mackie's rosette.'

Squinting over the heads of the two excited little girls, Louis tried in vain to concentrate on their chatter as he saw that Max was already talking animatedly to Abi. Her head inclined towards him, she seemed to be hanging on every word he said, smiling her beautiful smile. For Max. Only for Max.

'Out of your league, Bleachy,' muttered Louis miserably. 'A million zillion miles out.'

***

By the evening the fair had pretty much finished and the organisers were happy that the day had been a success. Lysander Trevelyan left with his wife and daughter as soon as the takings had been counted, a little tired of eager fairgoers draping arms round his shoulders for a photo with a famous Sponsor, and Lady Rosanna departed with her entourage at the earliest opportunity too, declining Alan Santiago's invitation to stay for the performance of his band. Her Ladyship was heard to comment on her way to her car that she'd rather pull out her own fingernails than be subjected to some faggot's attempts to play an instrument, and as a consequence she missed a very fine performance indeed, Alan being an extremely talented guitarist.

With Lady Rosanna and Lysander Trevelyan out of the way, Dex and Georgia decided The White Lion was Sponsor-free enough to risk reopening the bar. At a bit of a loose end now the fair had finished, undecided whether to stay and watch Alan's band or join the rest of his family back home, Louis followed a stream of thirsty fairgoers into the pub and almost tripped over a familiar wheelchair.

'Watch where you're going, numb-nuts,' snapped Gideon, draining the last mouthful from a pint glass. 'You nearly spilled my beer.'

'Gideon, you're drinking!'

'Aye, live dangerously,' replied Gideon with a grin, handing his empty glass to Louis. 'Get us another, would you? My challenged mobility makes it difficult to manoeuvre.'

Taking Gideon's glass and proffered ten pound note, Louis weaved his way across the crowded pub and squeezed in next to Alan at the bar.

'Do you want a beer on Gideon, Al?' he asked, generous to a fault with his mentor's money. 'Or are you about to help Dex and Georgie?'

'I am not! An artiste doesn't serve behind a bar before a big performance. Yes please, Louis dear, I'll have a gin and tonic. With lemon. For the vocal chords.'

'You don't sing, Al,' said Louis, laughing.

'So harsh,' Alan replied, laughing too. 'OK then, for the fingers. And don't say I don't play guitar either, or there will be tears!'

'Two lagers and a G and T please, Georgie.' Turning back to Alan, Louis then asked how come the pub was again allowed to serve alcohol.

'Today we were hosting the Sponsors' show,' Alan replied, nodding at Georgia to indicate that he did indeed want ice and a slice, 'so we worked to Sponsors' rules. Tonight we're freelance.'

'Isn't the pub – what do you call it? Endorsed?'

'Not as yet, Lou,' Dex replied, taking advantage of a lull in custom to join the conversation. 'The Scheme had only been around a few years when my folks came back from the States to take over The Lion after my grandad's stroke. Nanna and Grandad hadn't applied for endorsement – they were more concerned with Grandad's ill health, and coming from the US, Mom and Dad had no idea what it was all about. We seem to get along OK without it. Not sure how much longer, though.'

'Why not?'

'Goodness, Lou, doesn't your dad tell you anything?' Alan asked incredulously as Dex went off to serve. 'People who are sponsored are only supposed to use endorsed businesses. We'll end up with no customers if we don't take endorsement. I'm really not sure how we got the fair today – maybe because your dad grew up here.'

'Have either of you seen Chris anywhere?' Georgie asked, handing over Alan's drink.

'Why don't you go and look for him, Louis sweetie?' suggested Alan. 'Pet care tent's probably your best bet.'

'Louis,' called Gideon from across the room, 'thirsty!'

Struggling through the crowd again and putting both beers on a table beside his coach, Louis told Gideon that he'd be back soon then jogged out into the meadow before the older man had the chance to respond.

***

Chris was indeed in the Pet Care tent, having an animated conversation with his niece and nephew.

'Who was the guy then, Abi?'

'What guy?'

'You know very well what guy!'

'None of your business, little bro.'

'Come on, Abi, I'd like to know too,' said Chris.

'Mind your own, the pair of you!'

'Please?'

Abi burst out laughing.

'OK, you nosy gits. His name's Max. He's a freelance journalist at the moment, but I think he aims to head the Media Sponsors one day. Oh yeah, and he wants to take me out to dinner on Tuesday.'

'And?'

'And I said "Why not?"'

'What about Louis?'

'Why does everyone ask me about Louis when I start seeing another guy? He's not my boyfriend.'

'But you like him, though.'

'He's a nice bloke – what's not to like?'

'You know what I mean, Abi!'

'OK, Chris, yes, I like Louis a lot. As a matter of fact, I think he's damn gorgeous, even more so because he's totally oblivious of the fact, but what's the point? Whenever I go near him, he can't wait to get away from me. He can barely bring himself to speak to me, so now I'm giving Max a go. Get over it!'

'Abi…'

Cameron interrupted before his uncle could continue. 'Abi, if you're going out with a Sponsor now, how would you feel about me getting Sports Sponsorship?'

At this point in the conversation, Louis approached the tent and the words started to reach his ears. Torn between respecting the Farrells' privacy and grabbing the opportunity to learn more about Sponsorship, he chose the latter.

'Cam, I can't believe you asked me that! After what happened to Dad and all.'

'Well, Chris and Mam both have sponsorship, and I want to play football.'

'So play!'

'How can I without sponsorship? The local Sunday League team wouldn't look twice at me without it.'

'Just because Mam and Chris choose to betray Dad's memory and sell out to the bloody Sponsors doesn't mean that you have to as well.'

'Cruel, Abi,' said Chris. 'You know full well that neither your mother nor I could practise without sponsorship.'

'So what do I do? Give up all hope of a career? What are *you* going to do? You're a bloody hypocrite, Abi. You only got accepted at vet school because Chris has Medical Sponsorship.'

'I know that, moron, which is why I've dropped out.'

'Abi, no!'

'Sorry, Chris. I knew you'd be disappointed, but I can't sell my soul to the Sponsors like the rest of you. I can't bear it after what they did to Dad.'

'There's no proof, Abi…'

'Oh, get your bloody sponsorship then, Cameron.' Abi sounded as if all the fight had left her. 'Just try not to get yourself murdered, OK?'

Ashamed at himself for eavesdropping on such a private conversation, Louis backed up a few steps then re-approached the tent, calling Chris's name loudly.

'Hi, Louis,' said Chris, poking his head out.

'Georgie's asking for you, Chris.'

'OK, thanks. I'm pretty much done clearing up. Come on, guys,' Chris added, looking over his shoulder, 'I'll buy you both a beer.'

Cameron emerged from the tent with his uncle and whispered, 'Why don't you wait for my sister?' to Louis as he passed. Torn between desire to spend time with Abi and desperation to hide his feelings from her, Louis remained where he was, watching her through the open tent flap as she collected her things together.

When Abi exited the tent a few moments later, she looked absolutely delighted to see Louis waiting for her, but he was too mortified at having been caught ogling to notice.

'Hi, Louis,' she said. 'Are you staying for Alan's band?'

'Um, er, yeah…'

'Me too. Come on, why not walk back with me?'

Abi started walking towards the pub then turned and held out a hand to Louis, but as usual his crippling self-consciousness held him back.

'Babe!' Max Barrington seemed to appear out of nowhere, sauntering up to Abi and draping an arm round her shoulders. 'Fancy rocking the night away with me? Come on, I'll walk you back as Bleachy seems incapable of it.' Grinning smugly at Louis, he added, 'Naughty boy, Bleachy, I saw you having a bit of a letch at Abilene just now. Good God, man, don't you know when to give up?'

'He might not,' snapped Abi, glaring at the top of the tongue-tied Louis's head, 'but I sure as hell do. Come on, Max. I like a man who actually speaks to me.'

Startled by the sharpness of her tone, Louis looked up just in time to see the swirl of Abi's long, glossy hair as she turned her back, put an arm round Max's waist and walked away with him towards The White Lion. As they disappeared into the pub, Alan's band burst into life inside with a flawless rendition of the La's song *There She Goes*, providing the perfect soundtrack for Louis's hopes and dreams to come crashing down and lie in ruins at his feet.

Chapter 3 – Dory

A couple of days after the Sponsors' Fair, the weather changed dramatically, and by Tuesday morning the clouds had rolled in from the Irish Sea, sitting low on the Lake District fells. Nicola Trevelyan had sunk back into her drug-induced stupor following Lysander's return to London the previous day, and Jenny, unusually for her, didn't want to go to school. After grumbling all the way that she had tummy ache, she dissolved into tears as the first rainfall caught her and Louis by surprise, dodging her brother's attempt to hug her and stalking moodily into the school building without a backward glance.

Gideon's mood was also matching the weather, Louis observed miserably as the older man started yelling before he had even closed the door.

'Where the bloody hell have you been? I've been sitting here like a spare prick at a wedding for half an hour, and you waltz in as if you've a divine right to take the piss. And close the bloody door properly! Do you want me to catch my death?'

'Carry on like that, then yes,' Louis muttered, dragging his kit from his bag.

'What? Speak clearly, Trevelyan! Hurry up about getting changed, you've wasted enough of my time already. I hope you're going to put some effort in today – you were pathetic yesterday. Too much booze on Saturday.'

'I didn't see you exactly abstaining, Gid.'

'I'm not the bloody performing monkey, am I, and *stop calling me Gid!* If I don't see some decent gymnastics from you today I may seriously consider killing myself.'

'A minute ago you were worried about catching your death from cold,' shouted Louis, thoroughly fed up with bearing the brunt of Gideon's moods. 'I'll open the door again if you like, spare you a job.'

'Get on with your warm-up, Trevelyan,' screamed Gideon, purple with fury, 'now!'

Louis's day was as miserable as he'd suspected it would be, Gideon driving him harder than ever before. Nothing pleased the older man, and by the afternoon Louis was tired, aching and totally dispirited by the constant barrage of criticism. When he once again walked into the mysterious room instead of the shower, he didn't even make an attempt to communicate. He just stood by the door, arms folded, glaring at his visitor until the scene faded and the shower was once more a shower.

Stepping into the steaming jets of water, turned up as hot as he could bear in an attempt to ease his aching muscles, Louis immediately regretted his churlishness. The as-yet-unnamed man looked so unhappy; he was clearly trying to communicate, and Louis felt ashamed of being unreceptive. What did he want, though? He always seemed to be in that room – was he trapped? Furthermore, who the bloody hell *was* he?

***

Arriving at the school to pick his little sister up, hoping that she'd got over her earlier bad mood, Louis found her desperately hanging on to her best friend Alex and sobbing her heart out. Seeing Louis approach, Jenny threw herself, still crying, into his arms.

'Well, at least I'm getting a cuddle now,' he said, 'although why such a sad one?'

'Alex… has to… go away… for ever,' Jenny eventually managed between her tears. Picking up the distraught little girl, Louis made his way over to Alex's mother Jane who was comforting her own sobbing child.

'We've been moved,' Jane said to Louis without preamble. 'Trade Sponsors need more plumbers in Bristol, and my Bob's been selected to fill one of the posts. We're going at the end of the week, there's a house all ready for us.'

Jane's words brought fresh crying from the children.

'It's a very good move for all of us,' Jane finished in a monotone.

'You don't want to go, do you,' Louis observed.

Jane was quiet for a few moments. 'No, Louis,' she said eventually, 'I don't want to go. I want to stay here. My husband wants to stay here. My daughter wants to stay here. We love Blenthwaite.'

'Can't Bob turn the job down?'

'Louis, don't be so naïve,' snapped Jane. 'No, Bob can't turn the job down. You don't turn down opportunities offered by your Sponsors, otherwise the sponsorship is withdrawn. Bob would be out of work and we'd be homeless. Whatever happens, we can't stay here. People talk of choices, but in reality there are no choices for the likes of us. Only orders.'

'How about I talk to my dad, see if he can influence Trade Sponsors and get Bob a position in the north?'

Sighing, Jane shook her head.

'Thank you for the offer, Louis. I know it was kindly meant, but that would do more harm than good. If Trade Sponsors got wind of the fact I'd let anyone know I'm unhappy, then it would be curtains for Bob. We must be eternally grateful to our benevolent Sponsors and build a new life for ourselves in Bristol.'

Shocked at the harshness of Jane and Bob's situation, a very quiet Louis walked Jenny home from school, hugging her against his side as she continued to cry quietly. Once Jenny was safe in Sarah's arms, the kindly woman soothing the child's tears with loving words, Louis made his way back out into the gloom of the day to avail himself of the search engines on The White Lion's customer computers. The Trevelyans themselves didn't have a household computer: the bright monitors irritated Louis's eyes so he could never use one for long; Nicola had no need of one; Lysander used his laptop on the rare occasions he spent any time at home; and Jenny wasn't old enough to show an interest in the cyber world yet.

Louis found Dex alone in the pub, reading a letter with a concerned frown on his boyish face.

'You OK, Dex?' asked Louis. 'Everyone seems to be having a bad day today.'

'Yeah, I'm OK thanks, Lou. What can I get you?'

'Better stick to mineral water please, Dex. I'm in Gideon's bad books enough for drinking on Saturday night.'

'Sod Gideon!' said Dex, a grin lighting up his face briefly. 'I need beer, and I'm relying on you now not to leave me drinking alone like some old bum.'

'Go on then, I could do with something a bit stronger than water myself.'

'Tell me what's on your mind, Lou,' said Dex, placing two pints of lager on the bar. 'A problem shared is better than one in the bush, that's what they say.'

Not bothering to tell Dex that wasn't actually what 'they' say, Louis instead told him about Jenny's tears at losing her best friend.

'You're kidding me! You mean Jane and Bob Radcliffe's girl?'

'Mm-hmm. Bob's got a new job in Bristol, so they're leaving at the end of the week.'

Dex paused to have a quick look round the bar, out of the windows and behind the doors. Satisfied that no one was eavesdropping, he bent his head close to Louis and said, 'It's their Sponsors, huh, giving them no choice? No move, no sponsorship, no job, no home.'

'That's how it appears to work, Dex,' replied Louis, taking a long drink from his pint and savouring the taste for a couple of seconds. 'Considering I'm Lysander Trevelyan's son, I don't know much about sponsorship, but I'm learning fast and I can't say I'm impressed. By the way, Dex, people round here seem to trust me, which I'm beginning to find a bit odd given my parentage and the fact none of you trust the Sponsors.'

'We know you, Louis, we've watched you grow up.' Dex paused, frowning slightly for a few moments. 'There is a reason we all look out for you, Lou, but I'm not the right person to tell you what it is. I've probably blabbed too much already.'

'No one ever tells me a damn thing!' exclaimed Louis, frustrated yet again at his friends' reluctance to share anything of importance. 'Who is the right person then?'

'Gideon probably,' replied Dex after another small pause. 'Please don't get mad, Louis, I really don't know enough to tell you anything useful.'

'OK, Dex,' said Louis, calming down at the genuine look of regret on Dex's face. 'Your turn now. What's given you such a bad day that you're turning to the booze?'

Once again Dex paused before handing Louis the letter he'd been reading.

'This,' he said simply.

The letter was on notepaper of fine quality, bearing the Hotel and Catering Sponsorship logo at the top of the page:

Dear Mr Montfiore,

I have written several times to you, the senior owner of The White Lion Inn, Blenthwaite, regarding your continual rejection of the Hotel and Catering Group's generous offer to endorse your business. It has come to my attention that, following the highly successful Sponsors' Fair on July 2nd, you allowed a level of drunkenness in your bar that put both your business and the safety of your customers in jeopardy. It has also been brought to my attention that sponsored individuals are using your facilities, which must be brought to a stop with immediate effect. We will therefore be conducting random spot checks on your premises until such time as I receive your completed application for sponsorship. A form is included herewith.

I trust that you will appreciate the need to proceed in this matter with the utmost urgency. Therefore I wish to be in receipt of your completed application form by Tuesday July 19th. If I am not, I will be forced to consider alternative forms of communication.

Yours sincerely,

Anthony Wright

Director, Hotel and Catering Sponsorship Group

'Are you going to apply?' asked Louis, handing the letter back to Dex.

'Nope,' replied Dex without hesitation. 'My grandad was adamant to his death that this business should never be crippled by the limitations of endorsement. You heard the rules on Saturday: two alcoholic drinks per adult per day, maximum of eight per week. Pool and darts can only be played in front of a sponsored referee, drinking and chatting strictly forbidden. Food on the menu sacrificing flavour to strict Sponsor-controlled nutritional ideals.'

Dex smiled wryly, then added, 'No same sex couples allowed to share a bedroom.'

Louis started with surprise. 'Did you make that last bit up?' he asked.

'Not at all. Homophobia's alive and well in the land of sponsorship. You'll find it thinly disguised as an attempt to instil Christian morals and family values into the minds of the population.'

Dex ripped the letter and application form into tiny pieces, carefully dropping them into the bin one by one. Louis watched mesmerised for a while as the pieces of paper fluttered down, then he glanced over towards The White Lion's bank of computers.

'Is it OK if I go online, Dex? There's something I want to check.'

'Sure, go ahead, Lou,' said Dex, gazing across his empty pub and wondering how many of his regulars had already had the fear of God put into them by their Sponsors. 'That's what they're there for.'

Walking over to the computers, Louis booted one up, hunched over it to shield the monitor from Dex and typed 'St Benedict family' into a popular search engine.

Immediately a list of options appeared on the screen, most offering more information on the Sponsorship Scheme or potted histories, starting with its birth over a quarter of a century earlier. Finally, Louis found a site more suited to his needs and, after glancing over his shoulder, clicked on 'St Benedict family: images'.

Up popped Lord Bassenford, William St Benedict, on the monitor. Most recent pictures were of him and his daughter Rosanna, occasionally joined by a self-conscious-looking teenager. According to captions she was 'Lady Marina St Benedict, age 18' who clearly didn't like to be photographed and was usually pictured gazing at her feet. No sign of Louis's mysterious visitor, though.

Running his hand absently through his thick white hair, Louis clicked on 'Refine your search' and looked for images from further back in time.

Bingo! 'The St Benedict family in happier times,' said the caption, 'before the disappearance of Lord Bassenford's beloved wife, Isabelle (née Isabelle Farrell), and the subsequent breakdown of his son, Theodore.'

Louis blinked in amazement. Lord Bassenford's absent wife was Isabelle Farrell – the same Isabelle Farrell who used to visit her family in Blenthwaite many years ago, shaking off the trappings of her privileged lifestyle for a while in the sheer pleasure of being home. Isabelle Farrell: Chris's sister, Abi's aunt, mother of...

Smiling slightly, Louis realised exactly who his visitor was. Isabelle Farrell had a son pretty much Louis's age with whom he had shared many happy days when they were children. Memories crowded into his mind, including a solemn childhood ceremony they had performed in the branches of a huge old tree in 'Thwaite's Wood to proclaim themselves blood brothers, friends for life. Louis shook his head in disbelief that he could have forgotten.

'Dory,' he whispered, using his childhood nickname for the boy he'd always thought of as Theodore Farrell, 'it's you!'

***

If Louis had thought Gideon in a bad mood on the Tuesday, it was nothing compared to the temper he found his mentor to be in by Wednesday morning. Unlike the previous day, though, Gideon was quite specific about his reasons for launching into a furious tirade the moment Louis walked through the door.

'Do you know what those things are on either side of your head? They're ears. Do you know what they're for? They're for listening. Do you have anything where your brains are supposed to be? I don't think so. Stand over here, boy, in

front of me, and take those fucking glasses off!
It's like the middle of the night in here.'

Surprised, Louis did as he was told.

'Why the sudden interest in Lord
Bassenford?' snapped Gideon. 'I thought I told
you not to stick your nose in! I thought I warned
you how dangerous it is to get involved!'

'How did you know?'

'Search engines on computers show their
recent history, you imbecile. Anyone could have
found out. Luckily Dex had the presence of
mind to check out what you'd been looking at –
furtively, he said.'

'He had no right…'

'He had every right!' roared Gideon.
'Apparently, not five minutes earlier he'd told
you the Sponsors intend to carry out spot checks
on The Lion, and the first thing you do is put his
business in jeopardy by poking your nose into
Bassenford's business.'

'Oops,' said Louis, 'I didn't think. Is Dex
angry?'

Laughing mirthlessly, Gideon replied, 'What
do you think? Mr Laid Back Montfiore doesn't
have an angry bone in his body – he's more
concerned about you.'

'Why?'

'It would seem you're finding out a few
home truths about the Sponsors – the very

people we've been protecting… oh, never mind. We'll get to that.' Sinking his head into his hands, Gideon continued, 'OK, Louis, I've been dreading this day, but I should have known it was inevitable. So, I take it you now know who's trying, in a rather unorthodox fashion, to get in touch with you.'

'Aye,' replied Louis.

'No one knows exactly what happened to Theodore St Benedict, but I'll bet it's not something good.'

'I think he's a prisoner.' Louis was actually in no doubt that he was a prisoner, Theo having given his friend a few more glimpses of his awful life, including one in which he was chained to the bed.

'I don't suppose it's any use telling you not to go looking for Theodore, is it, Louis?' asked Gideon, finally raising his head.

'None whatsoever. Theo was my closest friend as a kid. He has appealed to me to help him, and I'm not about to let him down.'

Gideon was silent for a long time.

'Very well then,' he said eventually, 'as your mind is made up, you need to know what you're up against. You're dealing with a man in William St Benedict who, apparently, will even imprison his own son to achieve his ends.'

'Do you think it's Lord Bassenford who's imprisoned Theo then?'

'I have no doubt about it, Louis. Check the door's locked, then I'll tell you about my experience of the Sponsorship Scheme.'

Once he had returned from a short tour of the studio, making sure that all the doors and windows were securely closed and locked, Louis sat cross-legged at Gideon's feet.

'When the Sponsorship Scheme first took off a few years before you were born, it appeared that it would benefit everyone, from families struggling to make ends meet to businesses looking for guaranteed custom and quality workers. Bassenford and his cronies brought the two together, and before long their sponsorship groups had control of just about everything in this country. By the time people realised how much freedom they'd had to sacrifice to Bassenford, it was too late.'

'What sort of freedom did they sacrifice?'

'Where they could live, where they could work. You've seen what's happened to Jane and Bob Radcliffe – the decision to move wasn't theirs, it was their Sponsors'. Then there's leisure time. Want to join a gym? It must be Sponsor-endorsed so that the Sponsors can take a keen interest in your fitness regime. If you slack, if you don't stick to the programme, the Sponsors pay a visit and put you back on track.'

'How?'

'Persuasion they call it, but it's intimidation by any other name. Then, if that doesn't work, strange things start to happen. A car gets vandalised, a family member gets a beating, a beloved pet goes missing.'

'What, for not getting fit enough?'

'Not just that, Louis. It applies to anything people do if their behaviour doesn't conform to sponsorship standards. No one can enjoy a few drinks, or a bit of a gamble, or greasy food without expecting a visit from the Sponsors' heavies. Every aspect of life is open for scrutiny by the Sponsors, and action is taken if standards fall.'

'Why don't people complain?'

'To whom? The government lent its full backing to the Sponsors' proposals right at the start of the Scheme, and now the Scheme is so powerful that not one of the political parties will dare question it. The police are Sponsor-endorsed, as is the UK media. If people grumble among themselves, bad things happen. Really bad things.'

'Like what?'

'People disappear. Their family, friends and neighbours are told they've been moved for work, but no one ever hears from them again.'

'Don't people ask questions, though?'

'Not if they know what's good for them, no. They realise something's not right, but a lot of people are too scared to speak out now because they think they'll be next to vanish.'

Gideon paused for a moment, and when he spoke again his voice was flat and emotionless.

'Or sometimes they're involved in freak car accidents that leave them confined to a wheelchair for the rest of their lives.'

'You mean *you*, Gideon?' said Louis, shocked. 'Were you sponsored then?'

'To begin with, yes. When the Scheme was taking off I had premises in Newcastle, training young people who showed an aptitude for gymnastics. Some were quite good, although only one was your standard. Then in comes Sports Sponsorship and out goes freedom of choice. The strugglers were dropped, not by me but by the Sponsors, and of course this annoyed me straight away. I will teach anyone who has a love for the sport – they don't have to be the next Olympic gold medallist – and I just couldn't keep my mouth shut on the subject.

'That's when the visits started. A representative of Sports Sponsorship, sometimes even David Foster himself...'

'Who?'

'David Foster, Sports Sponsorship Director. He is to that group what your father is to Leisure and Fitness. Foster or one of his minions would visit and talk about the need for total cooperation between the Sponsor and the Sponsor-endorsed, such as my little enterprise. The Sponsors used the word "little" a lot in relation to my work, a constant reminder of where I stood in the grand scheme of... well... the Scheme! Foster would never fail to remind me, in very reasonable tones, that the future of all my protégés would be at stake if my endorsement was withdrawn, while a couple of thugs added just the right degree of menace by flexing their muscles in the background.

'Yet still I couldn't learn to keep my mouth shut, still I couldn't resist arguing every point made by the group, until one day it was only the thugs who paid me a visit.

'It was a month before I could come out of hospital. Every day, David Foster – and it was always Foster visiting by now, such was my nuisance value – would remind me that I was benefitting from the finest healthcare thanks to the Sponsors' support for hospitals up and down the land. Naturally, Sports Sponsorship had no idea who had attacked me, but sometimes *decent* people got a little upset with those critical of the Scheme. That I could readily have identified the attackers as the thugs I'd seen so often in my gym was of no interest to the group, or to the Sponsor-endorsed authorities, so it seemed no one was prepared to help me achieve justice.

'However, that's where I was wrong. Foster wasn't my only visitor in hospital. Another regular, timing his visits perfectly so as not to encounter Foster, was a young but already famous footballer by the name of Elliot Farrell.'

'Abi's dad,' said Louis, grinning.

'The very same. If Foster's visits were guaranteed to bring me down, Ell's had the opposite effect. We had so much in common: a love of sport, a rather offbeat sense of humour and, most pertinently, mistrust bordering on hatred for the Sponsorship Scheme. In no time at all we became firm friends, and that was the way we remained until the day…'

Gideon's eyes grew watery and he had to blink a few times before continuing.

'Until the day Elliot died,' he said gruffly. Louis opened his mouth to speak, but Gideon silenced him with a glower. 'When I was released from hospital I was allowed to carry on training the young gymnasts in Newcastle, but all the while I had a Sponsor Group heavy in attendance. Foster had the temerity to tell me it was for my own safety – we didn't want me to get another beating, now, did we? Elliot became the only person I could trust.'

'What about your family?'

Gideon's face darkened alarmingly with anger.

'My parents had their heads totally turned by the Sponsors. I was their only child, yet they chose loyalty to their Sponsors above their son. They disowned me, and I haven't seen them for over twenty years. Not even when this happened,' he finished, gesturing towards his irreparably broken legs.

Louis and Gideon were silent for a little while, Gideon preparing himself for the next part of his narrative, Louis digesting what he had already heard.

'You remind me a lot of your mother,' said Gideon, breaking the silence and smiling as Louis gasped in surprise. 'Nicola Brown, as she was back then, was one of the first young gymnasts to come to me for training when I started mentoring. She was immensely talented, and it's no surprise that her son is equally talented. She was also a very bright girl who shared my distrust of the Sponsors from the moment the Scheme first took off.'

'What happened then? Did she compete? I never knew she was a gymnast.' Thinking of his mother's vague allusions to 'that Giddy bloke' a few days previously, Louis realised he didn't even know Nicola and Gideon had ever spoken.

'That's because you've only known her since she met your father. Naturally!' Gideon chuckled briefly at his statement of the obvious. 'Lysander totally turned her head. I've never seen anyone fall so completely in love with someone so wrong.'

'My dad loves my mam too...'

'That's as may be, Louis, but your father's first loyalties lie with the Scheme. Nicola had to change her views very radically, at least to the outside world, and that meant no more contact with an old troublemaker like me. Anyway, that's not really relevant to the sorry tale I need to tell you, young man, so if you'll give me a chance to speak without interruption, I will continue.

'David Foster's visits became more and more frequent after my beating, especially once he realised I'd struck up a close friendship with Elliot Farrell. Ell was a constant thorn in the Scheme's side as he refused point blank to accept Sports Sponsorship and was very vocal about not wanting the Scheme to govern his life. He told me many times how worried his sister was about his public denouncement of the Scheme, but however much Isabelle pleaded with him to go with the flow, he was too stubborn. It's a trait his daughter has inherited.'

Louis shuddered at the idea of Abi falling foul of the Sponsors.

'It may amaze you that the Sponsors didn't deal with Elliot quickly and severely,' continued Gideon. 'The truth was they didn't dare. You see, from a very early age Elliot Farrell was widely considered to be the best footballer this country has ever produced. World greats were watching the progress of this young genius – he was far too much in the public eye for the Sponsors to touch him, and Ell wisely made sure it stayed that way, giving interviews to anyone who asked and keeping the international media focused on him. The Sponsors knew that all hell would break loose if Elliot or his family were hurt in any way, and the repercussions could be fatal for the Scheme.

'But finally, the Sponsors came up with the answer. It was ideal, sending a clear message to Elliot that his insubordination wouldn't be tolerated while teaching another troublemaker a lesson he'd never forget.

'Actually, I think they meant to *kill* me. When I woke up in hospital months afterwards, I often wished they'd succeeded. For anyone to lose their mobility is cruel. For a sportsman, it's pretty much unbearable.'

'Gideon, I…'

Once again, Gideon cut Louis's sympathy off with a glower.

'Elliot never abandoned me. He was there every day as I lay hovering between life and death, and he was there to help pick up the pieces during the long time it took me to come to terms with my new life. He was there when I left hospital, helping me to find somewhere to live out of the public gaze. It was he who brought me to this beautiful part of the world and helped me regain my independence, and it was he who first introduced me to you, Louis. Do you remember that?'

'Yes,' said Louis, recalling a blazing summer's day from the mists of his early memories. He must only have been Jenny's age at the time, but he could still remember his father dragging him by the hand around

Blenthwaite Primary's playing field. Bursting with pride to be hosting an event in his home village for Lord Bassenford and all the top names of the Sponsorship Scheme, Lysander hadn't stopped to think of the damage the sun was doing to his child's sensitive skin, and Louis was eternally grateful to the man who'd eventually rescued him from his plight. Murmuring that Louis would be better off out of the sun, Elliot Farrell had led him into the blissful shade of The White Lion's garden, leaving Lysander free to bask in the attention of his boss and colleagues.

'I hear you like sport, Louis,' Elliot had said, genuinely interested and putting the shy little boy at ease.

'Yes, I like running,' Louis had replied proudly, 'and gym-sticks.'

'Gymnastics? In that case there's someone I'd very much like you to meet.'

A number of weeks later, Sarah Lonsdale had met Louis from school, brimming with excitement and urging him to hurry as they had an appointment. The appointment had turned out to be in the training studio in which Louis and Gideon now sat, then newly acquired and equipped by Elliot Farrell. The footballer himself was waiting for them, beaming as he'd introduced Louis to Gideon and unfazed by the fact that his friend was scowling furiously at the terrified child in front of him.

'Gideon, this is Louis Trevelyan, a talented young gymnast. I'd be delighted if you would take him under your wing. Louis, don't be scared. Come and meet Gideon Wallis…'

'Wow!' the infant Louis had exclaimed at the mention of Gideon's name. 'You were the best gymnast *ever.*'

'Good to see the boy knows his stuff.' Gideon's expression had softened slightly at the child's heartfelt praise. 'Come on then, let's see what you can do.'

Beginning shyly, but becoming more confident as his love for gymnastics overrode everything else, Louis had proved to an increasingly impressed Gideon that he had raw talent. *Lots* of raw talent.

'All right, Ell, you win. I'll indulge your latest whim and train the boy,' Gideon had said as Louis landed with perfect poise in front of the adults.

'It makes sense, Gideon. You can help Sarah to keep an eye on him at the same time. He is good, isn't he?'

'Very,' Gideon had replied reluctantly.

So began the friendship between Gideon and Louis which, although often volatile, had remained strong and true to the present day.

The adult Louis, still cross-legged at Gideon's feet, asked, 'Why did Elliot feel that you needed to keep an eye on me?'

'This is going to sound a bit crazy,' replied Gideon, 'but a few days before you were born, one of Bassenford's inner circle, the revolting financier Mortimer O'Reilly, made a prediction.'

Louis started to laugh, stopping abruptly when Gideon slapped his face.

'Take this seriously! I don't want you to underestimate Bassenford. You must take everything I'm telling you seriously, Louis.'

'OK,' said Louis grumpily, the imprint of Gideon's hand still clear on his pale face. 'Carry on.'

'O'Reilly said that a boy-child would be born before the year was out, a fair-haired child who would bring about the downfall of the Scheme and all Bassenford and his greedy cronies held dear.'

'*Me?*'

'You fit the description. Your father was furious. As you probably know, he and O'Reilly loathe each other, and Lysander immediately accused O'Reilly of being a charlatan. That your parents were likely to have a fair child, both being fair themselves, was a reasonable assumption – although no one could have guessed *how* fair. By the way, sorry,' Gideon added, noticing the angry red handprint on Louis's face.

'How do you know all this?' asked Louis, less grumpy now he'd received a rare apology from Gideon. 'Surely my dad didn't tell you.'

'No, Isabelle told Elliot, and Elliot told me.'

'Did Isabelle believe it?'

'No. Like your father, she just thought it was O'Reilly's feeble attempt to stir up trouble. Unfortunately, though, Bassenford did believe it. Maybe not completely, but enough to put doubt in his mind. Isabelle became very concerned – she'd realised by then that her husband was totally ruthless in dealing with any perceived threat to the Scheme, and she confided her fears to her brother. Elliot wasted no time in ensuring that you would be protected from Bassenford as you grew up, hence Sarah Lonsdale became your live-in guardian. By the time you were born, Nicola was such a sad shadow of her former self that no one questioned the need for her to have permanent help. As she was apparently working for your father, no one questioned Sarah's lack of sponsorship either. Everyone sees the kindly woman you know so well, but few know she is also a very shrewd person who loathes the Scheme – the Scheme that destroyed her father, crippling his business, leaving him destitute and finally causing him to crack and take his own life. Heartbroken, her mother succumbed to ill health and joined her husband in the family grave less than a year later.'

'So,' said Louis sadly, 'all the time I thought Sarah cared for me, all my life has been a sham. She only stayed because she hates the Sponsors.'

'Sarah adores you, Louis,' snapped Gideon. 'Yes, she took the post in order to protect you. Yes, at the time it was her way of working against Bassenford, but that doesn't mean she doesn't love you. She does, you and your sister, so stop being so dense. Now, are we going to sit here talking all day or are you going to put in some work?'

***

As Louis began his day's training, a dejected Jenny sat in her classroom, an empty chair at her side. During the night, Bob, Jane and Alex Radcliffe had disappeared from their house in Blenthwaite, and by the time Louis walked his little sister home from school, their furniture was already travelling south in a removal van. A small group of people had gathered outside the Radcliffes' former home, talking earnestly, no one wanting to be the first to voice the suspicion that they'd never see or hear from the family again.

His resolve hardening, Louis made a silent vow.

Mortimer O'Reilly, you might just have been right. This can't go on happening, and if I'm the one to stop it, then so be it.

Chapter 4 – Abi Confesses

The warm weather returned for the start of the school summer break, and for a while Louis was distracted from his newfound burden by Jenny's excitement at being let loose for six weeks of fun in the sun. With the resilience of childhood, Jenny had taken the loss of her best friend on the chin, and as new pursuits took the place of Alex in her life, her memories of the Radcliffes began to fade. Louis wasn't so lucky, being only too aware that nobody had managed to contact Jane and Bob since their sudden departure from Blenthwaite. Both their mobile phones went straight to voicemail when called, and emails were returned unread from a now-obsolete email account.

And that wasn't the only thing bothering Louis. As the summer deepened, so did his irritation with the conceited Max Barrington – everywhere he turned, his rival for Abi's affections seemed to be there. Towards the end of July, when Max had followed him from the gates of his home to the doors of Gideon's gym for the fifth time in as many days, Louis's temper finally snapped and he asked pointedly if it was really Abi Max fancied, or whether the journalist was developing a taste for his own gender.

'Don't fret, Bleachy my old mate,' Max replied with a smug smile, 'you're not my type.'

'Well, leave me a-fucking-lone, then!'

Bursting into the gym and slamming the door in Max's good-looking face, Louis threw his kit bag across the floor and grumbled his woes to his mentor.

'He's not very subtle, this Max character,' Gideon replied with a chuckle. 'I think the Sponsors' patience will soon run out.'

Louis cast Gideon a quizzical look.

'Good job you're sporty, Louis, because you're very thick,' said Gideon, rude as ever. 'The Sponsors are watching you, remember? As long as it's someone as inept as Barrington on the case, we've no immediate cause for concern.'

Louis realised the truth in Gideon's words, but it didn't lessen his irritation at finding Max waiting for him when he left the gym at the end of the day.

'You *again*. Don't you have a life of your own?'

'Just trying to be friendly, Lewis,' replied Max. Louis cringed at the mispronunciation of his name and made a mental note not to annoy Gideon by calling him 'Gid' any more. 'I'd love to write an article about your training. Would it be OK to drop by and watch sometime?'

'No,' replied Louis shortly, walking away. Undeterred, Max followed.

'Oh go on, Lewis, I'd be good as gold. It'd be a wheeze, and I'd so love to meet this mystery mentor of yours.'

'Rest assured, he would *not* like to meet you, and my name's not Lewis!'

'Bleachy, then.'

'Oh, for God's sake!' Breaking into a run, Louis sprinted home and collided headlong with Sarah as she got out of her car.

'Gideon can't be working you hard enough if you've got that much energy at the end of the day!' she exclaimed.

'Barrington,' gasped Louis. 'He won't leave me alone, it's doing my head in.'

'Oh yes,' said Sarah, grinning. 'Max the Unsubtle. I shouldn't worry, I don't think he'll be around for much longer.'

'That's what Gideon said, but he's driving me mad.' Then, with an abrupt change of subject, Louis asked, 'When are we going to London?'

Far too wily to be wrong-footed that easily, Sarah assured him that they would go as soon as she could get things organised.

'We will go, though, won't we? You promised.'

Sarah had indeed promised to take Louis to London. When he had told her of his enlightening chat with Gideon, he'd also let her know everything that had preceded it, including the mysterious visions of Theo trapped in his room. The more his friend called to him for help, the more anxious Louis became to answer that call, but having protected him for his entire life, Sarah wasn't going to let him take the trip alone. There was also no way she was going to leave Jenny unguarded in Blenthwaite, so the child would have to come too.

'You know it takes planning, Louis,' she said, realising she would have to plan fast before the increasingly impatient young man took matters into his own hands.

***

While Sarah was reasoning with Louis, Max was trying a different tactic in his bid to learn more about the gymnast. He had been ordered by Lord Bassenford himself to observe and report on everything Louis was doing, and was determined to make the right impression with an accurate and detailed account. Lying in the sun next to Abi, her head on his chest as he stroked her hair, Max decided she was mellowed enough by his attentions and began asking questions.

'How long have you known Louis Trevelyan?'

'Most of my life, on and off. Why?'

'Do you know that bloke who trains him too? I heard he was a friend of your dad's.'

'I know of him,' she replied cautiously, alarm bells ringing in her head.

'Have you ever seen Trevelyan train? Is he good? Why doesn't he get sponsorship given who his father is?' Now he was getting into his stride, Max's questions came thick and fast until Abi, irritated, pushed him away and leapt to her feet.

'If you want to know about Louis, go and ask Louis,' she snapped, turning on her heel and sprinting over the meadow towards the village.

Arriving home, Abi gave herself a few seconds to get her breath back, then went into the living room where her mother, Dr Jessica Donatelli, was deep in conversation with Sarah Lonsdale.

'I don't like it,' Jess was saying.

'Hi, Sarah,' said Abi. 'Hi, Mam. What don't you like?'

'You tell her please, Sarah. Everything.'

Sarah turned to Abi and did as Jess had asked, telling her all about Louis's determination to travel to London and find Theo.

'Does Louis know how formidable an enemy the Sponsors can be?' Abi asked, concerned. 'Does he know what happened to my dad?'

'He knows the basics, but it might dissuade him from this madcap idea if you talked to him.'

'I doubt it,' said Abi, pulling a face. 'I don't think Louis likes me much.'

'What?' Sarah nearly shrieked in surprise. 'Do you really think that?'

'Well, yes. Why?'

'Abi, you have got to be the only person in Blenthwaite who doesn't know, then. Louis fancies you like crazy.'

'You're joking!'

'Never been more serious.'

'So why won't he speak to me? He pretty much runs in the opposite direction whenever I go near him.'

'He doesn't want you to guess how he feels. He's so desperately self-conscious.'

'Why?'

'Because – well, he feels like he doesn't fit in. He was quite badly bullied at school because of his albinism, I'm sorry to say.'

Abi snorted in disgust. 'People are such dicks sometimes,' she said. 'They were probably only jealous.'

'That's what I've been telling him for years, but I guess it's hard to stay positive when you're ridiculed on a daily basis for being a little different.'

'What about that girlfriend he had in the sixth form?'

'Briony? Yes, she was a nice kid.'

'That must have lifted his confidence.'

'It did. Shame she and her family were moved to Manchester.'

'Bloody Sponsors!' said Abi with feeling.

'My sentiments exactly.'

'Didn't they keep in touch? Manchester isn't that far away.'

'Not that I know of. It was all coming to a natural end by the time Briony left the area anyway.'

Abi gave a wry smile. 'I have to confess, I was so jealous of her at the time.'

'What, for being moved to Manchester?'

'No! For being Louis's girlfriend.'

Sarah's head snapped round and she gaped at the young woman.

'Are you telling me you…'

'Aye, Sarah, I fancy the pants off him too. I'd have to be blind not to. Fit as…'

'Abilene!' warned Jess.

'Relax, Mam, I was going to say fit as f… f…' Abi waved her hand around, her eyes gleaming, 'fit as a foxy… er… fit fella.'

'Of course you were, dear.'

The three women laughed together, Abi's mind spinning with thoughts of exactly what she was going to do with Louis Trevelyan next time she saw him.

'Mam,' she said, turning to Jess, 'you still haven't answered my question. What don't you like?'

Jess's smile vanished abruptly. Sarah answered for her.

'Max Barrington is causing us problems. He won't leave Louis alone.'

'Tell me about it! I just left him; all he'll talk about is Louis.'

'Have you fallen out with Max then, darling?' asked Jess hopefully.

'I wouldn't say we've fallen out exactly,' said Abi, narrowing her eyes suspiciously. 'But I certainly won't be going on any more dates with him. I'd decided that even before I knew I'd got a chance with Louis – I've had enough of Max's over-inflated opinion of himself. And his wandering hands.'

'Ah,' said Sarah, 'that could present us with a bit of a problem.'

'Why?'

'Because if I'm to get Louis out of Blenthwaite unnoticed, we'll need someone to distract Max.'

'OK, I get it,' said Abi, folding her arms. 'You want me to act as a decoy.'

'Could you not bring yourself to spend time with him? Just till Louis and I get back from this crazy trip to London.'

'Doing what? He's not got a very long attention span, you know.'

Sarah fell silent and Jess dropped her eyes, unable to meet her daughter's accusing gaze. Finally, Abi spoke, her voice sharp in the deafening silence.

'You want me to sleep with him.'

'I told you I didn't like it,' said Jess sadly.

***

Louis was curled up on the family room sofa in his parents' house, enjoying some rare peace and quiet. Jenny was at a sleepover party for the night and Sarah, unusually, was nowhere to be seen. Flipping idly through the latest edition of *The Gymnast*, he then chucked the magazine on to the table and lay back against the cushions, losing himself in daydreams of Abi. Although he knew she was seeing Max, and was a million zillion miles out of his league anyway, he couldn't resist imagining holding her close, kissing her passionately, running his hands through her hair and… there wasn't someone hammering on the front door.

However, there *was* someone hammering on the front door. Thoroughly fed up at being interrupted just as things with his imaginary Abi were getting interesting, Louis got up from the sofa without bothering to tidy his unruly hair and answered the door to the real Abi.

'May I come in?' she asked as Louis stood silent and stunned. 'I need to talk to you.'

'Y-yes, of course, come in,' stuttered Louis, making a vain attempt to smooth his hair with his fingers. 'Do you want something to eat? Drink?'

'Just a glass of water, please,' said Abi, settling herself on the very same spot where his head had lain a few minutes before. Returning from the kitchen with two glasses of water, Louis placed them on the coffee table then hovered in front of Abi, thoroughly confused.

'Sit down, Louis, make yourself at home,' she joked, patting the seat next to her. As he perched nervously on the sofa, she said once again, 'I need to talk to you.'

Preparing himself for Abi to tell him to back off, she would never love him, her heart belonged to Max, Louis was totally unprepared for what she really wanted to say.

'You're trying to find Theo, aren't you.'

'*What?*'

'Theo St Benedict. My cousin. He's been making contact with you, hasn't he?'

'Who told you?' gasped Louis.

'Sarah,' replied Abi. 'She's making plans.'

'For what?'

'For getting you out of Blenthwaite without dimwit Max and his Sponsor masters knowing, what do you think?'

Louis was silent, mulling over the things Abi had just said. She knew he'd been seeing visions of Theo and didn't appear to think he was mad. She seemed to know more about Sarah's plans than he did – was she a part of them? Finally – and this one lifted Louis's spirits no end – she didn't sound overly impressed when she mentioned Max.

Eventually, Abi asked, 'Are you sure you want to go through with this? Do you know how dangerous the Sponsors are?'

'Yes, and yes,' said Louis, now on sure ground. 'Theo and I were best friends as kids. He obviously considers us still to be so, and I'm not about to disagree.'

Leaning back into the comfortable sofa, Abi said quietly, 'They murdered my dad, you know. The Sponsors. Oh, there's no proof, but they did. Gideon's told you about Dad, has he?'

When Louis nodded his head, Abi continued.

'My dad was passionately opposed to the Sponsorship Scheme. I was aware of that from an early age, although I didn't understand why. I guess he saw where it would all lead – the oppression and the brutality. He was at the peak of his football career and constantly followed by the world's press, and he made sure he took full advantage of that attention, never missing an opportunity to call the Sponsors into question.

'Then something happened which knocked his confidence. Big time. I didn't know it then, but Mam's since filled in the gaps for me. He'd started receiving threatening letters – awful, evil things, getting increasingly nasty until the final one…'

Abi paused, pursing her lips.

'…arrived a week or so after my eighth birthday. It was a drawing of a gravestone with my dad's name and two dates. One was his date of birth. The other was the date of the following Saturday.

'We were at home that day,' she continued, referring to the football team her father had played for with so much success. 'Security was stepped up to the maximum for the match. Nothing was going to hurt Dad during the game, and afterwards we'd be heading straight back to Blenthwaite so he could surround himself with his family until the fateful day was over. Well, that was the plan, anyway.'

Abi stopped again to compose herself – her next words would recall the worst moments of her life.

'In the final ten minutes of the game we were awarded a throw-in directly in front of the hospitality box that I was in. Mam was there too, and Cameron. Thank God he was too young to remember. Dad went over to pick up the ball. He didn't take throw-ins, he was just nearest.

'As he picked up the ball, one of the stewards, who I now know was called Stephen Dyer,' Abi spat out the name, 'stood up and stabbed him repeatedly in the chest. In front of all those people watching the game, in front of the television cameras recording the action for the highlights programme later, and in front of me.'

Abi rammed her clenched fists against her mouth, composing herself with an almighty effort.

'Louis, I had to stand there and watch… and watch my dad die…'

Finally, she gave in to the tears that had been threatening, and finally Louis overcame his shyness. Wrapping his arms around her, he held her close and stroked her back gently as she sobbed on to his chest.

As Abi regained her composure, her sobs subsiding into sniffles, Louis handed her a tatty but unopened pack of tissues from his pocket.

'Thanks, Lou,' she said, blowing her nose. Reluctant to let her out of his arms, Louis was disappointed when she wriggled free and sat back to face him. For a split second he found himself wishing she'd cry some more so he could hold her again, but before he had time to feel ashamed of such an unworthy thought, she carried on speaking.

'The Sponsors made all the right noises following Dad's murder. What a terrible tragedy, how awful for the country to lose such a sporting talent in the prime of his life. If only he'd been sponsored, he would have been nurtured, he would have been protected. Even as spectators at the match were crying over the awful scene they were witnessing, they were already bleating like sheep that it wouldn't have happened if he'd accepted sponsorship – he shouldn't have been so stubborn. He shouldn't have criticised the wonderful Scheme, it made people angry, he got what he deserved. Stupid *morons*!'

Abi leapt from the sofa and paced round the room, pounding one small fist into her other hand as she spoke.

'The Sponsors must have been delighted. And Dyer? He got off with manslaughter! He took a knife to a football match with the sole aim of sticking it into my dad's heart and they called it *manslaughter?* How premeditated do you want it? Of course the Sponsors denied all involvement, and the Sponsored were either too stupid or too scared, or both, to question them. Dyer was paraded to the world as being a lone maverick, loyal to the Sponsors but acting on his own, and without my dad around to keep them interested, the media actually believed that crap. The Sponsors moved on to new heights of

103

oppression and intimidation unchallenged, happy their opposition had been silenced for ever, and *that*, Louis, is why I hate the Scheme so much.'

Tapping his knuckles against his lower lip, Louis looked up at Abi, his expression serious.

'Are you sure?' he asked.

Abi glared at him from the fireplace, where she'd unconsciously ended up using the stone hearth as a soapbox. 'Of course I'm damn sure!'

'I mean, are you sure the Sponsors' opposition has been silenced for ever?'

Returning to the sofa, Abi pulled him to his feet.

'Louis!' she said urgently. 'These people are so dangerous.'

'That didn't stop your dad,' replied Louis, relishing the touch of her soft fingers as she kept hold of his hands, 'so why should it stop me?'

'I'm scared for you, Louis.'

'I'm scared for me too, but I'm going to find Theo whether anyone helps me or not.'

'In that case, *I* will help you. I will do as Sarah asked, although you're not going to like it.'

'Like what?'

'Sarah's idea to get you out of Blenthwaite without the Sponsors finding out. You're going to need a decoy, someone to get Max off your case – and I'm the decoy!'

'What are you going to do to distract him?' asked Louis, not sure he wanted to hear the answer.

'Oh,' said Abi lightly, 'he's been asking all kinds of questions about you. I'll indulge him with some answers. Purely fictional answers, of course.'

'And if he gets bored? Or twigs that you're taking the piss?'

'Then I'll have to try something else.'

Louis immediately guessed what the something else would be.

'You're quite right. I don't like it.'

Before Abi could reply, Sarah burst into the room, slightly out of breath from her brisk walk back from visiting Jess.

'Think about it, Louis!' she said angrily. 'Someone's got to distract Max if this crackpot venture of yours has any hope of succeeding, and Abi's the most likely to make it work.'

'Have you been eavesdropping?' asked Louis, taken aback by Sarah's rare show of temper.

'Yes,' she replied unrepentantly. 'Don't worry, I didn't hear anything I didn't already know.' Her temper fading, she grinned pointedly at Louis and Abi's clasped hands and added, 'Cosy!'

Louis sheepishly returned her grin.

'Unfortunately,' she continued, 'it looks like the time has come for us to head for London.'

Louis's grin faltered. 'When?' he asked.

'Tomorrow?' suggested Abi. 'It won't be long before the Sponsors realise that Max is incompetent and replace him.'

'My thoughts exactly,' said Sarah. 'We can get our things together tonight without Jenny getting curious, then pick her up on the way out in the morning. She won't have time to alert anyone with her chatter then. I'm afraid your mother's going to have to look after herself, Louis.'

'I can look in on her,' suggested Abi, but Sarah shook her head.

'You'll be busy, dear,' she replied. 'I'll have a word with Chris before we go, ask him to tie up loose ends.'

Telling the youngsters she was going to make a start on the packing, Sarah hurried out of the room.

'I'm so sorry you've got to do this,' Louis said, absently massaging Abi's palms with his thumbs. 'You don't actually like Max, do you.'

'No, I think he's a conceited prat. I just haven't got round to dumping him yet, which is probably just as well given the fact I'm going to have to sweet talk him for a few days.'

Louis pulled a face.

'I know, Lou, I feel the same, but while we're standing here feeling squeamish about Max, life's not getting any better for my cousin. Anything I can do to help Theo – and piss off the Sponsors, of course – I'll do it gladly.'

'Not *too* gladly, I hope.'

'I'm not going to enjoy it, Louis. In fact, I can't bear him touching me. Doing anything physical with him will be a last resort, I promise you.' Abi paused, then added, 'If I have to have, um, you know with him, I'll get through it by pretending he's you.'

'All the same, I don't…'

Abi's words suddenly registered in Louis's brain.

'What… what did you say?'

'I said, I'll get through it by pretending he's you.'

Louis's mouth formed a perfect O.

'Abi,' he said, throwing caution to the wind, 'I… er… well… I love you.'

Abi's smile could have lit up the universe, but Louis couldn't see it as his eyes were tightly shut.

'Although I don't expect you to…'

'Shh,' she said, letting go of his hands and cupping his face instead. Louis's eyes flew open in surprise, then gradually closed again as his lips met Abi's for the first time. Sliding his arms around her waist, he pulled her hard against him, his tongue finding hers as their kiss deepened, and a fire that had been smouldering inside both of them for far too long exploded into life.

After a few minutes, Abi gently pushed Louis away.

'Wow,' he said, looking a little dazed.

'Wow,' echoed Abi, reaching out a hand to caress his face. 'Much as I'd love to tear your clothes off right now, the last thing we need is for Max to suspect anything's changed between us.'

Laughing, Louis added, 'I think Sarah might have a few choice words to say if she walked in on us shagging each other senseless, too.'

'I'd be tempted to take the risk,' said Abi with a cheeky grin, her hand travelling down from his face to the rather obvious hard-on in his shorts.

Louis groaned with pleasure. 'You'd better go right now, Abi,' he said breathlessly, 'because I can't control myself much longer. We've got the rest of our lives to make love. The priority at the moment is Theo.'

'Priority. Theo,' repeated Abi, reluctantly withdrawing her hand. Striding from the room, she took her jacket from the hall chair then grabbed Louis, who had followed her, for one final urgent kiss.

'Whatever happens in London, make sure you come back to me safely, Louis Trevelyan,' she murmured against his lips, 'because I love you too.'

Chapter 5 – Heading South

Jenny was delighted to be going on an unexpected road trip. As she and her brother left Blenthwaite and all that was familiar to them for the first time in their lives, she chattered away excitedly, providing a welcome relief for Louis from worrying about what lay in store for him in London. She had an observation to make about everything she saw, which soon morphed into a game of I Spy, keeping her and Louis amused as they passed from Cumbria into Lancashire on the first leg of the long drive south.

Unfortunately, though, when the novelty of the journey had worn off, Jenny's mood changed quite dramatically. Bored and fractious once the Lake District fells had slipped out of sight on the horizon behind them, she embarked on a whinge-fest that was far from amusing.

'I'm hungry. I need a wee. Are we there yet? Are we there yet?'

By the time the car slowed in heavy traffic around Manchester, Jenny was repeating herself relentlessly and driving Louis mad.

'Sarah, for God's sake stop at the next services,' he grumbled.

'I don't think we'll be able to, Louis love. They're all Sponsor-controlled.'

'Oh come on, Sarah, just so Jen can go to the toilet.'

'OK, Louis,' Sarah snapped back, 'but don't say I didn't warn you.'

The next motorway service station turned out to be close, only another five miles or so further on. Sarah parked up without any trouble, Louis giving her a smug look which lasted as far as the entrance doors, large signs on either side of which read: 'Insert Sponsorship Card to Gain Entry'.

'What?' said Louis, shocked. 'We can't even use the toilets?'

At that moment a security guard ambled past.

'Insert your card in either slot, lad,' he said. 'Don't matter which.'

'Err, I don't actually have…'

The guard interrupted, his previously friendly demeanour vanishing in an instant.

'No card, no entry!'

'But my little sister needs the toilet, and my father is…'

'I don't care if your father's the Sultan of Brunei. No card, no entry. We don't tolerate unsponsored scum around here, so get lost before I have to call the police.' Unmoved by Jenny's tears, the guard shoved Sarah and Louis towards the car park, and looked poised to do the same to the little girl until Louis whisked her into his arms.

Thoroughly confused by the unpleasant encounter, Louis was silent as they rejoined the motorway.

'I'm sorry I snapped earlier, Sarah,' he said eventually, 'I didn't know…'

'Of course you didn't, love. It's something we've been protecting you from, and I think maybe we've kept you too much in the dark. The reality is, in the more populated areas of the country the Sponsors control pretty much everything.'

'Where are we going to stay then? If we can't even take Jenny into a service station, I can't see many London hotels welcoming us.'

'All sorted,' replied Sarah with a smug grin.

'Sarah,' announced Jenny from the back seat, 'I still need a wee.'

'We'd better find a field then,' replied Sarah, leaving the motorway and driving deep into the Cheshire countryside.

'I can wee in a field?'

'Yes, young lady.'

'Like sheep do?'

'Absolutely.'

'Then can we have a picnic?'

'Of course we can, darling. I've packed lots of yummy food.'

'Cool,' said Jenny, eyes shining.

The break cheered the three travellers up no end. Jenny was asleep in no time once they rejoined the motorway, tired out by the excitement, and Sarah hummed along to the songs playing on her CD player, leaving Louis to lean his head against the window and watch the world speed by. It was a very different world to the quiet, tranquil one he'd always known in Blenthwaite. The further south they went, the heavier the traffic became, and the slower their progress as a result. Expressions grim, eyes fixed rigidly ahead, no one around them seemed to be in a particularly good place as they inched forward in their sponsored cars to their sponsored homes.

'Where are we now, Sarah?' he asked as her car ground to a complete halt.

'North Circular.'

'In London?'

'That's right.'

'So we'll be there soon?'

Sarah laughed in response. Having had no previous experience of anything to compare with either London's size or the volume of its traffic, Louis couldn't possibly have realised it would still take the best part of two hours to arrive at their destination.

The destination turned out to be the ugliest place Louis had ever seen. As Sarah steered her car into a desolate wasteland surrounded by graffiti-laden garages, the landscape backed by relentless high-rise blocks of flats, Jenny started to cry.

'It's horrid! I want to go home,' she sobbed.

'What is this place?' Louis asked.

'It's somewhere we'll be safe. Don't judge it on appearances, Louis. Don't cry, Jenny. Nice people live here.'

Louis was alarmed to see a strange man approaching them at a run until Sarah leapt from the car and flung her arms around him.

'Rick!'

'Sarah, so glad you've arrived safely,' the stranger replied, returning her hug. 'Lisa and the kids can't wait to see you.'

Turning to Louis, who had unstrapped Jenny from her car seat and was holding her hand tightly, the man said, 'You must be Louis, and this young lady must be Jenny. I'm Richard Lonsdale, Sarah's brother. Please call me Rick. Delighted to meet you!'

Returning Rick's smile, Louis took his proffered hand and shook it warmly.

'Now, Sarah,' said Rick, 'best get the car in here then I'll help you get your stuff upstairs.'

Walking over to one of the garages, Rick unlocked it so that Sarah could park her car inside, then, carrying as many things from the boot as they could manage, they all made their way to the nearest high-rise.

'Lift's working, luckily,' said Rick, punching a code into the keypad by the lift doors. With a ping they opened smoothly, and the four of them stepped inside to be carried up to Rick and Lisa's home. Louis looked around as they emerged on the tenth floor, noticing how well maintained the flats seemed to be. Their doors were nicely painted, windows sparkling clean, often well-kept plants decorating doorsteps or sills, and not a scrap of litter to be seen.

Seeing Louis's approving expression, Rick smiled and said, 'It's all we've got, so we take pride in it.'

'All who's got?'

'The Unsponsored,' said Lisa Lonsdale, appearing in the doorway of a particularly well-kept flat. 'The "underclass". This is where we live. Welcome!'

Hugging each of them in turn, Lisa then led them inside. Delighted to see toys everywhere, Jenny immediately made herself at home and was soon playing a raucous game of Buckaroo with the Lonsdales' children. Louis, far less confident than his outgoing little sister, perched awkwardly on the edge of the sofa and listened to Sarah swapping news with her brother and sister-in-law.

'Really?' said Lisa, unpacking Sarah's food into her fridge. 'They won't even let a child use the toilet?'

'Not without a sponsorship card, no,' replied Sarah. 'You know what the Sponsors are like.'

'Actually,' said Rick, 'we don't have much to do with the Sponsors. As long as we behave ourselves, they pretty much leave us alone.'

'How do you manage? Don't the Sponsored take all the jobs?'

'Not all of them. There'll always be some that the Sponsored view as being beneath them. We sweep their roads, collect their rubbish, clean their offices, that sort of thing. In return, we get food tokens and areas such as this to call home.'

'Where do you shop?'

'We get a market once a week, pretty much supplies us with all we need. It's stuff the Sponsored reject from their shops: misshapen vegetables, dented cans, the less popular cuts of meat. Perfectly good enough for us.'

'It's not the most pleasant experience in the world, though,' commented Lisa. 'The Sponsored who run the market consider it a huge imposition to have to mix with the likes of us, and they never miss an opportunity to tell us so.'

'What about the children's schooling?' asked Sarah, appalled.

'We teach them ourselves, in the community centre over there,' said Rick, pointing out of the window. 'Only the basics, though. The Sponsored don't want us getting qualifications.'

'Why do you put up with it?'

'Because anything, and I mean anything, is preferable to having our lives dictated by the Sponsors. You know that, Sarah.'

Nodding at the truth in Rick's words, Sarah asked, 'Who maintains the flats?'

'We do. We're a pretty skilled bunch, unbeknown to the Sponsors. We have to be – if something goes wrong, no one's going to fix it but us, so we learn fast.'

Later on, when the children were finally bathed and settled into bed, the adults reconvened on the Lonsdales' threadbare but comfortable sofas to discuss Louis's reason for being in London.

'No one's seen anything of the St Benedict boy for years,' said Rick. 'The official word is that he's too sickly to be seen in public, but some think he's dead.'

'He's neither,' said Louis with conviction. 'Lord Bassenford keeps him prisoner.'

'How can you know that?'

'He contacted me, um…'

'Go on, Lou,' said Sarah encouragingly.

'Er, OK. He contacted me with his… mind,' said Louis slowly. 'I guess he's been cut off for so long he's managed to find an… erm… alternative way to communicate. Yes, I know it sounds crazy, but I also know what I saw.'

Looking down at his hands folded in his lap, feeling slightly foolish, Louis waited for someone to speak.

'Why did he contact you?' asked Lisa. 'What, with your father being one of Lord Sponsor's cronies.'

'Theo and I were friends when we were kids,' replied Louis. '"Blood brothers", we called ourselves. He used to spend a lot of time in Blenthwaite back then, visiting his mother's family…'

'Ah, Isabelle,' said Lisa softly. 'Things were different when Lady Bassenford was around. The voice of reason keeping the power-hungry Sponsors in check.'

'Did you meet Isabelle?' asked Louis. 'What happened to her?'

'No one knows, dear. She just disappeared off the face of the earth about ten years ago. We were never fortunate enough to meet her in person, but we knew of her – her kindness was legendary. Anyone suffering misfortune of any kind, Sponsored or Unsponsored, she'd seek them out and offer her support. Wonderful person.'

'Unlike her husband and bitch of a daughter,' added Rick sharply. 'They stop at nothing to feed their addiction to money and power, and without Lady Bassenford to soften the blow they have made life increasingly difficult.'

'For you?'

'More for the Sponsored actually, Louis. They control their minions in every aspect of their lives. God, I'd rather be considered underclass than live like the Sponsored!'

Shuddering, Rick opened another bottle of his surprisingly good homemade wine and offered refills all round.

'So, young Louis,' he continued, sitting down again, 'do you know where Lord Sponsor lives?'

'Not exactly,' replied Louis, 'but I'd know it if I saw it. I can describe what I've seen if you like.'

Lisa and Rick both nodded.

'One time Theo contacted me he was standing by the window.'

Stopping for a moment, Louis looked helplessly at Sarah.

'Go on,' she prompted again.

'OK, I saw a wide tree-lined road. Big houses. The one opposite is a huge red-brick mansion, five storeys high with attic rooms at the top. The road is very clean, and all the cars are shiny. I don't know about cars, but they look expensive.'

'I thought you had bad eyesight,' said Rick, puzzled.

'I do, but Theo doesn't. He's the one in the room, so I guess I'm borrowing his eyesight.'

Lisa and Rick looked at each other.

'Are you sure you've never been to Lord Sponsor's house?' asked Rick. 'Not seen a picture maybe?'

'Never,' said Louis.

Walking over to a bookcase behind one of the sofas, Lisa picked up a magazine. Called *High Life*, it boasted on its front page that readers could enjoy full-colour photos of the St Benedict residence on pages 15 to 20. 'At Home with Lord Bassenford' proclaimed the front page proudly.

'Have a look,' she said, dropping the magazine on Louis's lap. 'See anything familiar?'

Louis looked, and gasped in surprise. There in the magazine was the tree-lined road, the collection of expensive cars, the red-brick mansion, all exactly as Theo had shown him. However, there was also a picture of something Theo hadn't been able to show him: the St Benedict family home itself. Theo's prison.

'I swear to you I've never seen this before,' said Louis, looking desperately at Lisa and Rick. Smiling kindly, Lisa reached over and ruffled his hair.

'It's OK, Louis love, we believe you.'

***

Louis slept remarkably well that night, and he woke refreshed the following morning to the unfamiliar sounds of London starting its day.

'Morning, Louis,' Rick said, appearing with three hungry children in tow and putting the kettle on. 'Cup of tea?'

'Love one, thanks,' replied Louis, sliding out of his makeshift bed on one of the Lonsdales' sofas and tidying his sleeping bag and pillow into a pile. The chaos of three children and four adults crammed into one small flat constantly distracted the apprehensive Louis as he enjoyed his breakfast and prepared to leave, but by late morning he was showered, dressed, smothered in a protective layer of sunblock and clearly procrastinating.

'Come on, Louis, let's get this show on the road,' said Rick as the young man busied himself wiping down the perfectly clean kitchen surfaces. Opening a pocket-size London *A to Z* and handing it to Louis, Rick tapped a map of Walworth with his finger. 'You are currently here. I'm not going to mark the map in case you lose this book – we find being overcautious is the best way to survive.'

Louis stared at the page in the *A to Z*, memorising the exact location of the Lonsdales' Walworth home before nodding at Rick to continue. Flipping the pages, Rick ran his finger over another area of London.

'Kensington,' he said. 'Home to the rich, the famous and the powerful. Lord Sponsor is all three. He could be called a lot of other things too – I won't list them now, but suffice to say none of them are good. Your tree-lined road is this one here.'

Once again Louis focused and memorised.

'Getting from here to Kensington is going to be a problem. The Unsponsored are only allowed to use public transport at designated times, and the next one is two days away. Sarah could drive you part of the way, but the roads in the more affluent areas of the city are closed to all but holders of Gold Sponsor Cards. So, that leaves two realistic options: walking or cycling. We do have a bicycle which you're very welcome to use, but not a lot of people cycle in the sponsored areas so it could make you a little conspicuous.'

'How long would it take to walk?' asked Louis, wanting to remain as inconspicuous as possible.

'A couple of hours, I should think. Probably for the best, though.' Referring to the *A to Z* once more, Rick said, 'You don't want to be stopping to consult this too much, so I'm going to work out as simple a route as possible for you.'

Rick talked Louis through the best route from the unsponsored flats to Westminster Bridge, then said, 'Once you're on the bridge you'll be able to blend in with the other tourists, so consulting the *A to Z* won't be a problem then. Now, have you got a hat? It would be an idea to cover that distinctive white hair of yours.'

Louis pulled his huge sunhat from his rucksack, dismayed when Rick burst out laughing.

'Louis, you can't walk through London in that thing. Here,' he handed over a navy-blue baseball cap, 'try this. Luckily it's a bright day so your dark glasses won't make you stand out. Right, I think that's pretty much it.'

Louis felt sick with nerves, but he swallowed his panic and squared his shoulders.

'Thank you for all your advice, Rick, and the book and stuff...'

'Stay safe, Louis. Be careful.'

'I will,' said Louis. 'Come here, Jen, give me a hug.'

'Where are you going, Louis?' asked Jenny vaguely, more interested in playing with the young Lonsdales than listening to her brother. Trying not to feel hurt, Louis told himself it was for the best as he knelt to kiss her. It would have been far more difficult to leave had she been clinging to him and crying.

'I'm off to see a friend,' he said. 'Bye, kids.'

'Mmm,' said the children without looking up from their game.

Walking with Louis to the lift, Sarah tapped in the code Rick had taught them the previous night and rode down to ground level with him.

'Do you have to go?' she asked desperately as they stepped out into the open air.

'Yes, Sarah, you know I do,' replied Louis, hugging her tightly. 'Please don't cry or you'll start me off.'

Sarah returned Louis's hug fiercely, then turned abruptly on her heel and walked back into the building, leaving him to fend for himself for the first time in his life. By the time her tears had subsided enough for her to present a brave face to the children, she had been gone so long that Jenny was worrying whether she was ever going to return.

***

Louis walked away from the warm, friendly blocks of flats, realising that he'd never think of them as ugly again, and passed shops, markets and food stalls as cheerful and diverse as the unsponsored people who ran them. Beyond the Elephant and Castle Roundabout, the surroundings became more affluent but less jolly, the passers-by all far too preoccupied with their Sponsor-endorsed lives to pay any attention to a pale figure in dark glasses and a baseball cap. There was only one heart-stopping moment when Louis heard a shout of 'Oi, unsponsored scum!' and the sound of running feet, followed by relief when he realised the shout had been aimed at the runners, not him.

Crossing over Westminster Bridge to the north side of the Thames, Louis allowed himself a minute or so to consult his *A to Z* before trudging on his way. Lake District born-and-bred, he always felt comfortable beside water, so it was with reluctance that he left the river behind to make his way through increasingly wealthy streets towards Kensington. As he walked deep into the Sponsors' territory, Louis's nerves returned with a vengeance, and by the time he reached the now-familiar tree-lined road he was feeling rather like a terrified rabbit caught in a vehicle's headlights.

'Oh God, I want to go home,' he muttered to himself, summoning up every ounce of his willpower. He had no idea what he was going to do once he got to his destination, realising all of a sudden how woefully unprepared he was, so it was just as well that no plan was needed. As he approached Lord Bassenford's house, Louis saw that a means of entry was right there in front of him, and without giving himself time to think, he took it.

Chapter 6 – White Rabbit

Remembering the name of Lord Bassenford's head of household staff from the article in Lisa Lonsdale's magazine, Louis walked up to the caterers' van parked in an alleyway beside the grand old London townhouse and spoke with a confidence he was far from feeling to the man in the back.

'Sorry, I got held up. Mr Mooreland asked me to give you a hand getting the stuff in.'

'OK, mate, cheers,' said the caterer amiably. 'Grab hold of that tray, will you? I guess you know where to take it.'

Nope, thought Louis, pretending to trap his finger and buying himself enough time for one of the other caterers to return, grab a tray and head back into the house. Louis followed him in through a side door further along the alleyway and up two flights of stairs, pushing through a swing door at the top to enter a wide and luxurious hallway.

The grand dining room that the caterer disappeared into, Louis close on his heels, was a hive of activity. A tall, thin man with the sourest face Louis had ever seen was barking out a stream of instructions, and household staff were rushing about, making sure the instructions were carried out to the letter. Putting his tray down on the nearest available surface, Louis didn't hang around to take in any more details, instead following his temporary colleague's example and leaving the room without hesitation.

The caterer had already disappeared through the swing door and the landing was deserted.

Now or never, Louis thought, sprinting up the next flight of stairs and ducking into a doorway at the top to assess his surroundings. His luck was holding nicely. Not only had he managed to get into the house without attracting attention, but the third-floor landing was as deserted as the one on the second floor, although he could hear Lady Rosanna's dulcet tones loud and clear as she yelled at someone behind one of the closed doors.

Just as Louis was about to make a dash for the fourth floor, the door behind him opened and he heard a frightened gasp.

'OhmyGod,' he babbled, swinging round to look into the startled blue eyes of a teenage girl. They stared at each other tensely for a few seconds, then the girl's face relaxed into recognition.

'Shh!' she hissed, yanking him into her room and shutting the door quietly behind them. 'I know who you are – Theo's friend from Blenthwaite. Er, Louis?'

'Well remembered,' said Louis, impressed.

'Not really. Theo and I had an albino rabbit when we were kids. We called it Louis.'

'Great. Fantastic. Thanks a lot.'

'Oh. We meant it as a compliment, honestly…' The girl blushed uncomfortably, and Louis took pity on her.

'Then I'm flattered… Marina?'

'That's me. OK, so, what exactly are you doing sneaking round my father's house?'

'Actually, I'm looking for Theo.'

'What, after all these years?'

'Well, yes. Look, I admit it seems a bit odd, but Theo and I kind of lost touch…'

'Yes, there's a reason for that. So, going back to my question…'

'What, why now? Because I've recently been made aware he's in some kind of trouble.'

'Trouble?' said Marina scathingly. 'That's the understatement of the century. How did you become aware?'

'Don't ask! The answer will only make you think I'm barking mad. Suffice to say I'm here now, and I'm not leaving without seeing Theo.'

'At last! Someone wants to help my poor brother. Brace yourself though, Louis – whatever you think may have happened to him, the truth's probably a lot worse.'

'Whoo, scary!'

Marina fixed Louis with a piercing stare.

'Don't take the piss!' she snapped. 'Be scared. And above all, be careful. Shh now, Louis, I'll check the coast is clear.'

Opening her bedroom door, Marina scanned the still-deserted landing and gave Louis a thumbs-up.

'Come on,' she whispered, 'before Rosanna stops bullying her boyfriend and decides it's my turn.'

Grabbing Louis's hand and dragging him up the staircase to the fourth floor, Marina gestured towards a flashing light on the wall and showed him a tag firmly clamped to her wrist.

'I can't go any further,' she said. 'Security would know the second I passed that alarm.'

'Why?'

'Because I care about Theo, and Father won't tolerate that. Now go, Louis. The door will be unlocked. Last one on the right.'

Not waiting for a reply, Marina tiptoed back down the stairs and into her bedroom. Creeping along the bare floorboards of the landing, Louis arrived at Theo's door and found that she had been right – it was indeed unlocked.

'Stop there!' Theodore St Benedict said urgently as Louis closed the door behind him. Continuing to look out of the window, his body language giving nothing away, Theo added, 'Camera, right-hand corner of the room. Whatever you do, keep out of its sight. It'll

129

remain trained on me, so as I move, you move. Get on the bed. Hide. Got it?'

'Aye,' said Louis. Doing exactly as instructed, he crept around the perimeter of the room as the camera's eye followed Theo and dived under the covers of the curtained four-poster bed. Exaggerating a yawn, Theo then ambled over to the bed and sat down, drawing the curtains all the way around and pulling the covers off Louis.

'Good to see you, Lou,' he said, grinning broadly.

'Back at you, Dory,' replied Louis, giving Theo a back-slapping man hug then nodding his head in the general direction of the security camera. 'Lucky that thing wasn't facing the door when I walked through it.'

'Yes, that could have been awkward, but as I spend most of my waking hours looking out of my window, I saw you arrive and made sure it wasn't. How did you manage to get in unnoticed, by the way?'

'Oh, there are caterers outside, delivering a load of food. I just grabbed a tray and tagged along.'

'Nicely done.' Theo grinned again. 'Sharp thinking.'

'Cheers,' said Louis vaguely, his mind still on the camera. 'Are we out of its view in here?'

'Yup. Security is happy that I can't go anywhere from the bed or the bathroom except back into the room, so they're my two little havens of privacy.' Lying back, Theo grinned at Louis once more. 'Believe me, Lou, there's no other reason I'd have invited you into my bed, but we can always go and sit in the bath if you prefer.'

Laughing, Louis settled himself cross-legged, facing his friend. 'No, here's fine, Dory,' he said. 'Good though it is to see you, I'd much rather share a bath with Abi. Or a bed, for that matter.'

'Ah, you've got the hots for my cousin, have you?'

'Big time, and amazingly she seems to feel the same way about me.'

Thinking of Abi, Louis felt delirious with happiness and dissolved into helpless laughter. Theo, pretty delirious at having some friendly company for once, joined in and it was some time before the two of them managed to control themselves enough to resume talking.

'What in God's name happened to you, Theo?' asked Louis eventually. Now that the euphoria had passed, the reality of Theo's situation hit home and childhood nicknames no longer seemed appropriate.

'What god?' asked Theo bitterly. 'I don't see much evidence of a god in the world I inhabit. What happened to me? Where do I begin? I believe Lord Bastardford, the liar, tells the world I lost my mind after my mother disappeared…'

Sitting up suddenly, every muscle in his body tensed, Theo clenched and unclenched his fists repeatedly as Louis waited patiently for him to calm down.

'I can assure you, Louis, I *never* lost my mind,' Theo continued. 'That particular lie is Lord Bastardford's convenient excuse to keep me locked away. I'll not deny I was devastated, though. Mum loved me so much… she *loves* me so much. She's still alive, Lou, I'm sure of it. I have to be – it's the only thing that keeps my spirits up. Oh, and my memories of 'Thwaite's Wood. I go there, you know, in my mind when things get too awful…'

'In your mind? Is that how you did all that weird telepathy stuff?'

Theo stared at Louis, a puzzled frown on his face. 'What weird telepathy stuff?'

'When you got in touch.' Theo still looked puzzled. 'With me, Theo. You didn't exactly invite me over via email.'

'Oh, *that* weird telepathy stuff. Sorry if I scared you – your face was a picture the first time I, er, popped by to say hello.' Clutching on to one of his bedposts, Theo opened his mouth and crossed his eyes in a parody of Louis's shocked expression weeks earlier.

'Dickhead!' said Louis, laughing.

'I'm not sure how I managed that, but I'm bloody glad I did. I guess because my heart has always been in Blenthwaite, it was only natural that's where my cry for help would head too. The only time in my life I was ever truly happy was there, staying with Mum's family, roaming around with you in 'Thwaite's Wood...'

'Blood brothers,' added Louis, nodding.

'Absolutely,' said Theo, sobering a little. 'You promised to be there for me if I were ever in trouble. And here you are, Louis, promise kept.'

After years of Gideon's training, Louis was far more used to criticism than praise, and he began to look a little disconcerted.

'Such loyalty, such commitment. Louis Trevelyan, a friend indeed.' The corners of Theo's mouth twitched as he regarded Louis with amusement. Now decidedly uncomfortable, Louis was fidgeting with his cuffs and glancing around at anything and everything to avoid making eye contact.

'Mind you,' said Theo, laughing out loud, 'it took you long enough to twig who I was, you muppet.'

'Your fault!' Louis retorted, back on familiar ground. 'Why didn't you just tell me?'

'Because I didn't want to force your hand. I wanted you to work things out then decide for yourself whether to come and find me or not. If I'd turned up in your head...'

'It was my bathroom, actually,' said Louis.

'Really? I'm jolly glad you weren't having a dump.' Chuckling, Theo continued, 'As I was saying before you started obsessing about details, if I'd turned up and said, "Hello, Louis, it's your old chum Dory and I'm in a spot of bother", you'd have...'

'Found you a lot sooner!' Louis shook his head at Theo. 'How was I supposed to work it out for myself? You always let me believe your surname was Farrell, not St Benedict. And you're titled too, I suppose, *Lord* Theodore.'

'That's generally the case with the offspring of the aristocracy.' Theo sniffed derisively. 'How I wish I didn't belong to this damn family. Even Marina's given up on me.'

'She hasn't.'

'How do you know?'

'She caught me sneaking in, gave me a few hints to see me the final stage of the way. Your father...'

'He's not my bloody father!'

Louis grinned and amended his words. 'OK, Lord Bastardford has put an electronic tag on her. If she passes the top of the stairs to this floor, the alarms will go off.'

'My gosh, security would tear her apart. If you see her on the way out, Lou, tell her *never* to risk it.' Then Theo's face broke into a huge grin as he realised his little sister did, in actual fact, still care for him.

'Please tell her I love her, will you, Lou? Tell her that knowing someone in this house gives a damn about me will make the world of difference. Tell her...'

'I don't think we'll have the chance for an in-depth chat, Theo.'

'Why not? You obviously talked on your way in. Incidentally, how did she know you weren't a burglar?'

'She remembered me,' replied Louis, casting Theo an accusatory look. 'Something to do with an albino rabbit.'

Theo snorted with laughter.

'Oh yes, Bunny-hop Louis. Now he was a character. We named him after you, you know...'

'I had guessed that. Can't think why he reminded you of me.'

'I'd have said it was obvious – the big teeth and twitchy nose, of course.'

Theo started to laugh again as a concerned-looking Louis put a hand up to his nose, then stopped abruptly and grabbed his arm.

'Shh, hide. Get under here, Lou.'

As Theo piled his bedclothes on top of his friend, the bedroom door opened.

'Food,' said an unpleasant voice. 'Personally I'd let you starve, you little shit.'

The curtains were pulled back, and Louis felt Theo's weight leave the bed.

'Ah, Mr Dyer, always a pleasure,' said Theo smoothly. 'Now, if you'd be so kind as to remove your hands from my collar, I really can't wait to tuck into this sumptuous feast.'

'You ungrateful fuck! You think you're so lah-di-dah.'

Louis heard Dyer walk towards the door, then he spoke again. This time his voice was triumphant.

'I'm busy tonight, but we'll have a bit of *physical* time soon. Have a nice little fuck, you little fuck, eh?'

Chuckling nastily, Dyer left the room and closed the door behind him. Still shielded from the security camera by the bed curtains that remained closed, Louis lifted the pile of blankets from his head.

'Surely that wasn't *Stephen* Dyer, was it?'

'The lowlife who murdered my uncle Elliot? Yes, that was Stephen Dyer. Do you want some food? *Stay there*, Louis – camera!'

Louis froze while Theo lifted the tray from the trolley Dyer had left and placed it on the bed, closing the curtain behind him. 'Mmm, this looks good,' he said, removing the tray's lid to reveal some of the food the caterers had delivered earlier. 'Help yourself, Lou.'

'What did Dyer mean by physical time?' asked Louis, tucking into a chicken leg.

'Don't worry about that. These beef and Yorkshire pudding things are delicious.'

'Tell me, Theo.'

Silence.

'Does that creep rape you?'

His quick temper flaring, Theo hurled his half-eaten Yorkshire pudding down, scattering cold roast beef and horseradish sauce across the tray, and fixed Louis with a glare.

'What good can it do you to know?' he snapped. 'I don't want to talk about that. We've far more important things to discuss before you have to go.'

Stuffing the beef back into the Yorkshire pudding, Theo nibbled on it moodily, still glowering at his companion.

Louis was undeterred. 'We could take him out when he comes back,' he suggested eagerly, jabbing the air with his fists to emphasise his point. 'Bish, bash, bosh! God, I'd love to give him the big boot in the bollocks on Abi's behalf…'

'*Camera*, Louis!' Theo said again, unable to keep himself from smiling at his friend's enthusiasm. 'Much as I applaud your sentiments, security would have us both in a stranglehold before you could blink.' Softening at Louis's downcast expression, Theo patted him on the arm. 'I know your intentions are good, Lou, but you've got to realise who we're up against here. These people are evil, and the most evil of the lot is Earl Bassenford.'

'You never call him "Dad", do you.'

'No. I used to, but not now. Once upon a time, he claimed he loved me.' Shaking his head sadly, Theo added, 'I won't ever fall for *that* lie again.'

The two friends ate in silence for a while, then Theo replaced the empty tray on the trolley.

'Back under the covers, Lou. Someone will come to collect this as soon as they see I've finished.'

True to Theo's words, Stephen Dyer returned within a couple of minutes.

'Pigged out tonight, haven't yer, shit brains,' he drawled. 'Keeping yer strength up for me?'

'Only for you, Stevie Boy, only for you,' replied Theo, voice heavy with sarcasm. Louis tensed slightly as he heard Dyer's hand connect hard with Theo's face. Hardly daring to breathe in case Dyer had noticed the movement under the pile of bedclothes, he was very relieved to hear the rumble of the trolley's wheels as Dyer crossed to the door.

Theo waited until the sound of Dyer's footsteps had faded away before once again closing the bed curtains and pulling the covers off Louis.

'Handy with his fists, that Dyer,' he said, rubbing the side of his jaw, 'who we are *not* going to spend any more time discussing.'

Settling down against his pillow, Theo resumed the telling of his sad story.

'When Mum disappeared, a few years after Elliot had been murdered, my Farrell grandparents were understandably distraught. I used to hope against hope that they'd adopt me, take me away from Lord Bastardford for ever, but within six months, both had died. My last connection with Blenthwaite, my last hope of escape, had been severed.'

Theo paused, a distant look in his eyes.

'But do you know what I believe now, Louis? There *is* still hope. Mum's – somewhere? – kind of trapped too.'

'Trapped? How?'

'Well, she can't just return.' Raising his voice an octave, Theo trilled, '"Oh hi, William, I had to escape because you were making my life hell, but now I'm back." There's no way she'd have left her children with… *him*… if there had been any alternative at all.'

'Was your father – I mean, Lord Bastardford making her life hell then?'

'Yes. It's a particular talent of his. Mum was so kind, to everyone. Even, shock horror, the Unsponsored.'

Nodding, Louis told Theo how fondly Lisa and Rick Lonsdale remembered Isabelle.

'I knew it! I knew people loved her. Sponsored, Unsponsored, it didn't matter to my mother. That, however, was the last thing... *he*... wanted. He wanted life to be a relentless hell for the Unsponsored, keeping the Sponsored so terrified of losing their endorsement that he could manipulate them any way he wanted. The rows between my parents were spectacular. This has always been my room, and *his* office is directly below. I could hear every threat, every time he hit her. I heard him goading her when Elliot was murdered, telling her she'd be next if she didn't toe the sponsorship line, making it harder and harder for her to visit Blenthwaite and enjoy the happy Farrell times. She never gave in though, Louis, and I'm proud to be her son.'

Theo smiled briefly, but it soon faded with his next words.

'After Mum disappeared and my grandparents died, there was no way I was going to let *him* know how upset I was. Instead, I told him I was going to tell the whole country what

I'd heard – let everyone know about his crimes and screw up his dictatorship for good.

'Big mistake! God, I was naïve. It was about then I allegedly parted company with my sanity, poor weak-willed little boy who couldn't cope without his mummy. I've been in this decaying old room ever since.'

'Seriously? You've been shut in here for years?'

'And years, yes.' Punching Louis lightly on the arm, Theo added, 'Don't look so forlorn, Lou. I've got used to it.'

'Hang on, Theo,' said Louis, frowning. 'If you can overhear conversations in Lord Bastardford's office, couldn't someone in there hear us?'

'I don't think so. I'm pretty sure the acoustics don't work that way. Anyway, we're whispering. They don't.'

'It's still a risk, though.'

'Look, if someone was listening to our every word I think we'd know by now. Surely you've realised that security round here doesn't exactly move subtly.'

'All the same…'

'Shh!'

Louis experienced the acoustics for himself as a plummy voice floated up loud and clear from the room below.

'Ladies and gentlemen, thank you for arriving early this evening. I wanted the chance to talk to you privately before the social event begins.'

'Lord Bastardford,' Theo whispered, his face a mask of contempt.

'You have all been with me since the birth of the Sponsorship Scheme. I'll never forget how you believed in me then, and as a result you are the people whose opinions I trust the most now. I would appreciate your thoughts on a certain matter.'

'Lysander,' Louis flinched as Lord Bassenford spoke his father's name, 'I'm sorry to say it's Blenthwaite giving me cause for concern – yet again.'

'Lord Bassenford, I'd like to propose that we go into Blenthwaite and go in hard,' said a nasal and rather whiny voice.

'Mortimer O'Reilly,' Theo whispered.

'The seer?' Louis whispered back, grinning. Theo returned his grin and nodded.

Below them, Louis's father was speaking.

'Your Lordship, what seems to be the problem? If you let me…'

'I've let you too many times before, Trevelyan,' roared Lord Bassenford, 'with little or no effect. I'm beginning to think your affection for that wretched village overrides your common sense sometimes.'

There was the sound of laughter from below, the nasal voice laughing louder and longer than anyone else.

'No, I think we need to send out a clear message. For too long we've let the provinces slip as we've concentrated on controlling the cities, now it's time to tie up loose ends. Right, the problem is this: the Hotel and Catering Group has repeatedly contacted that homosexual running The White Lion in Blenthwaite offering a very generous sponsorship package, but the idiot continues to reject the offer. He's had his chance, and I say we now make an example of him.'

Loud cheers greeted Lord Bassenford's words. In the clamour, Louis couldn't make out whether or not his father joined in.

'What have you in mind, Your Lordship?'

'I think a beating should do the trick, either for Montfiore or his boyfriend. The boyfriend, I think. They consider themselves in love!'

More sycophantic laughter.

'Yes, the boyfriend. I'll get Stephen Dyer on the case.'

Horrified by what he heard, Louis whispered, 'Oh shit! Alan won't stand a chance against that violent bastard.'

Downstairs another man was speaking.

'David Foster,' whispered Theo.

'Sports,' Louis whispered back before Theo could say more. 'Gideon told me about him.'

'Any news from Barrington?' David asked.

'Not for a couple of days, so we'll have to assume no news is good news.'

Upstairs, Louis breathed a sigh of relief. So far, it would appear his absence had gone unnoticed.

'The boy's keen, he'll do a job for us.'

'The boy's a bit thick in my opinion, Your Lordship.'

'Then I'll check on him right now. Put your mind at rest.'

There was a short silence, then Lord Bassenford's voice sounded clearly again.

'Maxwell, listen. I've got my most trusted Sponsors around me, and they're anxious to hear a report from you… Ill, is he?… You spoke to Wallis? Well done. Keep up the good work, and keep me informed.'

Lord Bassenford had clearly finished the phone call, and his voice became sarcastic as he addressed Lysander Trevelyan.

'Apparently your son's ill. Strange you didn't think to mention it.'

'I didn't know,' said Lysander coolly. 'I don't really have much time for Louis. Bit of a let-down as sons go.'

'Not as big a let-down as mine,' snorted Lord Bassenford. Then, a little impatiently, he added, 'What is it, Mortimer?'

'Your Lordship, please don't forget...'

'Your prediction? I know, Mortimer. Lysander, give home a ring. See how your son is, be the dutiful father for once.'

Theo rolled his eyes at the irony of Lord Bassenford's words. Again there were a few moments of silence from downstairs, then Lysander's voice carried up to him and Louis.

'Nikki, it's Lysander, darling. How is Louis? Just heard he's ill... Sunburnt?... Yeah, silly sod, will he never learn? May I speak to him?... No, let him sleep... Love you too, Nikki... Oh, hang on, Lord Bassenford wants a word.'

Louis held his breath, realising with surprise that one or other of his parents had been covering for him, and God help Lysander if he'd only been pretending to talk to Nicola.

The next words put his mind at rest.

'Nicola,' said Lord Bassenford, 'lovely to hear your voice again... I'm very well, thank you, and Rosanna and Marina are fine, but Theodore's not so good, poor thing.'

Theo curled his lip as the man he'd never again call 'Dad' chuckled.

'I understand your Louis's been sunbathing. Doesn't he have, um…'

'A rabbit named after him,' murmured Louis, glancing at Theo.

'…Albinism, that's it. I should think he is sore.'

Lord Bassenford said his goodbyes to Nicola, then his mockery drifted up to Theo's bedroom as he addressed Lysander.

'How did someone as bright as you end up with a son so stupid?'

Grinning, Theo fashioned his hands into bunny ears and twitched his nose at Louis, who gave him such a shove that he toppled through the bed curtains and landed with a thud on the floor.

'For God's sake, *shut up!*' roared Lord Bassenford, obviously directing his voice towards the ceiling. 'How did someone as bright as *me* end up with a son so stupid?' Lowering his voice, he then addressed the Sponsors again. 'I must say, Mortimer, that Trevelyan the Younger doesn't seem to present much cause for alarm. Come along now, people, I can hear my guests arriving downstairs.'

As the Sponsors left the room below, Theo climbed back on to his bed and faced a visibly shaken Louis.

'Shit, shit, shit, Theo, I am so sorry…'

'Stop worrying, Lou. Lord Bastardford's busy playing mine host, so I very much doubt there'll be any repercussions.' Theo was going to add 'At least, not tonight,' but seeing Louis so agitated he decided against it. Instead he picked up an old acoustic guitar from the floor beside his bed and played a string of popular songs, the music gradually having the desired effect of calming Louis down.

'They all know you're up here,' stated Louis eventually.

Theo paused his rendition of *Brown Eyed Girl* and nodded.

'Including my dad.'

'Afraid so.' Putting his guitar down, Theo wrapped his arms round his knees and rested his chin on top of them.

'And yet they do *nothing*.'

'Don't judge Lysander too harshly, Lou. You've seen what happens to people who cross Lord Bastardford.'

The two young men were silent for a while, then, his voice incredulous, Louis said, 'My mam covered for me.'

'Why wouldn't she?'

'Because she's always off her head on drugs, that's why,' replied Louis, wondering as he spoke if his mother had hidden depths he didn't know about.

***

Theo awoke the next morning and peered out from behind his bed curtains, finding to his surprise that it was already broad daylight outside.

'Louis,' he said urgently, shaking his friend who gradually and reluctantly woke up. 'You need to get out of here.'

'Why don't you come too?' asked Louis. 'You do know your door's unlocked?'

'Not if I go near it. Camera spies Theo making a bid for freedom, door locks immediately. Even if I were to get past it, you'd hear the claxons going off from Land's End to John O'Groats.'

'So how do I get out?'

'Same way as you got in. You open the door, walk through and close it behind you. After that, it's down to you.'

Theo, long accustomed to the routine of the house in which he was imprisoned, waited until the perfect moment for Louis to leave.

'This is it, Lou. Good luck, and thank you for everything. I'm going to give the camera something to watch. You know what you need to do.'

'Yes – I need to get you out of here, Theo. It may take time, but I'm going to do it.'

'I know. I never doubted you for a second, but that's not what I meant. Right, are you ready? I'm going to get off the bed now.'

'Theo…'

'Now!'

Marvelling at his friend's strength of character, Louis echoed, 'Now.'

Theo remained stock still by the window after he heard his bedroom door close behind Louis, staring down into the street below. His expression gave nothing away, neither his relief at seeing Louis emerge from the alleyway beside his father's house five minutes later nor his envy as his friend sprinted away to freedom.

Turning once Louis had disappeared from sight, Theo noticed something on his bed which had no right to be there.

'Oh, Lou, you muppet,' he said with a sad smile, glancing at the camera then picking up the book when he realised it was hidden from view behind the bed curtains. The appearance of a recent London *A to Z* in the room of a long-term prisoner would take some explaining, but Theo was reluctant to part with his one souvenir of Louis's visit, and besides, how was he going to dispose of it? Flicking through its pages for a few minutes, he then slipped it through a hole he'd made in his mattress where it joined a photograph of his mother: precious mementoes carefully hidden away from his persecutors.

Unable to keep his expression impassive any longer, Theo closed his bed curtains around him and curled into a foetal position. Burying his face in his pillow as his crushing loneliness returned with a vengeance, he resisted the urge to scream himself hoarse, but even the astonishing strength of will that had kept him sane for the last nine years wasn't enough to hold back his bitter tears of despair.

Chapter 7 – Lost and Beaten

Louis had managed to escape from Theo's prison without being detected. He had even managed to find his way from Kensington back to the river, despite having parted company with Rick's *A to Z*, but that was where his luck ran out. With the exception of the Thames itself creeping by in front of him, there wasn't anything in sight he recognised: no Westminster Bridge, no Houses of Parliament, no London Eye. The only notable building he could see was a huge four-chimneyed power station on the far side of the river which for some reason put him in mind of his parents' Pink Floyd albums.

Absently humming *Shine On You Crazy Diamond*, Louis looked up and down the river for inspiration and shook his head in defeat. He was hopelessly lost.

Concerned about still being deep in sponsored territory, Louis decided to cross over to the south side of the river then call the Lonsdales for help. It had struck him as strange that the Sponsors allowed the Unsponsored to have telephones, but Rick had explained it was only so they could make contact when they needed a menial task doing.

'Believe me, it's not to make life easier for us,' he had said.

Knowing that his use of a telephone box would reveal him as one of the Unsponsored, the

Sponsored all having mobile phones, Louis chose a quiet street from which to make his call and waited anxiously for the Lonsdales to answer.

'Hello?'

Louis sighed with relief.

'Lisa, it's Louis…'

Lisa shrieked in delight, then Louis heard a commotion start up in the flat. The next voice on the line was Sarah's.

'Louis, thank God you're safe! Where are you?'

'Hopefully not far away, Sarah. I got a bit lost, I'm afraid.'

There was the murmur of voices in the background, then Rick spoke.

'Hi, Louis, do you know the name of the street you're on at the moment?'

Louis told him, and Rick continued after a short pause.

'OK, I've found you on the map. Good God, Louis, which bridge did you cross over?'

'Umm… it wasn't Westminster Bridge…'

'Never mind the bridge for now,' said Rick, chuckling slightly as he outlined a simple route back to Elephant and Castle. 'Can you find your way from there?'

'I think so, Rick,' replied Louis. 'See you soon, I hope.'

Unfortunately for Louis, a group of sponsored teenagers strolled along his hitherto quiet street as he ended his call. Looking for a bit of underclass-bashing to brighten up their dull, stifled lives, they were delighted to see a lone man exiting a phone box and as one broke into a run, baying for blood. Even though Louis ran as fast as he could, the youths stayed hot on his heels, and he frantically wondered whether he'd ever be able to practise gymnastics again once they'd finished with him.

With a burst of adrenaline born of blind panic, Louis skidded round a corner and disappeared into a yard, slamming and locking the gate closed behind him. The youths rattled the gate a couple of times, but soon lost interest once their attention was drawn to a new quarry. Hoping that his replacement would escape unharmed as the sponsored youths took up the chase in full battle cry, Louis waited for his breathing to return to normal then turned to look at his new surroundings.

'Oh no,' he said.

***

Louis wasn't the only one having a bad morning. When Abi arrived at the Blenthwaite Hotel, The White Lion's sponsored rival, Max Barrington was still smarting from a recent phone conversation with Stephen Dyer.

'They're sending security up here,' he roared. 'They don't think I can do the job. How was I to know the cripple was lying?'

Suddenly rounding on Abi, Max added, 'Did you know?'

'No, Max, I don't know him that well…'

'Crap! You told me you'd known him all your life.'

Max had been instructed by Dyer to go and visit Louis Trevelyan. Lord Bassenford wouldn't be happy unless his watchman had actually seen Louis in person.

'Don't trust others to do the job, Barrington,' Dyer had snapped. 'That's not the way His Lordship expects his security staff to work. I have to say, we're very disappointed in you.'

'Have you any idea how I felt finding there was no sign of Trevelyan in that house? I had to explain that to Mr Dyer.' Abi winced at the mention of Dyer's name, but Max either didn't notice or didn't care. 'Now Lord Bassenford thinks I'm useless, and all because I trusted the crip. And you – I trusted you!'

'Max, Louis may be walking in the hills. He often does…'

'Yesterday he couldn't move from his bed, today he's gadding about on a fucking mountain? Do you think I'm thick or what?'

An ugly expression settled on Max's handsome face as realisation dawned.

'You've been distracting me for Trevelyan, you fucking bitch. Tell me, slut, where is he?'

Abi was silent.

'Don't tell me you've got feelings for that freak.'

'He's not a freak!'

'Looks like one to me – fucking freak.'

'He's not a *fucking freak*, as you so eloquently put it, he has albinism.'

'Same thing!'

'Completely different thing!'

'Well, that explains a lot,' sneered Max. 'All those excuses not to sleep with me – all the time you've been gagging for it from the freak show.'

Knowing it was useless to pretend any more, Abi offered a silent apology to Louis then said, 'I've no idea where he is, and even if I did know I wouldn't tell you.'

'Get out of here, you slut. I never want to see you again.'

'Fine by me,' retorted Abi, grabbing her jacket. 'You're an arrogant shit, Barrington, and I wouldn't sleep with you if you were the last man on earth.'

Max's fist connected with Abi's face, taking her by surprise and knocking her off balance for a second.

'Get out!'

Abi's fist, as unexpected as Max's had been, made far better contact with his face than his had with hers. As he fell to the floor, clutching his nose and crying like a baby, Abi put on her jacket then stood over him.

'Regard that as a lesson learned, Barrington. Goodbye.'

***

'Stephen,' said Lord Bassenford, beckoning Stephen Dyer into his office, 'do sit down. I hope I haven't called you away from anything urgent.'

Sitting opposite his boss, Dyer said, 'Thank you, Your Lordship. No trouble at all, anything I can do to be of service…'

'I do have a job for you, Stephen. Two, actually. Ah, here's Rosanna.'

Dyer leapt from his seat as Lady Rosanna entered the room.

'Morning, Father, you wanted to see me?' she said, ignoring Dyer and kissing Lord Bassenford lightly on the cheek.

'Indeed. I have a little something lined up I think you'll find entertaining, my darling.'

Dyer sniggered, guessing that he may well enjoy the entertainment too.

'Rosanna, Stephen here has discovered that Trevelyan Junior isn't ill in his bed after all. In fact, we don't currently know where he is. Now, Stephen, as we discussed earlier, we have the problem of The White Lion Inn to deal with. Have you decided on the men you wish to take with you to Blenthwaite? Good. While you're there, should you happen to encounter Nicola Trevelyan, perhaps you could instruct her *not* to lie to her husband's employer. Gently, of course.'

'It would be a pleasure, Your Lordship,' replied Dyer, feeling happier by the minute. Talk about job satisfaction!

In response to the sound of the doorbell, Lord Bassenford said, 'Ah, dead on time.'

A couple of minutes later, Mooreland ushered Lysander Trevelyan into his boss's office.

'Thank you, Mooreland. No, Lysander won't be needing refreshments. Now, Trevelyan,' Lord Bassenford rounded on his Director of Leisure and Fitness, 'where is your son?'

'Um, at home...'

'Liar!' roared Lord Bassenford, slamming his fist on to his desk.

'I… I promise you, Your Lordship, if he's not at home, then I have no idea where he is. Nicola…'

'She lied. She will be dealt with.'

'Your Lordship, please! My wife has, er, problems…'

'You're trembling, Lysander. Anyone would think you're scared of me all of a sudden.'

'Not at all…'

'Well, you should be! Your son is missing, and in the light of Mortimer's prediction, that makes me uncomfortable. And I don't like feeling uncomfortable. I am about to demonstrate what happens to those who oppose me, and I don't care who they are.'

Turning to his employees, Lord Bassenford said, 'Mooreland, Dyer, would you be so kind as to fetch Theodore and bring him down here?'

Lying in his bath in the room above his father's office, Theo let out a slow moan. He had heard every word and knew from bitter experience what was in store for him, but as ever, he was determined not to give Lord Bassenford, or the disgusting specimen called Dyer, the satisfaction of seeing how afraid he was feeling. Heaving himself out of the water, he wrapped a towel around his waist and, taking a few deep breaths to compose himself, made his way to the bathroom door, leaning, apparently nonchalantly, against the doorframe.

That was where his father's hired thugs found him.

'Morning, Mr Mooreland, Mr Dyer. I understand my presence is required downstairs. I don't think I need to dress, do I?'

'Shut up,' snapped Dyer, wrenching Theo's arms behind his back and frogmarching him down to Lord Bassenford's office behind Mooreland. To Theo's dismay, as they passed Marina's bedroom door, it opened and her startled face appeared.

'Mari, don't…'

'Shut up!' snapped Dyer again as Mooreland opened the office door.

Lysander stared in disbelief, doing his best to disguise his horror as Lord Bassenford's son, clad only in a bath towel, was shoved through the door and over to the far wall. He had idly wondered during the more boring moments of Sponsor meetings past why there were iron rings set into the wall of his boss's office; as Theo's wrists and ankles were firmly shackled to these rings, Lysander wished fervently that he had never found out the answer.

'Your Lordship,' said Mooreland, 'I hate to trouble you, but Lady Marina saw us bringing him down.'

'Really?' said Lord Bassenford, his tone more interested than anything else. Certainly not upset. 'Ask her to join us, will you, Mooreland? It's about time she toughened up a bit.'

'Please don't,' said Theo, his nonchalant act faltering momentarily.

'Silence!' roared Lord Bassenford. 'You are *nothing!*'

As Mooreland went to fetch Marina, Lysander glanced at Lord Bassenford and his elder daughter. His Lordship looked calm and relaxed, but it was Lady Rosanna's expression that horrified Lysander more. Her eyes were shining with pure pleasure, and she licked her lips once or twice as she anticipated the show to come.

Marina's face was a completely different picture when she entered the room with Mooreland. Seeing her brother chained to the wall of her father's office, she looked shocked and her eyes filled with tears.

'Father,' she said, 'you're not going to hurt Theo, are you?'

'Come here, darling, sit with your sister and me. It's just a little show for Lysander here. Stephen, you may proceed.'

Picking up a fearsome whip, Dyer strode over to Theo. As the whip cracked violently on Theo's back over and over again, as angry welts appeared on his skin, Lord Bassenford noted with satisfaction that neither Lysander nor Marina dared to look away. Lysander was obviously receiving his message loudly and clearly – if His Lordship's own son could come in for such punishment, whatever would be in store for Louis were he to stir up trouble?

Unable to escape to 'Thwaite's Wood in his mind, so tormented were his thoughts and so fierce was the pain in his back, Theo finally found blessed relief by slipping from consciousness, his last scrap of dignity vanishing as he lost control of his bladder.

'Father,' said Lady Rosanna, actually clapping her hands a couple of times, 'he's wet himself – how disgusting!'

Looking from the serene Lord Bassenford to Lady Rosanna, who was breathless with excitement as she witnessed her brother's torture, Lysander thought grimly that it certainly wasn't Theo who was the disgusting one.

***

Louis looked around in dismay as the shouts of his pursuers faded into the distance. Staring back at him was a group of about six or seven men, none of whom were looking very welcoming.

Eventually, a thickset bald man stepped forward from the group.

'Who the fuck are you?' he asked.

'Louis Trevelyan,' said Louis, immediately cursing himself for speaking without thinking.

'Trevelyan? You related to that twat Lysander?'

Before Louis could reply, a tall, athletic-looking man said, 'Bloody right, he is. Sponsor Twat Trevelyan has a son with albinism called Louis.'

'Cheers, Brains,' said the thickset man. 'Good job Brains here keeps up with current affairs, Louis Trevelyan. So, what the fuck do you want with us?'

'Nothing, I was trying to get away from…'

'You're a Sponsor – you've no place here!'

'I'm not a Sponsor!'

'You're Lysander Trevelyan's son. He's one of the worst of the lot, and we're supposed to believe you're not a Sponsor? Cos we don't, do we, lads?'

There was a murmur of agreement from the other men.

'Please, I seriously need to get back to Walworth. I'll just open these gates and…'

'Bring your Sponsor cronies to give us hell, no doubt. No way, young Trevelyan, you're going to stay a while.'

'No you don't, son,' said an older man, grabbing Louis's hands as he tried desperately to unlock the gates. Severely outnumbered, Louis was dragged from the yard into an old warehouse building, concluding that he appeared to have jumped out of the frying pan and into the fire.

***

Theo gradually regained consciousness, and then wished he hadn't bothered. His back felt as though it was on fire, and the pain became even fiercer every time he tried to move. Finally, gritting his teeth and hissing with pain, he managed to stagger to his feet and make his way into the bathroom. Knowing he had to cleanse his wounds but dreading the inevitable discomfort, he turned the shower on to cool and stepped under the spray.

Lord Bassenford was sitting alone in his office, regarding his computer monitor with an air of detached amusement as the security camera in his son's room relayed Theo's attempts to raise himself from the floor. After watching the young man make his unsteady way into the bathroom, Lord Bassenford then clicked off the monitor and went up to the fourth floor for the first time in years.

Over time, Theo had become a master at hiding his feelings, but even he couldn't conceal his surprise at finding Lord Bassenford sitting on his bed when he emerged from his painful shower.

'Your Lordship,' he said, sliding his hands under the waistband of his shorts and pulling it away from his unhappy back, 'this is a surprise.'

'I wouldn't put a top on if I were you, Theodore. Not until those wounds dry up a bit.'

'Good advice, Your Lordship, but if that's all you've come to tell me you could have saved yourself a journey. I'd already worked it out for myself.'

'No, Theodore, that's not why I'm here.'

Lying belly down on the bed, as far away as possible from his father, Theo said, 'What brings you to my humble abode then, Your Lordship?'

'I'm your father, Theodore.'

'If you say so, Your Lordship.'

'Are you incapable of replying without insolence?' roared Lord Bassenford, not wanting to admit to himself that he felt a grudging respect for Theo's nerve.

'Not even an hour ago, I was nothing. Your words, Your Lordship. Now I'm your son. Forgive my confusion, but you've lost me somewhere along the way.'

'Theodore, when you were born I was so happy. I desperately wanted a son and heir, someone to take over the running of the Sponsorship Scheme when the day comes for me to step down. Instead, I got you.'

'Hand over the running to Rosanna,' said Theo. 'She's probably got bigger balls than me.'

Still sitting on Theo's bed, Lord Bassenford slammed his hand down hard on his son's

164

wounded back, then wiped it indifferently on the sheets. As Theo cried out in agony, his father gave a grunt of satisfaction.

'It doesn't have to be this way, Theodore,' Lord Bassenford said. 'You only have to say the word and you can be my son again.'

'Be one of your brainwashed minions, you mean,' muttered Theo through gritted teeth. 'I'd rather stay locked in this room until I die.'

'Very well,' said Lord Bassenford. Getting up from the bed, he crossed to the door of Theo's room before adding, 'I understand you can hear conversations taking place in the room below. Therefore you must know that Lysander Trevelyan's son is missing. I'm also led to understand that you and Trevelyan Junior were once friends. Now listen to me and listen well, Theodore. If I find out Louis Trevelyan has managed to make contact with you in any way at all, I will kill him – slowly and painfully. Furthermore, I will make you watch every excruciating second of it.'

Meeting Theo's light-brown eyes, so similar to his own and yet so different, Lord Bassenford smiled grimly.

'I can see that you understand,' he said. 'Good.'

***

After an hour and a half of waiting for Louis, dodging an unusual number of Sponsored who were milling about, Rick was getting frantic with worry. He'd seen Sarah's anxious face appear from the entrance to his block a couple of times, but he'd waved her back inside. It certainly wouldn't do for the Sponsored to start asking *her* awkward questions.

One of the Sponsored was approaching Rick even as he was trying to decide whether or not to go upstairs again.

'Oi, underclass, what ya doing 'anging round out 'ere?'

'Umm…'

'You waiting for someone?' Without giving Rick a chance to reply, the sponsored man continued, 'You seen a bloke? Early twenties, very pale skin, white 'air?'

'No, sorry,' lied Rick quickly, thinking on his feet. 'I was just waiting for my mate to bring me some, er, paint. Said he'd be here an hour ago…'

'OK, underclass, I don't need yer life story. Looks like 'e ain't gonna turn up, so I want you to get lost – now. We've got enough on our plate trying to find this bloke without you getting in our way.'

His mind made up by the command of the sponsored man, Rick admitted defeat and returned to his home. Sarah's head shot up from the book she'd been reading to the children as soon as he opened the door, and Rick felt even more forlorn seeing his sister's hopeful expression fade as she saw that he was alone.

'Sorry, Sarah, there's no sign. The Sponsored are giving me a hard time too, so I daren't stay out any longer.'

Unable to hide her tears even for Jenny's sake, Sarah dropped her head and sobbed quietly. Jenny's own sobs weren't so subtle. Realising that something bad had happened to her brother, she began to howl fit to raise the dead.

'I… want… LOUIEEEEEE! LOUIEEEEEE!'

'Jenny, be quiet!' Rick said in alarm. 'I know you're upset, but don't shout Louis's name. Nasty people are trying to find him – we don't want them coming here.'

Jenny stopped howling Louis's name, but continued to howl nonetheless. The adults looked enquiringly at Rick, who was just starting to tell them about his chat with the Sponsored when the phone rang.

'Hello,' said Lisa, answering the telephone and doing her best to hear over Jenny's howls. 'Sorry, who?… *Really?*… Er… um… for real?… What on earth do you want with us?'

***

In his penthouse apartment, Lysander was talking to Lisa Lonsdale on the unregistered mobile phone he kept for emergencies. He could understand the unsponsored woman's disbelief at getting a call from one of the highest-ranking Sponsors in the land, but it was frustrating having to spend a couple of minutes convincing her that yes, it really was Lysander Trevelyan, and no, she wasn't in trouble.

'Listen, Mrs Lonsdale, you've got to warn my housekeeper that she and my children are in big trouble. Please get them out of London immediately. Especially Louis. It is imperative that Louis is not found in London...'

'Mr Trevelyan, what's this all about?'

'I really don't have time to explain. Don't insult my intelligence by telling me you don't know where my children are – I recognise the sound of my daughter crying in the background. Just get them out of London any way you can, I'm begging you.'

'*You're* begging *me*?'

Lysander sighed. 'Unbelievable though it may seem, yes, I am.'

'Well, well, well,' said Lisa. 'You want us – the Unsponsored – to get Louis and Jenny – the children of the all-powerful Head of Leisure and Fitness – out of London. Wouldn't it be far more effective if you just did it yourself?'

'Oh for fuck's sake...'

'Right, I'm hanging up the phone...'

'No-no-no-no-no, please don't.' Lysander's voice was about an octave higher than normal. 'Look, OK, I'll explain. Er – *someone* is after Louis, and if this, er… *someone* gets his hands on him, he'll… he'll…'

'*Someone* being Lord Sponsor, I take it.'

Lysander was silent for a moment, then whispered a barely audible, 'Lord Bassenford, yes'.

'Your boss, your problem.'

'Please, Mrs Lonsdale.' As unfamiliar concern for Louis overwhelmed him, Lysander swallowed back tears. 'You despise me, I get that, but Louis is not me. He's my son – my kind-hearted, scatty, humorous, loveable son…'

'Ah, now you're finally talking like a father. Hold the line please, Mr Trevelyan.'

Lysander heard a clunk as the telephone receiver was placed down. He waited meekly as a muffled consultation went on at the other end of the line, then a familiar voice sounded in his ear.

'Mr Trevelyan,' said Sarah, 'I'm here with Jenny. We've no idea where Louis is, though. He phoned a couple of hours ago to say he was south of the river but lost, and we've neither seen nor heard from him since.'

'That's n-not good news at all,' stammered Lysander.

'If I get Jenny out of London, my brother and sister-in-law will continue to search for Louis, although our chances of doing either are a little limited at the moment by the amount of your people patrolling outside.'

'Leave them to me. Now, here's a safe number on which you can contact me.' Lysander read out his unregistered mobile number, making sure Sarah noted it down correctly. 'Oh, and Sarah?'

'Yes, Mr Trevelyan?'

'If possible, don't head back to the house tonight. I've a feeling some, er, uninvited guests may be turning up in the near future, and I do not want them anywhere near Genevieve.'

Sarah was silent for a few moments.

'I know where we can go,' she said, 'but what about Mrs Trevelyan?'

'I've got an idea where Mrs Trevelyan's concerned. You concentrate on yourself and Genevieve.'

'Don't worry about Jenny, I'll keep her safe.'

'You always do, Sarah, and I can't thank you enough.'

'Oh... it's a pleasure, sir,' said Sarah, not quite able to keep her surprise at her boss's uncharacteristic show of gratitude out of her voice. 'Goodbye for now, and good luck. I'll let you know when Jenny and I are back in Blenthwaite.'

As he replaced the receiver, Lysander did his best to swallow his panic before making his next phone call. Anxious though he felt, this wasn't the time to turn into a screaming wreck.

'Dr Donatelli?' he said when his call was answered. 'It's Lysander Trevelyan. I know this is an unusual request, but my wife has attracted unwanted attention... Oh, they've arrived, have they?' Lysander went cold at the news that his boss's thugs had already been seen in Blenthwaite. 'God, I hope we're not too late. I don't think it's safe for Nicola at home, so would you go and check... You will? And can you keep her with you until I get home? Thank you so much.'

Ending the call, Lysander wondered for a second whether he should have mentioned that Dex Montfiore and his boyfriend were also in danger. He soon dismissed the idea, though; there were more pressing tasks.

Picking up his official phone, Lysander pressed the first number on speed dial.

'Lord Bassenford,' he said on hearing the familiar arrogant voice of his boss, 'I've been doing a lot of thinking since this morning. I really don't think my son is going to be a nuisance to the Scheme, but I respect your desire for caution. I've been putting out a few feelers,' he went on, lying through his teeth, 'and the reports seem to suggest Louis is in Chelsea.'

'Why Chelsea?' asked Lord Bassenford suspiciously.

'My brother lives there. Louis dotes on his uncle, and coupled with the reported sightings, I'm convinced he's trying to pay Fabian a surprise visit.'

'Fabian?'

Unseen by Lord Bassenford, Lysander rolled his eyes, long used to having to explain his own unusual name.

'My parents were both Shakespearean actors.'

'Oh, you luvvie!' said Lord Bassenford with a bark of laughter, and Lysander relaxed a little. 'Have you not phoned your brother?'

'Not yet, Your Lordship. My son's sense of direction is, quite frankly, hopeless, so my guess is he's wandering aimlessly around Chelsea, but I'm sure Fabian will call me if Louis does arrive on his doorstep.'

'Very well, I'll concentrate the search on Chelsea. Don't worry, Lysander, we'll find your boy.'

That's what does worry me, thought Lysander as Lord Bassenford ended the call. *For God's sake, Louis, don't choose now to pay Uncle Fabian a visit.*

***

Thoughts of Uncle Fabian were far from Louis's mind as the hot summer's afternoon progressed slowly into a balmy evening. His hands and feet bound with rope, he sat with his back to the wall of the old warehouse building into which the men had dragged him earlier, but although a prisoner, he wasn't being treated badly. His captors had given him plenty of food and a large cushion to protect him from the concrete floor, and as he learned more about them, he began to understand and forgive their caution. It turned out he'd run into one of the only places certain unsponsored people could call home. Couples without children, divorcees, singletons, gay couples – none were considered worthy of even a small flat like the one in which the Lonsdales lived. Persecuted and hounded by the Sponsored, they did their best to hide away and live their lives in peace.

'Right, Louis Trevelyan,' said the thickset man, 'what were you doing bursting into our yard earlier?'

'Escaping,' said Louis simply.

''Oo from?'

'Sponsored teenagers. I think they wanted to give me a kicking.'

'Sponsored were trying to beat *you* up?'

'They didn't know who I was, and I wasn't hanging around to tell them.'

'I still don't understand,' said the man affectionately known as Brains by his friends. 'Why did they think you were unsponsored?'

'Because they caught me coming out of a public phone box. And, in a way, I am unsponsored.'

'How come?'

'Well, I'm not sponsored,' replied Louis. 'And from what I've seen, I don't want to be.'

'You don't need to be, more like,' sneered the thickset man. 'Being Trevelyan's son must come with privileges.'

'Who were you phoning?' asked Brains

'Eh?'

'From the phone box.'

'Friends,' said Louis shortly. 'Look, I know next to nothing about you, so why do you expect me to tell you everything?'

Before anyone could respond to his question, a young woman, who Louis guessed to be about Marina's age, emerged from the shadows, shoulder-length black curls framing a pretty milk-chocolate coloured face, dark eyes full of warmth. Hugging Brains, she then grinned round at Louis's captors.

'Hi, Dad, guys. OK, so… why have you got a bloke tied up here?'

'It ain't as bad as it looks, Chloe,' said the older man, smiling affectionately at her. 'This is Lysander Trevelyan's son, and he just sort of arrived in the yard earlier. 'E seems 'armless, but we can't be taking chances considering the track record of 'is bastard father.'

'Fair enough, Jim,' said the young woman called Chloe, looking with interest at Louis. 'I'd guessed he's Trevelyan's son – he's the one the Sponsored are after.'

It was difficult to tell who was more surprised: Louis or the men holding him captive.

'Yeah,' Chloe continued, 'the place was crawling with the bastards until about half an hour ago. I would have popped over earlier, but every time I left Mum's I got a leaflet thrust in my face and a million questions about,' she gestured at Louis, 'him.'

All eyes in the room turned on Louis.

'Why are the Sponsored looking for you? Precious to them, are you?'

'Far from it,' snapped Louis. Looking into Chloe's friendly face, and figuring that if anyone had good reason to hate the Sponsorship Scheme it was this group of people, he then decided on impulse to throw caution to the wind and tell them everything that had happened since he, Sarah and Jenny left Blenthwaite.

A silence fell on the room when Louis had finished speaking.

'I still can't believe you know so little about the Sponsorship Scheme,' said the thickset man eventually, 'you being a Trevelyan.'

'I don't think we can blame the lad for who his father is,' said Brains before Louis could reply. 'We can't all be as lucky as Chloe here.'

Everyone chuckled as Brains hugged his daughter, then he added, 'I'm inclined to believe you, Louis.'

'I know nothing about the Sponsorship Scheme because I've been shielded from it my whole life – up until Theo made contact, anyway. Then people started to let me know what we're up against with the Sponsors, and I don't like what I've seen one little bit.'

'Why would people feel the need to protect you from the Sponsors, given who your father is?'

Louis had known he'd be asked this question before long, but anticipation didn't make him feel any less foolish about his answer.

'One of Lord Bassenford's right-hand men made a prediction just before I was born about a fair-haired boy who'd grow up to topple the Sponsorship Scheme. My father tried to laugh it off as rubbish – he's never got on with this bloke, apparently…'

'Was it O'Reilly?' asked Brains. 'It's well documented that O'Reilly and Trevelyan hate each other.'

'Aye, that's his name. Mortimer O'Reilly, Financial Sponsorship. My dad pooh-poohed his claims, but surprisingly Lord Bassenford took him seriously.'

'Not really surprising,' said Chloe. 'Tyrants often get paranoid. Who set up your protection, then – your dad?'

'No chance! My father and I aren't close. No, it was Isabelle St Benedict who warned her brother Elliot, and apparently he set it up.'

At the mention of Isabelle's name, the group smiled. Clearly their memories of Theo's mother were as fond as the Lonsdales' had been.

'Tell us more about Lord Sponsor's son,' said Jim. 'I still can't believe you just waltzed into the tyrant's house.'

'I didn't exactly waltz,' replied Louis laughing, then he became serious as he told the group just how badly Theo suffered at the hands of his father.

'My God, that's awful,' said Brains, shuddering. 'I thought Lord Sponsor couldn't sink any lower, but imprisoning his own son? Well, he's surpassed himself. I'm unclear on one thing, though, Louis. If Theodore is kept such a closely guarded prisoner, how did he make contact with you?'

Louis had been dreading this question more than any other.

'Er, he contacted me in my, er, head. The only thing his father can't imprison is his mind, so, er, he…'

''E made contact in your head, did 'e?' began Jim, but Louis interrupted, suddenly desperately tired of the whole conversation.

'Look, that's what happened. Believe me, don't believe me, I'm beyond caring. So, are you going to give me up to the Sponsors, let me go home or keep me on this cushion for the rest of my life?'

The men and Chloe looked at each other. Finally, Chloe answered.

'We're going to help you, Louis.' Slipping a knife out of her boot, she cut Louis's hands and feet free. 'First I think we should contact these Lonsdale people. They must be worried sick, so I don't think they'll mind a call at silly o'clock in the morning. Hopefully all the Sponsored will be in their beds – most of them are on strict curfews.'

Everyone smiled at Chloe's reminder of the rules governing the Sponsored. Tough though their lives were, Brains and the others cherished their freedom.

'Come on,' she said. 'Let's go.'

The group decided that safety lay in numbers, so they all accompanied Louis to the nearest phone box, which turned out to be the same one he'd used the previous afternoon. Hoping that the ring of their phone in the middle of the night wouldn't attract unwanted attention for the Lonsdales, Louis dialled.

'Hello,' said Rick, snatching up the receiver almost immediately, his voice alert.

'Rick, I'm OK. I'm safe.'

'Louis…'

'I'm sorry, can't explain now. I'm with good people, unsponsored, but we're vulnerable out here. Can we come back to the flat?'

'Of course, the coast should be clear. You know the lift's code? Good. Louis, be careful.'

'I will.'

This time, having the advantage of streetwise company, Louis did manage to make it back to the Lonsdales' flat. He introduced his new friends, all of whom crammed inside and sat on every available surface, then for the second time that night shared the details of his conversation with Theo and everything that had happened since. Once he'd finished, Rick and Lisa told the group about Lysander's unexpected phone call and Sarah's escape from London with Jenny. Right on cue, the phone rang just as they came to the end of their tale.

'Allow me,' said Louis, snatching up the receiver before anyone could stop him and grinning as Sarah screamed in delight from the north of the country.

'Louis…' she began, then a familiar grumpy voice came on the line.

'Where the bloody hell have you been?'

'Hello, Gideon, good to hear your voice,' said Louis honestly, his mentor's bad temper never having sounded so sweet.

'Good to hear yours too, Louis. Now, some of Bassenford's thugs are here. They arrived a few hours ago. Your mother…'

'She's in trouble, Gideon. She lied for me when I was with Theo…'

'Your mother is safe, thanks to a timely warning from your father of all people. Your home is not safe. If you're coming back to Blenthwaite, and I hope you are, I suggest you head straight to my place. Sarah and Jenny are here already.'

'I'll do that, Gideon, but in the meantime you need to tell Dex and Alan that the thugs are after them too. I think they mean to give Alan a kicking to teach Dex a lesson…'

'I'll warn them first thing in the morning, Louis. It's a tad late to ring them now. Get home quickly. I miss you.'

Without giving Louis time to reply, Gideon cut off the call.

'Louis, that was very foolish snatching up the phone like that,' said Rick. 'What if it had been the Sponsors?'

'Sorry,' replied Louis with an apologetic grin. 'Talking of Sponsors, I ought to phone my dad.'

The Unsponsored looked at him in alarm.

'I'll go back to the phone box if you prefer,' Louis continued, 'but he's put himself out to protect Jenny and me tonight – and my mam too, according to Gideon. Besides, he could be my best hope of getting home.'

'Phone from here,' said Rick, handing Lysander's unregistered phone number to Louis. Like Rick earlier, Lysander answered almost immediately – no one seemed to be getting any sleep that night.

'Dad?'

'Louis! How are you?'

'Er... safe.'

'Of course you're safe, Louis, I wouldn't expect you to be in danger from the Lonsdales.'

Laughing at Louis's gasp of surprise, Lysander continued, 'The Lonsdales' number appeared on my phone as soon as you called. You don't know much about phones, do you.'

'I don't know much about anything, Dad, but I'm learning fast. Now, I need to get home. Any ideas?'

Lysander was silent for a while, then said, 'Yes. It's risky, but I think it'll buy us time.'

'Us?'

'You're my son, Louis, and it's about time I started acting like a father. If the Lonsdales will be so good as to give you a bed for what's left of the night, I'll pick you up in the morning. Seven o'clock. Be ready.'

***

As soon as he'd finished speaking to his son, Lysander made another call, this time using his official phone.

'I've found him,' he said when the call was answered.

'Good,' replied Mooreland. 'We'll see you in the morning.'

Chapter 8 – Lysander's Plan

Unfortunately for Alan Santiago, Louis's warning came too late. Always an early riser, Alan was awake by six o'clock the morning after Sarah and Jenny's return to Blenthwaite, and seeing sun gleaming round the edges of the curtains, he decided to make the most of the gorgeous day by going for a run. Locking the door of The White Lion's living quarters behind him, mindful of the fact that unwelcome visitors had arrived in Blenthwaite the previous evening, Alan went through his warm-up stretches then set off at a steady pace along the main street.

'Bingo!' said Stephen Dyer, boss of the unwelcome visitors, watching Alan's progress from the window of the Sponsor-endorsed Blenthwaite Hotel. 'Job's a good 'un, boys.'

An hour or so after Alan had left for his run, Dex woke up alone in his bed. Showering quickly, he then pulled on his clothes and trotted downstairs, baffled by the uneasy feeling in the pit of his stomach.

Startled by the ring of the phone, Dex snatched it from its cradle.

'Dex,' said Sarah Lonsdale on the other end of the line, 'is Al with you?'

'I think he's out for a jog…'

'I hate to be the one to tell you this, but Al's in danger.'

Dex's uneasy stomach lurched.

'Danger?'

'Louis asked us to tell you Dyer's after him…'

Uneasy no longer, Dex descended into blind panic.

'Oh God, no!' he screamed. 'Alan!'

Not even bothering to put anything on his bare feet, Dex dropped the phone and ran out into the road, yelling Alan's name at the top of his voice. Doors opened as curious villagers appeared in the street, looking at each other in concern as The White Lion's normally chilled landlord dissolved into hysteria. Finally Abi Farrell, her face still bruised from Max's thump, caught him by the arm and attempted to calm him.

'Dex, running in circles won't achieve anything. What's happened to Al?'

'Dyer,' was the only answer Dex could manage. Abi's face blanched and she had to turn away to hide her horror from her already distraught companion.

'What do *you* want?' she spat, seeing Max hovering behind her.

'Follow me. Hurry!' he replied, setting off at a run. Glancing at each other in confusion, Dex and Abi came to a simultaneous decision and sprinted after him.

'There,' Max said five minutes later, turning to Dex and pointing to a narrow packhorse bridge.

'What?' asked Dex, but Max had already gone. Scrambling down the bank, Dex saw 'what' for himself and clapped his hands to his face.

'No, no, no,' he mumbled, kneeling beside the battered and motionless body of his partner lying half in and half out of a fast flowing beck. 'Abi? Abi, is your mom there?'

'I'm here, Dex. Oh my God!' Dr Jessica Donatelli dropped to her knees beside Dex and felt for a pulse in Alan's neck.

'Is he…'

'He's alive, Dex. We need to get him out of the water, though.'

'Shouldn't we call an ambulance?' asked Georgia, arriving at her brother's side.

'No,' he replied without hesitation. 'I'm not having a sponsored ambulance taking him to a sponsored hospital. It was Sponsors who did this to him. Sorry, Jess, it's down to you.'

'I'm sponsored, Dex.'

'You're not like them. I trust you.'

Smiling gently at Dex, Jess then called over her shoulder, 'Is Chris there? You got the van, Chris?'

It took a while to make up a stretcher from the contents of Chris Farrell's van, and even longer to lift the still-unconscious Alan into the back. Dex and Jess then sat on either side of him, keeping him as secure as possible as Chris drove back to the village.

'When is he going to wake up, Jess?' asked Dex, his voice unsteady.

'Not until we get him home, I hope, Dex,' replied Jess, trying to keep her own voice as light as possible. 'Otherwise it'll be a very painful journey for him.'

Alan did indeed stay unconscious while he was carried up the stairs he'd jogged down earlier in happy anticipation of a lovely day.

'Oh my,' said Jess as she and Dex laid Alan on his bed and gently removed his running top. His body appeared to be covered in one huge bruise. 'Now, I've not got the luxury of X-ray at my disposal, so I'm going to have to feel my way, Dex.'

'S'OK,' mumbled Dex, watching wide-eyed as Jess ran her hands over Alan in an attempt to find broken bones.

'Nothing's badly broken, Dex, which is good. I think he'll probably have a few cracked ribs, though, and that's going to give him some discomfort for a while. Apart from that it's bruising, cuts and concussion. We can get him through this, he's just going to need lots of TLC.'

'He's got it,' said Dex, the ghost of a smile on his lips.

'Has anyone let Matilda know?'

Before Dex could reply, a door slammed somewhere below them, followed by the sound of feet running at full pelt up the stairs.

'I think that answers your question,' he said as the bedroom door flew open and a young woman stood on the threshold, dark eyes flashing with fury.

'What worthless piece of Sponsor scum did this? I'll kill them!'

Rushing across the room, the young woman greeted Jess with a kiss on both cheeks then grabbed Dex in a bear hug.

'Dexy babes,' she said. 'Are you OK?'

'I'm cool, Matty darling,' Dex replied, returning her hug. 'Just wish I could say the same for...'

Dex's voice and smile both faded as he looked forlornly at his partner lying on the bed. Letting go of Dex and sitting down next to Alan, the young woman stroked his hair away from his bruised face and kissed him gently on the forehead.

'Matilda... baby... what... doing here?' mumbled Alan, his eyes fluttering open briefly before he slipped back into unconsciousness.

'What do you think, Dad?' said the young woman called Matilda, grinning affectionately at the man whose one brief foray into heterosexuality had resulted in her birth twenty years previously. 'I'm going to find the Sponsor scum who did this to you and I'm going to kick their arses into next week.'

***

As Jess left Alan in the loving care of his partner and daughter, many miles south Louis was saying farewell to his unsponsored friends and climbing into the luxurious car owned by the Director of the Leisure and Fitness Sponsorship Group. Sitting in the passenger seat as his father drove away from Walworth, Louis watched the streets of London going past – very slowly to begin with as rush-hour traffic built. Approaching the river through the more affluent streets that Louis had walked along two days previously, Lysander was able to leave the traffic jams and join the Sponsors' lane set aside for the elite such as himself. At regular intervals, traffic wardens scanned his number plate, realised the stature of the man driving and saluted as the Sponsor and his son passed by.

'Er, Dad,' said Louis, squinting through the car window as they crossed the river and the route started to look rather familiar, 'where are we going?'

Lysander kept his eyes fixed rigidly on the road ahead. 'Where do you think?' he murmured.

'Why?' said Louis, his voice sounding choked. 'You bastard! I thought I could trust…'

'Be quiet, Louis. For one thing, you can't trust people willy-nilly as you appear to have been doing up until now.'

'None of them has given me up to Lord Sponsor.'

'Lord *Bassenford*, Louis, show some respect! You've been spending far too much time with the Unsponsored.'

'Yeah, and as I said, none of them…'

'*Shut up*, Louis! *I'm* not giving you up to Lord Bassenford. Trust me.'

'What, willy-nilly?'

Sighing, Lysander replied, 'Lord Bassenford will keep looking for you. He will harass the people you love and who love you until you are found. Is that what you want?'

'No, but that doesn't give you the right to betray me without even…'

'Louis, I am not betraying you! The only way I can think of to get Lord Bassenford off your case is to show him you're no threat. I take it you know about O'Reilly's little prediction?' When Louis nodded, Lysander continued, 'Lord Bassenford thinks you're thick. Work with that. Let him think you're so painfully shy it makes you virtually incoherent. I'll do the talking.'

Lord Bassenford's office was full. All Lysander's colleagues were there, with the addition of Lady Rosanna, and a smirking Mortimer O'Reilly was actually dancing on the spot. Tearing his attention away from O'Reilly's quivering jowls before he burst into hysterical laughter, Louis squinted around the room instead. To his disgust, the huge framed photograph adorning the wall behind Lord Bassenford included a much younger Theo beside his father and sisters as if they were all one happy family. However, there was no sign of Isabelle in any photo in the room.

'Louis Trevelyan,' said Lord Bassenford, 'we meet at last.'

Slipping into the role his father had suggested to him, Louis shuffled behind Lysander.

'It's OK, Louis,' said Lysander, articulating his words carefully. 'This is Lord Bassenford.'

'Who? I want to go home, Dad.'

'Lord Bassenford, Dad's boss.'

'Oh,' replied Louis, his tone suggesting that he'd already lost interest in the man staring imperiously at him from behind a handsome oak desk.

'Your Lordship,' said Lysander, 'this is what I understand to have happened. My housekeeper decided to come to London and visit relatives. Foolishly, she brought my children with her.

Neither of them has ever left the Lake District before, and Louis in particular finds change very daunting, as you can possibly see.'

Sighing, Lysander paused to remove Louis's fingers from his mouth.

'My housekeeper spoke to me last night, telling me that Louis had strayed off. She was anxious to get back to my wife, who is unwell, and so left for Blenthwaite soon after we'd spoken. Luckily, Louis found his way back to her family in Walworth...'

'Not to Uncle Fabian in Chelsea?'

'Er, no... false lead...'

'No matter,' said Lord Bassenford, waving his hand dismissively. 'Carry on.'

'Right. Yes. My housekeeper's family looked after Louis until I was able to pick him up this morning, but he's traumatised and it's my wish to get him home as quickly as possible.'

'Home,' said Louis vaguely, tugging at Lysander's sleeve. The Sponsorship Scheme's elite looked at him, some with interest, some with contempt. Mortimer O'Reilly was delighted – Trevelyan's son had turned out to be an imbecile.

To O'Reilly's surprise, Lysander's next words were directed his way.

'Morti, old bean,' he sneered, 'this is the young man you're so scared of.' Turning back to

Lord Bassenford, Lysander added, 'Your Lordship, I will be having strict words with my housekeeper for putting my son at risk in this way, and I will be making sure he remains safely in the north.'

'How do you intend to get him home?' asked Lord Bassenford, looking at Louis. 'He doesn't look capable of arranging his own transport.'

O'Reilly sniggered. Lysander repressed the urge to strangle him.

'With your permission, Your Lordship, I'd like to take him myself.'

Lysander and Louis held their breath in the ensuing silence.

'Mortimer,' said Lord Bassenford, 'what do you think?'

'It would appear that I was mistaken, Your Lordship. Until now I was unsure whether my visions meant Trevelyan's son, but this idiot couldn't threaten a housefly.'

'Watch your mouth, O'Reilly,' snapped Lysander. 'My son is not an idiot…'

'Sorry, Lysander, but he looks like a common or garden idiot to me,' said Lord Bassenford, laughing. 'No wonder you keep him hidden in that little backwater up north.'

Raucous laughter greeted His Lordship's words, Mortimer's laugh louder than anyone else's. Lysander scowled with difficulty; inside he was starting to relax. Could his hastily conceived plan actually be working?

'Very well, Lysander,' Lord Bassenford said eventually. 'Take your idiot son home – and can't you stop him doing that?'

Louis had once again felt laughter threatening to burst out of him. It didn't help that he'd guessed, correctly, that Theo would be in paroxysms of laughter in the room above, and the only way he could control himself was to shove his fingers back into his mouth.

'Oh God, what a moron!' Lady Rosanna's scornful trill followed father and son as Lysander led the 'idiot' Louis from the room and down the stairs. Resisting the urge to glance up at Theo's window as he got into Lysander's car, Louis remained silent as his father drove away from the tree-lined road, away from Kensington and away from London. As the adrenaline rush of the last two days began to recede, he relaxed into the comfortable seat of the Mercedes and dozed intermittently as they sped past road signs and junctions, countryside and conurbations.

It was only once they were heading north on the M6 that Lysander finally broke the silence.

'Well that worked like a dream,' he said smugly.

Looking at his father, his expression impossible to read, Louis didn't reply at once.

'It did work, Louis, you've got to admit…'

'Next time, consult me first! How do you think I felt being dropped into that situation? What was your plan B?'

Lysander's grin faded. 'Um, didn't have one,' he mumbled.

'You didn't have one?' said Louis, then suddenly he burst out laughing. 'Good job it worked then. It was genius!'

Lysander glanced at Louis, who was smiling at him from the passenger seat.

'Genius?'

'Absolutely!'

At that moment relief got the better of father and son and they dissolved into fits of laughter, bonding in a way they had never done before.

Travelling north on the M6, Louis felt happier by the minute. He was going home. He'd soon see Abi again. He'd be able to resume his gymnastics training. Every once in a while, Lysander would ask whether he wanted to stop for refreshments, but anxious to get home as quickly as possible, Louis declined every time. Therefore, Lysander was very surprised when Louis suddenly said, 'Actually, can we get back to that service station over there?' shortly before they reached Manchester.

'It's on the southbound side of the road, Louis. There'll be one on this side before long.'

'Indulge me, Dad. After that stunt you pulled this morning…'

'OK,' said Lysander with a sigh, pulling off at the next junction in order to turn and rejoin the M6 southbound, 'but are you ever going to let me live that down?'

'Maybe,' said Louis, grinning, 'but I'm going to milk it for a while first.'

As they pulled into the service station, a security guard rushed over to see who was parking in the elite Sponsors' spaces.

'Oh, priceless,' Louis murmured.

'Welcome, Mr Trevelyan, sir,' said the very same guard who had reduced Jenny to tears a few days earlier. His demeanour was completely different today as he bowed and scraped in response to Lysander's Gold Sponsor Card, asking if there was anything he could do to make Mr Trevelyan's visit all the more pleasurable.

Lysander was about to brush the guard aside when Louis got out of the car.

'Hello again,' he said pleasantly. 'There *is* something you could do. Next time my little sister – Mr Trevelyan's daughter, that is – needs to use the toilets, I suggest you don't make her cry.'

'You did this?' Lysander rounded on the simpering guard. 'You made my little girl cry? She's only six – what sort of man are you?'

'Sir, Mr Trevelyan, sir, I didn't know who she was…'

'Oh yeah, that's another thing,' said Louis, enjoying himself. 'I did try to tell you who my father is. Can't quite stretch to the Sultan of Brunei, I'm afraid – will Lysander Trevelyan do?'

'It appears you managed to upset both my children. What's your name? I'll have your sponsorship withdrawn…'

Louis laid a hand on his father's arm.

'Don't, Dad. Let's go home now.'

'You're lucky,' said Lysander, glaring at the shaken guard, 'that my son's a nicer man than I am.'

Leaving the service station, Lysander headed south to the nearest junction so he could rejoin the northbound carriageway of the M6, a huge grin on his face.

'Did you listen to that sycophant?' he said, laughter in his voice. '"Ooh sir, Mr Trevelyan, sir, how about I kiss your arse a little bit more?" He's going to think twice before he makes a little girl cry again. I'll tell you what, Louis, that's the best fun I've had in ages.'

Louis gave a wry smile, but didn't reply. They travelled on without speaking for a while, Lysander occasionally chuckling to himself, until finally curiosity got the better of him.

'Are you going to tell me what the hell you were doing in London, Louis?' he asked. Again getting no reply from his son, he continued, 'Have you any idea of the danger you were in? Thank God that little stunt worked earlier, because I hate to think what His Lordship would have done to you otherwise.'

Shuddering as unwanted thoughts crowded into his head, Lysander decided to resort to shock tactics in a bid to break Louis's newfound vow of silence.

'Lord Bassenford put on a little show for me yesterday morning, taught me a clear lesson. If he's capable of having his own son flogged unconscious…'

Lysander's tactics worked.

'He did that to Theo? God, the man's a monster! Dad, is Theo… oh… umm…'

'When was the last time you saw Theodore St Benedict, Louis?'

Silence.

'Answer me, Louis! I'm trying to help here.'

'Dad, you got me out of a tight spot today, I'll admit that. I also understand you've put yourself out to protect Mam, but that doesn't mean it's all OK between us now. I don't trust you, and that's going to take some time to put right.'

Almost unbearably hurt by his son's words, Lysander took a while before he managed to regain his famous composure.

'OK, so you're not going to tell me why you were in London, and you're not going to tell me whether you've managed to make contact with Theodore. I'll work on the basis that you know nothing. About ten years ago, Theodore disappeared. As far as I can gather, he became a nuisance to the Scheme, and as a result his father keeps him imprisoned in his room and tortures him on a regular basis. This is how His Lordship treats his own son, Louis, and I never want him getting his hands on you. He's a very dangerous man.'

'I know,' was all Louis would say in reply.

Lysander drove on, hoping that Louis's mood would lift once they entered Cumbria and the ground started to rise all around, but if anything he became more and more sombre the closer to home they got.

'I thought you'd be beside yourself with excitement by now, Louis,' said Lysander eventually. 'What's the matter?'

Louis balled his hand into a fist and tapped it on his lower lip, unconsciously mimicking a gesture Lysander often used when he too was uneasy. This time, he decided to reply to his father's question.

'Before I left for London, Abi Farrell told me she loves me.'

'Oh,' said Lysander, totally taken aback and not quite sure how to proceed. 'That's good, isn't it?'

'Aye, I suppose,' began Louis, then the whole lot came out in a rush. 'But what if she was only saying it to make me feel better about going to London? She knew I was scared. What if she didn't mean it? What if it's really Max she wants?'

'Do you love her?' asked Lysander.

'Loads.'

'Did you tell her?'

'Yes,' said Louis in a small voice.

'Well, my experience of the Farrells is that they're people of their word. If Abilene told you she loves you, I'm confident that means she loves you.'

'Really?'

'Yes, Louis, really.'

Louis, immeasurably comforted by his father's words, suddenly became every bit as high-spirited as Lysander had expected him to be, and the final half hour of their long journey was raucous, loud and immensely good fun.

There was quite a gathering on the main street as Lysander drove into Blenthwaite, people milling around outside The White Lion, chatting earnestly in small groups. Parking up in the inn's car park, Lysander looked around him for Jess Donatelli, anxious for news about Nicola. So preoccupied was he that the scream of joy that rang out as his son emerged from the car made him physically jump with surprise.

A petite figure raced through the crowd and flung herself bodily into Louis's arms. Watching Abi Farrell kiss his son hungrily, Lysander realised he had been spot on – she clearly had meant it when she'd told Louis she loved him.

'Abilene,' Lysander said, tapping her on the arm, 'I hate to interrupt, but is your mam around?'

'Aye, she's at home,' replied Abi. 'And Nicola's with her – they're perfectly safe. They've been having a very interesting conversation, as a matter of fact.'

Lysander and Louis both stared at Abi, their curiosity piqued.

'About what?' Lysander asked uncertainly.

'About drugs. Do you have any idea how many tranqs your wife is taking?'

'She has issues…'

'Way more, and I mean *way* more than she needs.' Abi carried on as if Lysander hadn't spoken. 'Mam wants to try alternative ways of helping her.'

'She's under the care of Dr Turnbull, the best…'

'Ah yes, Fiona Turnbull. Head of the Medical Sponsorship Group. I know all about Dr Turnbull.'

'What are you trying to say?'

'What I *am* saying is that Mam will have Nicola's best interests at heart. If it turns out she needs the drugs, she will have the drugs, but Mam doesn't believe for one second that she does need them.'

'I'm sure Dr Turnbull has…'

'Lord Bassenford's best interests at heart. She's a Sponsor, just like you.' Becoming ever more animated, Abi broke away from Louis's arms and faced his father. 'So, where does your loyalty lie, Lysander? With your wife? Or with your lord and master?'

'My wife and family come first…'

Louis snorted derisively. 'Not so's I've noticed,' he muttered.

'Who dug you out of the shit you'd got yourself into in London, Louis? Who put his neck on the line to get Lord Bassenford off your case, eh? Well, answer me!'

'Yes, well done, Dad. It's only taken you twenty-two years to realise you're a father.'

Lysander sighed. 'OK, OK, I'll never be nominated for father of the year. But when I thought I'd lost you yesterday, Louis, I… I…'

Lysander's voice cracked and Abi took pity on him.

'I suspect under that Sponsor façade, there's a loving family man just waiting to be released, isn't there, Lysander?' she said, laying a hand on his arm. 'Work with Mam. She's an excellent doctor, and she'll do all that it takes to make sure Nicola gets the care she needs. Can you honestly say that of your Sponsor colleague?'

Lysander looked at his feet and didn't respond.

'That tells me all I need to know,' Abi said with a wry grin. 'Go and see your wife, Lysander. It always makes her day when she sees you. And at least hear what Mam has to say.'

Raising his head, Lysander smiled at the determined young woman in front of him. 'I will do that,' he said. 'And thank you, Abilene, for being honest with me. I have to say, I couldn't wish for a better girlfriend for my son.'

Louis and Abi looked at each other and burst out laughing.

'Glad we've got your seal of approval,' said Louis, grinning at his father. 'Go on, go to Mam.'

Lysander left the youngsters and headed in the direction of Jess Donatelli's home. They watched him walk away for a while, then turned back to each other, Louis's grin fading as he gently ran his finger under Abi's black eye.

'How did this happen?' he asked.

Abi pulled a face. 'Max,' she replied. 'I told him a few home truths, including the fact I'd rather pull out my own fingernails than sleep with him.'

'The bastard hit you? I'll kill him!'

'Looks like someone got there first.' Abi nodded her head towards Max who was sitting alone on The White Lion's wall, isolated from the animated crowd. 'I gave him a pretty good slap in return, but I didn't mess his nose up that much.'

As Louis glanced sidelong at Max's beaten-up face and grinned in satisfaction, Matilda Santiago emerged from the inn and the concerned villagers made a beeline for her.

'What's going on, Abi?' asked Louis, watching as Matilda sidestepped the crowd and headed in their direction.

'Oh,' Abi's face dropped, 'poor Al took one hell of a beating this morning.'

'No! If only I'd got a warning to him earlier...'

'It's not your fault, Louis,' said Matilda, now close enough to overhear. 'It's not Dex's fault for refusing to get the inn endorsed, it's not Dad's fault for going for a run alone. It's nobody's fault but the violent Sponsor scumbags', and if anyone else tells me it's *their* fault, I will scream!'

'Well, that's told me,' said Louis, laughing. Responding with a beaming smile, Matilda slapped Louis on the back and gave Abi a wink and a thumbs up.

'By the way, Lou,' she said, 'I understand you've been searching the mean streets of London for a certain Sponsor tyrant's missing son. Any luck?'

'Shh!' warned Louis, glancing nervously at the curious villagers lurking nearby. 'Probably not the time or place to discuss it.'

'You're right,' said Matilda with a chuckle, 'and I don't say *that* very often.' Stepping back, she folded her arms and gave Louis and Abi an appraising look. 'Anyway, welcome home, Lou. I would give you a hug, but you two don't look ready to be prised apart just yet.'

Louis and Abi gazed at each other and grinned.

'How is your dad?' he asked, turning his attention back to Matilda. 'Is he conscious? Would it be OK to see him?'

'Yes, he came round about ten minutes ago, and yes, I'm sure he'd love to see you. Be warned, though, all he's done since he woke up is moan about his ruined looks.' Matilda laughed for a second, then her face darkened. 'For some reason, he wants to see that… that Sponsor… *thing*.'

Unable to find a word to convey her disgust, she strode over to address Max.

'Sponsor, my dad wants to speak to you.'

'Who?'

'My dad. The bloke you helped beat to a pulp earlier.'

'What, the gay guy?'

'Aye.'

'Is your father?'

'Yes, scumbag. Problem?'

'How…'

'People experiment, yeah? I'm sure you've sucked Bassenford's cock enough times to secure your cushy little sponsored number.'

'I haven't…'

'My patience has just run out,' snapped Matilda, wrenching Max's arm behind his back and forcing him to his feet. As she propelled him towards the door of the inn, she indicated with a jerk of her head that Louis and Abi could come along too, and the four of them entered Alan's bedroom a couple of minutes later.

'I look that good, eh, Louis?' said Alan, smiling painfully as Louis gasped at the sight of his battered face.

'Alan, I'm sorry. It's just… that must hurt.'

'I have felt better.'

'I could have prevented this, if only I'd warned you in time…'

Matilda screamed.

'I *did* warn you,' she said, grinning.

'Matilda, please,' groaned her father. 'Headache.'

'Sorry, Dad,' said Matilda, sitting on the side of Alan's bed. 'I brought the Sponsors' worm to see you, as requested.'

'Max,' said Alan, turning his attention to the young man, 'thank you for coming. I'm sure my daughter's invitation wasn't very politely worded.'

'He helped beat you up, Dad…'

'He also risked a lot to lead Dex to me. I may have drowned otherwise. I wanted to thank you in person, Max.'

Amazed, Max raised his eyes to look at Alan.

'No problem,' he mumbled, shame burning his face. He had indeed been conscripted to go along with Alan's beating, and although he had always considered himself to be a dedicated supporter of the Sponsors, he had been sickened by the ferocity of the attack. Dyer in particular had been vicious, taking out his own repressed sexuality on the openly gay man even after it had become clear that Alan was unconscious. Still brimming with aggression an hour or so later, Dyer had caught the guilt-ridden Max returning from helping Dex to find Alan and had demonstrated his disapproval by breaking the young man's nose. Comparing Dyer's snarling anger to Alan's gentle gratitude, comparing the tension of Sponsor meetings with the relaxed and loving atmosphere around him, Max began to feel an unfamiliar emotion.

Humility.

It was the new humble Max who took a phone call from His Lordship as he left the White Lion to return to his soulless room in Blenthwaite's sponsored hotel.

'Barrington, Stephen Dyer tells me you went against orders this morning. Explain yourself.'

'Your Lordship, I believe I actually carried out your orders. I was under the impression you wished us to give Alan Santiago a bit of a kicking to teach Dexter Montfiore a lesson. With respect, Your Lordship, I thought Mr Dyer had killed him, which would have caused unnecessary trouble for the Scheme.'

'So,' said Lord Bassenford, 'it was concern for the Sponsorship Scheme, not for Santiago and his boyfriend, that motivated you?'

'Absolutely,' lied Max.

Lord Bassenford was silent for a couple of moments, then he said, 'Very well, Barrington, I will drop the matter this time. However, remember Mr Dyer is your superior, and I don't want you going against his orders again. Understand?'

'Yes, Your Lordship.'

'As you know, Mr Dyer and his men are now on their way back to London. Unfortunately they were unable to locate and educate Lysander Trevelyan's wife, but I am confident Trevelyan will, shall we say, *appreciate* lessons he himself has been taught recently. Now, I'm a reasonable man, Barrington, and I'm going to give you one more chance to prove yourself. You will stay in Blenthwaite. Watch, observe, report – not just on Trevelyan, I want you to report on the lot of them. There are too many loose cannons in that village. I'm sure you can sniff out anything I need to hear about – you are a journalist, are you not?'

'Yes, Your Lordship, I am,' replied Max, the seeds of rebellion germinating in his mind.

***

'Fab to see you home safely, Louis,' said Alan as soon as Max had left.

'It's good to be back,' replied Louis. 'I just wish you hadn't…'

'It's OK, I'll mend,' said Alan, laughing then wincing as pain shot through his fractured ribs. 'But if one more person alludes to the fact I'm currently an invalid, I may join my daughter in a scream. Now, we're waiting to hear everything, Louis.'

'I know, Al, but I'd rather tell everyone at the same time, if that's OK with you. If you're up to it, could we get them together here later on?'

'Fine with me, Louis sweetie, but what about getting Gideon up those stairs?'

'Leave Gideon to me,' said Louis, grinning.

'Who else will you want here? Matty can spread the word, can't you, darling?'

'No worries,' said Matilda. Her father and Dex exchanged amazed glances.

'What, no argument?' asked Dex.

'Not this time,' replied Matilda. 'I'll do whatever it takes to hear what went down in London.'

'Hah! Nosiness one, belligerence nil.'

Matilda pulled a face at Dex, then turned her back on him and faced Louis. 'So, Lou, who's in the loop?' she asked.

'Well, Sarah, obviously,' replied Louis. 'She and Jen are at Gideon's at the moment, so you can catch them all at once.'

'Mam should be here too, as she was in on the plans beforehand,' said Abi. 'Willing to sacrifice her only daughter to the evil clutches of Max…'

'I'd really rather not think about that,' said Louis as everyone else in the room laughed.

'OK, Jess is in, and no doubt Cameron will tag along too.' Matilda looked at Dex. 'I guess Georgie will have to run the bar, won't she? Or are you going to do it?'

'Dex stays with me,' Alan said plaintively, reaching his hand out towards his partner.

'I'll have a word with Georgie,' said Dex, 'promise to fill her in with all the details afterwards.'

'Cool. Chris can give her a hand, soften the blow.'

Knowing how busy her uncle's veterinary practice could get, Abi turned to Matilda. 'I'm not sure he'll agree to that,' she said.

'He will if I tell him he's going to,' replied Matilda with a grin. 'So, is that everyone, Lou?'

'Aye, I think that's got it covered.'

As Alan's head dropped back on to his pillow, shadows of exhaustion showing around his eyes, Matilda kissed him gently on the forehead, then ushered Louis and Abi from the room.

'Come on, guys. Let's leave my dad in the tender loving care of Nurse Dexy.'

The three youngsters clomped down the wooden stairs. Once outside, Matilda headed over to give the waiting crowds an update on her father, while Louis took Abi's hand and led her away from The White Lion.

'What are you going to do now?' she asked.

'I suppose I ought to catch up with Gideon, Sarah and Jen,' he replied. 'But what I really want to do is spend some time with you. Preferably alone.'

'Right answer, Louis. Any idea where we can go?'

'I have indeed,' he said, leading her up a familiar lane to a familiar door.

'This is where you train!' said Abi delightedly as Louis unlocked Gideon's gym and disabled the alarm. 'My dad bought this place.'

'I know he did,' replied Louis, locking the door behind them and taking off his dark glasses in the gloom.

'It's a shame you have to wear those things so often,' Abi whispered as they stared at each other. 'Your eyes are such an amazing shade of blue.'

'What, they're not red?' asked Louis with a wry smile, long used to the popular misconception about his eye colour.

'Maybe when you've got a hangover.'

Louis threw back his head and laughed.

'I don't do hangovers. I daren't, not with Gideon working me to within an inch of my life every day.'

'Mmm, good for Gideon. Now I get to reap the benefits,' Abi murmured, lifting her mouth to meet his as her arms slid round his muscular body. Pulling her hard against him, Louis revelled in the sensation of their tongues intertwining, his hands homing in on the little gap appearing between her camisole and skirt as she reached up to undo the buttons of his shirt.

Pushing the shirt from his arms, Abi came up for air as it dropped to the floor.

'Louis, you're so fit.'

'I'm a bit white…'

'You're gorgeous, Louis, and you're so… damn… fit…'

Trailing little kisses down Abi's neck, Louis slid his hands under her cami and pulled it over her head, stroking her breasts through the thin material of her bra. Abi undid the clasps, throwing the garment to one side as Louis sank to his knees, cupping her breasts in his hands and running his tongue over her nipples. Sitting back on his heels, his fingers still teasing her nipples, he gazed hungrily at the body he'd dreamt about so many times in the past.

'Better get those jeans off, Louis,' Abi whispered, pulling him to his feet and unbuckling his belt, 'before you burst out of them.'

Chapter 9 – Home Again

Louis and Abi arrived at The White Lion that evening just as Sarah was helping Gideon out of her car and into his wheelchair. Hearing his little sister excitedly squeaking his name, Louis trotted over to the car with a broad grin, opened the back door and undid the buckles of Jenny's child seat while she pulled at the straps impatiently. As he lifted her out and she wrapped her arms around his neck, their delight at being reunited was plain for all to see.

'Might have been nice if you'd paid us a visit this afternoon,' growled Gideon unconvincingly.

Shifting Jenny to his side, Louis slid his free arm around Abi's waist and said, 'Sorry, got a bit, er, distracted...'

Gideon's grin would have put the Cheshire cat to shame.

'You two been shagging all afternoon?'

'Cheers, Gideon, subtle as ever,' said Louis as Jenny asked what 'shagging' meant.

Despite being immensely happy to see Louis again, Gideon still complained vociferously at being carried up the stairs of The White Lion's living quarters, letting loose a loud 'Fuck!' when Louis and Abi, exasperated, dumped him down none too gently in Alan and Dex's bedroom. Jenny's eyes widened in curiosity and she tapped her brother on the shoulder.

'Louis, what's…'

'Nothing for you to worry about!' Louis glared at Gideon, while Alan threw back his head and laughed, regretting it immediately as pain shot through his damaged ribs.

'Please don't make me laugh again!' he said ruefully. 'Are we all here? Louis, do you want Jenny to go?'

Snuggling down beside Abi in an armchair, Jenny on his lap, Louis replied, 'No, let her stay. We've both been through so much in the last few days, I'm not quite ready to let her out of my arms yet. Gideon, if you could keep the gutter language to a minimum, I would appreciate it.'

It took a long time for Louis to recount everything that had happened to him since he'd left Blenthwaite a mere three days earlier. His tired mind muddled things up, and he was constantly having to backtrack when he realised he'd left out crucial details, but Sarah helped, telling the parts she knew and giving him a chance to collect his thoughts.

'You just walked in?' said Gideon when Louis shared how he'd initially gained entrance to Lord Bassenford's house. 'Wow, you've got a pair of balls after all, as I'm sure Abi knows by now…'

'Gideon!' snapped Louis, unable to hide his grin as Abi whispered, 'Oh yeah, baby,' in his ear. 'Yeah, I just tagged along with the caterers delivering food for Lord Bastardford's...'

Matilda fell about with laughter, even her injured father unable to resist joining in.

'Lord Bastardford? Brilliant!'

'Name courtesy of Theo,' replied Louis. 'And it's very apt.'

Seeing that Jenny had fallen asleep on his lap, Louis then told his friends what hell Theo's life had become. Even Matilda's natural high spirits were tempered as she listened, shaking her head in disbelief.

'Dad told me on the drive home that Lord Bastardford had Theo flogged unconscious, simply to send out a message that he'll stop at nothing...'

Louis choked on his words, and Abi gave his hand a comforting squeeze as she voiced the thoughts on all their minds.

'We have got to get my cousin out of there. How does he stay sane?'

'Simple,' replied Louis. 'Inherent strength. He's a Farrell.'

***

Louis was embarrassed to wake the following morning still curled up in Dex and Alan's armchair. During the night one of his friends had covered him with a blanket, and someone, probably Sarah, had taken Jenny from his knee.

Louis was disappointed to find Abi had also gone from his side; the only other people in the room were Dex, fast asleep at Alan's bedside, and Alan himself, wide awake and regarding Louis with amusement.

'Morning, Louis. Sleep well?'

'Morning, Al. I did, thanks, but why didn't someone wake me? I'm sure the last thing you need at the moment is me crashing in your bedroom.'

'Nonsense, you're always welcome in my bedroom, Louis. Oops, didn't mean it to sound quite like that!' Chuckling painfully, Alan added, 'We did try to wake you, Lou. I thought Dex was a heavy sleeper, but he's got nothing on you.'

Laughing, Louis pushed back his blanket and got up from the chair.

'Well, as I am here,' he said, 'can I get you anything?'

'Tea would be nice thanks, Louis, and Matilda if she's about.'

'Coffee,' mumbled Dex, raising his head from Alan's pillows.

'Coffee for sleeping beauty here, please. He normally likes the quality stuff, but he can make do with instant for now.'

Still unsure whether to be amused or embarrassed at having woken up in his friends' room, Louis made his way to the kitchen and found Dex was in luck. An early riser like her father, Matilda was already making a pot of fresh coffee along with three mugs of steaming tea so Dex wouldn't have to put up with instant after all.

'Hiya, Lou,' she said, handing him a mug. 'Didn't think you were ever going to wake up.'

Laughing, Louis took a mouthful of tea. 'I've been told I sleep like the dead,' he said. 'Sarah says World War III could break out and I'd sleep through it.'

'That I can believe,' said Matilda with a wry smile. 'How's your tea?'

'Good, thanks,' replied Louis. 'You read my mind. And Dex's,' he added, nodding towards the coffee pot.

'Not difficult! Dex lives on the stuff.' Picking up Dex's mug of coffee along with a garishly pink mug of tea, Matilda said, 'I'll just take these through to the beautiful ones then I'll be right back.'

True to her word, Matilda was back within a minute.

'So, Lou, how're things?'

'Couldn't be better,' replied Louis with feeling, and Matilda grinned knowingly.

'Yes, I see you and Abi have finally got it on. I was beginning to think someone was going to have to bang your heads together.'

'And I wonder who'd put herself forward for *that* job.'

'Aye, I'm up for a bit of head banging from time to time. Both the rockin' sort and the waking-up-two-friends-who-fancy-the-pants-off-each-other-but-won't-do-a-thing-about-it sort.'

'If you knew we both secretly fancied each other,' Louis narrowed his eyes at Matilda, 'why didn't you tell us?'

'Nah. Head banging's my thing, not go-betweening. Anyway, you got there in the end, thank God. So, you training today?'

'Not today, Matty. Gideon's given me the day off to catch my breath.'

'Oh no!' said Matilda, laughing. 'Don't tell me Giddy babes has gone soft.'

'Hah, would you call him Giddy babes to his face? Actually, on second thoughts, you're probably the only person who'd dare! So, how's uni?'

'Uni? Oh, Louis, you are so behind the times! I got in on merit, and got chucked out within five minutes for telling the first tutor I met where he could shove his sponsorship application form. No, I've been travelling around, doing a bit of sessioning with bands forward thinking enough to work with an unsponsored but – though I say so myself – mighty fine musician.'

'Modest as ever, Matty,' teased Louis, nodding nonetheless at the truth in her words. Every bit as talented as her father on the guitar, Matilda had also been blessed with a magnificent singing voice.

'I was actually recording with a band down in Manchester when the call came through about Dad.'

'Cool. Which band?'

Matilda named one of the UK's top bands of the moment, and Louis was suitably impressed.

'Fame and fortune, eh?'

'Not for me,' said Matilda, not looking in the least bit put out by the fact. 'No one remembers the session musicians, just the pretty boys who front the band. And try it on with the female guitarist,' she added with a grin, shaking her cascade of dark curls away from her stunningly pretty face.

'So, you heading back to Manchester now?'

'Nope. I told the band to shove it, too. I'm staying home with Dad and Dex. Perhaps form a band of my own, who knows?'

'That I would like to see. Cheers for the tea, Matty.' Louis finished his drink and rinsed out his mug. 'I'll catch you later, as you're going to be in Blenthwaite for a while.'

After coating himself in sunblock and donning his dark glasses, Louis popped his head round Alan and Dex's bedroom door to bid them farewell then walked the familiar route home. Showering and dressing in fresh clothes, Louis then hammered down the stairs in search of breakfast, the enticing aroma of cooking bacon making his stomach growl.

'Louis lazy bones!' commented Jenny when he entered the kitchen, shrieking with laughter as he crossed his eyes and attempted to touch his nose with the tip of his tongue.

'Watch the wind doesn't change direction, Lou, or you'll be stuck looking like that,' said Sarah with a grin, taking a pack of eggs from the fridge. 'Fancy a full English?'

'The works please, Sarah, black pudding and all. I'm starving.'

'Fat gymnast!' teased Jenny – a huge fry up wasn't on Louis's usual diet sheet.

'Shh, don't tell Gideon!'

'We won't,' promised Sarah, winking at Jenny as Lysander entered the room.

'Morning, Sarah, Louis, Genevieve.'

'Daddy,' Jenny said, exasperated, 'no one calls me Genevieve any more.'

'Wrong, young lady,' Lysander replied, ruffling her hair and kissing her, '*I* call you Genevieve. Cup of tea, Lou?'

'Got one, thanks, Dad,' replied Louis, holding aloft his full mug. Making an unhealthily strong cup of tea for himself, Lysander then added at least three sugars before sitting down opposite his son.

'You could stand your spoon up in that,' said Louis, his eyes crinkling with amusement as his father set the cup of sludge on the table with a contented sigh. 'The caffeine buzz alone will keep you going at least into next week.'

'And if it doesn't, the sugar rush will,' Sarah whispered in Louis's ear as she dished up the breakfast.

'I heard that, Ms Lonsdale,' said Lysander, grinning as Louis snorted with laughter. 'So, Lou,' he added, believing his son to have spent the night with Abi, 'did you sleep well?'

Louis's smile faded.

'Yes thank you, Dad. In an armchair. In Dex and Al's room.'

'Oh,' said Lysander, a little deflated. 'How is Alan?'

'Bearing up, but he's in a lot of pain. Your friends messed him up good and proper.'

'They're not my friends, Louis.'

'Your employees, then. Your Sponsored minions. Whatever you call them, they attacked a good friend of mine and left him for dead.'

Sensing the tension growing between father and son, Sarah put their breakfasts down on the table then ushered Jenny hurriedly upstairs to get dressed. Louis and Lysander ate in silence for a while, then Louis asked, 'So, when do you return to London?'

'As soon as I've eaten and got my stuff together. Don't look at me like that, Lou. You know it's not safe for me to stay here.'

'Would you, though, even if it was safe?'

When his father didn't answer, Louis found himself becoming inordinately upset. It wasn't as though he hadn't become used to Lysander never being home for long, but after the brief camaraderie they'd shared the previous day he realised he'd been hoping this time would be different.

'OK, go back to London. Kiss Lord Bassenford's arse in all the right places. Don't let me hold you back.'

'Louis,' said Lysander, 'you know what sort of man Lord Bassenford is…'

'Yes, I know what sort of man your boss is. One who imprisons and tortures his own son.'

Knowing it would be pointless to answer while Louis was so upset, Lysander carried on eating in silence. Finally, Louis asked, 'Do you still want to be part of the Scheme, Dad? I don't mean do you feel you have to, do you *want* to?'

'I still agree with the Scheme in principle…'

'That's all I need to know,' Louis interrupted, taking his empty plate to the dishwasher. 'Goodbye, Dad. Safe journey.'

Without waiting for an answer, Louis turned on his heel and walked from the room.

Part Two – Theo

Chapter 10 – Fish Have Rights Too

On a cool day in October, a couple of months after his summer adventures, Louis popped into the pub with Abi to find a disconsolate Alan tuning one of his guitars.

'You OK, Al?'

'No,' was all Alan would say. It was Dex who elaborated.

'The band wants to get Sponsorship. Al doesn't.'

'Why?'

'Dislocated jaw, three broken ribs, concussion, loss of my fine looks for weeks, lucky still to have all my teeth. Those enough reasons for you, Louis? I hate the bloody Sponsors!'

'I meant, Alan, why do the others in the band want Sponsorship?'

'Same reason anyone does,' said Dex glumly. 'It's the only way to progress. Al's had an ultimatum: either accept Sponsorship or he's out of the band.'

'But it's your band, Al,' said Abi. 'Why else would it be called The Pink Pound? There's no way they'll find another guitarist as good as you.'

Alan's smile was decidedly half-hearted.

'Thank you for that, Abi, but it doesn't alter the fact I'll soon be a guitarist without a band.'

'Not *still* moaning about the stupid Pink Pound, Dad?' said Matilda, bursting through the door with Max in tow. Since the summer, the two of them had struck up the most unlikely of friendships, Matilda having been as quick to forgive Max when she realised he was becoming disillusioned with sponsorship as she had been to loathe him in the first place. And she wasn't the only one reaping the benefits of having a mole in the Sponsors' camp.

'I've got the latest spot check dates, Dex,' Max said.

'Thanks, Max.' Dex took the page from the young man and scrutinised the list of dates when The White Lion could expect a visit from the Sponsors. 'What can I get you? On the house, of course.'

Max accepted a bottle of lager, then turned to Alan. 'Why don't you form a breakaway band?' he asked. 'Maybe call it The Blenthwaiters, or something like that?'

'Form a band with whom, sweetie?'

'People from the village – the Blenthwaiters.'

'OK,' said Alan, putting his finely tuned instrument to one side, 'so we've got a guitarist, we just need a singer, bassist, drummer, keyboard player…'

228

'I can play drums,' said Max unexpectedly. 'And Matty can sing, as you well know, Al.'

'Cool idea, Max,' said Matilda, eyes shining. 'I'm sure someone can learn to play bass, and we don't really need a keyboardist…'

'I used to play piano,' Dex interrupted.

'Stop, the bloody lot of you! Yes, this is all very fine, but it's not much use being able to play instruments if we've got no instruments to play.'

'I've got a keyboard somewhere,' said Dex. 'I think Georgie used to play on it when she was a kid so I don't know how good it'll sound, but then we're not talking about playing the Royal Albert Hall, are we?'

'And I've got my drums,' added Max. 'It'll be good to get them out and give them a blast again.'

Smiling round at everyone, the treachery of his former bandmates forgotten in the excitement of something new, Alan said, 'I think this could work. I love it! Well done, Max.'

Max beamed.

'I'm not working with the Blenthwaiters name, though. Any name suggestions?'

'The Anti-Sponsors,' said Dex without hesitation.

'The Unsponsored,' countered Matilda.

'The Underclass.'

'Bassenford Sucks.'

'Dyer Sucks.'

'And not in a good way,' said Alan with a wink. 'What about: Dyer's in the Closet?'

'Can we move away from the Dyer theme, please?' asked Abi, grimacing.

'How about: Theo's Avengers?' Louis suggested.

'You know, I quite like that, but we could hardly go public with it,' said Alan. 'May cause some bother for us, not to mention Theo himself.'

'OK then, Dory's Avengers.'

'Who's Dory?'

'I know,' said Abi, grinning. 'That's what Louis used to call Theo. No Sponsor would ever know who we meant – we could just say we're sticking up for the rights of John Dory fish or something.'

'I love it!' said Alan again, clapping his hands with delight. 'Fish have rights too you know, Mr Sponsor. Ha-ha!'

And so Dory's Avengers came into being. The keyboard Dex had mentioned turned out to be little more than a child's toy, but as luck would have it, the remaining Pink Pound members felt so bad about their desertion of

Alan, they were happy to help his new band in any way they could. As soon as they received their brand new instruments from their Sponsors, they rang him on the sly and offered to let him have his pick of their old kit.

'Don't know why they're persisting with the Pink Pound name,' Alan grumbled as the familiar keyboard, bass guitar and amplifiers of his erstwhile band were unloaded from Chris Farrell's van and brought into the pub. 'I was the only one who's gay.'

'Get over it, Dad,' Matilda grumbled back. 'The Pink Pound is *so* last season.'

As soon as the keyboard was in place, Dex and Georgie both made a beeline for it, each wanting to stake their claim to be the band's keyboard player.

'No, Dex, I do not want to play bass. You play bass. Listen to this, Al…'

'Get off it! *My* idea, *my* keyboard…'

'Piss off, Dexter!'

'Piss off yourself, Georgia!'

'Shut up!' yelled Alan. 'You want to be in the band? You audition. Dex, play something.'

'Oh yeah,' grumbled Georgie. 'We audition and you choose your boyfriend.'

'You audition and we choose whoever's better. Not just me, the whole band chooses. Dex sweetie, play something, please.'

Dex turned out to be a far more accomplished keyboard player than his casual suggestion had indicated and was the obvious choice for the band. Georgie ended up playing bass, which she actually found she loved, and for weeks after the brief audition she spent most of her free time with Alan, learning chords and playing techniques. Max's drum kit took up residence in the bar along with Dex's keyboard; the young man played with rather more enthusiasm than skill, but once he'd been persuaded that he didn't need to try and pound all the drums at once, he turned out to be perfectly competent at keeping the beat.

Bit by bit, Dory's Avengers came together.

***

It was during that autumn, as his avengers were attempting to make beautiful music, that life finally began to improve for Theo. Rather to his own surprise, Lord Bassenford was thinking about his son with increasing regularity – whenever yet another of his grovelling Sponsors had been seen out of the house by Mooreland, whenever one or other of his household staff had said all the right things to him, he found himself yearning for the company of someone who'd actually argue with him. Rosanna may have been blunt and outspoken with everyone else, but she always deferred to her father; Lysander could be cheeky, but he never disagreed with Lord Bassenford. The only person in His Lordship's world who had the nerve to tell him he was wrong was Theo, and to his amazement, he found he liked it.

As a result, he was visiting his son's room more and more often, to Theo's obvious dismay.

'You again, Your Lordship? I was hoping for a quiet day of looking out the window. I haven't had an opportunity to do that since… hmm, let me see… yesterday.'

'Can't you be nice for once, Theodore?'

'Not sure, Your Lordship. Can you?'

To Theo's surprise, Lord Bassenford roared with laughter.

It didn't take Theo long to realise that his father's increased visits were coinciding with a distinct improvement in his treatment. His back, although scarred, had healed from its summer flogging, and for a couple of months there'd been no repeat of the painful experience. If only Dyer's 'physical' time could be brought to an end as well, Theo's life would be positively comfortable.

Dyer's physical time did come to an end, quite dramatically, a few weeks before Christmas. Alone in his office after a particularly grovelly Mortimer O'Reilly had departed, Lord Bassenford was in need of some more scintillating company and flicked on the security monitor to see if Theo was awake. Theo was indeed awake; in fact, he was parading, stark naked, in front of his security camera.

There was no other way to describe it: the young man was putting on a show.

'Theodore, what the heck are you playing at?' murmured Lord Bassenford, switching off the monitor and making his way downstairs.

In the security room on the ground floor, Stephen Dyer sat alone in front of his own monitor, trousers round his ankles, eyes fixed on Theo. This was his closely guarded secret; he knew the ridicule he'd suffer if it became common knowledge that he found Theo attractive. More than attractive, actually – he fancied the young man so much it had become a physical ache. Over and over again, Dyer denied his true sexuality. He wasn't gay, of course he wasn't, he just enjoyed the sight of Theo St Benedict naked. Enjoyed it very much…

It was unfortunate for Dyer that at the moment Theo's show and his own right hand brought him to climax, the door of the security room opened and in walked Lord Bassenford. Taking in the scene before him: his chief of security masturbating in front of a large screen on which his son was striking seductive poses, His Lordship curled his lip slightly then composed himself with remarkable speed.

'Which are Theodore's keys, Dyer? These ones? Now, if you'll be good enough to make yourself decent and clean up your mess, I'd like to see you in my office.'

Leaving Dyer looking as if he wished the ground would open up and swallow him whole, Lord Bassenford went back upstairs, all the way to the fourth floor and Theo's room. Finding to his relief that his son had put some clothes on, he said, 'Bracelet, Theodore.'

Eyebrows raised, Theo held out the electronic security tag clipped firmly to his wrist. Lord Bassenford unlocked it and laid it on his son's bedside table.

'Follow me!' he barked.

'What, out there?' asked Theo incredulously, waving a hand towards the open door.

'Yes, out there.'

Too surprised to think of his usual smart answer, Theo followed Lord Bassenford out of his bedroom and walked freely down the stairs for the first time in years.

'Sit down!' commanded Lord Bassenford when they reached his office. Completely ignoring the seats in front of his father's desk, Theo headed instead for a large armchair, and when a timorous knock sounded at the door a few minutes later, he was already comfortable and relaxed. Not as good at hiding his surprise as the St Benedict father and son, Stephen Dyer started violently at seeing Theo in the armchair, long legs stretched out in front of him, hands clasped over his stomach. So calm. So devastatingly good-looking…

'Sit down, Dyer. Thank you for, er, coming so quickly.'

Catching his father's innuendo and failed attempt to disguise a snort of laughter as a sneeze, Theo immediately guessed what must have happened.

Oh boy, he thought, *I am going to enjoy this*.

'No problem at all, Your Lordship, and I can explain…'

'Yes, Dyer, I would like some explanations. Theodore, would you be so good as to explain why you were prancing around naked in front of your security camera earlier?'

'It amuses me, Your Lordship. I believe it amuses other people too. Did you enjoy the show?'

'No. However, you are correct – it was, ahem, *stimulating* a certain member of the household. Were you aware that Dyer masturbates over you?'

Dyer spluttered and went crimson. Smiling, Theo said, 'I thought there was a distinct possibility, Your Lordship, yes.'

'Don't you mind?'

Theo unclasped his hands and spent a few moments looking at his fingers. Finally, he said, 'It beats being buggered on a regular basis.'

Tick-tock went the grandfather clock into the deafening silence that followed Theo's statement. Lord Bassenford's frown deepened as he grasped the implications of his son's words; Dyer looked absolutely petrified. Only Theo remained calm, continuing his study of his fingers before raising his head to smile at the two older men.

'Dyer,' said Lord Bassenford slowly, 'have you been sexually abusing my son?'

Tick-tock, tick-tock. *Please let me wake up from this nightmare*, thought Dyer.

'Dyer, I'm waiting.'

'I, er, I thought it would be all right, Your Lordship. I thought, er, that you, er…'

'You thought what? That I'd totally given up on my son? What gave you the right to make such an assumption?'

'Well, er…' Once again Dyer broke off, waving helplessly at the iron rings on the wall where Theo had taken so many beatings.

'Ah, I see. Because I have ordered you to punish my son when I see fit to have him punished, you thought you could take matters into your own hands any time you wished. No wonder there've been times when the camera's been off in Theodore's room. I should have questioned it sooner.'

'With respect, Your Lordship, I thought Theodore…'

'*Lord* Theodore, Dyer.'

'Yes, Your Lordship. I thought, er, Lord Theodore enjoyed it.'

'Do you enjoy it, Theodore?'

Theo pulled a face. 'Not in the slightest.'

'Do you find men attractive?'

'No, Your Lordship. I see many nice-looking people walking by outside, and it's always the ladies who catch my eye.'

'Do you find men attractive, Dyer?'

'No, Your Lordship, I'm no bender...'

'Yet you seemed to find my son extremely sexually stimulating a short while ago!'

Lord Bassenford was silent for a while, leaving Dyer to suffer more of the clock's infernal ticking. Finally, he spoke.

'I've always been happy with your work, Dyer. You carry out your duties with enthusiasm and an attention to detail which I find pleasing. Therefore I'm not going to take this matter any further. I rather think this interview has been punishment enough for you.'

'Thank you, Your Lordship,' stammered Dyer, looking for a second as though he was going to prostrate himself at Lord Bassenford's feet.

'However, I can't have you in charge of the security in Lord Theodore's room any more. If you would be so good as to find Lee Fellows and ask him to come and see me, I will make arrangements for him to take over. Also, any abuse of Lord Theodore must stop, immediately. If he needs punishing, it will be carried out on my orders alone. Understand?'

'Yes, Your Lordship. Thank you, Your Lordship.'

'Now go. Send Fellows up.'

Dyer almost ran from the room, so great was his anxiety to be away from Lord Bassenford's disgust and Theo's mocking smile. Chuckling to himself, Lord Bassenford muttered 'Sycophant' as the door closed, causing Theo to roar with laughter.

'Couldn't have put it better myself, Your Lordship.'

'Why didn't you tell me?'

Lord Bassenford steepled his fingers under his chin and regarded his son, who stared steadily back at him. If Theo hadn't known better, he might have thought there was concern for him in his father's expression.

His Lordship was the first to break the uncomfortable silence.

'You're driving me mad with your constant chatter, Theodore. Make yourself scarce.'

Rising slowly from his comfortable armchair, Theo said, 'As you wish, Your Lordship,' and strode from the room. He wasn't surprised in the slightest to find Dyer hovering at the top of the stairs to the fourth floor.

Grabbing hold of Theo's lapels, Dyer slammed the young man into the wall.

'You little fuck! Don't think this is over…'

'Get your hands off me, Dyer! Didn't you hear Lord Bassenford? The abuse stops, now. Unless you want me to inform His Lordship that you are disobeying his orders, I suggest you remember that.'

As Dyer reluctantly let go of his collar, Theo smoothed his clothes and continued.

'Good. Now, I believe Lord Bassenford instructed you to find Lee Fellows, so don't you think you'd better carry out his wishes? Oh, and one more thing: it's "Lord Theodore", not "you little fuck".'

***

From that day, Theo's life improved dramatically. Lee Fellows was instructed to give him the run of the house, and Theo thrived in his newfound freedom, charging noisily up and down the stairs, exploring every nook and cranny, and watching anything and everything on television. Finding to his delight that there was a large flat screen in almost every room, he didn't take long to develop the bad habit of leaving them all switched on as he moved from one part of the house to another, infuriating the sour-faced Mooreland who was tasked with switching them off again.

Within days of Dyer's humiliation, Theo had discovered the household gym and embarked on an energetic exercise regime, determined to get properly fit after years of having to settle for press-ups and stomach crunches on his bedroom floor. Ravenously hungry after his workout, he would follow each session in the gym with a visit to the kitchen, helping himself to every tasty morsel the moment it emerged from the oven.

'You'll spoil your dinner,' the cook would warn.

'Unlikely,' he'd reply with a wink.

With the exception of Mooreland and Dyer, the household staff thoroughly enjoyed day-to-day contact with Theo, finding him to be a hugely entertaining young man despite his long absence from the social scene. Marina, of course, was delighted to have her brother back in her life, and even Lord Bassenford wasn't immune to his son's high spirits. He seemed far more inclined to smile rather than snarl since he'd freed Theo from his bedroom, and for the first time in years the grand old London townhouse felt like a home again.

As Christmas drew closer, Theo rediscovered sights, sounds and smells almost forgotten from childhood. The house was fragrant with the scent of pine as huge trees were brought in to adorn the rooms, and he was on hand the second each one was put into position, armed with a box of decorations.

'Tone it down a little, Theodore, or the tree will collapse,' Lord Bassenford said, laughing as his son hung ornaments from every inch of the impressive Norway spruce in the drawing room. 'This is the one people can see from the road, so it needs to be a work of art.'

'Don't let that prick near it then,' sneered Lady Rosanna, sitting aloof in the corner of the room. 'Life was so much nicer with him out of the way.'

'Many would disagree with you, Rosanna darling. Our adoring public is delighted that Theodore has recovered from his breakdown, and good popular opinion is always healthy for the Scheme.'

'Does he have to be so much in evidence, though, Father? He's…'

'Rosanna!' snapped Lord Bassenford. 'I find it refreshing having him around the place. Now, have you any more to say on the matter?'

'No, Father. Of course, you're right.'

Mildly disappointed at his daughter's sycophantic response, Lord Bassenford turned and caught Theo trying to drape tinsel on the already heavily laden Christmas tree.

'Theodore, I thought I said enough!'

'Of course, Your Lordship, you're so right, Your Lordship. May I kiss your arse now Rosanna's finished, Your Lordship?'

'If you're going to mock your sister, Theodore, I suggest you go to your room. Ah, actually, no. Stay. That'll be the photographer.'

Every year Lord Bassenford commissioned a top photographer to take pictures of his family, the best of which were made into Christmas cards for the privileged few. For the first time in a decade, Theo was to feature in the photos alongside his father and sisters.

'OK,' said the photographer when everyone was ready. 'Do you want a few with all of you, Your Lordship, or just the youngsters?'

'Just the youngsters for now.'

The photo shoot took a lot longer than expected, and Lord Bassenford wasn't sure whether to be amused or exasperated at Theo's disruptive influence. The young man questioned every pose he was asked to make, laughing out loud when the photographer suggested he hand a gift to Rosanna.

'How about I smash it over her head? That'd be a great picture.'

'Father, do I have to…'

'Yes, Rosanna, you do! Can you two please *try* to look like members of a happy family?'

In the end the photographer gave up on any attempt to get Theo and Rosanna to interact, settling instead on a series of pictures with Marina in between the two of them. He then took some photos of the whole family, even Theo behaving himself once his father was included. The formal photographs done, Rosanna stalked off to mix herself a gin and tonic, and the photographer got some shots of Theo and Marina relaxing together by the Christmas tree. These shots turned out to be by far the best of the lot.

The photographer was still packing up his equipment when people started arriving for the drinks party scheduled for that evening. Greeting his guests, Lord Bassenford was mildly annoyed to see his son throw himself down on the sofa facing the television screen and point the remote control in its direction, and as jangly cartoon theme tunes threaded their way through the polite buzz of conversation in the room, the red mist began to descend.

Eventually His Lordship snapped.

'Theodore, turn that off and join the soirée like an adult!'

A pair of light-brown eyes looked over from the sofa.

'Sorry, Your Lordship. I'll turn the sound down.'

'You'll turn the television off and join the company, Theodore!'

On his third glass of champagne and slightly tipsy, Lysander Trevelyan decided to offer an opinion.

'Oh, let him watch cartoons, Your Lordship,' he said carelessly. 'God knows, he's missed out on a huge chunk of his childhood.'

The buzz of conversation died down immediately as everyone in the room turned to stare at Lysander in astonishment.

'Turn the television off, Theodore!' hissed Lord Bassenford, eyes flashing ominously. Theo did as he was told, recognising that it would be the worse for Lysander were he to enrage his father even more.

'Are you questioning the way I treat my son, Lysander?'

'No, Lord Bassenford, of course not…'

'You are aware, are you not, that Theodore brought everything on himself? You are aware, are you not, of the need to teach him to show respect for the Scheme?'

'Really, I didn't mean…'

'What did you mean then, Lysander? I have been very generous in my treatment of my son, yet you feel the need to criticise. I could quite easily arrange it for Theodore…'

'Excuse me, I am here,' Theo said.

'Indeed, Theodore. So, do you feel that you've missed out on your childhood as Lysander here seems to think?'

Theo stood up, a look of mild amusement on his face that was uncannily reminiscent of an expression his father often wore.

'Not at all, Your Lordship,' he said. 'Being locked in a decaying room is every boy's dream, surely?'

'Answer without the insolence, you ungrateful little shit!' roared Lord Bassenford, totally losing his temper with his over-confident son, much to Rosanna's delight. 'And I am your father, for God's sake – stop calling me "Your Lordship".'

The room was perfectly silent as Theo walked, slowly and deliberately, until he was standing almost nose to nose with Lord Bassenford. Marina curled up in a ball on the sofa, offering a silent prayer that Theo wouldn't infuriate their father any more. As her brother spoke, she realised her prayer had gone unheeded.

'No, you are not my father. I will *never* call you "Father". You cannot demand my respect, *Your Lordship*, no matter how important you are in your... precious... Scheme!'

Theo pretty much spat the last word into Lord Bassenford's face. Taking a short while to compose himself, Lord Bassenford then turned to his chief of security.

'Mr Fellows, take my son to my office. Mr Dyer is well acquainted with the appropriate punishment.'

Knowing what was in store for Theo, Lysander murmured, 'I'm so sorry,' as the young man passed on his way to the door.

'It's fine,' he replied, grabbing Lysander's hand briefly. All eyes were on Theo as he left the room, head held high, and so no one noticed Lysander slip the folded piece of paper he'd just been handed into his pocket.

***

Heading home a couple of days later to celebrate Louis's birthday, Lysander was still mulling over Lord Bassenford's soirée. Why hadn't he held his tongue? Guilt overwhelmed him as he remembered the pain his foolish words had caused, and he checked yet again that Theo's precious piece of paper was safely tucked away in his jacket pocket. The least he could do was make sure he delivered it to its intended recipient.

Arriving in Blenthwaite, Lysander found The White Lion jubilant with the sounds of laughter and a live band playing, welcoming light pouring from the bar into the darkening street outside. As he approached, Jessica Donatelli appeared in the doorway and sent the cork from a champagne bottle flying, catching the first surge of fizz in a glass she'd had tucked under her arm. Grinning at Lysander, she indicated with a jerk of her head that he should follow her inside, then disappeared back into the warmth of the pub.

The scene that greeted him when he entered was so different to Lord Bassenford's stiff and nervous soirée that he couldn't help but smile with glee. The words 'Happy Birthday, Louis' were written in huge, colourful letters on the chalk boards over the top of the bar, and a large Christmas tree added its glow to that of the blazing log fire. The band was playing a selection of well-known songs, noisily but not too badly, and Lysander was surprised to see a beaming Max Barrington on drums. The birthday boy himself was jumping around in time to the music, one arm around Abi Farrell's shoulders. Sarah and Jenny were improvising an energetic jig by the fireplace, and a happy and alert-looking Nicola was tapping out the rhythm on the arm of Gideon Wallis's wheelchair.

As the revellers noticed Lysander hovering by the door, the party spirit faltered quite alarmingly. The band stopped abruptly, Max looking positively terrified at having been caught enjoying himself by a high-ranking Sponsor, and the dancing soon slowed to a standstill too.

Eventually, Louis broke the uncomfortable silence.

'Hello, Dad. Glad you could make it.'

'So am I. Please don't stop the party on my account. Happy birthday, Louis, these are for you.'

Louis accepted his father's card and present with a smile, then hugged Lysander in gratitude as he unwrapped a stylish and very expensive watch.

'It's cool, Dad, really nice,' he said, not having the heart to tell his father that he didn't like to wear any jewellery on his sensitive skin. 'Here, would you like some champers?'

As Lysander accepted a glass of champagne, the partygoers relaxed a little and demanded more music. Dex played the familiar opening bars of *Whiter Shade of Pale*, oblivious to the amused glances from his bandmates.

'Tactless, Dex,' said Matilda, her murmur amplified around the room by the microphone in front of her. Embarrassed, Dex stopped playing and mouthed 'Sorry' at Louis, who roared with laughter.

'Thought you were playing that in my honour,' he said.

'Don't think we'll run with that one, Bleachy.' Max twirled his drumsticks, happy now that Lysander hadn't in fact brought a legion of Sponsor thugs with him.

'Whatever,' replied Louis, a wicked grin on his face. 'If you're looking for something appropriate, how about *Journalists who Lie* by Morrissey?'

'Ooh, get you!' sang Max. Although Louis and Max were still a little mistrustful of each other, the insults they swapped, once designed to be hurtful, were now mellowing into banter.

'Play some bloody music!' called a gruff voice from the crowd.

'Manners maketh man, Giddy babes,' remarked Matilda, grinning as the gruff voice added a reluctant 'Please'. '*Long Live Rock 'n' Roll*!' she yelled, and the band burst back into life.

Placing a hand on Louis's arm just before he launched himself on to the dance floor, Lysander said, 'This is for you too.'

Louis took the folded slip of paper from his father. On the front was a surprisingly good drawing of a white rabbit eating a birthday cake, and Louis's face broke into a huge grin as he realised whom it was from.

'Look, Abi,' he said excitedly, holding the 'birthday card' open so she could see the message inside. Intrigued when Abi shrieked in delight and flung her arms round Louis, Matilda prised the piece of paper out of his fingers and read it, everyone in the room looking quizzically in her direction as her smile got wider by the second.

'Listen to this note, guys, just listen! "Happy birthday, Louis. Wish I could join you – I'm there in spirit. Have a good one, and get extra drunk for me, will you? Everything's cool here – really, it is! Love to you, Abi *et al*. Dory".'

Chapter 11 – What's Going On?

It took a long time for the jubilation that followed the news from Theo to quieten down enough for coherent conversation. To Lysander's dismay, he was the first topic of that conversation.

'Matty, do you think it was wise to read that out in front of him?' said Max, jerking his head in Lysander's direction. 'Especially as you've kind of blown the cover of Dory's Avengers.'

'Oh, I thought you were avenging a fish,' replied Lysander with a valiant attempt at humour.

'Told you,' Abi said, giggling tipsily, 'fish have rights.'

However, others in the room weren't so amused. Chloe, who'd managed to travel north for Louis's birthday with her father, Jim and the others who'd befriended him in London, said seriously, 'Max is right, you know. He might be your dad, Louis, but he's also one of Bastardford's lapdogs.'

Equally serious, Nicola defended her husband.

'Remember who brought the letter to Louis. Lysander had plenty of opportunity to read it on the way here. He could have not delivered it at all. He could,' she continued, rising from her place beside Gideon to cross over to Lysander and take his hand, 'have handed it to Lord Bastardford.'

'Yes, but all the same…'

'I'm with Nikki on this one,' Gideon interrupted unexpectedly. 'Lysander had every opportunity to betray us all. He didn't.'

Lysander started to thank Gideon, but didn't get very far.

'Save your grovelling for Lord Bastardford, Trevelyan. I still think you're an arrogant fuck who neglects his wife and kids deplorably.'

'Don't you *dare* call my daddy naughty names,' said Jenny, waving her hands furiously at Gideon and diffusing the tension in the room a little.

'I'm with Gideon on this one, and God knows how I hate the Sponsors,' Abi put in, sobering up a little. 'Also, bear in mind if Lysander was close enough to Theo to receive this note from him, he must have news to tell us. Chase him out of Blenthwaite with pitchforks later if you must, but first I would like to listen to what he has to tell us.'

'A good point, well made,' Chloe said with a grin. Chloe and Abi had got on well from the moment they'd met, recognising immediately the strength of character they shared. Helping herself to champagne and giggling again, Abi noticed that Chloe and Cameron were also getting on well, for somewhat different reasons.

'OK, Dad, it's down to you. What's going on in London with Theo? We want to hear everything too, not an edited version.'

'What about Genevieve?'

As Jenny protested that she was grown up enough to stay, for once letting the use of her full name go unchallenged, Louis said, 'Jenny's young, but she's strong. She stays.'

All eyes were still on Lysander, but they were a little less hostile now. Nicola stayed by his side as he spoke to the Unsponsored, and he wondered in an unusually humble moment what he'd done to deserve such devotion from his wife.

'OK, this is what I know. Something changed His Lordship's mind about Theo recently. No, young lady, I don't know what the something was.'

'Actually, I was going to ask you not to call that evil piece of shit "His Lordship". You're not with your bunch of kiss-arse Sponsors now.'

'Er – it's Chloe, isn't it? Point taken, Chloe. I'll compromise by calling him WSB.'

'Why WSB, Dad?'

'Lord Bastardford's initials, Lou – William St Benedict,' replied Chloe, turning to address Lysander again. 'I'd rather you called him Lord Bastardford...'

'A few minutes ago you were mistrustful of me. Works both ways, you know. What would my life be worth if it got back to WSB that I'd called him... er... what you said?'

Chloe nodded slightly, conceding the point to Lysander. 'I'm not sure it'd do your life a world of good if it got back to Lord Bastardford that you were having a cosy evening in the pub with us lot,' she said, 'but have it your way.'

'Right, I digress,' Lysander continued, warming to his task now he was on the familiar ground of addressing an attentive audience. 'A few weeks ago, Theo started appearing around the house. I believe he's still restricted from going outside, but he can wander around inside and talk to whoever he wants.'

'He must love that,' said Louis, grinning.

'He does. He particularly loves watching cartoons.' Tapping his fist on his bottom lip, Lysander remembered the trouble Theo's cartoons had caused at Lord Bassenford's soirée. Louis and his friends had asked for an account of everything, but dare he include that bit?

'Marina loves it too. It's been so nice to see her coming out of her shell, she's a great girl. Theo's amazing. All he's been through, he's still bright, humorous, entertaining. Everyone in the household adores him. All apart from Rosanna, that horrible man who heads security and...'

'Dyer?'

'Yes, him. By the way, I should have said *used* to head security. Now it's headed by some bloke called Fellows. Dyer's been demoted, and I think that may have something to do with Theo.'

Abi leapt up to exchange high-fives with Cameron and her mother, then grabbed another bottle of champagne and yelled, 'That calls for celebration!'

When the youngsters had calmed down a bit, Lysander continued.

'No, Dyer's not happy at all. Thank you, Abilene, I will drink to that. I've never liked the man, and I gather he's taken every opportunity to make Theo's life miserable. He's a bona fide scumbag.'

'Hear, hear!' said Max.

'What?'

'Just agreeing that Dyer's a scumbag.'

'He's your boss, isn't he, Maxwell?' asked Lysander, raising his eyebrows. 'Looks like I'm not the only one treading on thin ice. My theory is that WSB is actually sick and tired of his "kiss-arse Sponsors", to use Chloe's phrase. The only person who dares challenge him is Theo, and I think WSB enjoys that. Theo's gained his freedom through his sheer nerve.'

At last I seem to have said something right, Lysander thought as the Unsponsored smiled at the mention of Theo's nerve. However, his relief was short-lived, and it was his own son's question that shattered it.

'What about the torture – has *that* stopped?' Noticing his father tapping his fist against his bottom lip once again, Louis added, 'Tell us everything, Dad.'

'The torture seemed to stop for a while, but I don't know for sure. What I do know, I'm afraid, is that Theo took a beating a couple of nights ago.'

'Details,' said Louis relentlessly.

'WSB was hosting a soirée. He likes to have a little get-together after his festive family photo has been taken. I'm afraid I rather, erm, screwed up.'

The eyes in the room were hostile again.

'When I arrived, WSB was getting pissed off with Theo watching television. I'm afraid Theo does go a little far in antagonising his father sometimes…'

'Don't you *dare* blame Theo for his torture!'

'Really, I wasn't, Matilda. Theo was watching cartoons, laughing like a child. Actually I found it contributed nicely to the festive mood of the evening, added a sparkle that's been missing since Isabelle…'

Lysander coughed, trying not to catch Chris Farrell's eyes, then continued.

'WSB clearly didn't agree. He told Theo to turn the cartoons off, and without thinking, I stuck up for Theo.'

'That's cool, Dad…'

'No it's not, Louis. Hear me out, then decide whether or not you want to fetch your pitchforks. I opened my big mouth and told WSB that Theo should be allowed to watch cartoons as he'd missed out on a huge chunk of childhood. WSB hauled me over the coals a bit. That's fine, I can deal with it. Unfortunately, Theo got involved and told WSB a few home truths about his failings as a father. WSB had him…'

'Flogged?'

'I'm afraid so,' replied Lysander sadly.

'When did Theo give you the note, Dad?'

'As he walked from the room to take his punishment. He was so dignified, Lou. I tried to apologise, but he said it was OK… and slipped me the note.'

'He was that cool when he knew he was being led off to be flogged?' asked Matilda, eyes like saucers. 'This Theo is my kind of man.'

'Unlucky, Max,' murmured Alan, knowing full well that Max had been repeatedly trying to win Matilda's affections.

'WSB called me back to his house the morning after the soirée,' continued Lysander. 'I was expecting one hell of a grilling, but just as I'd sat down, Theo appeared.'

'How did he look?'

'Defiant! Theo's good at that. He walked in, Marina in tow as usual, and turned on the telly.'

'What did His Lordshit do?'

'He commented that Theo never learns. He actually sounded proud, too. Like I said, Theo's life is far from ideal, but it's improving.'

Lysander finished speaking, and tapped his fist nervously on his lips as he waited for a barrage of abuse. What he actually got amazed him.

'You stuck up for Theo, Lysander. I think that took some nerve,' said Jess.

'Yeah, you stood up to His Lordshit,' added Chloe, finding she was developing a slight admiration for Louis's father. 'I bet none of his other lapdogs would do that.'

'Don't be too hard on yourself, Dad. Theo wouldn't blame you.'

'How do you know?' asked Lysander, hoping to catch Louis off guard, but his son just smiled.

'Is Theo hot?' said Matilda suddenly, prompting hoots of laughter and a 'One track mind' that sounded suspiciously like it came from her father.

'I'm no expert,' Lysander replied, grinning at Matilda, 'but why not have a look for yourself?'

Crossing over to The White Lion's computers, Lysander booted one up. Once online he called up a popular search engine and typed in 'St Benedict Christmas'.

'By the way,' Lysander said to Dex as he looked through the options on the screen, 'how do you manage to get Internet connection in here?'

'What, being as the inn's unsponsored, you mean? The Wi-Fi account's in Chris's name. He's Sponsor-endorsed. Medical.'

'So don't even *think* about giving Dex any Sponsor hard sell,' added Alan. 'The answer remains no.'

'No hard sell, Alan, I was merely curious.' Turning his attention back to the computer screen, Lysander tapped in a password and found the images he wanted.

'Excellent, they're on,' he murmured, clicking on the recently taken photos of Theo and his sisters. 'Here you go, Matilda, judge for yourself.'

Everyone crowded around the screen, jostling for a place to get a good look at the latest pictures of the St Benedict siblings.

'How on earth did you manage to access these?' asked Dex.

'I got chatting to WSB's photographer,' replied Lysander. 'He'd been taking photos for His Lord... WSB's personal Christmas cards and was still there when my colleagues and I arrived for the drinks party...'

'So these were taken shortly before Theo was beaten unconscious?' Seeing Lysander lower his head in shame, Dex softened his tone and added, 'It's not your fault, Lysander. It's no one's fault but that monster you call your boss.' When Lysander still didn't respond, Dex prompted, 'You were saying?'

'Ahem, yes. I got chatting to the photographer. Nice bloke. He showed me some of the pics he'd taken, asked if I wanted any family photos doing myself and gave me the password to have a look at his work. So here we are.'

'Ah, I didn't think just anyone would be allowed to have a gawp at His Lordshit and family.' Dex scrutinised the pictures on the computer monitor again. 'Looks like Theo and Lady Rosanna want to kill each other,' he said, amused. 'Can't see any of these being suitable for the sponsored season's greetings.'

'Not the ones with Rosanna in, no. But look at these.'

Lysander flicked through the un-posed shots of Theo and Marina, taken after the evil eye of Rosanna had left the scene. Once again everyone crowded around him to get a better look.

'Oh yeah,' said Matilda, her eyes fixed on the photographs of Theo, 'he's hot.'

***

Lysander woke late the morning following Louis's birthday, rather hungover but feeling happier than he had done for a long time, warm and comfortable in his own bed. A fire was flickering away cheerfully in the grate, casting a pleasing glow around the bedroom, a cup of steaming hot tea sat on his bedside table, and Nicola was beside him, smiling.

'Nikki, you look wonderful!'

'*Compos mentis,* you mean?'

'Well, yes, that too. I guess Dr Donatelli was right – you didn't need all those stupid pills after all.'

'Mmm, I did have a little tranquilliser dependency going on for a few years, didn't I,' Nicola said, totally understating the extent of her addiction and the difficult time she'd had leaving it behind. If it hadn't been for Louis's determination to get to know his mother for the first time in his life, backed up by Gideon's desire to rediscover his one-time protégée and expert medical care from Jess, she'd never have got this far.

'Well, I'm just happy to have the woman I fell in love with back,' said Lysander. 'And I can only apologise for not realising sooner that… umm…'

262

'That your Sponsor friends had found a convenient way of keeping me quiet?' said Nicola with a wry smile.

Lysander gave her a searching look. 'I'm sure it wasn't like that…'

'You know full bloody well it was, Lysander!' As her husband's head dropped, his face burning with shame, Nicola softened her tone. 'Look, Sandy, I know you believed, or perhaps chose to believe, the official line that Dr Turnbull fed you. It wouldn't have done your career much good to do otherwise, would it? But I also love you too much to hold it against you. So, let's not speak of it again. I for one want to put that chapter of my life firmly behind me.'

'Have you spoken to Louis about this?'

'No, and I don't intend to. I'm not sure he'd be quite as forgiving as me.'

Thinking of Louis grilling him for information about Theo the previous evening, Lysander could only agree.

'Thank you for your support last night, Nikki. You were amazing.'

'So were you. It must have been pretty scary to start with.'

'Well, I got through it without a pitchfork in my backside,' said Lysander, grinning. 'Are the kids up yet?'

'Jen's at school. Louis… well, let's just say we leave Louis to it when Abi stays over.'

Chuckling, Lysander enjoyed his cup of tea while he and Nicola reminisced about the party the previous night. Dex had managed to get the best photos of Theo and Marina projected on to the inn's big screen, usually reserved for major sporting events, and the party had restarted in earnest. Dory's Avengers played better than ever before, everyone got extremely drunk and raucous (which probably contributed to the band sounding so classic), and many a toast was proposed to freedom and the pleasures of too much champagne.

'Ah, I think love's young dream may be awake,' said Lysander, finally hearing the sound of movement from his son's room.

Sliding back into bed next to her husband, Nicola replied, 'Well, I was just going to suggest that love's middle-aged dream stay in bed a little longer…'

***

It was well into the afternoon before everyone in the Trevelyan household was up and about. Lysander and Nicola found their son and Abi in the family room; Louis's birthday cards were displayed all around, the home-made one from Theo taking pride of place on the mantelpiece, and the youngsters were curled up on the sofa, watching cartoons.

'It's our tribute to Theo,' said Abi, laughing along with Louis as one of the baddies was squashed flat by a ten-ton weight. Leaving the young couple to their entertainment, Lysander and Nicola went to fetch Jenny from school, much to the excitement of the other parents at the gates. It wasn't often they got the opportunity to meet a famous Sponsor in the flesh, and they took full advantage, shamelessly scrutinising the increasingly embarrassed Lysander as they waited for their children.

Delighted to see her father was still in Blenthwaite, Jenny ran from her classroom as soon as the day's lessons ended and leapt into his arms, informing him that she'd be performing in the school Christmas play on Friday and asking if he would be there to watch. Hardly daring to breathe as she waited for Lysander's reply, Nicola crossed her fingers behind her back and hoped.

'Yes, Genevieve,' said Lysander, to the delight of both Jenny and her mother, 'I'll be home for a few days, actually.'

True to his word, Lysander stayed until the following Monday. Jenny's school play was a new experience for him, one he found he enjoyed immensely, and it was with regret that Lysander realised Louis had gone through his entire childhood without his father attending a single one of his school events.

'I bet you got loads of prizes, Louis,' said Lysander as the family ate dinner with Abi and

Sarah, his words sounding feeble and inadequate as he remembered Gideon's accusation of deplorable neglect. Without a word, Sarah left the room and returned with a box full of trophies.

'I didn't know we'd still got these,' said Louis, peering into the box.

'They're mainly sporting trophies,' said Sarah to her boss. 'Louis always was the active type, but I think there may be a "most improved at maths" prize from one year.'

'Athlete of the year. Gymnast of the year.' Lysander unpacked the trophies one by one, reading the accolades out loud. 'One hundred metres winner. Swimming. More running. Gymnastics. More gymnastics – Lou, did anyone else do sport at your school?'

'Of course,' said Sarah proudly, 'but no one was as good as our Louis.'

'You still practise gymnastics, don't you, Lou?'

Again, Louis didn't have a chance to answer, his mother cutting in this time.

'He does, and I've been to watch a few times. He's seriously brilliant, Sandy.'

'Well you're qualified to judge, Nikki. Lou, would it be OK for me to watch too?'

'Don't feel you have to make up for not coming to watch me at school, it really doesn't…'

'Louis! I'd like to watch – if that's OK with you, of course.'

'Well, I normally only train in the morning on Saturday, Dad. We go and watch Cam play football in the afternoon.'

'Who does Cameron play for, Abi?' asked Lysander.

'Blenthwaite Unsponsored,' Abi replied, unable to keep the pride out of her voice. 'He's good, Lysander, good enough to play in the top flight, but after what happened to Dad he refused to get sponsorship.'

'So there's an unsponsored league, is there?'

'There is indeed. Why not come along and watch the match tomorrow?'

'Do you know what, Abi, I'd like that – as long as I don't make the spectators run, screaming, for their homes.'

'You'll be my guest, Lysander,' said Abi, grinning at Louis's father. 'I'll make sure the locals behave themselves.'

***

Saturday dawned bright, sunny and cold. Snow had been decorating the fells for a few weeks, but the lower grounds were still clear and the football match was able to go ahead. Lysander woke up with a huge rush of excitement when he contemplated the day ahead, showered hurriedly, then went downstairs where Louis was already getting his kit together.

'Breakfast, Louis?'

'I ate earlier, Dad. There's no way I could train on a full stomach. You go ahead, though, we've plenty of time.'

Louis, his parents and Abi arrived at the studio just as Gideon was unlocking the door, Sarah having dropped him off before taking Jenny to see Father Christmas in Keswick. Grumpy as ever, Gideon rounded on Lysander as soon as he'd disabled the alarm.

'Bit late to take an interest in your son now, Trevelyan, and turn that spotlight off! Don't you know it hurts Louis's eyes?'

'Sorry,' replied Lysander meekly, snapping the lights off again. 'Didn't think.'

'No, you Sponsors never do. Except about making people's lives a misery…'

'Gideon, shall we begin?' Louis interrupted, already in his kit.

'Hmm. Have you warmed up, Louis? Well do it then! I'll be having to tell you when to wipe your arse next.'

Nicola sat next to Gideon, no longer scared of the 'Giddy bloke' of whom she'd been so wary during her drug-induced stupor, and Abi sat on the other side of him. Lysander stood a little apart from the others, hovering awkwardly by the door until Gideon roared at him to sit down and stop cluttering the place up.

Warm up exercises complete, Louis offered Gideon an exaggerated bow.

'What would be your pleasure today, Mr Wallis?'

'Parallel bars.'

Lifting himself from the ground, Louis performed the routine he and Gideon had been working on for weeks. Although they'd seen Louis train many times before, Abi and Nicola never grew tired of watching him, but it was Lysander who was the most enrapt, not taking his eyes from his son for an instant. When Louis landed on the ground with a light thud and perfect balance, Lysander sprang from his seat and applauded.

'Crap,' said Gideon. Lysander rounded on Gideon, determined to defend Louis's obvious talent, but Louis himself laughed.

'Chill out, Dad. If Gideon really thought I was crap they'd be able to hear him yelling in Australia.'

'Parallel bars, same routine again,' snapped Gideon. 'And concentrate on getting it right rather than showing off this time.'

As the morning progressed, an awestruck Lysander watched his son going through a series of complex routines, Louis's technique appearing flawless to his untrained eye despite Gideon picking up on every tiny mistake. Finally Gideon seemed satisfied with the day's work and called time on the training session just after twelve.

'Day of rest tomorrow, but that doesn't mean you can go and get drunk tonight, Louis. You were sluggish today. I want to see a huge improvement on Monday.'

'Why do you feel the need to be so nasty all the time?' snapped Lysander, thoroughly fed up with Gideon constantly criticising his son. 'I don't know why Louis puts up with you.'

'Because he's the best,' replied Louis, stretching his calf muscles.

'And there was me thinking it was because you liked me.' Gideon's half-smile faded abruptly as he turned to snarl at Lysander. 'What the hell do you know about gymnastics, Trevelyan? In fact, what the hell do you know about your son? Louis is immensely talented, but he can always improve, so if you're going to invade my studio in future I suggest you learn to keep your worthless opinions to yourself. Do you understand, you ignorant Sponsor twat?'

Unused to being spoken to so harshly, Lysander grabbed his coat and strode out of the room, slamming the door behind him. Looking immensely pleased with the reaction he'd elicited, Gideon turned his wheelchair around only to find himself face to face with a furious Nicola.

'You can bloody well apologise to Lysander!'

'Bit difficult, Nik,' replied Gideon with an unrepentant grin. 'Poor 'ickle Sponsor's run away.'

'Are you surprised? You were so damned rude to him.'

'Well he's…'

'My husband. The man I love. If you disrespect him, you disrespect me. Do *you* understand, Gideon?'

Once Louis had showered, he headed to The White Lion with his mother, girlfriend and uncharacteristically subdued coach. Matilda, Georgie and Dex were having an impromptu band practice on the stage in the corner of the pub, and to Nicola's relief, Lysander was sitting at the bar, chatting to Alan.

'Been training, Louis?' asked Alan, nipping behind the bar to serve. 'Wow, I bet you've got muscles where muscles have no right to be!'

'Settle down, Al,' said Dex with a grin. 'Abi's already laid claim to Louis's muscles. Hi, guys, you going to the soccer match?'

'It's *football*, Dexter,' grumbled Alan.

'We'll all be going, apart from Grumpy behind the bar there,' Dex continued. 'He drew the short straw.'

'Ha-ha, I'm splitting my sides.' Alan tossed his head and made a great show of rearranging clean glasses on the shelves.

'Yeah, well don't let those split sides make a mess. It's your turn on the cleaning rota too.'

Relaxing in the easy-going banter of The White Lion, enjoying a pint of ale and a bowl of chips in front of the roaring fire, Lysander found himself wondering if he could wriggle out of returning to London at least until after Christmas. *No chance*, he thought ruefully. His Lordship's latest text message had been quite specific:

Stop gadding about in that Godforsaken village and report to my office, Monday morning, nine o'clock sharp. This is not open for negotiation.

At ten to three, the pub emptied as people drank up and made their way to The White Lion's meadow, where a few makeshift terraces had been erected and large spotlights were serving as floodlights. On his way to join the crowd gathering to watch the football, Gideon wheeled his chair alongside Lysander and tapped him on the arm.

'I'm sorry, Lysander,' he said. 'I was unnecessarily rude earlier. Believe me, I do have Louis's best interests at heart.'

If anything, Lysander was more shocked by the apology than he'd been by the abuse.

The football match, against an unsponsored team from the Eden Valley, turned out to be far better than Lysander had expected and ended in an exciting 4–3 victory to Blenthwaite. Playing on the left side of midfield in a position similar to that of his late father, Cameron Farrell ran rings around the unfortunate defender commissioned with marking him and scored a spectacular long range goal two minutes into injury time to secure the victory. Having sung his way through the entire ninety minutes, Lysander cheered Cameron's goal as enthusiastically as the Unsponsored all around him, oblivious to both the cold and the laughter at his expense. Many Blenthwaite supporters would dine out for weeks to come on tales of the Director of Leisure and Fitness Sponsorship yelling 'Come on, the Unsponsored!' at the top of his voice.

'Enjoy the game, Lysander?' asked Cameron later, joining the company in the welcoming warmth of The White Lion after he'd changed from his kit.

'It was really good, Cameron. It's a shame…'

'A shame we don't get sponsored so the world can see what a wealth of football talent there is going to waste?'

'Actually, I was going to say… never mind.'

273

Cameron looked at Lysander quizzically, eyebrows raised.

'Oh, have it your way. I was going to say it's a shame you have to sacrifice your careers for your principles.'

'Do you mean it's a shame that in order to have a career we have to sell out to you Sponsors?'

'Yes,' Lysander replied eventually. 'That is what I mean.'

'Wowser!' yelped Max, reporter's notebook and pen in hand. 'I've just got to quote that in the…'

This time it was Max's turn to hold his tongue abruptly.

'Oh, come on, Maxwell,' said Lysander. 'You've got enough blackmail material from this afternoon alone to have me hung, drawn and quartered. Can't you risk giving me something in return?'

'OK then. We have a network, and a newsletter. For the Unsponsored.'

'What, locally?'

'That's all you need to know, Mr Trevelyan.'

It had been Max's idea to put his skills as a journalist to good use and produce a monthly newsletter for the Unsponsored, which started by simply reporting the goings on in Blenthwaite. However, his readership had grown

274

at a surprising rate as word spread from village to town, from town to city. Max and the Blenthwaite Unsponsored were now getting feedback from all over the UK, and the young journalist had his work cut out as the frequency of the newsletter increased from monthly to weekly in order to keep his readers up to date.

'You're living dangerously, Maxwell, do you realise that?' said Lysander.

'Yes, thank you, I know. I think His Lordshit's given up on me, though, and I'd rather live dangerously in Blenthwaite than kiss Sponsor arse in London. With all due respect, of course, Mr Trevelyan.'

'What changed your mind?'

'Alan, initially. He was amazing after that beating he got in the summer. God, Dyer tried to kill him! Instead of hauling me over the coals for being with the Sponsors, though, Al thanked me for helping Dex to find him. I asked myself who was the better role model – unsponsored Alan or sponsored Dyer? It kind of escalated from there.'

Alan looked absolutely delighted to have been the catalyst for Max's change of heart.

'Mr Trevelyan,' Max continued, 'where would you rather be? Relaxing with us or watching every word with your Sponsor cronies? You don't have to tell us, just be honest with yourself.'

***

Lysander left it until the last possible moment before departing for London. It was hard to leave Blenthwaite after such a wonderful few days with his family, but so entrenched was he in the Sponsors' world that he didn't dare disobey a direct order from Lord Bassenford. Driving down a quiet M6 in the early hours of Monday morning, he allowed himself to bask in the memories of the pleasant time he'd had at home, glad that this time Louis hadn't been angry with him for leaving.

'I know you've got to go, Dad. Don't antagonise His Lordshit, that won't help anyone. Besides, in London you can keep an eye on Theo.'

As he showered in his impersonal penthouse in London, Lysander laughed to himself. He was going to have his work cut out not to call Lord Bassenford 'Your Lordshit', not to mention the fact he kept catching himself chanting 'Blenthwaite' (clap-clap-clap) 'Unsponsored' (clap-clap-clap) in unguarded moments.

Lysander was one of the first Sponsors to arrive at Lord Bassenford's residence, noting to his dismay that Mortimer O'Reilly's car was the only other currently parked outside. He found Lord Bassenford and Mortimer already sitting in the office on the third floor, with the surprise addition of Theo sprawled in a comfortable armchair.

'Lysander,' said Theo, leaping to his feet. 'Welcome back.'

Shaking Theo's outstretched hand, Lysander greeted the young man warmly.

'How are you feeling, Theo?' he asked as the other Sponsors filed through the door.

'Much better, thank you. I can lie on my back now...'

'Yes, yes, very nice,' interrupted Lord Bassenford. 'Theodore, haven't you got some childish nonsense to watch on the goggle box?'

'I'd rather stay here actually, Your Lordship. I've listened to so many of these little get-togethers from upstairs, thought it'd be nice to see one in the flesh.'

Looking round the room and finding that all his most trusted Sponsors were now in attendance, Lord Bassenford shrugged, an expression of mild amusement on his face.

'Stay or go, Theodore, it's all the same to me,' he said. 'Perhaps, however, you would be so kind as to place whatever Lysander just passed to you on the table in front of me.'

Tick-tock, went the old grandfather clock. Lysander felt his blood freeze, and even Theo was too shocked to come out with a smart retort. How on earth had Lord Bassenford clocked that there had been more to their greeting than a simple handshake? Theo could have sworn he'd got sleight of hand down to a fine art, so many

277

hours had he spent over the long years of imprisonment practising card tricks in front of his bedroom mirror.

When Theo finally did speak, it was one word. 'No.'

So absolute was the Sponsors' silence that the clock's volume seemed to have notched up a few decibels. Drumming his fingers on the table, Lord Bassenford regarded his son through hooded eyes.

'Theodore, put it on the table or I'll have Dyer break your arms and take it from you forcibly. Either way, I'm going to get to see what's in your pocket. So what's it to be – the easy way or the painful way?'

I seem to bring nothing but trouble to Theo, thought Lysander miserably as the young man put his hand in his pocket and drew out the scrap of paper from Louis. Placing it on the desk in front of Lord Bassenford, he then backed away a couple of steps and crossed his arms defiantly. It seemed to take Lord Bassenford an age to unfold the note, and most in the room suspected he was milking the moment.

'"Happy crissmuss theo from Louis",' he read out loud before raising his eyes to look at Lysander. 'I'm not too happy with the teaching at Blenthwaite School if this is the usual standard of spelling, or is it just because your son's a halfwit?'

'Louis finds things difficult, Your Lord... erm... ship. I believe the standards are perfectly acceptable. My daughter's doing very well.' Stopping himself before he started gabbling, Lysander inwardly applauded his son's genius at giving him a decoy note for Theo.

'Actually, I'm bored already,' said Theo, closing his fingers round the tightly folded note still in his pocket. 'I think I'll make myself scarce.'

Before anyone could reply he left the room, treating Lysander to the ghost of a wink as he passed, and sprinted up to the privacy of his curtained bed to read the real message from his 'halfwit' friend:

Hi there, Theo Dory.

'Ehh, what's up, doc?' (Lol)

I hope my dad doesn't get caught handing you these notes, but if he did I hope the decoy worked. If you didn't need it, then ignore the other note – it's from my imbecile alter ego!

We were soooo pleased to hear from you on my birthday. Nice card, I'll treasure it for ever! Dad came in for a bit of a grilling from my mates, but he took it well and was able to tell us what's been going on with you. I gather His Lordshit's eased up on you a bit, and the Dyer scum has been demoted. Fan-flipping-tastic! However, we also know His Lordshit still isn't above a bit of torture. We're on the case, I promise you, and we'll get you out of that hellhole one day. The Unsponsored are getting stronger by the day, and they're all on your side.

By the way, we've put a band together here in Blenthwaite, called Dory's Avengers. Hope you like the name!

Love to you and Marina. Spit in the eye to His Lordshit and Lady Bitch.

Louis (AKA Bugs Bunny, lol)

The writing then changed, became gentler and more feminine:

Not much to add to Louis's note, just echo that we're thinking of you all the time and we'll never desert you. Can't wait to see you again, Cuz. Miss you and love you loads, Abi xxx

> PS So pleased to hear the Dyer
> scum is off your case. Wish I'd
> been there to witness his demotion!

I wish you had been too Abi, thought Theo, *you'd have loved it*. Finally, one more change in the handwriting:

> Hi there, Theo, allow me to
> introduce myself. My name's
> Matilda Santiago and I think you
> are HOT, so if it's OK with you we
> are so going to get it on when we
> meet xxxxxxx

Laughing silently, Theo couldn't remember ever feeling so happy in his adult life. Knowing it was risky to keep the note but reluctant to part with it, he contented himself with stuffing it deep into the hole in his mattress where it joined his other treasured possessions. Delighted though he was at word from Louis and Abi, Theo admitted to himself as he lay back against his pillows that their messages paled into insignificance next to the postscript from the mysterious Matilda.

'I do hope we meet soon, Matilda Santiago,' he murmured, wondering if she was as hot as she seemed to find him. 'I like your style.'

Chapter 12 – Olympic Gymnast

While Theo was lying on his bed enjoying some pleasant daydreams, Lysander was getting a very hard time in the room below.

'So, Trevelyan, let me get this straight. Your imbecile son decided, out of the blue, to send Theodore a note. How nice of him.'

Seeing Lysander squirm, Lord Bassenford warmed to his task.

'You expect me to believe, after all these years of no contact, that your barely articulate son would send Theodore this touching Christmas greeting.' Picking up Louis's decoy note, he screwed it into a ball and threw it in Lysander's face.

'Have you been passing notes back and forth between Theodore and – what's his face?' he bellowed suddenly. Even in his fury, Lord Bassenford was impressed to notice that Lysander was the only one in the room who did not flinch.

'No, Your Lordship. This was an impromptu greeting, and my son's name is Louis…'

'I don't think you're in a position to question whatever I choose to call your freak of a son.' Lysander winced and glared at his boss, knowing how offended Louis would be by his words, but Lord Bassenford either didn't notice or didn't care. 'Impromptu greeting, was it? After all this time?'

'With respect, Your Lordship, there haven't been many opportunities for me to pass on notes to Theodore in previous years…'

'Are you questioning how I treat Theodore yet again?' Slamming his fists down, Lord Bassenford stood and leant over his desk, glowering at Lysander. 'Has Theodore ever asked you to pass a message to your son?'

At that moment the door opened and Theo came back into the room.

'It's all right, Lysander, I'll take it from here. Your Lordship, Louis sent me his little Christmas card in response to me sending him a birthday card last week.'

'So it wasn't impromptu at all, Trevelyan. You were lying…'

'Lysander was covering for me, for which I thank him wholeheartedly.'

'Why would he do that?'

'Probably because he feared the consequences would be pretty harsh for me otherwise.'

'You sent the Trevelyan boy a birthday card?'

'Yes, Your Lordship. A birthday card. It's a thing people send to their friends. On their birthdays.'

'*Enough*, Theodore! Your insolence is not helping. Both of you, listen to me. There will be no more correspondence between Theodore and Louis. None. If I find this order disobeyed, the consequences will be harsh for *both* of you. Understand?'

Lysander and Theo had the good sense to nod, even Theo realising that a smart answer wouldn't be a wise move.

'Now,' said Lord Bassenford, sitting down again and addressing everyone in the room, 'I'm sorry that this meeting seems to be all about Lysander here, but there's one more thing I'd like him to explain. Lysander, what in the name of heaven were you doing... here?'

Rousing his computer from its slumber, Lord Bassenford played the film that had been standing by. To Lysander's horror, the Blenthwaite Unsponsored versus Eden Valley football match he'd attended the previous Saturday filled the screen.

'Here we have some underclass attempting to play football. This,' Lord Bassenford tracked one of Cameron's runs on the screen with his pen, 'I understand to be Elliot Farrell's son. I suppose that would make him your cousin, Theodore.'

Theo settled in his favourite armchair and watched the football match with interest.

'Some of these players, my man in Blenthwaite informs me, are pretty useful.

Farrell Junior falls into that category. However, they have all spurned the benefits of Sponsorship and are paying the price. Sponsorship equals a fine career, possibly playing in the Premier League. No Sponsorship equals cold Saturday afternoons playing on a field in Cumbria. Ladies and gentlemen, need I say more?'

Lord Bassenford's lapdogs all applauded right on cue, with the exception, Theo was pleased to notice, of Lysander.

'That's not actually why I wanted to show you this film, however.'

The camera panned round from the match to the spectators, particularly to Lysander.

'Lysander isn't the only person we wouldn't expect to see fraternising with the Unsponsored.' Tapping the screen, Lord Bassenford pointed out Max Barrington. 'I've suspected for some time that this young man has been relaxing his loyalty to the Scheme, and I've had undercover men and women keeping an eye on him. Barrington has made his choice – his sponsorship has been cancelled and he can rot with the rest of the underclass.'

Watching Max roaring with laughter along with a couple of young women, Theo decided that rotting with the underclass seemed rather a pleasant option.

'Ah look, Lysander – it's loopy Louis.' Lord Bassenford regarded Lysander with the air of detached amusement he usually reserved for Theo as Louis wandered into view on the screen. His arm was round the waist of a young woman who was so clearly a Farrell that, even if Theo hadn't been aware of his friend's affections, he would have known at once she was Cousin Abi.

'I must say he looks a little more with it than last time I saw him,' murmured His Lordship, watching Louis swapping quick-fire banter with Max.

'Lord Bassenford…'

'I haven't forgotten, Mortimer. I never forget your prediction for a moment, so please be quiet. We're reaching the bit I find the most interesting.'

The Sponsor spy at the football match had focused the camera on Lysander. His face loomed large on the screen, and no one in the room needed to be an expert in lip-reading to make out the words he was singing.

'Blenthwaite Unsponsored!' he chanted along with the people around him. 'Blenthwaite Unsponsored!'

Pausing the film with Lysander's face still filling the screen, Lord Bassenford sat back in his chair and stared at the man himself.

'So, Lysander,' he said eventually, 'would you please tell us why one of the highest-ranking Sponsors in the land spent his Saturday afternoon very visibly and vocally supporting a team of underclass? What sort of message do you think this sends out to the Sponsored? Whatever were you doing?'

Realising there was no chance of him being able to lie his way out of this tight spot as he'd done so many times before, Lysander elected to tell the truth.

'I was having fun, Your Lordship.'

The atmosphere in the room was electric as everyone stared at Lysander and Lord Bassenford.

'Would you like to elaborate, Lysander? You were in the underclass-loving hole you call home for days, so please share with the group what kept you there. What other… fun… activities did you enjoy with the Unsponsored?'

'I attempted to make up for all the years I've neglected my family. I watched my daughter perform as a very convincing angel in her school play. I watched my son training. I spent some quality time with my wife, the details of which stay between Nikki and me…'

'Boring,' said Lady Rosanna, shocked to find herself chastised sharply by her father.

'Not boring, Rosanna. I suggest you don't interrupt again or I will have you removed from the room. Don't taunt your sister, Theodore!' he added in response to Theo licking his finger and drawing a 1 in the air. Turning back to Lysander, Lord Bassenford asked, 'You watched your son train in what? How to conduct himself in company?'

Mortimer O'Reilly started to laugh, but was hushed by Lord Bassenford.

'Gymnastics,' replied Lysander.

'Is he good?'

'Very.'

'Interesting.' Lord Bassenford sat in quiet contemplation for a while before turning to David and Julia Foster, the husband-and-wife team who headed Sports Sponsorship.

'I'd like one of you to go to Blenthwaite and watch Trevelyan's son train. Take a camera crew with you. I want a film of his performance beamed back to my office – I'll give you today to get it organised, tomorrow to travel, so we'll say Wednesday morning. Everyone be back here at 10am Wednesday when we'll see if the lad really is any good.'

Glaring once more at Lysander, Lord Bassenford said, 'For your sake, Trevelyan, he'd better be. Your hold on the Directorship of Leisure and Fitness is very tenuous at the moment.'

***

Two days later, the Sponsors were once more sitting in Lord Bassenford's office, looking curiously at a huge blank screen adorning the wall behind the desk, completely covering the family photograph.

'Ladies and gentlemen,' said Lord Bassenford, switching on his projector, 'welcome to the show!'

As live footage from Blenthwaite came into focus on the big screen, Gideon Wallis was in full voice.

'What the *bloody hell* is going on here? And get that light out of Louis's eyes!'

Louis appeared on the screen, hastily putting his dark glasses on as a bright camera light shone in his face. Gideon, looking furious, wheeled his chair in front of Louis in an attempt to protect his protégé, and in doing so caught sight of Lysander sitting awkwardly in the London office via David Foster's monitor.

'Trevelyan!' he yelled. 'What is the meaning of this? I let you visit, and what happens? You sell your own son…'

'Mr Wallis!' said Lord Bassenford, his voice so sharp that even Gideon stopped in mid flow. 'I have commissioned this film. I want to watch Lewis, who is apparently a talented gymnast.'

'Why?' retorted Gideon. 'What makes you so interested? I can speak for Louis, he doesn't want Sponsorship…'

'I'd rather he spoke for himself, Wallis. Good morning, Lewis, do you know who I am?'

There was no response whatsoever from Louis.

'Trevelyan, I asked you a question, and when I ask a question I expect the courtesy of a reply.'

'Oh, I do beg your pardon, Your Lordship,' said Louis, his face a mask of innocence. 'Were you talking to me?'

'Of course I was talking to you, you bloody imbecile. My God, you are astonishingly stupid...'

'Only I thought you were talking to someone called Lewis.'

Theo tried and failed to stifle a laugh.

'Theodore, you are lucky to be in the room at all,' snarled Lord Bassenford, rounding on his son. 'Behave or leave. The choice is yours.' Turning back to the screen, he spoke to Louis once more. 'Very well, Lou-*ee*, as you're so particular, I'll indulge you. Can't you take those glasses off? It's the middle of winter.'

'Only if you have that light dimmed,' replied Louis.

'Turn the lights down!' barked Lord Bassenford at the camera crew. 'Now, Louis,' he added as Louis took off his dark glasses, 'I'm going to ignore the fact that you seem to have miraculously learned some social skills since the summer. The situation is simple. You're a gymnast. The country needs a gymnast.'

'Why?'

'For the Olympic Games, of course.'

'You want *me* to compete in the Olympics?'

'I want to see if you're good enough.'

'Don't I have to qualify?'

'A British gymnastics team looks set to qualify, but unconvincingly. It's a weakness…'

'But don't the gymnasts who qualify have to be the ones to compete? If you're serious about this, I'd better take part in the rest of the qualifying events.'

'No. I want to play you as a wild card next summer…'

'He doesn't want to give any publicity to an unsponsored competitor, more like,' said Gideon in a none-too-quiet aside to Louis.

'Wallis!' snapped His Lordship. 'I wasn't talking to you. As I was saying, Louis, I want to play you as a secret weapon, and anyway it's too late for you to appear out of nowhere and take part in the qualifiers…'

'It'll be even more too late next summer…'

'If I say you're going to compete with the British team, then you compete!'

'And if I refuse?'

'I'll use other methods of persuasion. Your father is at my mercy – you wouldn't want Mr

Dyer to get upset with Lysander, would you, Louis?'

Gideon started to wheel himself over to the camera again, but Louis stopped him.

'OK,' said Louis, 'what do you want to see?'

'Address me as Your Lordship, Trevelyan, I demand respect!'

'I wasn't aware respect was something that could be demanded,' replied Louis, much to Theo's delight. 'However, as you so rightly say, my father is at your mercy. Morning, Dad, by the way. What do you want to see, *Your Lordship*?'

'Gymnastics!'

'I meant, Your Lordship, with all *due* respect, Your Lordship, do you want to see floor work? Rings? Parallel bars?'

'Anything! Just get on with it.'

Louis turned to his mentor for input.

'Gideon?'

'Pommel,' replied Gideon with an amused gleam in his eyes, naming Louis's least favourite discipline.

'I knew you were going to say that.'

Crossing over to the pommel horse, Louis got on with it. Not a word was uttered, either in the London office or the Blenthwaite studio, as he executed his complicated routine with effortless skill.

'Next!' barked Lord Bassenford the second Louis landed on the floor.

Selecting the rings, Louis nailed another series of difficult moves with his natural grace and talent.

'Next!'

This time Louis raised a hand. 'Let me get my breath back first,' he said.

Louis had to demonstrate every one of the six disciplines of men's gymnastics for Lord Bassenford, who then asked to see another routine on the parallel bars before he was satisfied.

'Come over to the camera, Louis,' he said. 'David, what do you think? Is Louis good enough?'

'Without a doubt, Your Lordship,' replied David Foster.

'Julia?'

'Totally agree with David, Your Lordship. What a talent!'

'Theodore?' asked Lord Bassenford without warning.

'Your Lordship?'

'Don't act stupid, Theodore, that's more young Trevelyan's area of expertise. What did you think of the gymnastics?'

Walking over to the camera beaming the scene in Lord Bassenford's office up to Gideon's studio in Blenthwaite, Theo bypassed his father and addressed Louis in person.

'I think you're an absolutely brilliant gymnast, Lou. You've bowled me over – I've never been so impressed in all my life.'

'Thank you, Theo,' replied Louis with a smile, just managing to stop himself calling his friend Dory.

'All right, stop the little love-in, you two,' Lord Bassenford said. 'That's settled then. Louis, I'm going to put your name forward to perform with the British gymnastics team next summer. With the Olympics being held here in London, I want the strongest competitors possible, so you'll be getting top Sponsor-endorsed training. I know the very place…'

'Whoa, Your Lordship, whoa!' interrupted Louis, holding up his hand again. 'If – and it is a big if – I go along with this, I will not be trained by anyone but Gideon, and I will not train anywhere but Blenthwaite.'

'Remember your father is at my mercy…'

'Remember I have something you want, Your Lordship. If you continue to threaten my family, you're going to be disappointed.'

'Proud of you, Louis,' whispered Gideon.

'Don't you *dare* speak to me like that!' roared Lord Bassenford. 'You're even cockier than your father. I make the rules…'

'Not this time, Your Lordship. I still don't believe I can rock up and compete instead of the gymnasts who actually qualified, but I'll go along with your crazy idea nonetheless. It has to be on my terms, though.'

'What are your terms then?'

'Simple. One: Gideon, and only Gideon, trains me. I wouldn't be the gymnast I am today without him. Two: I train in Blenthwaite, and only leave here when required to compete. Three: stop threatening my father. These are my terms, Your Lordship, and they're non-negotiable.'

Unable to hold his tongue any longer, Mortimer O'Reilly whined into the silence that followed Louis's statement.

'Your Lordship, is it wise putting Trevelyan's son into the public eye in this way? The world's media will be focused on the Olympics, I beg you to reconsider…'

'Thank you, Mortimer, that will do! Unless you can find a better gymnast than Louis Trevelyan, he will be performing at the Olympic Games next summer. Have it your way, Louis.'

'Thank you, Your Lordship, I'm glad we were able to come to an agreement,' replied

Louis, raising his head from his warm-down stretches. 'Good morning, Mr O'Reilly – that crystal ball of yours thrown up anything interesting recently?'

***

Gideon didn't make Louis train any more that day. After the departure of David Foster along with Lord Bassenford's camera crew, they stared at each other in amazement for a few minutes, both finding it hard to believe what had just taken place.

'You know I don't give praise lightly, Louis…'

'That is the understatement of the century, Gideon,' replied Louis with a grin, sitting cross-legged in front of his mentor's wheelchair. 'Sorry, do go on.'

Tell-tale dimples appeared either side of Gideon's mouth, then a huge smile lit up his face.

'Louis, I'm so proud of you I could burst. That little stunt of His Lordshit's – I thought you'd go to pieces, but you were brilliant. Your performance was as good as I've ever seen you produce, and the way you handled His Lordshit…'

'Careful, Gideon! You'll make my ego so big I won't be able to get through the door, let alone perform at the Olympics.'

'I'm amazed you agreed to do it, Louis, you used to be so shy. What made your mind up?'

'To start with, it was His Lordshit threatening Dad. I know you don't have much time for him, but he's still my father. He does his best.'

'Which is pretty piss poor…'

'He does his *best*, Gideon.'

'Why didn't he warn us about this morning's little stunt then?'

'Bloody hell, Gideon, I thought I was meant to be the dense one. You heard His Lordshit – Dad's at his mercy. Anyone who can imprison and torture his own son won't flinch at doing the same to one of his Sponsors.'

Louis shuddered as unwanted thoughts filled his head about the possible horrors his father may have had to endure.

'I'm sure Dad would have warned us if he'd been able to. He's changing. Anyway, that was my first reason. Funnily enough, it was Mortimer O'Reilly who gave me a second good reason. The eyes of the world's media will be on the Olympics. Let's say His Lordshit does manage to swing it so I can compete despite not having qualified…'

'Which, I hate to say, is highly unlikely…'

'But what if he does? Imagine if I win gold. Everyone knows about Sponsorship in this country, how all our sportsmen and women have to be sponsored. Then, an unsponsored Brit wins gold at the Olympics. It gives us publicity, Gideon. We can show the world the extent of the Sponsors' oppression…'

'Louis…'

'It may even give us a platform to overthrow…'

'*Louis!* I applaud your wild notions, God knows I applaud them, but remember Elliot Farrell was in the eyes of the world's media too. Remember what happened to him.'

'I know, Gideon. Of course I understand your concern, but what happened to Elliot won't happen to me.'

'How the fuck do you know that?' growled Gideon.

'Oh hello, Gideon – I'm glad you're back and that strange nice bloke has gone. I know it won't,' Louis started to laugh, 'because Mortimer O'Reilly foresaw it.'

Gideon roared with laughter, and he and Louis were pretty much helpless for a few minutes. Eventually, Louis said, 'There's one more reason I said yes.'

'What's that, lad?'

'Think about it, Gid,' replied Louis, his face glowing with excitement. 'I could end up competing… at the Olympic Games!'

***

Abi dropped into the studio while Louis and Gideon were still discussing their eventful morning and listened wide-eyed as Louis, almost incoherent with excitement, let her know what had taken place. Torn between euphoria and anxiety, she was full of questions.

'Louis, be careful! I don't want to lose you like I lost Dad. Aren't you nervous?'

'What about – His Lordshit's thugs or performing at the Olympics? I'll be fine, Abi, I promise,' he added as Abi shuddered, 'but we've got to use this opportunity to challenge the Sponsors. As for the Games, I can't help but daydream a bit. The Olympics, Abi…'

'How did His Lordshit know you were a gymnast?'

'Not sure, but I think it may have had something to do with Dad.'

'You mean your bloody Sponsor father sold you out to His Lordshit? I really thought he was changing his views.'

'Couldn't have put it better myself, young Abi.'

'Shut up, the pair of you!' snapped Louis. 'As I've already explained to Gideon, I don't think Dad had any choice. His Lordshit was at great pains to tell me that Dad's at his mercy – what if he's been tortured like Theo?'

'Theo's never sold you out.'

'I don't think Dad did either. So he may have told His Lordshit I'm a gymnast. Aren't parents meant to be proud of their children's achievements? There's no way anyone could have guessed His Lordshit would want me to perform at the Olympics.'

'His Lordshit wants what?' asked Nicola Trevelyan, entering the studio at that moment and closing the door with difficulty on a blast of icy wind.

For the benefit of his mother, Louis went through the story once more.

'That's fantastic, Louis, I'm so proud! I'm amazed your dad didn't tell us himself…'

'Louis thinks His Lordshit's imprisoned and tortured Lysander, just like he did with Theo…'

'Well done, Gideon,' muttered Louis as the colour drained from his mother's face.

'You think he's torturing my husband?' Not waiting for a reply, Nicola took a mobile phone out of her bag.

'Didn't know you had one of those, Nik,' said Gideon, but Nicola waved at him to be quiet.

'Lysander? Are you OK?… Yes, I've just heard. Our Louis at the Olympics!… I'm so proud too… Where are you?… Still there? Put His Lordshit, I mean Lordship, on will you, darling?'

Nicola switched the call to speakerphone so everyone in the studio could listen in. There was a slight pause, then Lord Bassenford's voice came on the line.

'Good morning, Nicola. I take it you've heard the news.'

'Indeed,' said Nicola. 'I'm with Louis now. That's not what I wanted to talk to you about though, Lord Bassenford. I'll be brief – is my husband free to leave your house?'

'Well, yes, I suppose so,' said Lord Bassenford. 'So much has happened this morning, I hadn't really thought...'

'So he can come home for Christmas?'

'Of course, Nicola. I'm holding a Christmas soirée on the twenty-third which he will be expected to attend, but he will be free to leave London on Christmas Eve.' Impulsively, Lord Bassenford added, 'Why don't you attend my soirée too?'

It was Nicola's turn to hesitate, contempt for the Sponsors competing with curiosity and a desire to be with Lysander. Finally she said, 'Thank you, Your Lordshit, I will.'

Lord Bassenford ended the call abruptly, not giving Nicola a chance to speak to Lysander again. Turning to face her companions, she found them doubled up with laughter.

'What?' she asked, baffled.

'You… said… "Your Lord*shit*"!'

'Oh my goodness, so I did.' Chuckling, Nicola added, 'Did you hear that? I've been invited to Lord Bassenford's pre-Christmas get-together.'

'Not selling out to the Sponsors, are you, Nik?'

'Not at all, Gideon, although I confess I'm intrigued. Mainly I want to be there for Lysander. If I find my husband's been hurt, I'll rip His Lordshit's sponsored head off and ram it up his sponsored arse!'

***

As word of Louis and Gideon's eventful morning was spreading round Blenthwaite, Lysander was still hanging around the St Benedict residence. The company of the high-spirited Theo and gentle Marina was infinitely preferable to time spent alone in his luxury apartment, and Lord Bassenford seemed indifferent to his presence, so he stayed, sipping wine by the drawing room fire and catching up with the latest goings on in *EastEnders*.

Entering the room and noting, to his approval, that all the characters in the soap opera were sponsored, Lord Bassenford sat in his favourite armchair and opened his laptop.

'Marina,' he said, glancing up as his screen glowed into life, 'what do you want for Christmas?'

'Umm, not sure, Father.'

'Well, you'd better make your mind up soon, dear, there are only a few days left. What about you, Theodore?'

Theo looked round in amazement, the world of the sponsored *EastEnders* forgotten for a moment.

'*Me*, Your Lordship?'

'Yes, Theodore, I would like to get you a Christmas present. You are, after all, my son.'

'In that case, please may I have a whore?' replied Theo. Lysander nearly choked on his wine, and Marina, although quite used to her brother coming out with the unexpected, giggled nervously. Only Lord Bassenford remained unruffled, merely raising his eyebrows a little.

'A whore?'

'Yes please, Your Lordship, a whore. The dirtier, the better – I'm a little frustrated…'

Lord Bassenford held up a hand, smiling slightly. 'I think I can do better than that,' was all he would say.

***

The day before Christmas Eve, Lysander felt like the proudest man on the planet when he arrived at the St Benedict residence with his wife at his side. He thought she was by far the most beautiful woman in the room, and judging by the number of admiring glances she was getting from the male guests, it would seem that others agreed. Even Lord Bassenford's eyes shone with approval as he lifted her hand and kissed it.

'Nicola,' he said, 'wonderful to see you. You look – well – wonderful!'

'Lord Bassenford,' replied Nicola shortly. Taking a tissue from her bag, she pulled a face and wiped her hand where his lips had touched it as soon as his back was turned.

'I'll get some disinfectant for you if you like, Nicola,' said Theo with a grin, approaching with hand outstretched.

Nicola roared with laughter. 'Cheeky, Theodore!' she said, swatting Theo with the tissue then hugging him warmly, her pleasure at seeing him contrasting starkly with her contempt for his father. 'My, you've grown up to be a dish.'

'And you're looking lovely.' Shaking Lysander's hand warmly, Theo added, 'You're a lucky man, Lysander.'

'Circulate, Theodore!' snapped Lord Bassenford, grabbing his son's arm and leading him away from the Trevelyans. As he and Theo crossed the room, he said, 'I've been giving some thought to your rather unorthodox present request, and the answer's no. However, I appreciate that you're a young man, and your opportunities to meet the fair sex have been a little... limited, shall we say?'

As Theo raised his eyebrows at the understatement, Lord Bassenford continued.

'I've an idea to put to you which I'm hoping will suit your needs rather better than a dirty whore.'

'It's not Stephen Dyer in drag, is it?'

'No, Theodore, it's not,' replied Lord Bassenford, laughing. 'It's the young lady over there.'

Following the direction of Lord Bassenford's gaze, Theo spied the young woman in question. Dressed in an over-fussy pink dress, golden blonde hair neatly pinned up behind her head, she was standing awkwardly next to a man who had to be her father, so strong was the family resemblance.

'What, the pink bunny?'

'That is Catherine Lorimer, Theodore. I'll be brief, I think she's noticed you gawping at her. Her father Philip heads the British branch of a Europe-wide logistics firm. I don't think I need to name them – they pretty much control haulage and shipping throughout the continent. Being part of a European firm, the British branch isn't Sponsor controlled, and therefore I want to develop a good business relationship with Philip Lorimer. I want regular contact with the man. I want…'

'…me to start shagging his daughter so you've got an excuse to invite him into your lair. Am I right, Your Lordship?'

'I'd rather you didn't put it quite so crudely, Theodore. Woo her, romance her, flatter her. I'm given to believe that you're a very good-looking young man…'

'You want me to help your Scheme? You know my views on your oppressive regime, Your Lordship.'

'Shut up, Theodore! I'm not interested in your opinions. One way or another I will get Lorimer onside, I was merely furnishing you with a means to satisfy your desires. Unless,' Lord Bassenford's eyes gleamed with amusement again, 'you'd prefer Stephen Dyer in drag.'

Without waiting for an answer, Lord Bassenford strode over to Philip Lorimer and engaged him in conversation, leaving the painfully shy Catherine alone. She had indeed noticed Theodore St Benedict looking at her, and was wondering why someone that good-looking would even acknowledge her existence. A moment later she was even more baffled – Theodore the Gorgeous was standing by her side, smiling warmly as he introduced himself.

'Hello there, you're Catherine, aren't you? I'm Theo. The old men are talking business, I suppose.' He jerked his head at Lord Bassenford and Philip Lorimer. 'So boring! How about we get something to drink?'

Offering his arm to Catherine, Theo led her over to the drinks laid out on the huge antique sideboard. Lord Bassenford was right in one respect: Theo was a very frustrated young man, and in the absence of the enigmatic Matilda, Catherine may be his best option. She was quite pretty, really…

'What do you fancy?' asked Theo, selecting champagne for both of them before she had a chance to reply. 'Nice dress, by the way.'

'No it's not,' said Catherine, finally finding her voice.

'OK, you're right,' he said, laughing. 'I'm so glad it wasn't your choice. I've had to wear some pretty ghastly things too from time to time, although never pink frills.'

Relaxing gradually as the champagne and Theo's easy charm worked their magic, Catherine actually found herself enjoying the soirée she'd been dreading all week. Even the awful dress, chosen by the personal shopper she was too shy to question, was forgotten as she basked in his company. His ready smile, his sparkling eyes, the way his hand brushed hers as he handed her more champagne, the warmth of his leg pressed against hers all combined in a heady mix, and before long a smile of pure pleasure lit up her face.

Watching Theo's skilful manipulation of the young woman until he virtually had her eating out of his hands, Lord Bassenford was greatly satisfied with the night's work. *Ah, Theodore*, he thought, *it would appear you're not as unlike me as you seem to think.*

Chapter 13 – It's Christmas!

Lord Bassenford's Christmas soirée turned out to be a very enjoyable evening, but that didn't alter the fact that both Nicola and Lysander were relieved to be travelling north on Christmas Eve, back to the uncomplicated friendship of the Blenthwaite Unsponsored. Nicola decided to drive to give her husband a chance to catch up on some sleep, but Lysander was so happy to be going home that he spent the whole journey chatting to his wife instead. There was a lot to discuss too: the Olympics; Theo's apparent new love interest; Lysander seeming to be constantly in His Lordship's bad books.

'I can't do anything right at the moment, Nikki,' he said, grinning.

'Just be careful, Sandy,' she replied.

Unbeknown to Mr and Mrs Trevelyan, though, it was actually Nicola who was the topic of conversation in the St Benedict residence. Summoning Lee Fellows and his security team to his office, His Lordship informed them that there seemed to be a bit of a problem, and it needed addressing immediately. The only member of the team missing was Stephen Dyer – the discussion being delicate in nature, Lord Bassenford had commissioned him to keep the ever curious Theo well out of the way for the duration of the meeting.

'I can't have Theodore listening in on this one, Stephen. Keep him occupied any way you see fit, just make sure he's nowhere near my office.'

Dyer sniggered. His Christmas had come a day early.

'Gentlemen,' Lord Bassenford said, entering his office and looking round his security staff, 'Nicola Trevelyan. She looked rather too alert for my liking last night. Fellows, as head of security, explain to me why she is no longer dependent on drugs. Has her supply dried up?'

'Your Lordship, she was totally dependent until her son and Gideon Wallis got involved. We weren't prepared for...'

'You got complacent, you mean.' Lord Bassenford sat down and leant back, cupping his hands behind his head and fixing Fellows with a piercing stare. 'For years she's been no threat to us, now she is again. I want her watched closely. Get your best people on to it, Fellows, immediately. She was a big troublemaker in the early days of the Scheme, her and that bloody Wallis.'

Dismissing the security guards from his office, Lord Bassenford remained sitting at his desk, staring into the middle distance and mulling over the problem that was Blenthwaite. He was still deep in thought when Theo slammed into the room half an hour later, fresh from the shower and angrier than Lord Bassenford had ever seen him.

'What the fuck are you playing at, Your Lordship? A few weeks ago you forbade that creep to go near me, today you give him carte blanche to…'

Breaking off abruptly, Theo waved his hands in disgust and prowled round the office like a caged animal. His father regarded him with amusement for a few moments, then said, 'Just keeping you focused, Theodore. Keep the sweet Catherine happy, or it'll be Stephen Dyer from now on…'

'Fuck off!' yelled Theo, slamming his fists down on Lord Bassenford's desk. 'This is *not* a joke. What am I, Dyer's fucking Christmas present?'

'Theodore, control yourself and stop swearing.'

'Control myself? How can I control myself when my own father hates me so much?'

'I don't hate you…'

'Oh, save your fucking lies for your Sponsors.'

'Theodore! This conversation does not continue until you calm down and stop swearing.'

Theo walked over to the window of the office and leant his head against the pane, hands tightly clenched into fists, breathing heavily. Anyone looking up from the street below would have seen an extremely angry young man on the third floor, so at odds with the cheery Christmas tree displayed directly below him.

After five minutes of uncomfortable silence, Lord Bassenford joined Theo by the window, laying a hand on his son's shoulder. Theo flinched as though he'd been stung and jumped out of his father's reach.

'Don't touch me! Don't you *ever* touch me!'

To Lord Bassenford's amazement, Theo had tears flooding down his face.

'Yes look, Your Lordship. You've achieved it. You've finally broken me. You must be so proud...'

Running to the door, Theo wrenched it open, fled through it, and slammed it with all his might behind him. Lord Bassenford heard his feet pounding up the stairs, then the sound of another door slam as Theo shut himself in his bedroom. More shaken by his son's rare show of emotion than he wanted to admit, Lord Bassenford stared up at the huge family photo on his office wall, his eyes resting on Theo's ten-year-old face, frozen in a happier time before his father made his life a living hell.

'No, Theodore, I'm not proud,' he murmured. 'I made a wrong decision this morning. A big, ugly wrong decision.'

***

By the afternoon of Christmas Eve, Marina had persuaded her brother down from his bedroom, tempting him with promises of cartoons and mince pies. When Lord Bassenford joined his family in the drawing room for the beginning of the Christmas festivities that evening, he was relieved to see Theo sprawled out over his favourite beanbag, watching repeats of old comedy shows and eating his way steadily through a bowl of nuts.

'Don't spoil your appetite, Theodore. Remember Catherine and her parents are joining us for dinner tonight.'

Without speaking, or even looking at his father, Theo replaced the bowl of nuts on the sideboard, throwing himself back on to his beanbag as the doorbell announced the arrival of the Lorimers two floors below.

'Marina darling, go and find Rosanna. Our guests have arrived.' As soon as Marina left the room, Lord Bassenford sat next to Theo on the beanbag she'd just vacated.

'These things are quite comfortable, aren't they. I'm surprised.'

Silence.

'I've not got long, so I'll come straight out with it. I'm sorry, Theodore.'

His eyes fixed on the television screen, Theo said, 'For what? Being the worst father in history?'

'Well, no. I mean for letting Dyer do, er, *that* to you...'

'What, rape me? "Rape" is the word you're looking for, Your Lordship. Dressing it up with euphemisms won't make me feel any less violated.'

Wincing at Theo's brutal words, Lord Bassenford said, 'Theodore, it won't happen again. You have my word...'

'Your Lordship, your word is worthless. You promised me that once before. You lied.'

Recovering with admirable speed as the Lorimers were shown into the drawing room, Theo leapt to his feet with a huge smile and greeted them warmly, leaving Lord Bassenford marvelling yet again at his son's strength of character.

Christmas Eve dinner in the St Benedict residence was a thoroughly enjoyable affair, Philip and his wife Simone proving to be engaging company. Theo found that neither the amount of nuts he'd consumed earlier nor the nasty experience with Dyer had dampened his appetite at all, and he enjoyed every mouthful of the excellent meal. After dinner, which had been fairly informal, the evening became even more relaxed when Theo fetched his old guitar from his bedroom and played a selection of well-known Christmas carols for the assembled company, even Rosanna glowing with Christmas cheer as she sang the familiar songs in her surprisingly sweet voice and held hands with her boyfriend Adam. The only light in the drawing room came from the Christmas tree and the roaring fire, and Lord Bassenford found himself happier than he could remember feeling for many years. Concentrating on his son strumming the guitar while everyone sang along, more and more heartily as the wine took its effect, Lord Bassenford tried not to let the thought run its course: he hadn't felt this happy since Isabelle had left his life.

Eventually Theo put his guitar down and held his hand out to Catherine as the group got up to fetch drinks, mingle and chat. Leading her from the room, he took her to the more informal family room at the back of the house and, laughing, nodded his head towards an overladen Christmas tree in the corner.

'All my work, I'm afraid. His Lordship asked me not to put so many decorations on it. I hate to say it, but I think he may have been right.'

'It looks fab to me.' Then, unable to resist satisfying her curiosity, Catherine asked, 'Theo, why do you call your father "His Lordship"?'

Theo replied casually, 'Just a little family joke, Cathie. Do you mind being called Cathie?'

Catherine replied that Theo could call her Medusa if he wanted.

Theo cupped her face in his hands. 'You're far from being the Medusa,' he murmured, then he leant forward and kissed her. Expecting him to be as confident and experienced at kissing as he appeared to be at everything else, Catherine was surprised to find his kisses little more than tentative brushes of the lips, and in the end it was she who moved them on to something more passionate. Holding him close, she opened her mouth against his and he responded with typical Theo-like enthusiasm, slowly sinking down on to the sofa and pulling her on top of him as their tongues entwined.

Looking into the family room half an hour later, Stephen Dyer came crashing down from the cloud he'd been riding around on all day. There, lying on the sofa, was the object of his desires, wrapped in a passionate embrace with a young woman. A *woman!*

'Disgusting,' he muttered, closing the door behind him and grunting in alarm as he walked straight into Lord Bassenford.

'Looking for someone, Dyer? Not my son, I hope.'

'No, Your Lordship…'

'Is Lord Theodore in the family room?'

'Yes, Your Lordship.'

'Alone?'

'No, Your Lordship.'

'Well, don't be shy, who's he with? Young Catherine? That's nice. It is Christmas, after all, which is why I'm prepared to overlook you helping yourself to a little festive treat this morning.'

Dyer predictably coloured up with embarrassment, and Lord Bassenford smiled without warmth.

'My son does not want your attentions again, Dyer. Ever.'

'Lord Bassenford, you said…'

'Ever! I thought I had made that clear. Stay away from Lord Theodore, or the consequences will be *dire* for you, Dyer.' Lord Bassenford chuckled at his little quip, then added, 'Now, off you go. Merry Christmas.'

***

As the evening came to a close, Lord Bassenford saw his guests out, then led his family, with the addition of Adam, back upstairs.

'Jolly glad your parents can join us tomorrow for presents and Christmas dinner, young Foster,' he boomed, Adam being the son of David and Julia, the Sports Sponsorship Directors. Glancing over his shoulder, he smiled indulgently at his son and added, 'Theodore, you were magnificent tonight. Catherine would jump through hoops if you asked her to. Well done – I think I'll be seeing a lot more of the Head of Euro Logistics UK from now on.'

Theo gaped at his father in surprise. 'Actually, Your Lordship, I genuinely like…'

'Tomorrow, Theodore. I'm tired now, and Santa won't visit if I'm not asleep like a good boy. Sponsored Santa, naturally! Goodnight, all.'

Chuckling, Lord Bassenford disappeared up the stairs. Turning his attention to Marina, intending to ask if she fancied a glass of wine before going to bed, Theo was taken aback by the hostility in her eyes.

'I'm tired too,' she snapped. 'Tired and disillusioned. Goodnight.'

'Mari…'

'*No*, Theo! I thought you really liked Catherine, now I find it's just a ruse to help Father and the Scheme. She's already crazy about you, and you're going to break her heart…'

Turning abruptly, Marina ran up to the third floor and slammed her bedroom door behind her.

'Nice one, Theodore,' said Rosanna, smiling smugly at her brother. 'Ads and I have better things to do than chat to Father's latest lapdog. Sweet dreams, little bro.'

Left alone with his thoughts as Rosanna and Adam headed for the stairs, his high spirits dampened by Marina's stinging words, Theo almost found himself longing for the uncomplicated Christmas Eves spent locked in his bedroom.

***

Many miles north of Lord Bassenford's Christmas Eve gathering in Kensington, the defiantly unsponsored White Lion Inn was playing host to a very different evening. As usual, the entertainment was provided by Dory's Avengers, and the pub was packed with revellers, all euphoric about having an Olympic gymnast in their midst and deaf to Gideon's sporadic attempts to put things into perspective.

'Even His Lordshit doesn't have control over the Olympics,' he protested as a tipsy Sarah draped a homemade 'gold medal' (a disc of yellow card strung on a length of Jenny's hair ribbon) around his neck, 'despite the fact he thinks he rules the world.'

Matilda, unsurprisingly, had embraced what Gideon had called Louis's 'wild notions' about challenging the Sponsors at the Olympic Games with alacrity, and by Christmas Eve she was full of ideas, each one more farfetched than the last. Relaxing in the warm camaraderie of the pub, the Unsponsored howled their encouragement as she used the gaps between songs to propose suitable comeuppances for Lord Bassenford.

'Matty!' Max said, leaning over his drum kit and prodding Matilda in the back as she followed the band's rendition of Kasabian's *Fire* by pondering the possibility of floating His

Lordship down the Thames on a burning boat. 'Remember there's a Sponsor in our midst.'

'Aye,' replied Matilda, laughing uproariously. 'You, Maxwell.'

'I meant…'

'I know, Max. Just remember, we accepted you. Lysander's got to have his chance too.'

Walking over to Lysander, Matilda clinked her bottle of beer against his pint glass and kissed him soundly on the lips.

'Good job I'm not the jealous type, Matty,' said Nicola, laughing.

'Saving myself for Delicious Dory, Nik, don't you fret. Besides, your husband's too Sponsor-endorsed for me, not to mention the fact he's older than my dad.' Dodging playful swipes from both Nicola and Lysander, Matilda sprang back on to the stage and led the band in a high-speed version of Madonna's *Papa Don't Preach*.

Lifting a sleeping Jenny in his arms a little later on, Lysander said his goodnights to the people around him, readily accepting their invitation to join them in the pub for lunchtime beers on Christmas Day.

'It's a big day for little girls tomorrow,' he commented, gently kissing his daughter's head. 'Best get this one home so Father Christmas can pay a visit.'

'I'll take her…'

'You stay, Sarah, I'd like to be the one to take her home. God knows, I've got some catching up to do with my kids.'

Lurking outside, a couple of Lord Bassenford's watchmen shivered in the December air, blowing on their hands and grumbling that they'd rather be in the warmth of the Blenthwaite Hotel. Nudging his mate, one of them nodded towards the inn as the door opened and a couple emerged, the man carrying a child.

'Trevelyans! Do you want to follow them?'

Watching Lysander and Nicola walking off chatting happily, Jenny sleeping in her father's arms, the other replied, 'Nay, lad, it's Christmas. Santa's got to visit the little 'un…'

Unable to continue, so acute was his longing to be home with his own children, the man lapsed into quiet contemplation. Being sponsored meant good prospects, good homes, happy families… didn't it? No, actually, at that moment being sponsored meant standing in the freezing cold on Christmas Eve, miles from his family, while the Unsponsored enjoyed drinks in the warm.

By the time the party in The White Lion broke up, the doubt-filled sponsored watchman had long since returned to his impersonal hotel room. Seeing the Unsponsored pass by, some making their way home, others responding to the peal of the church bells inviting them to

Midnight Mass, all exchanging cheerful season's greetings, the watchman came to an abrupt decision. Pulling his phone from his pocket, he scrolled down to his wife's number and pressed call.

***

Theo awoke in a state of confusion on Christmas morning, fully clothed and tucked under a blanket on one of the drawing room sofas. Raising a tousled head from his makeshift bed, he cast his eyes around the room, noticing that a number of presents had appeared beneath the Christmas tree while he slept.

'Morning, Annie,' he said, turning to his favourite housemaid who was making up the fire as quietly as she could.

'Morning, Lord Theo,' she replied. 'Bit too much vino last night, was it?'

'I think you may be right,' he said with a rueful grin. 'My head's a bit woolly.'

Sitting back on her heels as the fire flickered into life, Annie asked, 'Can I get you anything? Black coffee, maybe?'

'A latte would be lovely, please, two sugars.'

'Oh, get you, Lord T, bog standard instant not good enough for you?' said Annie with a cheeky grin, dodging the fat cushion Theo pulled from underneath his head and hurled at her as she made for the door.

'And a merry Christmas to you too, you little minx!' he called after her.

Within five minutes, Annie was back with Theo's latte and a sizeable slab of Christmas cake.

'Enjoy!' she said before heading back downstairs to help serve breakfast. Theo devoured the cake in three monster bites, then savoured his latte, his eyes constantly drawn to the glowing Christmas tree and the exciting pile of presents around it. When he'd finished, he returned his mug to the kitchen two floors below, finding it a hive of activity. Preparations for the family dinner were in full swing, popular seasonal songs were blaring from the radio, and all the staff seemed to be in high spirits, apart from the eternally miserable head of household, Mooreland.

'Lord Theodore,' he said stiffly, finding it difficult to treat the young man with respect after so many years of being permitted to treat him like rubbish. 'One of the servants would have fetched that mug, there was really no need…'

'It's fine, Mr Mooreland. I wanted the opportunity to wish everyone a merry Christmas before it all gets too manic. Oh, and thank you whoever put the blanket over me last night. It was much appreciated. Was it you, Mrs White?'

Going over to kiss the amiable cook on the cheek, Theo declared her to be 'kindness personified' as he helped himself to a mince pie from the tray she'd just taken from the oven. Immensely irritated by the way his staff all clearly adored Theo, Mooreland began snapping out instructions with even less festive spirit than before, doing his utmost to dampen the mood.

'Go easy on them, Ebenezer, it is Christmas Day,' suggested Theo as he headed for the door. He hoped his wisecrack wouldn't make Mooreland even harder on the staff, but judging by their gales of laughter as he left the kitchen, they'd probably hardly notice if it did.

So engrossed was Theo in trying not to burn his mouth on the still piping-hot mince pie as he trotted up to his bedroom to shower, he almost walked into Marina at the top of the stairs to the third floor.

'Oh!' he said in surprise. 'Didn't see you there, so sorry. Merry Christmas, Mari.'

Stooping to kiss his sister on the cheek, Theo was dismayed when she turned her face away.

'OK, Mari,' he said, 'I'm not putting up with any more of this. Come over here!' Not giving Marina any chance to reply, he took her hand and dragged her to the window seat overlooking the handsome back garden of the St Benedict residence.

'Hit me with it. Shout, scream, slap my face if you want, but don't give me the silent treatment. It'll only spoil your day as much as it'll spoil mine.'

'You know what's wrong, Theo,' said Marina, trying and failing to free her hand from her brother's. 'I told you last night. I can't believe you're using Catherine to help the Sponsorship Scheme...'

'Well, if you can't believe it, why are you believing it then?' interrupted Theo. When Marina didn't reply, he continued, 'I thought long and hard about what you said last night, Mari. Actually, I never got to bed – I've just woken up on the drawing room sofa. Do you actually think I'd do *anything* to help the Scheme?'

'No, I don't think that, Theo. However, I still don't think your motives are pure and true. I heard what you asked for as a Christmas present, remember? Is it Catherine you want, or could she be anyone as long as you get laid? And if you're just using her for your own purposes, not bothered that she stands to end up badly hurt, how does that make you any different to Father?'

Marina finally managed to free her hand from Theo's and she sat back, looking moodily at her fingers.

'I thought about that too, Mari. I admit it was His Lordship's suggestion I chat Cathie up in the first place. I also admit I did it to start with because I could see that... God, this is going to sound big-headed...'

'You could see she fancied the pants off you?'

'Er, well, yes. And I was thinking with…'

'Your cock?'

'Yes, Marina, once again concise and to the point. But,' seeing Marina about to speak, Theo held up his hand to hush her, 'the truth is I like Cathie, and it's got nothing to do with what *he* wants. I can't wait to see her again. I want to make her laugh, hold her, smell her hair…'

'Take her to bed?'

Theo laughed. 'Yes, that too, but only because I really like her.'

'Why? What do you find so special about Catherine?'

'Bloody hell, Mari, a minute ago you were accusing me of not liking her enough! What is so special about Cathie is quite simply this: she reminds me of Mum. Cathie's kind, gentle, thoughtful, all those wonderful things our mother was… *is*, and do you really think I'd deliberately break the heart of someone like that?'

Marina, looking for all the world like a younger version of their mother, relaxed and smiled warmly at her brother.

'Merry Christmas, Theo,' she said, hugging him. 'I didn't really think you were turning into Father.'

'You did for a moment, Mari, but it's OK,' said Theo, returning her hug. 'You were wrong.'

Chapter 14 – Philip's Suspicions

By the time Theo had showered and dressed in fresh clothes, David and Julia Foster had arrived at the St Benedict residence, looking forward to spending Christmas Day with their son in such opulent surroundings. Theo too was determined to enjoy this Christmas – his first proper one in a decade – and he entered the drawing room with a beaming smile, scanning the pile of presents, which had grown considerably since he'd woken up on the sofa, then settling himself on a beanbag.

'Good of you to join us at last, Theodore,' said Lord Bassenford, rubbing his hands together gleefully. 'Now we're all here, let the celebrations begin!'

Glowing with his uncharacteristic love of the season, His Lordship pulled a Santa hat on to his head and presided over the festivities with a 'Ho-ho-ho', taking the entire morning to hand out the gifts one by one. Not only was there an impressive amount to get through, but Lord Bassenford insisted that each gift was opened as soon as he handed it to its recipient so everyone could savour the moment.

Shortly before pre-dinner drinks were due to be served, only one present remained unopened: a large and curiously shaped parcel, almost hidden behind the huge tree. Sliding it out into the open, Lord Bassenford looked fit to explode with excitement.

'This one's for you, Theodore,' he said, handing it over to his son.

Reading the tag, Theo said, 'To Theodore, Merry Christmas…'

'Come on, then, who's it from?' asked Lord Bassenford, clapping his hands together impatiently.

'You, Your Lordship, as I think you probably know.' The tag actually continued with the words 'Love from Father', but there was no way Theo would be reading that bit aloud. Instead, he said, 'What is it?'

'Open it and see! Open it!'

Theo unwrapped the mysterious present to be faced with an equally mysterious box. Opening the box, Theo gasped before he could stop himself when he saw what was inside. Almost reverently, he took out the beautiful guitar and placed it on his knee.

'It's a Les Paul,' he whispered.

'Do you like it? Do you love it, Theodore? There's an amplifier too, but that was too bulky to wrap. Mooreland, go and fetch Lord Theodore's amplifier, please.'

Mooreland left the room and returned a few minutes later with a Marshall amplifier, dumping it on the floor in front of Theo before returning to sit, stiff and miserable, in the far corner of the room. Plugging the guitar in, Theo tuned the instrument then started to pluck out some songs, his mouth open all the while in surprise at his father's thoughtful and perfect present.

'I didn't know you could play, Lord Theodore,' said David Foster.

'Oh yes,' said Lord Bassenford, almost babbling in his jubilation. 'He's very good, actually. Do you love the guitar, Theodore? Do you?'

'Yes,' Theo replied simply, raising his head and for once looking at his father without animosity. 'Thank you... er... Your Lordship.'

***

Lord Bassenford celebrated Christmas Day with a childlike exuberance, buoyed (although he'd never have admitted it) by Theo's genuine delight at his new guitar, but the following day was the indisputable highlight of the Head of the Sponsorship Scheme's social calendar. By early afternoon, a number of Sponsors, along with anyone else His Lordship considered worth cultivating, had arrived at the St Benedict residence for his legendary Boxing Day gathering, and he greeted each guest personally, exchanging pleasantries and circulating like the perfect host. Feigning interest in Mortimer O'Reilly's financial predictions for the new year, Lord Bassenford allowed himself a quick glance around, noticing to his satisfaction that his son, new guitar in hand, had made a beeline for Catherine Lorimer and was attempting to emulate Jimi Hendrix as she gazed adoringly at him.

'Nice work, Theodore,' he murmured, scanning the room in search of Catherine's influential father.

Engaged in scintillating conversation with Philip and Simone Lorimer half an hour later, Lord Bassenford was annoyed to be approached by an anxious Lee Fellows.

'Your Lordship, I hate to disturb you, but Pete Lomax is on the phone…'

'Who?'

'Pete Lomax, Your Lordship. One of our security men in Blenthwaite…'

'That fucking village!' hissed Lord Bassenford through clenched teeth, his eyes flashing with fury. 'Put the call through to my office, Fellows.' Noticing Philip Lorimer's quizzical expression, His Lordship reined in his temper with a huge effort and added, 'Just a rather vocal bunch of Unsponsored, Philip, nothing to worry about. Please excuse me for a few minutes.'

As Lord Bassenford strode from the room, Philip Lorimer smiled uneasily at his wife. Whatever the Blenthwaite Unsponsored had done, it was clearly going to be bad news for them once Lord Bassenford had been put in the picture.

Upstairs in his third-floor office, Lord Bassenford was incandescent with rage.

'He did *what*?'

'He renounced his sponsorship, Your Lordship.'

'Where's he from? Glasgow? Get on to the security up there, round up his wife and children…'

'With respect, Your Lordship, his wife and kids are nowhere to be found. I alerted Glasgow security right away, but the house is all locked up and quiet.'

'So where is he now?'

'We don't know, Your Lordship. He left a note…'

'Read it.'

'Your Lordship, I'd rather…'

'*Read it!*'

Pete Lomax wished heartily that anyone but he had been the one to find out that his fellow watchman had defected.

'"Hi, Pete, sorry to drop you in it, lad, but I can't do this sponsorship lark any more. I quit. Watching the Unsponsored has only taught me one thing: they're a lot happier than we are. Why are we watching Nicola Trevelyan anyway? It strikes me all she wants to do is spend quality time with her family, and quite frankly, that's all I want too".'

'Nicola Trevelyan!' snarled Lord Bassenford. 'It comes back to Nicola bloody Trevelyan. And when, pray, did you find this oh-so-informative note?'

'Yesterday m-morning,' stammered Lomax. 'I didn't want to ruin your Christmas Day, Your Lordship…'

'And so you decided to ruin my Boxing Day instead.' On the London end of the phone, Lord Bassenford was angrier than ever. 'Lomax, listen to me. I'll be sending men up first thing in the morning. They'll have instructions that *must* be carried out to the letter. I'm going to teach that bloody village a lesson it won't forget in a hurry. Understand? Still with me? Good!'

Ending the call, Lord Bassenford took a while to compose himself before joining his guests downstairs, all pleasure in the festive season over as far as he was concerned.

***

As Lord Bassenford despatched Stephen Dyer and a team of thugs up to Blenthwaite the next morning, Philip Lorimer was embarking on a difficult conversation with his daughter.

'Cathie, my darling, come and sit with your old dad for a while. There's something I want to discuss with you.'

Sitting beside her father, Catherine asked, 'What is it, Daddy?'

'I'll come straight out with it… Theodore St Benedict…'

Seeing his daughter's face light up at the mere mention of Theo's name, Philip realised just how difficult the conversation was going to be.

'You like Theodore a lot, don't you, Cathie.'

'Loads and loads, Daddy. He's so funny, kind… gorgeous too,' she added with a grin.

Sighing, Philip ploughed on. 'I'm not sure he's good for you. I'm not sure any of us being involved with that family is good…'

'Why?' Catherine's voice was quiet and composed, but Philip couldn't miss the horror dawning in her eyes.

'I think Lord Bassenford is a dangerous man. He, er, had a phone call yesterday afternoon. It wasn't a welcome call, and it made him very angry. Oh, he tried to hide it, but his eyes! They were evil – the devil's own eyes.'

'Theo's not like his father though, Daddy. They couldn't be more different.'

'I know that, darling, but there's still a lot of mystery around Theodore. Where's he been all these years?'

'He had a breakdown, after his mother disappeared…'

'Really? Do you think Theodore comes across as someone who had a breakdown so serious it kept him out of the public eye for a decade? Then there's the fact he never leaves that house. Has he offered to take you out? Of course not. Why?'

'He's agoraphobic, Daddy. He told me he's too nervous…'

'Nervous? Theodore? Cathie, I think he's lying to you.'

Catherine went silent. Much as she hated to admit it, she shared her father's fears about Theo's history. It just didn't add up somehow.

'Darling,' Philip went on, 'your mother and I love you so much. You're our world. We don't want anything bad to happen…'

'Daddy, I know.'

'So you'll stay away from Theodore? I have a little suspicion the whole romance may have been commissioned by His Lordship to get me onside…'

'No, Dad, I will not be staying away from Theo. In fact, I'm going to see him right now. I won't deny I've had the same worries as you, but I care far too much about him simply to give up on him. I've got to give him a chance to tell me his side of the story.'

'And if he doesn't? Or confirms our fears?'

Catherine sighed. 'I'll never see him again in that case, Daddy. Just let me give him this chance.'

***

Lord Bassenford's cook Mrs White, alone in the kitchen, was surprised to hear the sound of the doorbell – no guests were expected, and impromptu visits were unheard of. Making her way along the grand entrance hall and opening the door, thinking she'd have to tell a group of Jehovah's Witnesses that Lord Bassenford wasn't seeking salvation, she was pleasantly surprised to find Catherine Lorimer on the doorstep instead.

'Come in, dear,' she said kindly, ushering the nervous girl through the door.

'M-may I see Lord Theodore, p-please?' stammered Catherine.

Before Mrs White could reply, Mooreland appeared on the stairs.

'This is most irregular,' he growled. 'I'll have to speak to His Lordship.'

Mrs White led Catherine into the warmth of the kitchen and made her a cup of tea while they waited for Mooreland to return. Catherine found herself relaxing in Mrs White's friendly company, but that didn't stop her jumping violently when the kitchen door opened ten minutes later. Bracing herself to be escorted from the premises by an angry Mooreland, she virtually sagged with relief as Theo entered the room instead, his hair still damp from a recent shower.

'Cathie,' he said, taking hold of her hands and kissing her. 'This is the best surprise ever.'

'Why don't you take the young lady upstairs, Lord Theodore?'

'Good idea, Mrs White.'

As he led her into the hall, Catherine just had time to whisper, 'Theo, I need us to talk in private...' before Lord Bassenford appeared in their path.

'Ah, love's young dream,' he bellowed. 'Can't get enough of each other, eh?'

Knowing exactly how to work his father, Theo winked and grinned.

'That's right, Your Lordship. I was just going to take Cathie... um... you know...'

'You devil, Theodore. Don't let him take advantage of you, Catherine. Off you go, now, I'm sure you're anxious to be alone.'

Lord Bassenford stepped aside to let the youngsters pass, chuckling knowingly as they disappeared up the stairs.

'Here we are,' Theo said as he and Catherine reached the fourth floor, closing the door to his bedroom behind them and throwing himself down on his bed. 'I'm sorry my room doesn't quite measure up to the opulence of the rest of the house, but we'll be alone here.' As Catherine continued to hover nervously by the door, he added, 'It's OK, Cathie, I really won't take advantage of you.'

'It's not you, Theo, it's… that…'

Following Cathie's horrified glance, Theo looked up at his redundant security camera and smiled.

'Don't worry about that, Cathie, it's switched off…'

'I *am* worried though, Theo, and that's given me one more thing to worry about.' Sighing, she added, 'Daddy doesn't want me to see you any more. He…'

Stopping abruptly as Theo held up a hand, she watched in confusion as he stood up, crossed over to the door and checked that the landing was deserted. He then turned and said in a low voice, 'Cathie, please come and sit on the bed. I promise I won't take advantage of you. I won't even touch you if you don't want me to, but we'll be more private talking there. Walls have ears in this house.'

Cathie allowed herself to be led over to the bed, still longing for Theo with every fibre of her being despite her misgivings about his past.

'OK,' she said when they'd sat down. 'My dad doesn't believe that you had a breakdown. He doesn't believe that you're agoraphobic. He thinks something sinister's going on here and he doesn't want me involved.'

'And what do you believe, Cathie?' Catherine was silent for a while, and it was Theo who said, 'You think the same.'

'My dad said you're probably only seeing me so that Lord Bassenford can have regular contact with him. You know, Dad being the head of Euro Logistics UK and not being sponsored…'

'Your father's a shrewd man, Catherine.'

'So it's true?'

'It's true that His Lordship asked me to forge a relationship with you. That was *not* why I did it, though.'

'What were your reasons then, Theo? And why do you really call your father "His Lordship"? I don't buy the family joke excuse any more.'

Theo rested his arms on his knees, staring into the middle distance as he replied.

'Brace yourself, Cathie. If you want the truth, I will tell you the truth, but it's grim. I call him Lordship because I will never call him Father. I *hate* him. I hate him more and more with every breath I take, and I would never do anything to help him, or his Scheme.

'You're right – I didn't have a breakdown. I was imprisoned for the best part of a decade. Hence the security camera. My crime? I spoke my mind about the Scheme, told him I thought it cruel and oppressive.'

Catherine was as white as a sheet. 'He imprisoned you?' she said incredulously. 'Your own father? Isn't he afraid you'll tell someone?'

'He limits my contact with the outside world. Look.' Theo showed Catherine the security bracelet on his wrist. 'This is not a watch, Cathie, and I'm not agoraphobic. How I'd love to leave this house and never return, but if I pass the threshold, this thing will set off alarms all over London.'

'So, you've not been outside in ten years?'

'That's right. Until recently, I hadn't even left this rotten bedroom. I'm not sure what mellowed him on that one. Remarkably, I think he enjoys my company. I argue with him, no one else does. No one else dares – actually, I think they're the sensible ones.'

'My father thinks Lord Bassenford's got a violent temper. Apparently he got a call yesterday which made him look... well, Dad said he had the devil's own eyes.'

Theo laughed a little at Philip Lorimer's choice of words.

'His Lordshit does have a violent temper. I should know.'

'His Lord*shit*?'

'That's what Dory's Avengers call him, and it suits the bastard down to the ground.'

'Sorry, you've lost me, Theo. Dory's Avengers?'

'Oh yes, I'll come to that.'

'Please do, I'm intrigued. Now, I hardly dare ask, but why should you know? About His Lordship's violent temper, I mean.'

Theo hesitated for a few moments. 'Don't be alarmed, I'm not about to pounce on you. I just need to show you something,' he said, removing his shirt. Catherine had a moment to admire his body, nicely toned now thanks to his freedom to use the household gym, before he turned over and lay on his belly. He heard her gasp in shock, then her fingers started to trace the scars on his back.

'Your father does that to you?'

'Not personally, no,' said Theo. 'His Lordshit doesn't like to get his hands dirty. He has his thugs do it.'

'Do what?'

'They whip me, Cathie. They flog me, often until I pass out with the pain. His Lordshit watches. Sometimes my sister watches too.'

'*Marina* watches?'

'No, I meant Lady Bitch, although His Lordshit did force Marina to watch once.'

Catherine continued to stroke Theo's back as she digested the awful truth about his life. Eventually, she said, 'How did you stay sane? I think I'd have gone mad in the first week.'

'Now, this is going to sound a bit mad, Cathie, but bear with me. I've learned to go off in my mind, to a place I loved as a child. When I was young, we often used to visit my mother's family in the Lake District, a village called Blenthwaite. They were happy times…'

'You must miss your mother a lot.'

'I miss her every second of every day.' Theo turned away as tears blurred his vision. 'My mother was the polar opposite of His Lordshit: kind, generous – to the Unsponsored as well as the Sponsored. It went against everything he believed in to have a wife uniting everyone as he was trying to divide them. Gradually he put more and more limitations on her freedom, stopped us going to Blenthwaite, stifled her compassion.

'And then she disappeared. No one knows where. No one dared to ask, except for me. I couldn't let it go without challenging him – unfortunately I've inherited some of his temper. I was only thirteen, Cathie, but the row was spectacular. I think I'd have been scarred for life from the beating I received that day even if there hadn't been plenty more since. He then had that disgusting specimen Dyer, newly released from prison after serving his paltry sentence for murdering my uncle, lock me in this room…'

'Dyer murdered your uncle? No wonder he gives me the creeps.'

'He gives you the creeps because he's a creep, Cathie.'

'Yet your father employs him?'

Theo laughed bitterly. 'His Lordshit's concept of what is acceptable is a bit under-developed, to say the least. Like me, Uncle Elliot was vehemently opposed to the Scheme, and wasn't afraid to say so. I'm sure it suited His Lordshit down to the ground to have him silenced.'

'Hold on – are you saying your father ordered Dyer to…'

'Shh,' said Theo, rolling on to his side and holding a finger to Catherine's lips. 'Best not travel on that particular train of thought.'

Catherine shivered. 'How come His Lordship lets you speak to me alone? Doesn't he fear you'll tell me everything?'

'I'm under strict instructions not to tell you a thing, hence the stupid agoraphobia tale. Whatever happens, he must never know that I've opened up to you. I think you realise how dangerous His Lordshit is now, don't you?'

'Trust me, Theo, I won't tell a soul. I know what would happen to you.'

'I'm more concerned about you, Cathie. His Lordshit will hurt *anyone* to achieve his own ends. He must think that I'm a selfish prat whose only interest is getting laid, and you're a ditsy girl hopelessly in love…'

'I don't have to pretend to be hopelessly in love with you, Theo…'

Theo grinned and raised his eyebrows suggestively, making Catherine laugh and relax a little. Not leaving anything out, he then told her all about Louis and Dory's Avengers.

'I don't know how I managed it, but lying here alone day after day, going up to Blenthwaite in my head, I eventually made contact with Louis. Telepathically. I know it sounds insane, and I can't do it now. I think I could only do it then because there were no distractions.'

Smiling wistfully, Theo recalled the day Louis had turned up in response to his cry for help.

'I'll never be able to express how much that meant to me, Cathie. For the first time in years, I had someone to talk to. Someone who actually liked me. God, I was so lonely…'

Theo's voice caught, and Catherine held him while he gave in to his emotions. Finally he composed himself, sat up and blew his nose.

'This is the latest news from Blenthwaite,' he said, taking Louis's note from its hiding place and showing it to Catherine.

'Who's Matilda?' she asked when she'd read it.

'I don't know. Sorry, I forgot about that bit.'

'She sounds hot.' In her head, Catherine added: *confident, exciting and far more suited to Theo than shy, nervous little me.*

'She sounds desperate. You're my girlfriend now, Cathie, if you want to be.'

'Of course I do, Theo.'

'What, even considering all I've just told you?'

'Yes,' she said simply.

The two of them fell silent for a while, lying side by side as Catherine stroked the muscles of Theo's stomach. As her fingers got closer and closer to the waistband of his trousers, his breathing became ragged and he groaned with desire.

'Cathie…' he began.

'Shh.' Undoing his belt, Catherine slid Theo's trousers off then ran her hands back up his long legs, wrapping her fingers around the straining bulge in his boxer shorts and squeezing it gently.

'Oh… my… God…'

Theo closed his eyes in ecstasy and threw back his head, his words coming out in a drawn-out moan. Misinterpreting his moan, Catherine abruptly pulled her hand away.

'What is it?' she said. 'What have I done wrong?'

Returning his head to its natural position and opening his eyes, Theo stared at her in disbelief.

'Wrong?' he said. 'You, my vision of beauty, have done nothing wrong.'

'Only I thought perhaps you didn't want...'

Pushing Catherine gently on to her back, Theo leant over her, silencing her with a hungry kiss.

'Catherine,' he said, coming up for air, 'I have never wanted anything so much in my life.'

Chapter 15 – Nicola

That evening, after Catherine had departed for home, Lord Bassenford found all three of his children in the family room. Theo was curled up on his beanbag watching cartoons with Marina, while Rosanna sat filing her nails, aloof as ever. His Lordship perched on the sofa for a few moments, then decided the time had come for a father-and-son chat.

'Theodore,' he said, 'I don't think anyone in the household has any doubt what you were up to all afternoon.'

Theo ignored him. Lord Bassenford ploughed on regardless.

'Now then, Theodore, did you take precautions?'

'Did I take *what*, Your Lordship?'

'Precautions. Precautions, you silly dolt.'

'Against what?'

'Against getting the young lady pregnant, of course. Oh…'

Lord Bassenford's voice trailed off as realisation dawned on both him and his elder daughter at the same moment. Looking up from her fingernails, Rosanna shrieked with laughter.

'He doesn't know the facts of life, Father! He's twenty-two years old and he doesn't know how a baby's made.'

'Do you, Theodore?'

Lord Bassenford and Rosanna were gratified to see Theo blush slightly.

'No,' he mumbled. 'Should I?'

'Given your activities this afternoon I think it would be as well, yes. Rosanna, would you pop down to the kitchen and fetch a carrot, please?'

Waiting for Rosanna to return, Lord Bassenford turned back to Theo.

'How much do you know?'

Glancing helplessly at Marina and finding even she was desperately trying to keep her laughter in check, Theo resorted to looking at his fingers.

'I'm guessing it's got something to do with sex,' he said eventually.

'Well done,' said Lord Bassenford sarcastically. 'I should have thought of this sooner. No one's taught you the facts of life. Ah thank you, Rosanna, a nice, big carrot.'

Theo looked at the carrot in confusion, wondering what it had to do with making babies. Rosanna had guessed exactly what the carrot was for and she sat down beside her brother, laughing helplessly.

Fishing in his pocket, Lord Bassenford said, 'This – look at it, Theodore – this is a condom.'

'Jolly good, Your Lordship. I haven't a clue what that is.'

'Here. Open the packet.' Theo did as he was told and Lord Bassenford continued, trying to ignore the amusement of his daughters.

'Now, when you have sex, Theodore, and you… you know… finish off…'

Sensing his father's discomfort, and that his sisters' laughter was more at Lord Bassenford's expense than his, Theo felt the corners of his own mouth twitch.

'You… finish off and… your sperm goes into… well, it goes inside the lady and, erm, sometimes meets her egg. If this happens and your… er… sperm fertilises the egg, nine months down the line we've got a baby Theodore on our hands.'

Pulling himself together, Lord Bassenford injected some authority back into his voice.

'Stop laughing, all three of you! This is serious. Theodore, I don't want you making babies with Catherine Lorimer. God knows, you can barely look after yourself.'

Theo would have argued that point, but he was incapable of speaking.

'Right, the trick is to stop your sperm getting to Catherine's egg, and that's where the condom comes in. Have a look at it. How do you think it works?'

Theo examined the condom, then started to blow it up like a balloon.

'No!' roared Lord Bassenford as his offspring rolled on the floor, crying with laughter. 'I'm beginning to wish I'd worn one of these things myself a bit more often. Give it here, Theodore!'

Liberated from Theo's hand, the inflated condom flew across the room with a satisfied fart, reducing the young St Benedicts to hysterics. Gritting his teeth, His Lordship took another pack out of his pocket, then prodded Theo with his foot.

'Right, Theodore, pay attention. You put the condom on like so.' Using the carrot, Lord Bassenford opened the new packet and demonstrated. 'Once it's on, nice and secure, you can go ahead and have sex. Your semen collects in the condom, which you carefully dispose of afterwards. It doesn't reach Catherine's egg, and we don't have any silly accidents. Do you understand?'

'Yes, Your Lordship,' replied Theo, his voice wobbly with laughter. 'I put the condom on the carrot and there'll be no baby Theodores.'

'Oh, for God's sake!' Thoroughly exasperated, Lord Bassenford threw the carrot at his son before stomping from the room, leaving his children rolling around, screaming with laughter, on the family room floor.

***

The same day Theo learned (and experienced) the facts of life for the first time, Lysander was brought back down to earth with a bump following the euphoria of Christmas. Checking his phone, he was alarmed to find a message from Lord Bassenford that had gone ignored since the previous afternoon.

Get back to London, immediately.

Nervous that he'd already let time elapse before obeying His Lordship's command, Lysander packed his things and prepared to leave without further ado, all under the accusatory gaze of Louis.

'I thought you were staying for a few days, Dad.'

'I can't, Louis, I've got to go back to London.'

'You said you'd stay!' said Louis in an unusual fit of petulance. 'You said you'd watch me train today! You said you wouldn't look at your phone!'

This was all true. Carried away by the warm unsponsored camaraderie, Lysander had declared over Boxing Day drinks in The White Lion that he wouldn't check his phone until after the New Year.

'Let His Lordshit wait!' he'd yelled, basking in the approval of the Unsponsored. However, in the cold light of day, he'd had a change of heart.

'How will it help anyone if I antagonise His Lordship… er, I mean, Lordshit?'

'Once a Sponsor, always a Sponsor,' grumbled Louis, looking at his father through narrowed eyes. 'By the way, Dad, did you know His Lordshit was drugging Mam?'

Lysander froze. He'd hoped to get away without Louis asking that question.

'Louis…'

'Just bloody answer, Sponsor!'

'I won't lie to you…'

'That'll make a refreshing change.'

'Let me speak! I knew to start with. I was commissioned by His Lordshit to court your mother, win her affections, get one of the Scheme's main critics off our case…'

'You bastard!'

'Thank you, Louis. Thank you for hearing me out, then coming to a measured and intelligent conclusion. You're young and impetuous, just like I was then…'

'There's no comparison! I'd *never* let anything bad happen to Abi.'

'You've got the benefit of hindsight, I didn't. I'll admit I thought the Scheme was the be all and end all, but… *but*…' Lysander held up a hand to hush his son, 'I did fall in love with your mother. I love her to this day. She knows the truth. I don't want us to part on bad terms again, Louis. I love you too…'

'Bollocks!' yelled Louis, kicking his half-packed kitbag across the room, scattering training gear and protein drinks in its wake.

'Well done,' said Lysander sarcastically. 'Very mature.'

'Think yourself lucky it was only the kitbag I kicked, you Sponsor bastard…'

'Louis, I haven't got time for your histrionics.'

With a heavy heart, Lysander walked out to his car and chucked his briefcase and laptop on to the back seat, slamming the door shut with rather more force than was necessary. As he turned to get into the driver's seat, he found his wife at his side.

'You've told him,' she said simply.

'Yes. Please try to calm him down – I'm pretty much his least favourite person at the moment, and quite frankly, I can't say I blame him. I'm so sorry, Nik…'

'I know that, silly,' said Nicola. 'Go on, I'll deal with our Louis.'

Kissing Lysander and reassuring him that she'd always love him, Nicola then went back inside the house as he drove away.

'Louis,' she said, entering the family room and finding her son talking animatedly to Sarah. Leaping up, he flung his arms around her.

'Mam, I can't believe that bastard…'

'Shut up, Louis! Don't ever talk about your father with that lack of respect again. No, listen to me,' Nicola continued as Louis tried to interrupt. 'It's true that Lysander was complicit when Dr Turnbull first put me on the drugs. Young and naïve, he was torn between loving me and wanting to do well in the Scheme. He didn't realise what they were, thought they were some super new vitamins, and by the time he did realise, it was too late. His Lordshit's tame doctor kept me supplied, and hopelessly addicted, I kept taking the drugs. I'm so sorry, darling, I've been a useless mother. I was off my head by the time you were born, let alone Jenny…'

'You were drugged, Mam. It wasn't your fault. Why didn't he stop it?'

'Your father was told I was ill. He was told that Dr Turnbull was keeping me sane, when actually she was supplying me with drugs I didn't need in order to keep my rebellious mouth shut. It was only when you, Gideon and Jess intervened… well, you know the rest.'

Louis was silent for a while, collecting his scattered kit together and packing it back into his bag. Finally another thought struck him.

'Why did Dr Turnbull treat you? Why not Jess?'

'Jess is a GP. His Lordshit told Lysander that Dr Turnbull was a specialist – which she is, but unfortunately one without scruples – and I'd probably do something stupid without her care. Look, Louis, your father's begged me for forgiveness and I've forgiven him. I love him. He loves me. We move on from here.'

'But…'

'Louis, we move on! Avenging Dory is the priority now – the future, not the past.'

'I'm not happy that he knows about Dory's Avengers. What if he…'

'He won't. I know you're angry, Louis, but your dad loves you. I love you, and we're both so proud of you. Now get off to training before Gideon skins you alive.'

Still fuming, Louis stormed into Gideon's studio ten minutes later.

'You're late…'

'Don't start, Gid, I'm not interested. You've not got a monopoly on bad moods, you know.'

No more would Louis say until he'd changed and warmed up, then, mostly from an upside down position on the parallel bars, he shared the whole sorry tale.

'I can't believe she still loves him,' he said, landing neatly on the floor.

'How much would you forgive Abilene?'

'Abi would never…'

'Nor did Lysander. I admit I hated the fact that Nik was falling for a Sponsor, but he loved her, Louis. He still does.'

'But he…'

'Made a mistake. Everyone makes mistakes – apart from me, of course.'

Louis harrumphed at Gideon's attempt to lighten the mood.

'I can't believe you're sticking up for him, Gid…'

'Stop calling me Gid! Just because you're cross doesn't give you special dispensation.'

'Oh, get lost!'

'Get back on those parallel bars!'

With an exaggerated sigh, Louis turned his attention to his training.

Leaving the studio at the end of the day, eyes cast down miserably, Louis almost walked into Abi waiting for him outside.

'Oops!' she said with a grin, pulling him into her welcoming embrace and lifting her lips to meet his. 'Whatever's the matter? You look like Gideon's sold all your favourite apparatus and filled the studio with pommel horses instead.'

Louis managed a watery smile in response. 'I wouldn't put it past him,' he said, 'so don't go giving him ideas.' Taking Abi's hand, he set off towards the village with her, their footsteps crunching satisfyingly in the freshly fallen snow. 'For once it's not Gideon who's pissed me off,' he continued. 'It's my bloody Sponsor father.'

'Lysander?' said Abi in surprise.

'Yes, Ly-bloody-sander. Why, do I have an alternative father? Please tell me I do – he couldn't be any worse than the moron I'm currently saddled with...'

'I've a feeling Theo might disagree with you there,' said Abi quietly. 'So what's Lysander done that's so bad? I thought you two were getting on well these days.'

'So did I,' grumbled Louis. 'But that was before I discovered that he not only knew all about Mam being drugged, he bloody well condoned it.'

'Seriously?' Abi looked up at her boyfriend as they walked. 'I guess Nicola's filing for divorce then.'

'Is she heck. *She* thinks Ly-bloody-sander was duped by His Lordshit. *She* thinks he thought the drugs were keeping her sane. *She* thinks he believed she'd lose the plot completely without them. She's adamant she still loves him and he loves her and he loves Jenny and me and we've all got to look to the future and avenging Dory's the priority and…'

'For God's sake, Louis, breathe!' said Abi with a light laugh. 'So the wronged party here – your mam – has forgiven the man who apparently wronged her.'

'Yup.' Louis's sigh emerged in a cloud of vapour.

'Doesn't that suggest to you that it might not have been Lysander's fault?'

'Nope.'

'So you think your mam's stupid?'

'No, of course not…'

'She must be if she'll forgive a man who's deliberately drugged her for the last couple of decades.'

Louis pursed his lips but didn't reply.

'Look, Lysander's a decent bloke, for a Sponsor.'

'But that's the whole point, Abi – he *is* a Sponsor. That's top priority with him, always was, always will be.'

'A few weeks ago I would have agreed with you, now I'm not so sure. I genuinely believe he's changing his views. And more than that, I believe he *does* love your mam… and you.'

Louis snorted derisively.

'Right,' snapped Abi, snatching her hand away from Louis's, 'so your mam's stupid and I'm a liar. Great. You seem to be on a mission to alienate everyone who loves you, so I'll leave you to it until your hot head has cooled down a bit.' Turning on her heel, Abi stormed off a few steps then swung back to face him. 'Meet your dad halfway, Louis. Build bridges. What have you got to lose?'

'What have I got to gain?' snarled Louis. 'I never want to see the man again. I couldn't care less if he died…'

Abi took a sharp breath, but it wasn't the lungful of freezing air that brought tears to her eyes.

'You don't mean that,' she said. 'Louis Trevelyan, you do not mean that.'

'Oh, my big stupid gob,' moaned Louis, momentarily clapping his hands over his mouth as the penny dropped. 'Abi, that was crass in the extreme, and I'm so, so sorry.'

Abi crossed the distance between them and wrapped her arms around him again.

'I know,' she whispered as he enclosed her in a hug. 'Just tell me you didn't mean it.'

'I didn't mean it,' replied Louis with conviction. 'I was angry and lashing out. Of course I don't want my dad to die…'

'And you'll build those bridges?'

'And I'll build those bridges. You're quite right, I've got nothing to lose and a good relationship with my father to gain.' Relieved to see Abi's tense expression relax into a smile, Louis responded with a smile of his own. 'That's better,' he said. 'Perhaps today's not going to be completely crap after all…'

'Miss Farrell!' Stephen Dyer's sneer interrupted Louis's words as the thug emerged from a black people carrier on the Blenthwaite Hotel's forecourt across the street.

'Or perhaps it is,' muttered Louis.

'Silly me,' Dyer continued, 'I should have brought flowers for your daddy's grave…'

Furious, Louis started towards Dyer, stopping abruptly when Abi pulled him back.

'Louis, leave it. He's not worth it.'

'Oh hello, Whitey. Didn't see you there in the snow.'

As Abi restrained Louis, Dyer warmed to his task.

'Miss Farrell, it can be *murder* keeping these boys in check. Or should that be manslaughter? I'm never sure – what's the difference?'

Louis once again tried to get across the road, yelling that Dyer was a piece of shit.

'Louis, no, don't rise to him…'

'I'll fucking kill him!'

'I'll let that go, Whitey, as you're His Lordship's new plaything. I'm a generous man… ooooof!'

So intent was Dyer on baiting Louis and Abi that he didn't notice a little whirlwind approach until her boot made violent contact with his groin.

'You really need to learn not to stand with your legs so far apart,' advised Matilda, sprinting away before anyone could react, her laughter echoing around the village street. Doubled up with pain and no longer enjoying his encounter with Abi, Dyer yelled at his companions to take it out on her boyfriend.

'Get the albino twat, you idiots. He started it…'

'Mr Dyer, His Lordship won't like that. Stick to the plan, eh?'

Regaining his composure a little as he remembered the 'fun' Lord Bassenford's plan held in store, Dyer smirked across the road at Abi and Louis.

'Yeah, let's behave with some dignity,' he said with unconscious irony. 'You'll learn, Unsponsored scum.'

***

Louis was far too easy-going to sulk for long. Following his conversation with Abi, he put his anger at his father behind him and sat down to talk things over a lot more calmly with Nicola.

'I've been thinking, Mam. I really believe Dad's trying to make amends…'

Not letting her son say any more, Nicola enveloped him in a bear hug.

'Darling, you're right. Your father's not a bad man – the worst he's been is naïve. He's been entrenched in the Scheme for so long, and now doesn't know how to get out. But he does love us. Really, he does.'

'I know, Mam,' said Louis, returning her hug. 'I gave him such a hard time this morning, do you think it'd be OK to give him a ring to put things right?'

'OK? Louis, he'd love that.'

Louis was eternally thankful he'd had this conversation with his mother, coming when it did. Following an emotional phone call to Lysander, which ended with both of them in fits of laughter as they saw the funny side of Louis's tantrum that morning, he went to bed feeling optimistic about the forthcoming New Year, and the next day headed off to training with a spring in his step, looking forward to Nicola joining him and Gideon after she'd put some washing on. Later he would recall that morning a thousand times, searching his memory for any feeling of foreboding, but he would always come to the same conclusion.

He had no idea of the horror to come.

Ten minutes after waving goodbye to Jenny and Sarah as they left to catch the sales in Carlisle, Nicola Trevelyan was feeling as cheerful and optimistic as her son. Collecting the laundry together, earphones on and listening to her favourite songs on her MP3 player, she boogied her way from room to room upstairs, singing along tunelessly.

She never heard Lord Bassenford's thugs entering her house.

'Silly cow!' said Dyer, laughing as he walked, bold as brass, through the Trevelyans' unlocked front door. 'Talk about sealing her own fate.'

Nicola took a second to register the scene in front of her as she walked down the stairs: Dyer and his thugs waiting in her hallway, some with baseball bats, all with nasty smirks.

'Ahh, Mrs Trevelyan…'

A basket of dirty washing flew down the stairs, hitting Dyer in the face as Nicola ran back to the landing. Immediately, she realised her mistake. Where could she go from here? Sooner or later, the thugs would find her. Deciding she couldn't bear to be dragged from either of her children's bedrooms, Nicola headed instead for the room she'd shared with Lysander for so many years.

She'd almost made it to the door when an arm wound round her neck.

'Got her, Mr Dyer,' called the thug, dragging the struggling Nicola back into the midst of his companions as the sound of cheerful music continued to come from her headphones. Walking up to Nicola, Dyer punched her in the face, breaking her jaw with one blow.

'Very silly move, that washing basket thing,' he snarled. 'Goodbye, Mrs Trevelyan. Should have stuck with the drugs…'

***

Louis had just executed a perfect Maltese cross and was dangling from the rings, grinning smugly at Gideon.

'Yes, you've nailed it, well done,' growled his coach. 'Now could you *please* incorporate it into the rest of the routine? I want to see…'

But whatever Gideon wanted to see at that particular moment would be lost to the mists of time.

The door into the gym flew open. Looking over with a smile, expecting to see Nicola arriving to watch her son train, Gideon was surprised to see a wild-eyed and distressed Jess Donatelli instead.

'Louis…'

Jess could say no more before bursting into tears. Louis dropped to the ground and was at her side in an instant.

'What the bloody hell's happened?' asked Gideon.

'Sponsor thugs, Louis,' Jess managed through her tears, 'your house…'

'Mam!' Louis pulled his shoes on and ran out into the cold December day, not even pausing to take his coat from its hook. Grabbing Gideon's chair and wheeling him through the studio door, Jess locked up then followed as quickly as possible, attracting plenty of attention as she pushed him through the village behind Louis. By the time Jess and Gideon caught up with Louis outside the Trevelyans' house, they'd been joined by quite a crowd, and within minutes Abi and her uncle arrived too, Jess having put a hysterical phone call through to Chris on her way to Gideon's studio.

'Oh no,' Abi whispered, jumping out of Chris's van and almost slipping over on the icy ground in her anxiety to reach her boyfriend. Louis was standing stock still in front of the silent crowd of Blenthwaite Unsponsored, his eyeballs dancing uncontrollably as the scene in front of him impressed itself indelibly on his shocked brain.

Nicola Trevelyan, beloved wife of Lysander and mother of Louis and Genevieve, was hanging by the neck from a large tree in the garden, cold and dead.

Chapter 16 – The Bleak Midwinter

In the office on the third floor of the St Benedict residence, a Sponsors' meeting was in full swing. As usual, Lord Bassenford was anxious to tie up any loose ends before the New Year, and he was listening to each member of the group reporting on the progress of their particular endorsements. Wanting to make amends for being late back from Blenthwaite, Lysander had stayed up into the early hours of the morning putting together a detailed presentation on Leisure and Fitness, and he was delivering this presentation when his boss's phone rang.

Glancing at the caller display, Lord Bassenford said, 'Sorry, Lysander, I'm going to have to take this.'

The call was brief. 'Good morning, Stephen… Exactly as planned?… Excellent. Now listen, I need you back here. Leave three – no, make it four – men behind, and return today. Well done.'

Replacing the receiver, Lord Bassenford turned back to his inner circle of Sponsors. 'Sorry about that,' he said amiably. 'Please continue, Lysander.'

Lysander didn't get the opportunity to continue before his own phone rang.

'Your Lordship, I really should…'

'Kill the call and get on with your presentation, Trevelyan. You're on very thin ice these days, so don't push it.'

Lysander did as he was told, but his mind kept wandering and he stammered his words. Then his phone shrilled again. Curious as to why Jessica Donatelli would be repeatedly trying to call him, Lysander looked pleadingly from his ringing phone to his irascible boss.

'My doctor… my kids…' he mumbled, reluctantly rejecting Jess's call again as the expression on Lord Bassenford's face darkened.

In the room below, the sound of Theo's guitar stopped abruptly and the television was turned up.

'Breaking news, just in.' Lord Bassenford's inner circle could clearly hear the words blaring from the drawing room. 'We now cross over to our reporter in the north…'

The television presenter's voice trailed off in confusion, and the next voice the Sponsors heard was that of Maxwell Barrington.

'Good morning. I'm in Blenthwaite, Cumbria, reporting on…'

'This is highly irregular,' interrupted the presenter, trying to regain some composure. 'We've got sponsored reporters onsite. Where's…'

It was Max's turn to interrupt.

'No Sponsored. Only Unsponsored allowed beyond this point. Do you want to know what's happened? Then you'll have to make do with me reporting.

'As I was saying,' Max continued, his voice sombre, 'I'm in Blenthwaite, reporting on the mysterious death of Nicola Trevelyan, who was found hanging from a tree by her son earlier today. Louis Trevelyan was alerted by local GP, Jessica Donatelli, who had noticed some irregularities around the Trevelyan household as she'd driven past. I've yet to confirm what these irregularities were…'

Not a sound could be heard in Lord Bassenford's office beyond the ticking clock and Max's voice as he went on to say that the official word was suicide. He then gave some general background information about Nicola – two children: Louis, twenty-three, a gymnast potentially of Olympic standard; Genevieve, six, pupil at Blenthwaite Primary School. Husband Lysander, forty-six, Director of Leisure and Fitness Sponsorship.

All of a sudden the television was switched off, the sound of running feet came up the stairs, and Theo burst into Lord Bassenford's office.

'Lysander, you need to get home, now, urgently…'

'We heard, thank you, Theodore,' Lord Bassenford interrupted. 'Very tactless, I must say, having the television on that loud. What a way for Lysander here to find out…'

'You knew.' Lysander's voice sounded choked as he looked at his boss. 'That call from Dyer. You knew!'

Sinking into a chair, Lysander took out his phone and scrolled down to Jess's number. She answered pretty much on the first ring, clearly in tears.

'Dr Donatelli?… Yes, I've just heard Max's report. I'll leave straight away…'

'You'll stay here,' growled Lord Bassenford. Lysander ignored him.

'Yes, thank you, I'm OK to drive. Is Louis there?… May I speak to him?… No, that's understandable.'

There was a long gap while Lysander listened intently to Jess Donatelli. Finally, his face unreadable, he said, 'Really? We'll talk more when I get home.'

Ending the call, Lysander stared at his phone without speaking. Never blessed with compassion, it was Lord Bassenford who broke the uncomfortable silence with a highly inappropriate comment.

'Louis not talking again, Lysander? Shame, his social skills were coming along so nicely…'

'He's just lost his mother, you inhuman bastard!' yelled Theo, slamming his fists on to

Lord Bassenford's desk and causing Mortimer O'Reilly to jump violently. 'I know how that feels, remember?'

Still staring at his phone, Lysander said, 'You knew, didn't you, Your Lordshit.'

'Given that you're overwrought, I'll let that slip of the tongue go, Trevelyan. Yes, I'll admit I knew. Suicide, poor Nicola. If only she'd continued with her course of medication…'

'Might it not have been – shall we say, considerate? Yes, might it not have been *considerate* to share the news with me? Being as it concerned… my wife…'

'Lysander, I would have shared the news with you after the meeting had my son not decided to take matters into his own hands. Now, continue with your presentation…'

Standing up, Lysander said, 'No. I'm going home.'

'After the meeting, Lysander. Of course I understand your need…'

'No. I'm going home, now.'

'You're disobeying a direct order?'

'I'm beyond caring, Your Lordshit. Here.' Taking out his wallet, Lysander threw his Gold Sponsor Card on to Lord Bassenford's desk. 'Have it. I'm through with your Scheme. Oh, and for the record, I don't believe for one second that my wife committed suicide. Dr Donatelli saw your thugs leaving my home this morning, shortly before my son made his awful discovery. Oh yes, and if… *if* Nik did commit suicide, apparently she beat herself up pretty badly first…'

As Lysander turned to go, Theo hugged him briefly.

'Please pass on my condolences to Louis,' he said, 'and to your little girl. My heart goes out to you all, Lysander. I'm so sorry.'

Lysander squeezed Theo's shoulders, not trusting himself to speak. As he walked across the room, Julia Foster said, 'I'm sorry too, Lysander. Drive carefully.' Lysander paused at the door while these sentiments were echoed by everyone else in the room, with the exception of Mortimer O'Reilly and Lord Bassenford. Then, nodding slightly, he left.

***

In Blenthwaite, the Unsponsored had formed a human wall around the scene of Nicola's death. Sponsored reporters stood idle and annoyed as Max delivered the news which could have been the scoop of a lifetime for them.

'Nicola Trevelyan was discovered,' said Max to the host of television cameras surrounding him, 'after Dr Donatelli became suspicious when she saw a group of men, known to be in Lord Bassenford's employ, leaving the Trevelyan residence. One of the men was identified as Stephen Dyer, who inflicted a fatal stab wound on professional footballer Elliot Farrell, Dr Donatelli's partner and father of her two children, fourteen years ago. We don't yet know whether the presence of Lord Bassenford's employees was in any way connected to Nicola's tragic death, but before her alleged suicide she apparently sustained several injuries, including a badly broken jaw. Rather a severe injury to inflict upon oneself.'

As Max continued to hold the television cameras rapt with his insinuations, Jess wrapped a coat round Louis, who was still shivering in his gym kit, and led him into the house. Abi and Gideon followed, while the rest of Louis's close friends stayed outside to help keep the sponsored journalists at bay.

'I don't want Sponsors taking her away,' Louis said, finally finding his voice as he huddled next to the Aga in the kitchen. 'I don't want them involved with… you know… funeral…'

Abi heard the catch in Louis's voice and hugged him close, understanding his pain only too well.

'No sponsored scum is going to get near your mother, Louis,' said Gideon. 'You just have to see the solidarity of the human wall out there.'

Alan Santiago put his head round the door.

'Sorry to barge in, Lou, but do you want us to… um… move your mam?'

Louis looked up from Abi's embrace, surprised by Alan's words.

'What about the police? Don't they want to look for evidence or something?'

Alan pulled a face. 'Apparently not. They're convinced it's... well... er...'

'Suicide,' Louis finished for Alan, his voice croaking halfway through the word. Clearing his throat, he continued bitterly, 'Of course, that'll be the official Sponsor line, then.'

'Exactly,' replied Alan. 'But it does mean we're now free to move your mam somewhere a little more, um, private.'

'Would you, Alan? That's very thoughtful. Sarah will be back soon, I don't want Jenny seeing...'

Once again Louis's voice gave up. Alan crossed the room and knelt in front of him.

'We're all with you, Louis. We all feel for you – Dex, Matty, Georgie, Chris, everyone – and we'll do anything we can to see you through this. You just say the word.'

'Thanks, Al, I never doubted it for a moment.'

'Now,' Alan continued, looking uncharacteristically ill at ease, 'I wish I didn't have to be the one to ask you painful questions, but where shall we take, er, your mam? Do you want us to take her to The Lion?'

'No thanks, Al,' replied Louis, doing his best to collect his thoughts. 'Would you put her in the living room for now, please? It's on the right as you come through the front door. It's a horrible room – we never use it normally, but that's not going to worry Mam now.'

Going back outside, Alan passed on Louis's wishes. He was only just in time – as he and Dex were carrying Nicola's body into the cold, impersonal living room, Sarah was driving up the lane to the Trevelyans' house. She'd heard the news on her car radio and returned from Carlisle as quickly as possible, doing her best to ward off the horde of sponsored journalists and photographers who recognised Nicola Trevelyan's daughter and started banging on the car windows, camera flashes reflecting in the frightened blue eyes of the little girl.

'She's only a child,' yelled Sarah desperately. 'Leave her alone!'

It didn't take long for the unsponsored human wall to realise what was going on, and Max cut short his television report to help shield Sarah's car as she drove into the Trevelyans' drive.

'Come on, Jenny,' she said, ushering the confused child into the house and away from the crowds as Dex and Alan emerged from the living room.

'Why are you sad face, Alan?' Jenny asked as he lifted her into his arms. 'Is it because the Sponsors made my mammy dead?'

'I've told her that Mummy's with the angels now,' said Sarah. 'I don't know how she's picked up on the Sponsors.'

'Sponsors are nasty, Sarah,' said the child. 'They do nasty things, and I don't like them…'

Holding Jenny close as she started to cry, Alan whispered, 'I don't like them either, darling. One day we're going to make the nasty Sponsors go away, then we can all be happy.'

'Dory's 'Vengers,' said Jenny through her tears.

'Sarah! Jenny!' said Abi, appearing at the family room door. 'I'm so glad you're home safely. Louis's in the kitchen with Gideon and Mam. Dex and Al, you're welcome to come on through too.'

As soon as Louis saw Jenny in Alan's arms, he leapt up and ran over to her.

'Thanks, Al,' he said, taking the sobbing child. 'Thanks for everything.'

'Do you want us out of the way, Lou?'

'No, please stay. I need my friends round me more than ever at the moment. That is, unless you and Dex want to get back to the pub.'

Alan shook his head. 'The pub's closed for now. If you need us, Louis, this is where we stay. So, is there anything you'd like done next?'

'Tea next,' said Sarah decisively, putting the kettle on. 'Then we wait for Mr Trevelyan.'

***

As the feeble winter sun sank behind the western fells of the Lake District, Max popped his head into the kitchen to let everyone know he'd finished his TV report and had drafted an emergency newsletter ready to release whenever Louis wanted.

'We're not deciding anything until Dad gets back,' said Louis. 'Thanks though, Max. Of course, we'll keep you informed.'

Max accepted a cup of tea gratefully, patted Louis on the arm and passed on his condolences, then went back into the darkening winter's day to help reinforce the unsponsored wall. At that moment the wall needed all the help it could get as the sponsored journalists were becoming very excited at the arrival of Lysander Trevelyan.

'Mr Trevelyan! Mr Trevelyan!' they called, desperately trying to reach through the human shield and bang on Lysander's car. 'How do you feel about your wife's death? Was it suicide? What does Lord Bassenford think? Will the funeral be sponsored?'

Ignoring the questions, just about holding it together, Lysander drove through the crowds and the human wall closed the gap behind him. Thanking the Unsponsored for their support as he left his car, not even caring to lock the expensive Mercedes, he finally walked into the place he'd been longing for all day: his family home. Knowing exactly where everyone would be gathered, he made for the big, friendly kitchen, but pulled up short at the sight of the Christmas tree which, only a few days earlier, had presided over the joyful family festivities.

'Bittersweet memories,' he mumbled, his eyes blurring with tears. 'Get a grip, Lysander.'

'Dad,' Louis said, appearing at the kitchen door. Dropping his bag, Lysander crossed the family room in three strides and wrapped protective arms around his son, and Louis finally lost the composure he'd been hanging on to so desperately since the morning. Clinging to his father as if he'd never let go, his fat tears soaking Lysander's shoulder, he began the grieving process in earnest as Lysander murmured, 'Louis, I'm so sorry,' over and over again.

***

With nightfall, the temperature outside plummeted and the sponsored journalists gave up and drifted away from the Trevelyan household, enabling the Unsponsored to get out of the cold too. Inside the house, Lysander visited his wife's body with Louis, and it was a good twenty minutes before they returned to the kitchen. Both were red-eyed, and Lysander's face was as pale as his son's.

'Thank you, Sarah,' he said, accepting a glass of wine. 'Better make the most of this. Not sure how much longer I'll be able to afford fine wine…'

He then went on to tell everyone how he'd thrown his Gold Sponsor Card at Lord Bassenford.

'Probably wasn't the best career move of my life,' he said, 'but perhaps I should have done it sooner. Then Nikki might still be…'

Lysander flopped down on a chair and sank his head into his hands.

'Don't blame yourself, Dad,' said Louis gently. 'None of this is your fault.'

Lysander looked up gratefully at his son, then blew his nose and regained his composure.

'Who told you, Lysander?' asked Jess. 'About poor Nikki, I mean. I tried to phone you but kept getting cut off.'

'Yes, sorry, Dr Donatelli…'

'Jess.'

'Sorry, Jess. His Lordshit forbade me to answer. He knew himself by then, of course. He'd had a call from that… murdering… scum…'

'Dyer?' asked Abi through clenched teeth.

'The very same. God, that man spreads so much misery! Yes, His Lordshit had a call, made him very satisfied. "Well done" is what he said.'

Staring into the middle distance, haunted by the memory, Lysander repeated, 'Well done,' in a hoarse whisper. Jenny climbed on to his lap, knowing with her child's intuition that Daddy was in need of a cuddle, and strengthened by his daughter's affection, Lysander continued.

'His Lordshit wanted me to continue with my presentation. Said he would have told me when I'd finished. He hadn't banked on his son, though. Theo was downstairs, playing his guitar as usual. Anyway, he must have had the telly on silent, and turned it up when a news flash came on about Blenthwaite. We could clearly hear Max's report in His Lordshit's office…'

Lysander shook his head in an attempt to collect his thoughts.

'As you know, I then rang Dr… Jess and got a few details from her. Theo had burst into the office by then – one day I'm going to tell that young man just how grateful I was for his support at that moment. Anyway, cue big row. I tell His Lordshit a few home truths. Theo tells His Lordshit a few home truths. By the way, Louis, Theo said… he said…'

Louis looked at his father, waiting patiently for Lysander to carry on.

'He said his heart goes out to you. To all of us. He said he… understands how it feels to… lose your mother.'

In the silence that followed Theo's message, the vibrating of Lysander's mobile phone was clearly audible.

'You have got to be kidding!' he said, looking in disgust at the caller display and cutting off the call. 'His Lordshit.'

'My God, the man's devoid of compassion…' began Gideon, stopping abruptly as the house phone rang. Louis stormed over and answered it, ready to give Lord Bassenford a piece of his mind.

'Louis, please don't hang up,' shouted Theo from London.

'Theo?' said Louis incredulously, lifting the receiver to his ear. 'What the…'

'Lou, are you OK? His Lordship's allowing me to call you under the circumstances. I tried your dad's phone first.'

'Oh, sorry, Theo. We thought that was His Lordshit…'

'Who's sitting right next to me, Louis,' warned Theo. 'Anyway, this isn't about me, it's about you. I'm so sorry, my friend. If there's anything I can do… well, in my rather limited way, that is…'

'Theodore,' Louis heard Lord Bassenford say in the background, 'I've very generously granted you this liberty. I can just as easily take it away.'

'Yes, Your Lordship,' said Theo in a deadpan voice, becoming animated once more when he spoke to Louis again. 'Listen, Louis, I wish I could be there with you, help you through this. I know the pain of losing someone you love that much. I'm with you in spirit, I assure you.'

'Theo, you've already helped no end by phoning. It means a lot to me, and my dad says thank you for supporting him earlier too…'

Everyone crowded round, hoping for a word with Theo themselves, but Louis shook his head in disgust as Lord Bassenford came on the line.

'I worry about you and my son, young Trevelyan,' he said jovially. 'You're far more loved-up than befits red-blooded young men. Now, how's that training coming on?'

'I don't believe you, Your Lordshit. My mother died this morning, and you're asking about gymnastics? The training's fine, OK? Fine! You'll have your gold medal in the summer to add to the rest of your trinkets. Now, I've had a *really* bad day, so please may I speak to Theo again?'

'I'll overlook your insolence in light of your bereavement, Trevelyan,' snapped Lord Bassenford, all pretence of joviality vanishing. 'I was mistaken to allow this call. I indulge my son's whim, and the pair of you take liberties.

Theodore does not make the decisions governing his life, and neither do you. *I* make them, and I'll thank you to remember that.'

Lord Bassenford cut off the call without another word. After looking for a few seconds at the humming telephone receiver in his hand, Louis then replaced it in its cradle and turned to his companions.

'We have got to get Theo away from that man,' he said. 'Preferably sooner rather than later.'

Chapter 17 – The Darkest Hour Is Before the Dawn

The New Year began as the old one had ended: cold and bleak. Snow had fallen upon snow in Cumbria, and Lysander and Louis huddled by the family room fire as they made plans for Nicola's funeral. To Lysander's amazement, he'd discovered he still held plenty of influence in the world of Sponsorship, despite having tendered his resignation so dramatically on the day of Nicola's death, and he was arguing that it made sense to take advantage wherever they could.

'The funeral isn't something we can do by ourselves, Louis, and it's not as if all sponsored people are bad. They're just scared, most of them. It's the Sponsors who are the enemy. Like me,' he added bitterly.

In the end, father and son came to a compromise. Sponsored would be involved, but always under the watchful eyes of the Trevelyans, Sarah or Gideon. Sponsored television companies then expressed a desire to broadcast the funeral, and Lysander was amazed when Louis readily agreed.

'I'm not letting the country forget, Dad,' Louis explained. 'Let Lord Bastardford's vile crime be in the public eye for as long as possible.'

Lord Bassenford finally managed to contact Lysander three days into the New Year, finding the unshaven and haggard Director of Leisure and Fitness getting drunk in The White Lion Inn.

'Lysander, in the pub again? You won't find the answer at the bottom of a beer glass, you know.'

Lysander's only reply was to drain the glass in front of him and replace it with a full one.

'Are you in The White Lion?' Lord Bassenford asked, peering via his computer monitor at the sign behind Lysander's head welcoming guests to the inn. 'You shouldn't be in unsponsored premises…'

'Why not?' Lysander said, perfectly coherent despite his lack of sleep and excess alcohol. 'I resigned, remember?'

'Ah, well, you were upset.' Holding up Lysander's Gold Sponsor Card, Lord Bassenford continued, 'I've held on to it for you. It'll be waiting in London on your return.'

'Who said I'm returning, St Benedict? You never listen, do you.'

'We'll discuss this after the funeral, Lysander, and preferably when you're sober. I'm making a lot of allowances for your grief, I hope you realise that. Now – the funeral. I'll attend, of course…'

'You'll do no such thing! I don't want you anywhere near Blenthwaite on that day, do you hear? The Unsponsored don't want you anywhere near here.'

'I don't care what the Unsponsored want…'

'And I don't care what you want any more. Stay away. Now, if you'll excuse me, I've got some serious drinking to do.'

Not waiting for a reply, Lysander cut the visual link with London and shut down his laptop.

***

The day of Nicola's funeral dawned bright, but very cold. Fresh snow had fallen on Blenthwaite during the night, and the glare of the winter sunlight on this snow was almost more than Louis's sensitive eyes could bear as he glanced out of the window. Outside, the crowds were phenomenal: Unsponsored had moved hell and high water to travel from all over the country and line the route, jostling for space with the sponsored camera crews and reporters. Meanwhile, Louis's London friends and Sarah's family arrived in luxury transport, courtesy of Lysander's still active Gold Sponsorship status.

The funeral procession moved off slowly, and the Unsponsored lining the route bowed their heads as the cortège passed by. Jenny walked behind the hearse in between her father and brother, holding on to their hands as she struggled to understand what was taking place, and Abi, Sarah and Gideon followed them. Louis had drawn the line at using sponsored pallbearers; instead, Chris, Cameron, Alan and Dex were waiting with Sarah's brother Rick and Lysander's brother Fabian to carry Nicola into the church. Lysander walked behind his wife's coffin with his two children, his face rigid with grief, and their friends followed.

Confident that Theo would be one of the many people around the country watching the funeral on television, Louis held himself together throughout the service. He even held himself together as his mother's coffin was carried from the church and lowered into the cold ground. It was only when the time came for him and Jenny to throw the first handfuls of dirt on to the coffin and say a final goodbye to their mother that Louis found he could no longer rein in his emotions. Arms tightly wrapped around his little sister, he looked up to the sky in despair and the whole country watched his heart breaking.

**

No Sponsored were involved in the wake following Nicola's funeral; instead, all the catering was organised by Georgie, who'd excelled herself. Louis, surprised to find he still had an appetite, ate heartily, then thanked Georgie over and over again for the delicious food.

'It's OK, Louis, really,' she said with a smile after the fifth or sixth thank-you. 'I'm glad to have helped.'

As the afternoon progressed into evening and the alcohol flowed freely courtesy of Dex and Georgie, the conversation eventually turned once again to Theo's predicament.

'There's no way we'll be able to get him out of that house,' said Louis. 'Not with that security tag on his wrist and the… scumbag… guarding him so closely.'

'Which kind of handicaps us a little,' commented Chloe, who had been so busy renewing her acquaintance with Cameron that everyone was amazed she'd been following the conversation.

'We can't get Theo out of the house,' said Brains thoughtfully, 'but His Lordshit can…'

'Yeah, Dad, Genius! "Oh hello, Your Lordshit, would you mind removing Theo's security tag so we can rescue him from your evil clutches?" "Oh no, unsponsored ones, of course I don't mind". I don't think it's going to work.'

'Put like that, Chloe love, of course not. However, what if we gave His Lordshit a reason to take Theo out of the house? Even better, a reason to bring him to Blenthwaite?'

Everyone's attention was on Brains now.

'Do you have something in mind, Brains?' asked Chris.

'Yes, as a matter of fact…'

'Thought you might,' Chloe interrupted, laughing. 'Dad usually has an idea.'

'Yeah, I have an idea, and actually, Chris, it involves you. You and Georgie are planning to get married, aren't you? Why not make the wedding sooner rather than later?'

'What on earth has our wedding got to do with…'

'I think I know,' Georgie said suddenly, her eyes shining. 'Weddings have guests, don't they? It would be only right to invite the groom's nephew, for example…'

'Yes, Uncle Chris,' yelled Abi, leaping up from Louis's side in excitement. 'Yes, yes, yes! It's about time you two set a date. Invite Theo and…'

'Hold on, all of you,' said Louis. 'You're forgetting His Lordshit doesn't let Theo out for *anything*. Don't you think he would have been here today otherwise? You can invite him all you want, but I don't think there's any way His Lordshit will let him come…'

'Well, we invite the whole family, of course,' said Georgie. 'I didn't think for one moment His Lordshit would let Theo and Marina come by themselves. It'll mean putting up with His Lordshit for a day, but it'll be worth it to get Theo…'

'What you'll get is His Lordshit, if you get anyone at all,' said Louis. 'It's a great idea in principle, but remember who we're talking about. It's going to take more than a wedding invitation to get Theo out of there.'

'What if someone were to persuade His Lordshit that it'd be a good idea to accept?' asked Chloe.

'Who, Chlo?' asked Cameron, briefly breaking off from nuzzling her neck. 'Lysander?'

'I don't think that'll work,' said Lysander. 'I'm still waiting for His Lordshit to accept my resignation, and I'm in no hurry to return to London in the meantime.'

'It's OK, Lysander, I wasn't thinking of you,' replied Chloe gently, respectful of his acute grief. 'I was thinking we could use Theo's girlfriend…'

'What girlfriend?' asked Matilda sharply.

'Ah sorry, Matty, didn't you know?'

'You mean Catherine Lorimer?' said Lysander. 'How did you find out about her, Chloe?'

'She found us, actually,' replied Chloe, getting up from Cameron's knee, much to his dismay, 'two or three days after Christmas via an unsponsored family she knows. Her father's head of Euro Logistics UK…'

'Sponsored?'

'No, that's the beauty of it,' said Lysander. 'It's a European firm, so the UK branch doesn't have to accept endorsement. Also His Lordshit's anxious to keep Philip Lorimer onside, especially with the Olympics coming up, so if anyone has influence over him...'

'You're leaping ahead, Lysander, and I think you've lost a few people,' said Chloe, laying a hand on his arm. 'Catherine's free from sponsorship, as is her father, so she can associate with the Unsponsored any time she wants. My God, she's shy. It must have taken a lot for her to pluck up the courage to come and talk to us.

'Anyway, she told us that Theo had explained his whole horrible life to her the previous day. Her father, Philip, had apparently guessed, correctly, that His Lordshit put Theo up to starting a relationship with her so he could tempt Philip into regular meetings...'

'So Theo doesn't really fancy her, then?' asked Matilda hopefully.

'Sorry, Matty, but I think he does,' said Lysander, and Louis nodded in agreement.

'If Theo's seeing this Catherine, he must like her. There's no way he'd do anything to help His Lordshit out.'

'You've always got me, Matty,' said Max, patting Matilda's bottom and earning himself a slapped face.

'We're kind of moving away from Chloe's point here, guys,' said Brains.

'Thanks, Dad,' said Chloe, continuing once everyone had settled down. 'Catherine went to talk to Theo, gave him a chance to put his side of the story across. Theo was completely honest with her. He even showed her the scars on his back.'

Chloe drew in a breath through bared teeth.

'He also told her all about Dory's Avengers, and showed her a letter you'd sent just before Christmas – is that right, Louis?'

'She read the letter?' asked Matilda, perking up again.

'Yes,' said Chloe, laughing. 'She did mention your name, Matty. I gather you outlined rather explicitly what you'd like to do with him…'

'Oh yeah, baby!' said Matilda, laughing as she danced round the pole she'd talked Dex into having fitted in the pub.

'I think you're too late, Matty, sorry. Anyway, my point is this: Catherine will do anything to help Theo. She's crazy about him, and I think we could use that.'

'How?'

'Simple. Chris and Georgie – you choose a date for the wedding. If you don't mind, that is.'

'We'd be delighted.'

'Two – we get the invitations sent out, including one to His Lordshit. Three – I liaise with Catherine and her father, find a way to persuade His Lordshit that it's a good idea for his family to attend the wedding…'

'We could invite the Lorimers,' said Georgie.

'We've never met them…'

'*We* know that, Chris, but *His Lordshit* doesn't. We can say, what's his name – Philip? Philip always stops off here when he visits that haulage place in Carlisle. We could say he had a happy holiday here once – anything.'

'Brilliant, Georgie!' said Chloe. 'The Lorimers get their invitation, and it's the most natural thing in the world for them to bring the subject up with His Lordshit. Catherine can get all excited about going, and as she's Theo's girlfriend of course she'll want him to go too. His Lordshit wants to stay in Philip's good books… you know, I really think this could work. What do you think, Louis?'

Louis was silent for a little while as he thought over the conversation, then suddenly he smiled for the first time since his awful discovery before New Year.

'I really think this could work too. Chloe, you're a genius!'

Part Three – Wedding Bells

Chapter 18 – The Invitation

As winter slowly gave way to spring, plans for Chris and Georgie's wedding were well underway. There was a little difficulty in getting a licence to marry, Georgie being one of the defiant Unsponsored, but Lysander used his continuing influence to resolve the situation (even Louis having to admit that sometimes a Gold Sponsor Card came in handy), and from then on preparations ran smoothly. Once they'd set the date for the second weekend in June, the happy couple selected the main players for the big day: their father having died a few years earlier, Georgie decided she'd like Dex to give her away; Alan appointed himself chief of décor; and Abi, Matilda and Jenny were all delighted to be lined up as bridesmaids.

However, no one was more delighted than Gideon when Chris phoned him one evening and asked him to fulfil the best man's duties.

'I'm so honoured!' he repeated over and over again to Louis the next morning, his grinning protégé taking full advantage of his unusually good mood to spend the first half hour of the training session doing absolutely nothing.

Chris and Georgie sent the invitations out at the beginning of March. Chloe and Brains had explained the wedding plan to a highly receptive Philip a few days after Nicola's funeral, and as soon as he learned that the invitations were imminent, he contrived to be at the St Benedict residence on a daily basis, using discussions about the forthcoming Olympics as a handy excuse. Catherine always came along too – so convincing was her 'ditsy girl hopelessly in love' act that Lord Bassenford never suspected for a moment she spent much of her time alone with Theo updating him on plans for his escape. Truth be told, a fair bit of their time together was spent doing exactly what His Lordship *did* suspect they were doing, too.

Calling round shortly after breakfast on the day their own invitation arrived, Philip and his daughter were gratified to see the post still unopened in Lord Bassenford's hand.

'Coffee, Philip?' said His Lordship, waving the letters languidly as he ushered his guests into the drawing room.

'Coffee would be lovely, thank you, Lord Bassenford,' said Philip, mouthing 'Perfect' at his daughter as His Lordship began to open his post. Catherine grinned back conspiratorially, then sat with Theo and Marina on the beanbags, all desperately trying to look unconcerned as they waited for Lord Bassenford to get to the crucial envelope.

'Well, well!' His Lordship exclaimed eventually. 'Well I never! Christopher Farrell's getting married.'

'Oh,' said Philip, apparently surprised. 'Do you know Chris and Georgie, Your Lordship?'

'Christopher is, er… my wife's brother.'

'Goodness me! Of course, I should have realised. I've known Chris and Georgie for a while, stop at that lovely inn whenever I've got business in Carlisle. Our invitation arrived this morning too – tell you what, why don't we all travel together?'

'It's so exciting, Your Lordship, I love weddings,' added Catherine, eyes shining. 'I told you Theo would be coming too, didn't I, Daddy…'

'Not so fast, young lady,' said Lord Bassenford, amiably enough. 'Theodore's got his little agoraphobia problem. It's a big step for him.'

'Oh, Theo, please…'

Theo kissed Catherine's nose then looked at his father.

'I'm willing to try, Your Lordship…'

'Theodore,' Lord Bassenford cut in, his voice sharpening a little, 'I'm really not sure it would be a good idea. Perhaps I should go, maybe with Rosanna…'

'What about me, Father?' asked Marina. 'I'd like to go too.'

'Surely Theodore would cope, Your Lordship,' said Philip. 'He'll have his family around him, and Catherine. My daughter's such a calming influence…'

'Wait, wait, the lot of you! I haven't said *anyone*'s going yet.'

'Going where?' asked Rosanna, choosing that moment to walk into the room. When Lord Bassenford showed her the invitation, she immediately made her feelings clear on the subject.

'I'm not going to that bloody backwater to attend some poxy wedding.'

Cursing his older sister inwardly, Theo said, 'It's not always about what *you* want, Rosanna. Your Lordship, I'd like to go – for Cathie's sake. I'm sure with her support…'

'Will you all stop clamouring and let me think!' shouted Lord Bassenford. 'Rosanna – if I say you're going, then you go. Theodore – if I think you'd be better off staying here, then you stay.'

'Your Lordship,' said Philip, his calm voice belying his churning stomach, 'it's merely a suggestion, but wouldn't this be a fine opportunity to get some positive publicity for the Scheme?'

'How do you mean?' asked Lord Bassenford, torn between curiosity and telling Philip to mind his own business.

'With the greatest respect, Lord Bassenford, I'm in a position to see things from the Unsponsored point of view. There are those who still say Theodore is mad. Do you want people talking about your son like that?'

'Why should I care?'

'Because rumours are dangerous. They get out of hand. Before you know it you've got the Sponsored thinking the same, or worse. If you turn up at this wedding, the TV cameras are sure to follow. You'll be seen as having made a huge effort to extend the hand of friendship to the Blenthwaite Unsponsored, despite their continued disrespect for the Scheme, and the wave of public sympathy will be entirely in your favour. I have heard some say that Theodore isn't permitted to leave this house – the country's full of weak-minded fools who'll believe any rubbish. Then, *voilà!* Theodore appears at his uncle's wedding. Another false but potentially damning rumour quashed. To my mind, you've got so much to gain and nothing to lose by attending this wedding. By *your whole family* attending this wedding.'

As Philip fell silent, not a word was spoken in the room. Marina and Theo continued to watch the television as though it really didn't matter to them one way or another, while Catherine turned pleading blue eyes in Lord Bassenford's direction. Rosanna helped herself to coffee, being the only one in the room who genuinely couldn't care less about Chris Farrell's wedding.

Finally, Lord Bassenford spoke. 'I could have people find the roots of these rumours, deal harshly with the culprits…'

'Once again I speak with the utmost respect, Lord Bassenford. I have nothing but respect for you and the Scheme,' Philip lied. 'But if you fight this with force, you will only breed resentment. Cut down one adversary, two more will appear. In your position, I would take the Unsponsored by surprise. Do precisely what they don't expect. What weight will their rumours hold when they're so clearly seen to be untrue? The credibility will be yours, and yours alone.'

'You're a powerful speaker, Philip,' said His Lordship. 'If ever you fancy a change of career, you'd be welcome to join the Scheme.'

Silence fell once more as Lord Bassenford stared broodingly into the middle distance. Philip tried unsuccessfully to gauge his mood, while Theo, Catherine and Marina concentrated with all their might on an advert for washing-up liquid. In the end, it was Rosanna who broke the silence.

'Well, Father,' she said, her voice petulant, 'do we have to go to this stupid wedding or not?'

Ironically, it was Rosanna interrupting his thoughts that made Lord Bassenford's mind up for him. Suddenly finding himself immensely irritated with his daughter's constant whingeing, he took out his mobile phone and dialled the number on the invitation.

***

In Blenthwaite, no one was doing any work. Only too aware that Lord Bassenford's wedding invitation was likely to reach him that day, Dory's Avengers had congregated in the bar of The White Lion, Gideon contenting himself with ordering Louis to stay off the booze. Much to Gideon's disgust, instead of drinking, Louis was passing the time helping Matilda improve her pole dancing skills by demonstrating how to grip the pole with his legs and hang upside down.

'For God's sake, Louis,' Gideon grumbled, 'you're supposed to be an Olympic gymnast, not a bloody lap dancer.'

Alan was equally unimpressed, but for different reasons.

'If your skirt were any shorter, Matilda, it would qualify as a belt. Hang upside down on that pole and Louis will be able to see what you had for breakfast.'

Matilda grinned unrepentantly at her father and was covering what she could of her modesty with her extremely short skirt when Chris's mobile phone rang.

'Please don't let this be someone with a sick parrot,' he muttered, answering the call. 'Hello?'

The bar fell silent as everyone held their breath, then Chris started to smile and nod.

'Good morning, Lord Bassenford… Yes… How many?… Wonderful. You'll all be more than welcome… See you in June, then.'

Ending the call, Chris grinned inanely at his phone for a few moments then looked round at the eager faces peering in his direction.

'It worked,' he said.

***

Taking into consideration he was meant to be so friendly with Chris and Georgie that they would invite him to their wedding, Philip Lorimer arrived in Blenthwaite a few days later with his wife and daughter to make their acquaintance.

'Welcome, *old friend*,' said Georgie, laughing and hugging the Lorimers once Philip had introduced himself and his family. 'I'll have some rooms made up for you in no time. You are staying, aren't you?'

'Yes please, that would be lovely,' replied Philip. 'It'd be rather too long a drive back to London tonight.'

Word soon spread round the village that the Lorimers were staying at The White Lion and the Unsponsored turned up in their droves, all wanting to hear about the day Lord Bassenford's invitation had arrived.

'It was a nightmare trying to play it cool,' said Philip, going on to entertain the assembled company with a highly amusing account of His

Lordship's reaction. 'I thought we'd blown it when Rosanna turned up and started whingeing.'

'It's something she's very good at,' added Simone. 'But as Philip believes it was actually her moaning that swung things in our favour, I guess we should be thankful for it.'

'Ah, Lady Bitch, the hero of the Unsponsored,' said Gideon, laughing. 'Sadly she's not here to accept our gratitude, so please allow me to buy you and your family drinks instead, Mr Lorimer.'

'There's really no need…'

'There's every need, Mr Lorimer. Joking aside, we owe you so much for ensuring Theo can come to Blenthwaite.'

'In that case, thank you. A pint of bitter and two dry white wines would be just the ticket. Oh, and please call me Philip. "Mr Lorimer" is way too formal, especially as we're all meant to have known each other for years.'

'Philip it is, then. I'm…'

'Gideon Wallis, I know.' Grinning at Gideon's astonished expression, Philip added, 'I've always been an avid fan of the Olympics. Seem to remember a certain British gymnast wowing the judges and collecting gold medals back in the eighties.'

Gideon coloured up slightly, unsure whether to feel flattered or sad that Philip remembered his glory days. 'That seems a long time ago,' he said, smiling wistfully. 'I had a bit more hair back then. Oh, and functioning legs. Legs always help…'

Before Gideon could descend into self-pity, Sarah perched on the side of his wheelchair and put an arm round his shoulders.

'And this summer you'll be involved in the Olympics again,' she said.

'Of course,' replied Gideon, perking up immediately. 'Philip, you must meet the future of British gymnastics. Louis, come over here a minute.'

Shaking hands with Philip and Simone, who were delighted to meet him and bombarded him with questions about his training, Louis then sat down next to Catherine and smiled warmly at her.

'Hi, Catherine, I'm Louis – Theo and I have been friends for ever.'

'He said,' whispered Catherine, blushing profusely.

'When did you and Theo meet?'

'Christmas.'

'Cool. Do you see him often?'

'Mmm.'

'Great. Is he excited about the wedding?'

'Mmm.'

'I bet he is. We still can't quite believe His Lordshit said yes.'

'Oh.'

'You and your dad are heroes.'

'Oh.'

After five minutes or so of monosyllabic answers, Louis finally accepted defeat and drifted off to find Abi, saying something that sounded suspiciously like 'Good luck' as he departed.

Oh no, don't tell me another one's coming for a chat, thought Catherine, staring at the floor and sighing as a pair of feet clad in ballet pumps appeared in her line of vision.

'Hello, Catherine, I'm Matilda,' said the owner of the feet.

No, no, not you. Anyone but you.

'Would you mind passing me those glasses?'

Catherine's reluctant eyes travelled upwards, taking in long, toned legs, the most exquisite hourglass figure and finally a flawlessly beautiful face framed by masses of dark curls. The vision smiled encouragingly and waggled a finger towards the empty glasses on the next table, and Catherine passed them over without a word, trying desperately not to cry.

Her rival for Theo's affections wasn't just gorgeous, she was breathtakingly so.

'Cheers,' said Matilda, stacking up the glasses and bounding over to the bar, graceful and athletic.

On the other side of the room, Gideon had watched the interaction between the two young women with interest, and as Matilda entered into fast paced banter with Dex while Catherine slipped quietly away to the sanctuary of her room, he turned to Sarah with raised eyebrows.

'I know,' Sarah said, reading his mind. 'She's not what I was expecting either.'

Later on, Gideon caught a quiet moment with Louis, curious to know his opinion on Theo's girlfriend.

'She's very, er, sweet…'

'But?' prompted Gideon.

'Well, she loves her parents, looks good, ticks lots of the right boxes…'

'*But*, Louis? Go on, this is strictly between us.'

'But, unfortunately, I don't think she's right for Theo.'

'And who is right for Theo?'

Louis looked over at Matilda, who was now belting out Beyoncé's *Single Ladies*, booty shake and all.

'I think we both know the answer to that, don't we, Gideon.'

Chapter 19 – Goodbye, Kensington

Lord Bassenford had decided his family and Rosanna's boyfriend Adam would make the long journey north the day before Chris and Georgia's wedding, and Theo awoke early that morning in a fever of excitement. Padding silently downstairs to make himself a coffee, he looked at the outside world through the kitchen window as the rising sun gradually lit up the far end of his father's garden.

'Sunshine,' he murmured, a smile of wonder on his face, 'it's been a long time since I last felt your warmth…'

'Morning, Lord Theo,' said the housemaid Annie, as always the first of the staff up and about. 'Talking to yourself again?'

'Well I have to live up to my barking mad reputation,' replied Theo, laughing. 'Morning, Annie. Coffee?'

'Love one, Lord T, then I'll give you a hand with your packing, if you like.'

Armed with a pot of coffee and two mugs, Theo and Annie made their way up to the fourth floor. Theo had a huge affection for the irreverent and humorous housemaid, always thoroughly enjoying time spent in her company, and if he was going to be completely honest with himself, he was rather enjoying the sight of her pert backside going up the stairs before him, too.

'Will you feel safe alone in here with me?' he asked, opening his bedroom door. 'I'm sure you've heard tales about feckless lords taking advantage of serving wenches in days of yore.'

'Now there's an offer,' replied Annie, looking appreciatively at Theo's toned torso clad in a body-hugging vest. 'To be honest, Lord T, I wouldn't kick you out of bed for farting.'

'I'll have you know, I'm far too posh to fart,' said Theo, laughing as he opened his wardrobe and started chucking clothes on to his bed. Continuing to flirt, he and Annie fell into a vague system of sorting the clothes, packing them in Theo's holdall, then unpacking the whole lot again when they realised they weren't going to fit in everything he wanted to take.

'Woolly jumpers?' said Annie, looking pointedly at the sun streaming in through the window. 'Why? It's bloomin' twenty-five degrees out there already.'

Sobering a little as Theo continued to line his holdall with winter clothes, Annie fixed him with a penetrating gaze and stated, 'You ain't coming back, are you.'

Halting his packing, Theo looked up and shook his head slightly.

'Please don't…'

'Of course I won't drop you in it, what do you take me for?' Smiling sadly, Annie added, 'I was here, you know, that night he locked you away.'

Theo shifted from foot to foot uncomfortably, rubbing the back of his head with his hand.

'I had to clean your blood off his office floor. I could hear you screaming for help, and there was nothing I could do...'

Taking Annie's face in his hands, Theo lightly kissed her forehead. 'There was nothing anyone could have done,' he murmured against her skin, then he leant back and grinned at her. 'Now you'd better scarper, wench, or I might just live up to my feckless ancestors' reputation.'

'Shame,' she replied as sounds of movement came from the third-floor bedrooms. 'I wouldn't have minded a little roll between the sheets to remember you by.'

'I am spoken for, you know,' protested Theo, a tad unconvincingly.

'Unfortunately Catherine ain't here, so you're going to have to deal with that impressive bulge in your shorts yourself. His Nibs will have kittens if his breakfast's not laid out 'cos I'm too busy laying his son.'

Theo roared with laughter. 'Annie! Don't let Mr Mooreland catch you talking about His

Lordshit in that disrespectful tone. His Nibs, indeed!'

'I'd better not call him "His Lordshit" either,' replied Annie, grinning at Theo as she jogged from his bedroom.

It was mid-morning before the St Benedict family was ready to leave Kensington, by which time an exasperated Lord Bassenford had decided he'd better supervise his son's extensive packing or they'd never get away.

'What the bloody hell do you need winter clothes for?' he roared, grabbing a couple of fleeces out of Theo's holdall and chucking them back into the wardrobe. Remembering how easily Annie had put two and two together earlier, Theo reluctantly decided he'd have to leave the majority of his clothes behind and finally closed his bag on those he considered to be the essentials. After all, what did a few clothes matter when his freedom, so nearly within his grasp, was at stake?

'At last!' grumbled Lord Bassenford, picking up the holdall and sliding it across the floor in the general direction of Annie, who had just reappeared at Theo's bedroom door to ask if he needed anything carrying downstairs. 'Take this, girl. And you, Theodore,' His Lordship added, propelling his son towards the stairs, 'hurry up. We're leaving in five minutes, and if you're not in that limousine, you'll be left behind.'

And so it came to pass that Theo's long incarceration in his father's house ended with a shove in the back from the very man who'd imprisoned him a decade earlier. Stumbling over the threshold, Theo trotted down the steps to the clicks and flashes of a multitude of press cameras, turning his face up to the sky and feeling the warmth of the sun for a blissful second before an impatient Lord Bassenford hauled him unceremoniously into the waiting limousine.

***

As His Lordship and family were travelling north, several police motorcyclists ensuring they had an unencumbered journey all the way from Kensington to Cumbria, preparations for the wedding were in full swing at The White Lion. A marquee had been erected in the meadow, a smaller but more luxurious one than the huge effort that had graced the Sponsors' Fair the previous summer, and inside was a mass of balloons and ribbons. Tables were set out all around, a top table for the bridal party taking pride of place under the most elaborate of the decorations, and Alan was buzzing around flapping about minutiae.

'I'm sure this table's not level. Look, that one's fractionally turned at an angle, this one isn't.'

'They all look fine to me,' said Dex, failing to see any difference between the two tables.

'No, Dexter, look! It doesn't look straight to me.'

'Nothing looks straight to you,' replied Dex, laughing.

'*Don't lean on that!*' shrieked Alan, pushing Dex away from the top table and smoothing an imaginary crease in the tablecloth. 'If you're not going to help, Dex, then shoo! Scoot! Oh hello, Matty darling, is that the centrepiece?'

Taking the display from his daughter, Alan arranged it this way then that way in front of the bride and groom's seats.

'This could take a while,' Matilda whispered to Dex, nodding towards her father. Alan was standing, hands on hips, regarding the top table with a frown. 'And I bet he's been giving you a hard time, hasn't he, Dexy babes – he's just *sooo* stressed!'

'I can deal with your dad's mood swings, don't you worry,' replied Dex, grinning at Matilda.

'And I can hear you two whispering about me,' called Alan, still rearranging the centrepiece.

'All nice things, Daddy dear. Don't forget the wedding rehearsal's at five. Oh, and Dory's arrived.' Not waiting for a reply, Matilda sprinted back into the pub, and Alan and Dex rushed out to the main street, the wedding decorations forgotten for a moment. They were too late to see Theo himself, Lord Bassenford already having ushered his family into the Blenthwaite Hotel, but Alan was rewarded with a glimpse of Theo's guitar being unloaded from the limousine.

'My God, Dex,' he said, eyes shining. 'He's got a Les Paul…'

At five o'clock sharp, the wedding party filed into the church for the rehearsal, not one of them appropriately dressed. The bridesmaids' clothing in particular was more suited to playing in the sun than a solemn ceremony rehearsal: Abi had her very short shorts on, Matilda was sporting her usual micro miniskirt, and Jenny was in bikini and flip flops. The bride walked up the aisle wearing cut-off denim shorts and an AC/DC T-shirt, hanging on to the arm of her brother who still had foliage in his hair following an earlier pruning frenzy to make The Lion's garden wedding day perfect. The happy couple and their attendants had planned the rehearsal with every intention of taking it seriously, but as the Vicar of Blenthwaite attempted to talk them through their roles for the following day, their playful sides got the better of them and they started finding the whole thing hilariously funny. Georgie's vows came out in a wobbly squeak as she and her fiancé tried desperately not to burst out laughing, and when Gideon whipped a joke shop ring from his shirt pocket and squirted water into Chris's face while practising one of his more important best man's duties, the rehearsal completely descended into farce.

'OK, OK,' said the Vicar, holding up her hands and admitting defeat. 'Let's just go through the walk down the aisle one more time.'

As soon as Georgie and Chris emerged into the sunshine outside the church, 'la-la'ing the tune of the *Wedding March* and followed by their attendants, Alan tried to head for the marquee yet again.

'Enough tinkering, Al,' said Georgie, grabbing his arm. 'I know you – you'll be changing things round all night if someone doesn't stop you.'

'But, Georgie…'

'But nothing! I'm the bride, and what I say goes. You are not to enter that tent again until the flowers arrive in the morning. OK?'

'OK,' said Alan reluctantly.

'Good man. Right, who's up for a game of rounders? Oh look, Philip's here!'

Running over to greet Philip as he emerged from the inn, Georgie asked how his journey had been.

'Busy,' replied Philip. 'Unfortunately we weren't accommodated by His Lordshit's police escort and we got stuck in traffic God knows how many times. So nice to arrive and freshen up – Simone and Cathie will be down as soon as they've finished discussing what makeup they're going to wear for the wedding.'

'Glad to hear they've got their priorities right,' said Georgie with a grin. 'Sorry we couldn't greet you personally when you arrived – wedding rehearsal and all that jazz.'

'Not a problem at all, Georgie,' replied Philip, returning her grin. 'Being as I don't have to worry about important issues like makeup, I thought I may as well enjoy this glorious sunshine. And is this a rounders match I see starting up? I love a game of rounders…'

***

Emerging from the shower in his sponsored hotel room, Theo heard the cheers and laughter as the rounders match got underway on The White Lion's meadow. Much as he wanted to go and join in the fun, he knew it was highly unlikely his father would let him simply walk out the door. Peering through his open window, he considered the possibility of shimmying down a handily placed drainpipe, but that idea was scuppered straight away when he discovered Stephen Dyer on guard duty outside, leering up at him. His stomach turning in disgust, Theo retreated into the privacy of his room, where he stood rubbing the back of his head for a few minutes in a most uncharacteristic fit of indecisiveness.

All of a sudden he was inspired by a plausible excuse, and with a grin made his way downstairs to test the water.

'Theodore!' boomed Lord Bassenford as his son appeared in the hotel bar's doorway. 'Won't you join us for drinks?'

Relieved to find his father in a heartily good mood, Theo crossed his fingers behind his back and replied, 'I was hoping to go and see if Cathie and her parents had arrived at The White Lion yet, Your Lordship.'

'Oh,' said Lord Bassenford, his expression unreadable. 'Now?'

'Yes, Your Lordship.'

'I wouldn't mind a little walk round the village too,' said Adam unexpectedly. 'How about you, Rose?'

'No, I bloody well don't want a little walk. I want a little drink, and then I want another one. It's the only way I'm going to survive this bloody weekend.'

'I'd like to go too, Father,' said Marina. 'Please…'

'That inn's unsponsored. I can't have you…'

'We'll have to go in there for the wedding reception tomorrow, Your Lordship,' interrupted Theo. 'And I thought we were supposed to be demonstrating to the Unsponsored that their rumours are a load of tosh.'

'Oh, very well,' said Lord Bassenford, and Theo only just managed to stop himself from punching the air. 'But you're not going without security. I will stay here and keep Rosanna company. Fellows, Lomax, escort Lord Theodore and Lady Marina to the unsponsored inn.'

'I could escort them.'

Theo shuddered as Dyer appeared very close behind him.

'No, Stephen, I think you'd be better off here. No point upsetting the Farrells unnecessarily, you know how sensitive they are.'

Content with the idea that his mere presence could upset the Farrell family, Dyer shrank back into the shadows, sniggering.

'Now then, off you go. Don't be back too late…'

Not giving Lord Bassenford any opportunity to change his mind, the supposedly agoraphobic Theo was out of the door like a shot, Adam and Marina right behind him. Theo didn't care about Lomax and Fellows stomping alongside them – very shortly he'd be reunited with Louis and meet all the people who'd been supporting him while he languished in his luxury prison, and he couldn't be happier.

'Hold on,' he said, smiling gleefully at his companions when they arrived at The Lion. 'I'd like to savour every moment of today, but I didn't have much of a chance when we left *chez* St Benedict as His Lordship virtually threw me down the steps.'

Nodding their acquiescence, Marina and Adam stood with Theo on the periphery of the inn's meadow and watched the rounders match for a while. Theo was pretty sure the bowler was his cousin Cameron, but he didn't think he recognised the person in bat – a stunningly beautiful young woman wearing a huge smile and a tiny skirt.

'Wow!' he said, his mouth dropping open. 'Who's the goddess?'

'Good job Catherine's not with us, Theo,' said Adam with a grin, rather admiring the view himself.

'Good job Rosanna isn't too,' replied Theo, winking at Adam, 'being as you're doing a passable impression of King *Leer* yourself.'

Laughing, both young men turned their attention back to the goddess, their eyes following her every move until an exasperated Marina prodded her brother in the stomach.

'Have you savoured the moment enough yet, Theo?' she asked. 'Let's go over and say hello.'

Baseball cap pulled down low on his head and dark glasses covering his eyes, Theo was determined to stay incognito for as long as possible. No one was paying much attention as he, Adam and Marina approached – the rounders players were convinced Lord Bassenford wouldn't allow Theo a public appearance before the wedding, so all their attention was focused on deciding who should bat next.

'May I?' Without waiting for an answer, Theo loped over to the bat and nodded at Cameron to bowl the ball his way.

'Er, OK,' said Cameron, looking a bit confused. 'You're welcome to play, but... who are you?'

'Good grief,' said Lysander, laughing at the baffled faces around him, 'don't you know?' Crossing over, he removed the mystery batsman's baseball cap and threw it, Frisbee style, at Cameron. 'Honestly, Cam, *now* do you recognise him?'

Grinning, Theo took off his dark glasses and saluted Cameron, who dropped the ball he'd been about to bowl and collided with Abi as they raced towards their cousin. Before either of them could reach Theo, though, a jubilant Louis sprinted over and engulfed him in a bear hug.

'Unreal! Un-bloody-real, Theo, I can't believe His Lordshit's let you out today.'

'Quite frankly, Lou, neither can I.' Theo threw out his arms and bent over backwards, soaking up as much sunshine as humanly possible. 'Have you any idea how good those rays feel?'

'Nope, afraid I'm going to have to pass on that one.'

'Ah, Louis Trevelyan, the fairest of them all.' Theo roared with laughter and pulled Louis's sunhat over his face. 'Don't worry, Lou, I'll happily take your share of ultraviolet. It's been a long time.'

Turning to his family and friends, who were surging around him as the rounders match descended into pandemonium, Theo sang, 'Been a long lonely, lonely, lonely, lonely, lonely time,' in a fair imitation of Led Zeppelin's *Rock and Roll* as he hugged and high-fived right, left and centre. Eventually, happy that he'd greeted everyone, he put an arm around his sister and led her over to where Louis was still standing grinning at him.

'Mari, you remember Bunny-hop Louis, don't you?'

'Of course,' said Marina, smiling at Louis. 'Been sneaking round anyone's house lately?'

'Not recently,' replied Louis, chuckling. 'I'm more of a burrow man by nature.'

Marina laughed, relieved to know that she hadn't irretrievably offended Louis the previous year, then turned her attention back to her brother.

'For your information, Theo,' she said, 'Ads is chatting up your goddess.'

'The dirty devil,' Theo murmured, looking over to where Adam was flirting shamelessly with the beautiful young woman in the tiny miniskirt. 'Who *is* she, Lou?'

'Your number one fan – Matilda Santiago.'

'Seriously? That is Matilda Santiago?'

'Mm-hmm.'

'The one who so wants to get it on with me?'

'Mm-hmm.'

'Oh, my stirring loins!'

'Your *what*?'

'My stirring loins,' repeated Theo, grinning at Louis. 'I've just discovered the hottest woman I have ever seen is also the woman who wants to get it on with me, so what do you expect my loins to be doing?'

'To be honest, Theo, I'd rather not think about it.'

Laughing, Theo punched Louis lightly on the shoulder. 'Matilda Santiago, eh?' he said, looking over at the goddess again. 'Best I go and say hello.'

'Theo, have you even said hello to Cathie yet?' asked Marina.

'I've not seen her yet,' replied Theo vaguely, already heading in Matilda's direction. Offering his hand to her, he said, 'Hello, I'm Theodore Farrell. Actually, I suppose I should say St

Benedict. No, not St Benedict, I *do* mean Farrell…'

Matilda threw back her head and laughed.

'I can't resist a man who doesn't know his own name,' she said, taking Theo's hand, her touch sending shock waves through his body. 'I'm…'

'Matilda Santiago.' Theo kissed her hand and caused her to go a little breathless. 'We meet at last.'

'Er, Theo,' said Adam, 'I was talking to Matilda, actually.'

'You've got a girlfriend,' Theo replied, not taking his eyes from Matilda's.

'So have you. And she's looking this way right now…'

Ignoring Adam, Theo said, 'So, Matilda, am I as hot as you'd hoped?'

'Hotter, I'd say, Theodore Farrell or St Benedict,' replied Matilda with a wink. 'Your photos don't do you justice – I didn't realise you'd be so tall.'

'You like your men tall, do you?'

'Oh yeah, baby. And fit.'

'And am I…?'

'Fit. Yeah. Oh yeah.' Matilda's words were coming out more and more huskily as she stared into Theo's eyes, and Adam realised he wasn't likely to get any more sense out of either of them. Wandering off towards the pub to treat himself to a cold cider, a wry smile on his face, he encountered Louis wheeling Gideon in the opposite direction.

'Mind you chaps don't get burnt up over there,' he warned. 'There's some impressive chemistry going on between those two.'

Grinning, Louis and Gideon continued on their way and saw for themselves what Adam meant. Theo and Matilda seemed oblivious to the world around them, and despite the fact that she was explaining to him that they wouldn't 'so be getting it on' as it wasn't her style to make a move on another woman's boyfriend, the air was almost crackling with the sexual tension between them.

'I hate to interrupt,' Louis said, waving a hand in Matilda's face, 'but your dad asked if you'd go and help behind the bar.'

'Oh. OK. Cheers, Lou. Catch you later, Theo.' Reluctantly letting go of Theo's hand, Matilda dropped a noisy kiss on Gideon's bald head and said, 'Lookin' good, Giddy babes,' before sprinting off towards The Lion.

'Giddy babes?' said Louis delightedly.

'Don't even think about it!'

'How come Matty can get away with Giddy babes and I can't?'

'Work it out for yourself, moron. You're a bloke, and she's…'

'The most drop-dead gorgeous woman ever to walk this earth,' said Theo, still gazing wistfully in the direction Matilda had disappeared.

'Oh heck,' said Louis to Gideon, 'he's likely to give us the low down on his stirring loins any minute…'

'They're doing more than stirring, Lou.'

'Theo!' said Gideon, wrinkling his nose. 'Way too much information.'

'Hold that image, Mr Wallis.' Theo finally turned his attention away from the pub's door and grinned at Gideon. 'I've been particularly looking forward to meeting you. I believe you shout at Louis a lot. Anyone who shouts at Louis is a friend of mine…'

'Dickhead,' said Louis.

'Pleased to meet you too,' replied Gideon, shaking Theo's hand. 'But please call me Gideon. "Mr Wallis" makes me feel about ninety years old…'

'I thought you were ninety years old,' murmured Louis.

'Looks like Louis fancies spending the next month training on pommel,' said Gideon conversationally to Theo, grinning sidelong at his protégé. 'And we all know how much he *loves* pommel.'

'Oh, that old chestnut,' grumbled Louis.

'Does he really?' asked Theo, genuinely interested.

'No!' replied his companions in unison, Louis adding, 'It's just Gideon's feeble attempt at humour. Not bad for a grumpy git, I suppose.'

'Er, talking of grumpy,' Gideon said.

Theo and Louis exchanged baffled glances.

'Talking of grumpy what?' Theo asked.

'Seriously pissed-off girlfriend, approaching from the west…'

As Theo turned in the direction of Gideon's gaze, Catherine stormed over to join them, her face like thunder. Slipping an arm round her waist, Theo noticed to his dismay that he didn't feel anything like the intense jolt of desire he had with Matilda.

'Good to see you, Cathie,' he said. 'This is Gideon Wallis and…'

'I know. I've met them before. So, what did – what's her name? Martha? Matilda? What did Matilda want?'

'Oh, just introducing herself. She's the lead singer of a band formed in my…'

'Yes, it's all about you, isn't it, Theo? It's *always* all about you.' Jealousy overcoming shyness, Catherine screamed at her boyfriend while Louis and Gideon fidgeted awkwardly. 'You've got your own way, so now it's "Goodbye, Cathie, I'm off to screw some slut in a stupidly short skirt". Now you're back with your fucking albino friend, I've served my useful purpose...'

Totally losing control, Catherine fled sobbing into The White Lion.

'Apologies for that, gentlemen,' Theo said, turning to Louis and Gideon. 'I didn't know she had that much passion in her. Sorry about the dig she made at you, Louis.'

'Not to worry, Theo, I've been called far worse. Besides, I *am* albino. It's no different to describing you as... let's see... a cad and a bounder.'

'Oh, I say,' replied Theo in his best Terry-Thomas voice, grinning unrepentantly.

'Poor Catherine,' said Gideon. 'Perhaps you should have a *little* more sympathy, Theo.' Turning his wheelchair around, he added, 'Right, I've got a date with Sarah and a cold beer, so I'll catch you two later.'

Sitting cross-legged in the shade as Gideon disappeared into the pub, Louis said, 'So, what are you going to do now, Theo?'

'About what?' asked Theo, sprawling ecstatically in a patch of sunlight.

'About the Catherine or Matilda situation, of course.'

Theo sighed and looked away from Louis, over towards 'Thwaite's Wood.

'I'm not going back to London, you know, Lou,' he said eventually. 'Now I've tasted freedom, it'd be the death of me, so my contact with Cathie's going to be limited…'

Theo's face suddenly lost its faraway expression and he rolled his eyes in exasperation.

'Oh damn, I'd forgotten about them.'

One of Lord Bassenford's security guards was approaching.

'Lord Theodore, don't wander off again. His Lordship wouldn't want the underclass poisoning your mind.'

'As you wish, Mr Fellows. We were only talking about women. Come on, Lou, I could murder a beer. Are Olympic gymnasts allowed to drink?'

'Not usually, but I think I can risk one or two this weekend.'

Walking over to the pub behind Lee Fellows, Louis whispered to Theo, 'For what it's worth, I don't think Cathie's right for you anyway, and neither does Gideon…'

'Stop whispering to Lord Theodore, Trevelyan! If you weren't His Lordship's great white hope for the Olympics, I'd teach you a little lesson right now.' Chuckling at his tremendous wit in describing Louis as the 'great white hope', Fellows positioned himself behind the two young men and shoved them both into the pub.

'Theo, sweetie!' Flamboyantly dressed as ever and sporting a couple of diamante grips in his hair, Alan held out a hand from behind the bar as Louis and Theo walked over. 'Welcome to The White Lion.'

Looking at Alan, Theo was struck by two things – he was quite clearly gay, and he was quite clearly Matilda's father.

'Well, how did that happen then?' Theo clapped a hand over his mouth when he realised he'd spoken out loud, but Alan, far from being offended, threw back his head and laughed uproariously.

'The usual way. Had a little dabble with heterosexuality before I met Dex. It didn't suit me.' Ostentatiously adjusting his sparkling hairgrips to illustrate his point, Alan added, 'I'm Alan Santiago – I gather from your question you've already worked out that Matilda is my daughter…'

'Who was last seen upstairs with *my* daughter,' said Simone Lorimer, her sudden appearance at the bar taking Theo completely by surprise. After ordering drinks for herself and Philip, Simone glared at Theo and hissed, 'Put things right,' nodding towards the door leading to the guest rooms.

Looking round, Theo spotted Catherine hovering awkwardly in the doorway and crossed over to join her.

'Cathie…'

'I'm sorry…'

'Let's start the conversation again, shall we?' Theo said gently, leading Catherine over to a quiet table and sitting down with her.

'Cathie, I'm sorry about earlier. You're quite right, this isn't all about me…'

'But it is, Theo! This whole weekend's about getting you away from…'

Catherine stopped abruptly and glanced around.

'I behaved like a jealous fool,' she said when she was happy Lord Bassenford's thugs were out of earshot. 'I admit I was upset when I saw Matilda talking to you, especially because of… you know… what she wrote in that letter.'

'I don't think she knew I had a girlfriend…'

'She didn't, Theo. And, if you remember, you and I hadn't actually met at that time. Matilda and I have been talking. Yes, it rather took me by surprise too when she turned up at the door of my room. Mum was sitting with me, and I'm afraid she had a few choice words to say to your Matilda…'

'Cathie, she's not my…'

'Not yet. But she will be. Shush, Theo, let me finish. Matilda said she needed to speak to me, and I wanted to hear what she had to say, so Mum reluctantly joined Daddy in the bar. They're not very happy with you, I'm afraid.'

'I gathered that!'

'Matilda told me about *that* message – she'd heard all about you, liked the look of you in photos and decided it would cheer you up. She does fancy you, but she won't make a move on another woman's boyfriend, and she's sorry about upsetting me this afternoon.'

As Catherine fell silent, Theo looked over to where Matilda was dancing seductively around her pole. Try as he might, and despite knowing it was highly inappropriate, he couldn't tear his eyes away from her.

'I guessed right from the start that this would happen,' Catherine said. 'I knew all along our relationship was too good to be true. Now look me in the eye – that is, if you can bear to stop ogling Matilda for a second – and tell me you'd have chosen me if you'd been free to go out and meet other women. Meet someone like Matilda, for example.'

Theo looked into Catherine's eyes, but found he couldn't say the words she wanted to hear. Brushing tears away angrily, she held his gaze.

'If I'm honest, she's far more suitable for you anyway. Although I'm disappointed, I'm not actually hurting as much as I thought I would be, so perhaps you're not suitable for me, either.'

'Well, that's something,' said Theo, finally having the good grace to look ashamed of himself. 'But it doesn't alter the fact I behaved like a total bastard today. Like father, like son, eh?'

'Don't be ridiculous! You're not the first man to be governed by his groin, and you won't be the last, but that doesn't mean you deliberately set out to hurt people. His Lordshit, on the other hand, does, and no one knows that better than you. You've suffered enough, Theo. Get away from him. Get far away. Run away with Matilda for all I care, it makes no difference to me now. We're finished. Consider yourself dumped.'

Theo watched Catherine walk over the room, speak briefly to her parents, and then leave the bar with her head held high. It struck him as slightly sad, but he had more respect for her at that moment than he'd had at any time during their relationship.

Chapter 20 – Run Like Hell

The first thing Georgia Montfiore heard when she woke on the morning of her wedding day was the rain pouring through her open bedroom window and splashing on to the floor.

'Typical!' she exclaimed, wide awake in an instant and leaping out of bed to slam the window shut. 'It was a scorcher yesterday.'

Dressing in casual clothes and humming Alanis Morissette's *Ironic*, Georgie grinned in delight at the beautiful wedding dress hanging from her wardrobe then made her way to the kitchen, not surprised one iota to find Matilda and Alan already sitting at the table sharing a pot of tea.

'Don't you two ever sleep?' she asked with a laugh, helping herself to coffee.

'Loads to do, Georgie dear, simply masses,' Alan replied with an exaggerated sigh. 'If only you'd allowed me into the marquee after the rehearsal yesterday…'

'Alan! There's *nothing* you need to do until the flowers are delivered three hours from now, and you've got even longer to wait before the unsponsored volunteers arrive to set out the food.'

'I wish you'd let me set out the food, Georgie.'

'You'll be at the wedding, remember? Your boyfriend's sister's wedding, yes? You've talked the volunteers through every detail so many times, I'm sure they could set things out in their sleep by now.'

Alan was mollified for a second, then his brow furrowed once more.

'Are you sure you can't get the florist here earlier? I'll need time to get myself looking gorgeous…'

'I'd give up now in that case,' said Matilda, grinning at her dad and putting the kettle on again.

'Oh yes, young lady, going back to the subject of getting no sleep last night…'

'Oh, do give it a rest, Dad.'

'Matilda! I know Theo's gorgeous, but what if one of those thugs had caught you?'

'What's this?' asked Georgie. 'You and Theo, Matty? What about Catherine Lorimer?'

'She dumped him. I helped him find solace by sneaking into his bedroom and…'

'Spare me the details, darling,' said Alan, getting up to make more tea. 'It's more than your old dad can bear.'

'So, Matty,' said Georgie, 'are you and Theo an item now?'

'As far as we're concerned, yes. As far as His Lordshit's concerned, better keep it quiet. He was banging on the door at one point last night...' Matilda started to laugh '...banging on the door while we were banging away...'

'Matilda!'

'His Lordshit was hammering on the door going: "Theodore, keep the noise down! The rest of us would quite like to get some sleep tonight. We all know you've got Catherine in there". Oh yeah, like little Miss Prissy would ever have sucked him off...'

'*Matilda!* Not listening.'

'I'm sorry, Dad, but think of poor Theo. He'd never had a blow job until last night...'

'AAARGH!' Alan clapped his hands over his ears and fled to the bathroom, leaving Georgie and Matilda helpless with laughter.

'I don't really think your dad wants the graphic details of your sex life,' said Georgie, wiping her eyes.

'I know, Georgie, I just can't help winding him up sometimes. Oh good grief, here comes the walking dead.'

Dex had drifted, bleary-eyed, into the kitchen, poured himself a coffee and sat down at the kitchen table opposite Matilda and Georgie.

'Who's been upsetting Al this time?' he asked, looking at Matilda over the top of his mug. 'As if I don't already know. Has it got anything to do with you spending the night with Theo?'

Georgie and Matilda started laughing again as Alan walked back into the kitchen.

'Don't talk about it!' he said. 'As if I haven't got enough on my plate today.'

'Like what, Al? Putting a few flowers on tables?'

'Dexter, how could you? This is serious, and I'm so nervous…'

'You're nervous? I've got to make a speech!'

'And all I've got to do,' said Georgie, smiling serenely, 'is get married to the man I love.'

***

The wedding of Georgia Montfiore and Christopher Farrell was due to take place at two o'clock in the afternoon. By twelve noon the marquee was looking beautiful, the team of unsponsored volunteers was all ready to prepare the food for the reception while the wedding was taking place, the floral displays were stunning, and even Alan couldn't realistically find anything else to move around. Torn between one last tweak of the décor and getting himself ready, Alan finally decided on the latter, Georgie having laid down the law earlier.

'If you're not in and out of the bathroom by 12.30,' she'd said, 'then you won't get in at all.' Knowing her brother's partner as she did, Georgie guessed that the only thing Alan feared more than the marquee not being perfect for the wedding was not being perfect himself, and she was right. By 12.30 Alan was showered, clean-shaven, dressed unusually soberly in a brand new suit and enjoying a drink with the growing crowd of wedding guests in The White Lion.

About forty minutes before the wedding, Gideon and Chris left the pub to take their place at the front of the church. Chris was as calm and collected as his fiancée, while his best man was a quivering mass of nerves.

'Good grief, Gideon,' said Chris, laughing, 'if you're this nervous today, what state will you be in when Louis performs at the Olympics?'

'I dread to think,' replied Gideon shakily, gnawing the side of his fingernail.

As the guests filed into the church, Chris watched Alan and Louis hurrying about, showing them to their seats.

'Where on earth is my nephew?' he murmured, scanning the church and shaking his head. 'As if I can't guess.'

Grabbing Louis's arm as the young man whizzed past, Chris said, 'I thought Cameron was supposed to be helping you. Hasn't he managed to prise himself away from Chloe yet?'

'I'll nip outside and see,' replied Louis, grinning. Exiting the church, he nearly collided with Cameron who was wrapped around Chloe in the porch.

'Oh, hi, Lou,' said Cameron sheepishly. 'I was, er, just going to show Chloe to her seat...'

'No, *I'll* see Chloe to her seat. You can deal with the stragglers,' Louis replied, nodding his head in the direction of the church gate. An imperious looking Lord Bassenford was emerging from his limousine, closely followed by his extremely mardy elder daughter.

'Thanks a lot...' began Cameron, but Louis had already vanished into the church with Chloe. Sighing, Cameron summoned up as welcoming a smile as possible, introduced himself and offered Lord Bassenford an order of service.

'Carry it for me, Farrell,' barked His Lordship.

His smile a little strained now, Cameron greeted Rosanna.

'Hi, Rosanna, order of service?'

'Who the hell are you?'

Cameron's eyebrows shot up in surprise. 'Y-your cousin, actually,' he stammered.

'What, the illegitimate son of the dead unsponsored footballer? Hardly qualifies you to be my cousin.'

Cameron recoiled in shock and drew in a deep breath as Rosanna strutted after her father.

'Bite your tongue and count to ten, Cuz,' advised Theo quietly, patting Cameron on the shoulder. 'She gets off on hurting people.'

'I don't qualify as your cousin, apparently,' replied Cameron, his eyes still haunted.

'You're Uncle Elliot's son. Qualifies you in my book.'

'Elliot's *illegitimate* son. Mam and Dad never did tie the knot.'

'I see your illegitimacy,' said Theo with a grin, 'and raise you being His Lordshit's legitimate son.'

Relaxing, Cameron laughed and ushered Theo, Marina and Adam into the church, his smile fading almost immediately.

'Oh, give me strength!'

Lord Bassenford and Lady Rosanna had laid claim to the front pew. Breaking into a run, Cameron sprinted up the aisle and skidded to a halt next to them.

'Excuse me, Your Lordship, this pew is reserved for my mam and the bridesmaids. Your pew is this one behind...'

'No!' snapped His Lordship, not even deigning to look at Cameron.

'Never mind, darling,' said Jess, smiling at her son as she picked up her bag and moved to the pew originally intended for the St Benedicts. 'Change of plans.'

Theo, as stubborn as his father, sat down next to Jess.

'Theodore!' roared Lord Bassenford, grabbing Theo's tie and hauling him to his feet again, all eyes in the church now fixed on the entertainment. 'You are going to sit here, next to me, and bloody well behave yourself.'

Theo was clearly heard to say 'Embarrassing' as his father manhandled him none too gently into the front pew. Trying not to laugh as he imagined what Matilda's reaction was going to be on discovering His Lordship had ousted her from her seat, Cameron turned towards the church door and gave Alan a double thumbs-up, a signal Alan then relayed to Dex watching from The White Lion. The guests were finally seated, and the wedding could begin.

***

Three quarters of an hour later, the familiar music of the *Wedding March* boomed from inside the church and the bells started to ring, their joyful sound echoing through 'Thwaite's Wood and up into the fells. As the bride and groom emerged from the church, their faces glowing with happiness, a sudden beam of sunshine burst through the rain clouds, and the group of Unsponsored who'd gathered in the street to watch proceedings cheered and whistled. The photographer flitted around, taking full advantage of the brief dry spell to get a few shots in the garden, but within minutes the rain had returned with a vengeance, driving the wedding party back into the church and the cheering Unsponsored to their homes.

Once the church photographs were complete, the wedding guests splashed over to The White Lion under an assortment of umbrellas, Georgie and Chris greeting each person as he or she walked through the door of the inn.

'Lord Bassenford,' said Chris, holding out a hand to his despised brother-in-law with an admirable attempt at hospitality, 'we're glad you could make it.'

His Lordship looked at Chris's outstretched hand as though it were something threatening for a second, then shook it and mumbled his congratulations. Following on behind her father, Rosanna didn't even acknowledge her uncle and his bride. Instead, she snatched a glass of champagne from the tray Matilda was offering round to the guests and gulped it down in one.

'Don't mention it. Oh, hang on a minute, you didn't,' muttered Matilda as Rosanna slammed her empty glass down and took another full one.

'What did you say, underclass?'

'I said, "I hope you slept well",' replied Matilda with a laugh, disappearing into the crowd and leaving Rosanna too baffled to come back with a suitable retort.

Unlike his rude girlfriend, Adam Foster offered warm congratulations to Chris and Georgie, giving both a friendly hug and a big smile.

'What a nice lad,' Georgie said to her new husband as Adam went off to face a stinging barrage of abuse from Rosanna. 'Why on earth is he with Lady Bitch?'

'It's one of life's mysteries,' replied Theo, next in line to offer his congratulations. 'Lovely bridesmaid – I mean, wedding! Congratulations, both of you. Georgia, you look stunning.'

As Theo hugged his uncle and new aunt, Georgie laughed and said, 'Almost as stunning as Matilda, eh, Theodore? You're looking good on so little sleep.'

Grinning wickedly, Theo kissed Georgie on the cheek then went off in search of champagne.

As the guests filed into The White Lion and congratulated the happy couple, Louis was having a rather intense conversation with Chloe and Brains.

'So, what's the plan, Louis? We're often a bit out of touch in London despite Max's newsletters, and this isn't exactly something he can write about.'

'What isn't?' asked Louis, genuinely confused. 'What's what plan?'

Brains and Chloe looked at each other, then Brains tried again.

'Well, the plan for today, of course, Louis – today being the day of Theo's great escape and all that.'

Abi joined the group as Brains was speaking and heard his last few words.

'Ooh, shit,' she said.

Looking from Abi to Louis, Chloe shook her head in disbelief.

'Don't tell me Dory's Avengers haven't formulated a plan to get Theo away from His Lordshit. That's what getting him here today was all about, wasn't it?'

'Umm,' mumbled Louis, tapping his fist against his bottom lip. 'Actually we didn't think beyond Theo coming to Blenthwaite…'

Chloe turned as Alan and Dex approached, Dex carrying a full bottle of champagne in case anyone needed their glass topping up.

'What about you guys? Do you have any thoughts on how to get Theo away from His Lordshit and the thugs today?'

Looking as awkward as Louis and Abi, Alan replied that they didn't.

'We thought maybe you'd think of something, Brains…'

'Did you now, Alan. And what would be the point of me formulating a plan in London? We've got Theo away from London. It's the Blenthwaite escape we need to think of now.'

'Theo's coming this way,' added Chloe. 'So who's going to tell him there's no plan?'

'Hello, everyone. Yes please, Dex,' said Theo, grinning round and holding out his empty glass for more champagne. 'What's this plan that doesn't exist then? As if I can't make an educated guess.'

'I'm sorry, Theo,' said Louis, still tapping his lip, 'but as Brains has so rightly pointed out, while we were all busy being excited about you coming to Blenthwaite, we should have been working on a plan to get you away from His Lordshit once and for all.'

'It's OK, Lou, stop looking so worried. For what it's worth, I haven't been working on a plan either.' Theo laughed, then added, 'I suppose I thought I'd just stay. Refuse to go back to London.'

'Won't His Lordshit force you to go?' asked Abi.

'I'm sure he'll try, Cuz, but he's a bit outnumbered by the Unsponsored today. Besides, Philip Lorimer's here, and His Lordshit's anxious not to show Philip what an evil, worthless apology for a human being he really is.'

Theo virtually spat out the last few words, but his frown cleared instantly as Matilda approached.

'I could get trapped in Matty's bedroom,' he said, grabbing her hand and pulling her close. 'I'm quite used to being shut in a bedroom, and I certainly wouldn't want to escape if it were Matty's. Once she's got those thighs wrapped round me, I'm more likely to be coming than going... oh, sorry, Alan...'

Alan rolled his eyes as everyone else in the group roared with laughter.

'OK, Theo,' said Alan, a smile tugging at his lips, 'I'll let you off that lewd comment about my daughter if you'll allow me to play your Les Paul.'

'My guitar? Good grief, yes, I need to liberate it from that sponsored hotel – it's one of the only possessions I actually care about. Of course you may play it, Alan. I'll go and fetch it now, before the wedding breakfast begins.'

Dodging through the cheerful throng of guests, Theo made for the door and was about to push it open when Lord Bassenford roared his name.

'Theodore! Where the bloody hell do you think you're going?'

Turning away from the door reluctantly, Theo answered in the deadpan voice he reserved for his father.

447

'I was going to fetch my guitar, Your Lordship.'

'You'll do no such thing. I want you here where I can keep an eye on you.'

'Shall I fetch it, Your Lordship?' asked Adam, appearing by Theo's side.

Grunting his acquiescence, Lord Bassenford replied, 'Yes, off you go. Theodore, come here.'

Smiling gratefully at Adam as he handed over his room key, Theo then walked slowly over to face Lord Bassenford, grabbing a handful from a large bowl of dry roasted peanuts en route.

'Now, Theodore, would you like to explain what's gone wrong between you and Catherine?'

Theo took his time chewing and swallowing the peanuts before answering.

'She dumped me.'

'Why?'

'Because... well, we weren't really compatible.'

'I thought I told you to keep the young lady sweet,' hissed Lord Bassenford. 'It's crucial that I am able to liaise with her father, especially with the Olympics coming up...'

'For the last time, Your Lordship, I didn't have a relationship with Cathie to help out your damn Scheme. I had a relationship with her because I liked her, but it's run its course now and we've split up. Your business with her father has nothing to do with me, or Cathie.'

Lord Bassenford snorted derisively.

'I suppose she caught you sniffing round that unsponsored tart – the one who was so disrespectful to me during the wedding service.'

Cameron had guessed correctly that Matilda wouldn't take kindly to being ousted from her seat in the church, but no one could have predicted her reaction. On finding the all-powerful Head of the Sponsorship Scheme in her rightful place, resolutely refusing to move, she had resolved the situation by sitting on his lap, much to Alan's alarm and everyone else's amusement.

'Disrespectful?' scoffed Theo. 'Don't give me that, Your Lordship, you enjoyed every minute of it.'

His Lordship had in fact enjoyed every minute, but he wasn't about to concede the point to his son.

'Listen to me,' he growled, jabbing a finger into Theo's chest. 'You will keep your hands off that tart – yes, I saw you helping yourself to a little feel earlier – and make things up with Catherine.'

'Let's get one thing straight, Your Lordship,' said Theo furiously. 'Matilda is not a tart, and if you ever call her that again…'

At that moment, Adam returned, Theo's guitar slung from his shoulder. Glad of the excuse to get away from his father before he said something he'd regret (probably for another ten years), Theo plugged his precious guitar into the amplifiers on the stage then beckoned Alan over. Grinning like the Cheshire cat, Alan stroked the Les Paul reverently a couple of times then tuned it to perfection, testing it out with a medley of complex riffs while Theo and Adam watched, spellbound.

'He's pretty damn good, isn't he,' said Matilda, appearing at Theo's side and smiling proudly at her father. Nodding, Theo announced that he couldn't resist joining in any longer and jumped back on to the stage.

'May I?' he asked, picking up one of Alan's guitars and holding it out.

'Of course!' replied Alan, his riff medley morphing seamlessly into the familiar melody of Bob Marley's *Jammin'*. Following the placement of Alan's fingers carefully, Theo picked up the right notes and was soon playing along with the expert, while Matilda added vocals – an impromptu Dory's Avengers performance featuring Dory himself.

***

Louis caught up with Theo again as the wedding party moved over to the marquee for the feast.

'Any idea what you're going to do, Theo?'

'Well, nothing for now, apart from eat.'

'If you do make a break for it, head for 'Thwaite's Wood. You know where.'

'I'd rather head for Matilda's bedroom,' replied Theo, sticking his hand out into the pouring rain from underneath his umbrella. 'Nice weather for ducks.'

'Quack, quack,' said Louis, chuckling. 'Come on, you southern softie, a bit of good honest Lake District rain never hurt anyone.'

'I'd still rather take my chances in Matilda's bed…'

'Which is probably the first place His Lordshit'll think to look for you, going on the amount of times you've had your hand on her arse this afternoon. That reminds me – I take it it's all over between you and Catherine.'

'Yes, she dumped me – something to do with me being a cad and a bounder – and pretty much told me I'd be better off with Matty. You and Gideon were spot on, Lou: Cathie wasn't right for me.'

'And Matty is?'

'Hell, yes – what a woman! She sneaked into the sponsored hotel last night and was sitting on my bed when I got back from The Lion. Wow, Lou, what a woman.'

'So you said,' replied Louis with a grin. 'I guess your stirring loins are happy now.'

'My stirring loins are exhausted! Lou, she completely blew my mind – not to mention other parts of me too. What a…'

'What a woman. Yes, Theo, I get the general idea.'

Laughing, the two young men entered the marquee, where Lord Bassenford was waiting to pounce.

'Ah, there you are, Theodore. Our table's over here. Should you be drinking, Trevelyan?' His Lordship added, looking dubiously at the glass of champagne in Louis's hand.

'I find it keeps me from dehydrating.'

'Don't be facetious! I meant, should you be drinking alcohol?'

'It's a one-off. Don't worry, I usually stick to water.'

'Your Lordship,' prompted Lord Bassenford.

'No, really, I'm just plain old Louis.'

Laughing, Louis sprinted away before His Lordship could roar at him.

Philip and his family were seated at the same table as Lord Bassenford, it being too late to change the plans around following Catherine and Theo's recent split. It was lucky for the unsponsored waitress assigned to serve the St Benedict table that the Lorimers, Theo, Adam and Marina were there, as they did their best to atone for the continual rudeness of Lord

Bassenford and his elder daughter. Rosanna in particular was on a mission to be as obnoxious as possible, and nothing was to her liking, despite the food being declared delicious by everyone else in the room.

'Oi, unsponsored scum, I can't eat this muck!'

'Don't look at me like that, you unsponsored moron.'

'Get me more champagne, unsponsored filth!'

'Do you really think you need any more booze, Rosanna?' asked Theo, regarding his sister's bleary eyes and dishevelled hair with amusement.

'If Rosanna wants more champagne, she shall have it, Theodore,' roared Lord Bassenford. 'More champagne here – *now*, Unsponsored!'

Theo shrugged and tucked into his sister's discarded meal, having already finished his own, while everyone else in the room did their best to hide their disgust at her bad behaviour.

With the exception of Rosanna, all the guests thoroughly enjoyed the speeches that followed the wedding feast. Dex summed up with his well-chosen words the love he felt for his younger sister, and how happy he was to see her married to someone as perfect for her as Chris. Welcoming Chris to the family, he then led the guests in a toast to the bride and groom, and even Lord Bassenford stood to raise his glass. Only Rosanna stayed slumped in her chair, Theo whispering to Marina that their sister was probably too drunk to stand.

Chris's speech was equally moving, but it was Gideon who really stole the show. Hidden beneath the gruff exterior was a very humorous man, and everyone roared with laughter at tales of Chris's mishaps when he'd just qualified as a vet, his tentative courtship of Georgia and his drunken attempts to play football 'better than Elliot' one silly night in Carlisle. Taking Abi's hand, Gideon concluded his speech by commenting how much Chris's brother and sister would have enjoyed the day's celebrations. Jess wrapped her arms around Cameron while Marina squeezed Theo's hand, then Gideon raised the mood and followed the sombre moment with another rousing toast to the bride and groom.

'And more champagne!' demanded Lady Rosanna with a belch, so drunk she didn't realise the ensuing roar of laughter was at her expense.

Once the cake had been cut signalling the end of the formalities, the wedding party moved back through the pouring rain and into the pub for the evening. Dory's Avengers took to the stage, Adam standing in as bass player so Georgie could continue to chat to her guests, and as soon as they'd tuned up, they burst into an enthusiastic rendition of *Girls Just Wanna Have*

Fun. Several female guests, including, to everyone's surprise, Catherine, got up to dance in front of the stage, while most of the menfolk elected to jostle for a prime position at the bar.

To Lysander's dismay, he found himself cornered by Lord Bassenford.

'Nice wedding, wasn't it, Lysander. I do love a celebration, don't you?'

'Well, it beats a funeral, Your Lordship,' replied Lysander tartly, looking around for someone else to talk to.

Lord Bassenford wasn't going to be put off that easily. 'Of course it does,' he boomed, slapping Lysander on the back. 'Any chance of you returning to London sometime soon?'

'Perhaps. As you said, this is a celebration, so let's not discuss it now. Is that a free table over there? Why not go and take the weight off your feet?'

'Don't worry, Dad, I'll save you,' said Louis, appearing out of nowhere and clinking his glass against Lysander's. 'Cheers!'

'Cheers, Lou,' replied Lysander gratefully, draping an arm around Louis's shoulders. Turning away from the affectionate father/son interaction, Lord Bassenford scanned the room with a slight frown on his face, concerned that he wasn't currently aware of his own son's whereabouts. As it turned out, Theo wasn't at all difficult to locate – he'd climbed on stage with

Dory's Avengers and was hogging the limelight, belting out *Long Live Rock 'n' Roll* while a grinning Matilda played lead on the Les Paul and Alan sulkily strummed one of his own guitars.

'Think you've left it a bit late to build bridges, Your... er... Lordship,' said Louis bluntly, following the direction of Lord Bassenford's gaze.

'Dory's Avengers?'

'Yes. We stand up for the rights of fish.'

Turning to Louis with a cold smile, Lord Bassenford said, 'So it has nothing to do with the fact you used to call my son Dory, then? Aha, you thought I didn't know, didn't you, young Trevelyan. I can guess your opinion of my fathering skills, or rather my lack thereof, but believe it or not, I do love Theodore.'

Laughing at the disbelieving expressions on the faces of the Trevelyans, His Lordship made his way through the growing crowd of people on the dance floor and positioned himself in front of the stage, singing along to *Living on a Prayer* with gusto. For the next hour or so, the wedding guests and His Lordship's security guards were amazed to see him partying alongside the Unsponsored with ever increasing enthusiasm – even Theo yelling, 'I'd like to dedicate this one to His Lordshit,' before the band burst into *I Hate Everything About You* couldn't dampen his spirits. He simply shrugged at the people around him then redoubled his efforts to look up Matilda's skirt.

As the live-music set came to a close, Alan donned a rainbow-ribbon-bedecked trilby and took lead vocals. The radiant bride clambered on stage, a double bass in hand, and the band brought the house down with a highly entertaining version of *Stray Cat Strut*. Having thoroughly enjoyed the show, the crowd roared its appreciation as the musicians took their bows, His Lordship completely forgetting himself in the joy of the moment and cheering every bit as loudly as the rest of the wedding guests.

However, one person wasn't enjoying the evening at all – Lady Rosanna. Having hardly eaten all day, she'd been on a mission to down as much champagne as humanly possible, and by the time the band reached its finale, she was paralytic. Paralytic, and very belligerent.

'I can't believe you, Father!' she yelled, staggering over the dance floor, arms flailing. 'You hate the unsponsored scum… *you hate them*… What are you *doing*?'

Finally facing her father as he turned to see what the commotion was all about, Rosanna tried desperately to grab hold of his shoulders but only succeeded in doubling up and vomiting on his expensive shoes.

457

'Now!' whispered Louis as Theo leapt down from the stage. 'Get out of here now, Theo. I'll meet you at the tree when I can.'

'Go, Theo,' added Matilda, landing on the floor beside him.

'But…'

'*Go*, Cuz,' hissed Abi.

Glancing briefly at Lord Bassenford, who was yelling at his security men to take Rosanna back to the hotel and clean up the mess on his shoes, Theo then made full use of the unexpected distraction and sprinted out of The White Lion. Caring nothing for his expensive suit, he fled across the meadow and into 'Thwaite's Wood, knowing the way instinctively. Running headlong through dense woodland, bushes and branches caressing him as he passed before closing the gaps behind him, he eventually reached the old tree in which he and Louis had made their childhood pact many years earlier – the pact Louis had honoured so loyally the previous summer.

About to haul himself into the tree, Theo noticed something out of the corner of his eyes as they adjusted to the gloom – something that had no right to be in the middle of the wood. Letting go of the tree's branches and investigating more closely, he discovered a piece of white paper, protected from the elements by a polythene bag, attached to an igloo tent, fully erected and ready to inhabit. Tugging the paper free, Theo crawled inside the tent and grunted with approval as his hand came into contact with a torch.

Drawing the piece of paper from the polythene bag, he shone the torch on it and gasped in amazement. It was a note, and it was addressed to him.

Dearest Theodore,

A few things to make you comfortable. Enjoy. Use the torch sparingly – light travels.

Stay safe. Your ever loving Fairy Godmother xxx

Heeding the advice, Theo switched off the torch and felt around a bit more, gratified to find his fairy godmother had left him a dry set of clothes, a towel and a box of food inside a large sleeping bag. He hastily changed from his soaking wet suit then tucked into a hearty ham and cheese sandwich, wondering as he ate who on earth his mysterious fairy godmother could be, and how she knew he loved ham and cheese sandwiches above all others. Finally, replete, warm and dry, he snuggled into his sleeping bag with a huge smile on his face, the euphoria of being free at long last enveloping him at the exact moment the shouts started from The White Lion.

'Never mind Rosanna, the stupid little drunk,' Lord Bassenford's hysterical voice carried into 'Thwaite's Wood as clearly as the peals of the wedding bells earlier in the day, 'where the *hell* is Theodore?'

Chapter 21 – Gideon's Secret

The shouts of Lord Bassenford's henchmen sounded long into the night, His Lordship himself joining in the search despite the continual rain soaking him to the skin. From time to time he'd return to The White Lion to grill the Unsponsored about Theo's disappearance, and every time he re-entered the bar he became increasingly annoyed to find them carrying on with the wedding celebrations as if nothing had happened.

When he discovered the band had started playing again, he completely lost his temper.

'Stop that racket!' he roared, the music he'd enjoyed so much earlier in the evening now sounding like mockery. Unplugging the Les Paul from the amplifiers and cutting Alan off in mid-solo, Lord Bassenford rounded on the guitarist.

'Put that bloody guitar down! I didn't spend all that money for you to get your unsponsored hands all over it. Give it…'

His Lordship tried to snatch the guitar, but Alan was too quick. Leaping from the stage, guitar hugged to his chest, he disappeared rapidly into the living quarters of the inn, leaving a seething Lord Bassenford to take his temper out on Louis.

'Where is he, Trevelyan? You've been planning…'

'Er, how exactly, with me up north all the time and Theo a prisoner in your big house in London?'

'He is *not* a prisoner, you insolent…'

'So what's the problem, Your Lordship?' asked Philip Lorimer, appearing at Lord Bassenford's shoulder. 'Theodore's an adult, and as you say he's not a prisoner, so why shouldn't he leave the party any time he wishes?'

'Theodore's agoraphobic…'

'I think we can drop the agoraphobia story now, Your Lordship. Theodore positively revelled in being outside yesterday. I don't know the true story of his life, and I don't actually care now he's no longer with Cathie, but it would seem he wants a break from it.'

'Philip,' said His Lordship, reining in his temper with a mighty effort, 'I am probably the most powerful, influential and stinking filthy *rich* man in the country. Has the possibility that Theodore's been *kidnapped* not occurred to you?'

'That would be unfortunate, Your Lordship, but judging by the friendliness and hospitality we've experienced here today, I would doubt that to be the case. Besides, even if Theodore has been kidnapped, I can't see how it's Louis's fault.'

At the mention of Louis, Lord Bassenford turned once more in the young man's direction and found him flanked by Lysander and Abi.

'I'm beginning to wonder if Mortimer was right all those years ago, Lysander. God help your wretched son if he is planning anything against the Scheme. I'll have every bone in his body broken. Your boy will make *him*,' Lord Bassenford pointed at Gideon, 'look like the active type.'

'I won't do too well at the Olympics then, Your Lordshit,' said Louis, arms folded defiantly.

'Ah yes, the Olympics…'

Lord Bassenford stopped abruptly as Lee Fellows entered the bar.

'Fellows, what news?'

'He's nowhere to be found, Your Lordship. That forest round the village is pretty much impenetrable, so unless he's up on that mountain, I'd say he's far away from here now.'

'He won't be up on the mountain in this weather, imbecile! Search the bloody village – I'll wager one of this lot,' Lord Bassenford jerked a thumb at Louis and his companions, 'is hiding him.'

'We're doing all we can, Your Lordship, but obviously it's very late…'

Fellows's attempt to reason with Lord Bassenford only served to annoy him more than ever.

'I don't care! Get out there, knock on doors. Get men patrolling the village all night. I want Lord Theodore found, sooner rather than later. What I don't want is excuses.'

Face like a thundercloud, Lord Bassenford turned to his younger daughter.

'Marina, we're returning to the sponsored hotel. *Now.*'

Marina had been enjoying a lively discussion about the eventful day with Catherine and was reluctant to leave. Adam interceded, arguing that he could see her back to the hotel later on, but unfortunately for him, his good deed backfired.

'Absolutely not, Adam. I'm not letting Marina out of my sight after tonight's unfortunate events, and I'm not sure I approve of Rosanna's beau fraternising with this unsponsored rabble either, so you'd better come back with me too.'

Muttering that Theodore had been nothing but trouble since the day he was born, Lord Bassenford strode from the pub, his security men surrounding him to ensure his safety and escort the reluctant Marina and Adam behind him. As all eyes in the room followed their departure, a slim figure shrouded in waterproofs slipped out unnoticed through the back door, heaving a rucksack on to its back then heading at a run towards 'Thwaite's Wood.

***

The following morning, Lord Bassenford sat at the best table in the Blenthwaite Hotel's dining room, his mood as dark as the heavy rainclouds outside. Laptop open in front of him, he emailed his inner circle to demand their presence at an emergency meeting in his office the following morning, then turned his attention to Adam sitting opposite him.

'Where's Rosanna?'

'Still in bed, Your Lordship.'

'Go and get her.'

'She's feeling a bit…'

'*Now*, Foster!'

Sighing, Adam handed his empty breakfast plate to the passing waitress with a smile of thanks, then did as he was told. Five minutes later, a very fragile-looking Rosanna was propped up in the corner opposite her father.

'You look awful, Rosanna, and you were a bloody disgrace yesterday,' said Lord Bassenford without sympathy. 'How *dare* you let me down like that!'

'Sorry, Father,' mumbled Rosanna, looking at the table and hoping she wouldn't have to rush off to be sick.

'I suppose you know Theodore's gone. That rumpus you caused took everyone's attention, and off he went.'

'We'll be better off without him…'

'We will *not*, you stupid girl!' Rosanna wisely shut up, and Lord Bassenford continued more quietly, 'We'll be leaving in an hour. Get your things ready, Rosanna, and if you're sick in the limousine I'll have you thrown out on to the motorway.'

'Adam,' snapped Rosanna, turning to her boyfriend who was drinking coffee and chatting amiably to the hotel owner, 'stop talking to servants and get my stuff together. Give me coffee too.'

'No,' replied Adam. 'Do it yourself.'

'*Adam!*' shrieked Rosanna, pausing briefly as another wave of nausea hit her. 'Adam, if you want to remain my boyfriend, I suggest…'

'Well, that's just it,' Adam put his coffee cup down and faced Rosanna, 'I don't want to. I used to think you were beautiful, now all I can see is the nasty, bitter woman you are inside. I've got my own things together, Lord Bassenford,' he continued, addressing His Lordship who was suddenly very interested in the conversation, 'but I'm not returning to London right now. I told Mum and Dad I'd watch Louis train for a few days, then I'll get a lift back with the Lorimers.'

Lifting his hand to silence any protests, Adam finished what he wanted to say.

'It's all arranged. I spoke to Philip yesterday and he said he'll drive me home, no problem.'

'Very well, Adam. Although I'm saddened to hear you won't be continuing your relationship with my daughter,' Lord Bassenford looked contemptuously at Rosanna, who was hiccoughing into a napkin, 'I can't say I blame you. Talking of daughters, you don't happen to know where Marina is, do you?'

'White Lion, Lord Bassenford. She ate an early breakfast then went straight up there to see Catherine. Philip's delighted that the girls are such good friends.'

'Excellent,' said Lord Bassenford, smiling slightly as he realised Marina's friendship with Catherine would be every bit as advantageous as Theo's relationship with her had been. 'But it doesn't alter the fact that Marina's coming back with me. I will be returning to Blenthwaite as soon as I have concluded my business in London, so she can resume her friendship with Catherine then.'

Adam picked up his holdall. 'I'll be off then, if you don't mind, Your Lordship,' he said. 'I've arranged to go for a bit of a workout this morning.'

'No, I don't mind at all. Goodbye, Adam.' As Adam left the hotel, Lord Bassenford turned back to his elder daughter and added, 'I hope you realise what you've lost, Rosanna. Adam's a good man.'

Rosanna was still far too concerned with her nausea to worry about the pain of losing Adam. That would come later.

**

While a brooding Lord Bassenford was travelling back to London with his daughters, one sulking at having been dragged away from Blenthwaite and the other too hungover to speak, his errant son was still hiding in an igloo tent in 'Thwaite's Wood. The heart of the wood, so recently declared impenetrable by Lee Fellows, had welcomed Blenthwaite girl Matilda Santiago with open arms, and she and Theo were lying entwined on top of his sleeping bag, basking in the afterglow of some energetic sex and discussing what to do next.

'His Lordshit's got thugs crawling all over the village, Theo, so we can't head back there yet.'

'Including Dyer?'

'Afraid so.'

Feeling Theo tense, Matilda gently massaged his shoulders as she recounted an incident that had taken place the previous evening.

'The Dyer Creep's not having it all his own way, I can assure you, Theo. He kept slithering about annoying everyone in The Lion, so Dex told him in no uncertain terms to sling his hook.

Creep got all mardy and replied he's glad he's not gay like Dex, then Dex replied he's glad he's not in denial about his sexuality like Creep is. Creep reared up and made a grab for Dex, so I decided it was time to practise my karate kicks. On Creep's bollocks. Hard.'

Theo laughed, and Matilda was gratified to feel him relax in her arms.

'Priceless,' he said. 'Dex is a legend, and so are you.' Kissing her soundly, he added, 'And so's your dad. What an amazing guitarist!'

'You don't have any problems with my dad being gay, then?'

'None at all. Why would I?'

'Oh, just some nasty small-minded condition called homophobia, which I'm delighted to know you don't suffer from.' Matilda straddled Theo and plunged her tongue into his mouth, then pulled back with a teasing grin the moment he responded.

'Not a good look, Dory babes,' she said, laughing at his tongue waggling out of his mouth. 'Talking of Dad and Dex, they'll be worrying about me. I'd better make a move…'

'Not yet, you're not,' Theo replied huskily, pulling her back down on top of him.

Half an hour later the conversation resumed, a little breathlessly.

'Ye gods!' said Theo, sniffing his armpit warily. 'I need a shower. I'm starting to fester.'

'You smell fine to me...'

'Well, I won't before long, so you're right – we'd better make a move. Although where to, I don't know...'

'All sorted,' said Matilda, grabbing her rucksack and producing a key. 'Come on then, Sexy. Sad though it is to see the body beautiful covered up, it's time you got dressed.'

Once they were ready to go, Matilda set off at her usual brisk pace, leading Theo by the hand and only slowing when the trees gave way to more open land. Cautioning him to stay where he was, she then ventured out of the woods and checked the coast was clear.

After a few minutes, she beckoned Theo over to an old farm cottage which looked as though it had seen better days a long time ago.

'I can shower in that?' he asked incredulously. 'With what – rainwater?'

Laughing, Matilda said, 'Just you wait,' as she unlocked the door of the cottage and led him into its surprisingly modern kitchen, kitted out to allow its wheelchair-bound owner to move around freely and be totally self-sufficient.

'You could have knocked first, Matty,' said Gideon with a grin, entering the room.

Matilda just had time to reply, 'I wasn't sure if you were home, Gideon,' before her father shot past him and enveloped her in a bear hug.

'My baby, my baby girl, I'm so glad you're safe. Thank you, Theo, for bringing my baby back safely…'

'Oh, stop blubbing, Dad!' said Matilda, returning Alan's hug affectionately.

'Actually, Alan, *she* brought *me*,' said Theo.

'Of course she did!' Dex greeted the youngsters warmly, if a little less tearfully than Alan. 'Matty isn't one of life's followers. Good to see you both.'

'Good to see you too, Dex. Matty tells me you gave Dyer a few pointers on being honest about his sexuality last night.'

Dex grinned wickedly. 'Yeah, shortly before she did some more damage to his family allowance. It was hilarious – you should have been there, Theo.'

'Probably just as well I wasn't there, or I may not be here now.'

'That's true,' said Gideon, eyes twinkling. 'Jolly decent of your sister to provide the perfect opportunity for you to escape.'

Theo roared with laughter.

'Yes, Gideon, she's thoughtful like that.'

'So, Theo – I take it you don't want us to call you Lord Theodore?'

'I'd rather you didn't – I don't want anything from Lord Bastardford, including his wretched title. From now on I'll be Theo Farrell, Gideon. Mister.'

'Well, *Mister* Theo Farrell, best you get in the shower. You stink.'

As Theo burst out laughing again, Dex passed his holdall over.

'Adam dropped this off at The Lion earlier. He's staying for a few days, by the way. Oh, and he's dumped your sister.'

'Good news! Ads is a decent man, he deserves so much better than Lady Bitch.'

Showering with Matilda, Theo took rather longer than he'd intended, and by the time they returned, Alan looked as though he was chewing on a wasp.

'Yes, Dad, we did have a quick shag,' said Matilda, grinning. 'And don't pull that face, I left sweet sixteen behind a few years ago.'

Alan's face relaxed into its ready smile. 'Oh 'eck,' he said, 'my baby's all grown up. I must be getting old.'

'Yup,' agreed Matilda cheekily. 'OK, we need to swap news.'

'I'll begin, shall I?' said Theo, settling down on the floor. 'The main thing baffling me is…'

'Never underestimate 'Thwaite's Wood.'

'No, not that, Alan. I never doubted that I would be safe in 'Thwaite's Wood, but I wasn't expecting it to provide a fairy godmother.'

'It did *what*?'

'There was a tent set up next to the big tree Louis and I virtually lived in when we were children, and attached to it was this.'

Theo held out the note. Alan and Dex read it curiously then passed it on to Gideon, who merely fanned himself with it, an enigmatic smile on his face.

'Your fairy godmother?' said Alan, his brow furrowed. 'Who could that be, Theo?'

'No idea.'

'Do you think it was Louis?'

'I'm not sure Louis would appreciate being thought of as a fairy,' said Theo with a laugh. 'And he and Abi were both so embarrassed at their lack of planning when Chloe and Brains confronted them yesterday, I think we can count them out. It wasn't anyone from London as they'd assumed you lot had made plans.'

'What about Max?'

'Doesn't really qualify as a fairy either.' With a teasing grin, Matilda added, 'It wasn't you, was it, Dad? You fit the description.'

'The clue *is* in the name,' said Gideon.

'Aye, *fairy* godmother. It was Dad, then.'

'Are you saying I'm camp?' said Alan, affecting a pose that was excessively camp even by his standards.

'Course not, Dad,' replied Matilda, sucking in her cheeks in an attempt to keep a straight face and failing abysmally when Dex let out a huge snort of laughter.

'I was thinking more of the "mother" bit of the name,' said Gideon quietly, his murmur lost in the general hilarity.

'Hang on a minute,' said Theo, sobering a little as a thought struck him. '"The clue's in the name"? Gideon, that suggests you know who…'

Theo stopped abruptly as a voice spoke from the doorway – a voice he'd spent the last ten years hoping to hear again one day.

'Shall I take it from here, Gideon?'

'Am I dreaming?'

'No, Theodore, you're not. Come on then…'

Theo didn't need asking twice. Shooting up from the floor, he hurled himself into his mother's embrace and clung on to her as if he'd never let go.

***

It took a while before a very emotional Theo had calmed down enough for the conversation to continue.

'My gorgeous boy,' said Isabelle, sitting on the floor and doing her best to cradle her strapping six-foot-plus son. 'I bet the ladies all love you.'

'Matilda…'

'Ah, yes.' Isabelle grinned over at Matilda. 'I guessed you two were rather more than friends when you disappeared into the shower together. It's so good to see you all again.'

'Good to see you too, Izzy,' said Alan. 'But why didn't you tell us you were here?'

'More to the point, where have you been?' the ever forthright Matilda added. Alan frowned a warning at his daughter, but Isabelle just laughed.

'Matilda's right, Alan. I'm sure you all want to know the answer to that one.'

'Well, yes,' admitted Alan. 'So, when did you get back?'

'Couple of days ago,' replied Isabelle. 'And Gideon kindly offered to put me up.'

'So you knew all along, Gideon! Why didn't you tell us?'

'What, with His Lordshit and his henchmen in the village…'

'Is that what you call him, Gideon?' Isabelle interrupted, laughing. 'His Lordshit?'

'Yes,' said Matilda. 'It's a choice between that and Lord Bastardford. They both suit him so well.'

'You don't mind, do you, Izzy?' asked Alan. 'Izzy might still love him, Matty, he *is* her husband…'

'Alan, I hate him,' Isabelle interrupted again, her voice hard and bitter. 'I hate him with every fibre of my being. I hated him ten years ago when he drove me away from my children, and now I know how he's been treating Theodore – his own son…'

For the first time, Isabelle's composure slipped and she wrapped her arms tightly around Theo, lowering her head for a minute or so before continuing.

'In answer to your question, Matilda, I've been in Italy. Staying with Jess's family. Jess and I have been friends since childhood – much like you and Louis, Theodore – so if I could trust anyone, I could trust her.

'I had to leave. William… I mean, Lord Bastardford made it impossible for me to stay. I was too much of a threat to his obsessive ambition to be the most powerful man in the country, with a multitude of sponsored minions all unquestioningly loyal to his wretched Scheme.'

'He still thinks he's in the right,' murmured Theo, the first coherent thing he'd managed to say since Isabelle's surprise appearance.

'Yes, he always did.'

'Why didn't Jess…'

'She didn't tell anyone because I asked her not to. When Lord Bastardford forced me to leave the country, the last thing he said to me was that he would kill me, slowly and painfully, if he ever found out that I had returned, and he'd make my children watch.'

'He threatened to do something similar to Louis once,' said Theo, sitting up and stretching.

'His threats haven't become any more original, then. Yes, he threatened to kill me, just because I did what little I could to make life bearable for the unfortunate people he sought to oppress. There was no doubt that he would carry out his threat, so I truly believed it was better for my children if I stayed away.'

Isabelle's voice faltered as she struggled to find her next words.

'What I didn't even contemplate was that he would stoop so low as to hurt his own son…'

Curling up in his mother's arms again, Theo said, 'I know, Mum. I never doubted you for a second.'

'I didn't realise Jess had been protecting me from the truth over the years. Poor Jess, I gave her such a hard time when I found out. She did it because she cares about me, though – she knew I'd have been straight back if I'd known for one moment how His Lordshit was treating

Theodore, and that would have been the end of Isabelle Farrell.'

'So what made you come back now?'

'Everything aligned to make now the right time – my brother getting married, Theodore being freed from His Lordshit's house for the wedding, and finally having the opportunity.'

'What opportunity?'

'Philip Lorimer,' replied Isabelle. 'I believe you all know him. Jess introduced us in Italy earlier this year, and having an influential ally free from the limitations of Sponsorship opened up a whole world of transport options for me.'

**

As Isabelle was telling her tale in Gideon's cottage, Louis was hosting an exercise class in his mentor's studio. The workout had begun sensibly enough, with Louis leading his friends through a series of callisthenics, but then Abi spied a football under one of the benches around the perimeter of the studio and decided to flick it out with her foot, dribbling it expertly across the room and challenging the others to tackle it from her. Suspecting that their footballing abilities wouldn't measure up to those of Elliot Farrell's daughter, Chloe and Adam elected to leave Cameron to rise to the challenge, deciding instead to strike poses on Louis's gymnastic apparatus while Louis barked out instructions, Gideon-style.

When Adam slipped and straddled the pommel horse painfully, Louis suggested, through howls of laughter, that maybe a run would be a more successful way to get some exercise.

'That is, if you can still walk, Ads.'

'Yes. Thank you all for your sympathy, but I'm OK,' replied Adam tartly.

The playful mood of the youngsters didn't last long, though. Leaving the studio, they were dismayed to be confronted by His Lordship's security men, led by the hated Dyer.

'Off for a jog, boys and girls?' he drawled, smirking. 'Or maybe a little visit to Lord Theodore.'

'Piss off, Dyer,' snapped Chloe, grabbing hold of Cameron who had tensed at her side, fists clenched. 'We don't know where Theo is.'

'You're *lying*, unsponsored bitch!' Turning to Louis, Dyer added, 'We'll be watching you especially carefully, Whitey. I want my plaything back, and you'll be the one leading me to him. OK, where are we jogging to?'

'Tell you what,' said Louis, ignoring Dyer and turning to his friends, 'I've lost the urge to exercise. Shall we go to The Lion instead? The company stinks out here.'

'Don't you think you ought to go easy on the booze, Whitey?' sneered Dyer.

'If I wanted a worthless opinion,' replied Louis furiously, 'I would find a dog shit and ask what it thinks. I'm sure it would talk more sense than you.'

Dyer flew towards Louis, fists raised, but Cameron was quicker. Full of anger at never having had the opportunity to get to know his father, he slammed a punch with full force into Dyer's face, grunting with satisfaction as blood spurted from the thug's nose.

'I'll get you for that, Farrell,' Dyer howled. 'I'll stick a knife in you like I did to your fucking father…'

'Very interesting, Mr Dyer,' said Philip Lorimer, suddenly appearing behind the thugs, mobile phone in hand. 'I think I'd better give Lord Bassenford a call. I'm sure he'd be interested to know that his security men are brawling in the streets instead of searching for Lord Theodore.'

'Mind your own business, Lorimer,' snarled Dyer.

'His Lordship's number's right here on my screen, Dyer. All I have to do is press…'

Like all bullies, Dyer was really a coward, and he backed down the moment he realised Philip was serious. Holding a handkerchief to his bleeding nose, he offered a grovelling apology to the unsponsored man who held so much influence over his boss, then contented himself with glowering at the youngsters as they filed past.

Once in the safety of The White Lion, Philip rounded on Cameron and Louis.

'What do you think you were doing, antagonising Dyer like that? How's that going to help Theodore?'

When they didn't answer, Philip softened a bit.

'Look, I know you both loathe Dyer. I know you've both got good reason to hate Dyer, but getting yourselves beaten to a pulp won't be the most constructive move, will it, lads?' Smiling kindly as Louis and Cameron shook their heads, Philip added, 'OK, what do you all want to drink?'

Everyone asked for a beer, except Louis who chose mineral water. Helping Philip to fetch the drinks, Louis was surprised to see his father serving behind the bar.

'New job, Dad?' he said. 'Where are Dex and Al?'

'They went to find Matty,' replied Lysander. 'You can imagine the state Alan was working himself into with his daughter in 'Thwaite's Wood and all those thugs on full alert. No one expects the newlyweds to work the day after their wedding, so I'm covering.' Smiling wryly, he added, 'It's nice to be doing something worthwhile for once.'

'It's nice to see you doing something worthwhile for once,' said Louis with a laugh, picking up the last drinks of Philip's order and carrying them over to his friends.

'Now,' said Philip when Louis had sat down, 'have you had a chance to see Theodore since he left the party last night?'

'Not yet, Philip. I told him I'd meet him in the wood, but my opportunities are going to be a little limited with that lot on my tail.' Looking out into the street where Lord Bassenford's thugs were still swarming around, Louis pulled a face. 'Theo must think I've deserted him.'

'I'm sure Theodore's shrewd enough to know how tenacious his father's security guards can be, Louis.' Smiling at Jess as she came over to join them, Philip added, 'Do we tell them now, Jess?'

'I think it's about time, Philip, yes. My children especially have a right to know.'

All the youngsters looked at Jess and Philip questioningly, Abi wondering fleetingly whether her mother was going to confess to a passionate affair with Catherine's father.

Reading Abi's mind, Philip smiled and said, 'Don't worry, Abilene, I'm still very happily married to Simone and there's nothing untoward going on between myself and your mother. There are two things you need to know. When Matilda left to find Theodore last night she took a key to Gideon's cottage with her. Lovely though the wood is, Theodore can't hide there for ever. Gideon's place is out of the way and unlikely to attract attention.

'I'm still a little angry about the manner in which Theodore moved on from my daughter as soon as he made Matilda's acquaintance, but I'm man enough to realise that these things happen. Besides,' Philip looked over to Catherine who was sitting at a table across the room, sharing what appeared to be a hilarious joke with Max, 'it doesn't seem to have done Cathie any harm. Anyway, I digress. I'm sure Dyer wouldn't have been able to resist a gloat if Matilda had fallen into the thugs' hands, so I think we can assume she reached 'Thwaite's Wood and Theodore safely. By now, Theodore should not only be in the safety of Gideon's cottage, he should also be reunited with his mother...'

Philip smiled as his words were greeted by uproar, as he'd expected them to be. Of all the people currently in the bar, only he, Simone and Jess were aware that Isabelle had returned, so he'd taken the youngsters totally by surprise. Eventually he shushed them, especially Abi and Cameron who were very vocally celebrating the fact that their aunt was alive, well and back in Blenthwaite.

'Hush now, hush! I know you're delighted, but remember who's just outside. If it gets back to His Lordshit that Isabelle's returned, he'll tear the place apart to find her.'

'OK, OK!' Abi calmed herself with difficulty and sat down beside Louis. 'Auntie Izzy's back home, though. Theo must be…'

'Theo never doubted she was alive,' said Louis. 'He told me when I went to London.'

'He told me too,' said Catherine, coming over with Max to join the conversation, 'and I told Mum and Daddy.'

'When Cathie acquainted Simone and me with the horrors of Theodore's life, we became determined to do whatever we could to help the poor lad. We were more than happy to play our part in Chloe and Brains's plan to get Theo away from His Lordshit and up to Blenthwaite for the wedding.'

'With the plan in motion,' said Jess, taking up the story, 'we realised it was the perfect time to get Izzy back home too. I spoke to Philip and Simone when they first came up to Blenthwaite and broached the idea of them meeting with Izzy…'

'Hang on a minute, Mam. Did you know where Izzy was, then?'

'Yes, Abilene. In Italy.'

'You knew all along and didn't tell us?'

'Izzy asked me not to tell you. It's not that she doesn't trust you, but… well, look at your reaction when you first heard she was back. You're young, you're impetuous…'

'And you thought we'd give her away?'

'No…'

'Did Chris know?'

'Yes, but no one else. Believe me, nothing you can say can match the tantrum Izzy had when she realised I'd been keeping things from her – things concerning her children. I'm going to have to live with the decisions I made, and I think – hope – Izzy now realises I made those decisions in good faith…'

'Would you have told Izzy if you'd known exactly how awful Theo's life had become?'

'I really don't know, Abilene. I'd want to know if someone was being that cruel to you or Cameron, be there to protect you, but in Izzy's case that would have meant walking to her death…'

'Don't beat yourself up, Jess,' said Lysander, collecting up empty glasses left over from the wedding celebrations. 'If anyone should be hanging their head in shame, it's me. I *did* have a fair idea how awful Theo's life had become – as did your parents, Adam, and all my former colleagues – but we did precisely nothing beyond burying our stupid sponsored heads in the sand. I'm amazed Theo can bring himself to speak to me…'

'Theo doesn't blame you, Dad,' said Louis.

'Do you know that for a fact, or are you just trying to make me feel better?'

'It's a fact. He told me last summer.'

'*Last* summer?' Lysander put a stack of empty pint glasses on the bar, then folded his arms and turned to face his son, realisation dawning. 'Oh, last summer when you disappeared in London and worried the life out of everyone. So you *did* see Theo, you git!'

Laughing, Louis nodded. 'I think it's safe for me to fess up now, Dad,' he said.

'You finally trust me, eh?'

'I finally trust you.' Lysander glowed with pride, but Louis wasn't going to let him off that easily. 'I must admit I was disappointed in the extreme when I realised you knew full well that he was locked away right above His Lordshit's office, but Theo told me not to be too hard on you. If anyone knows the repercussions of crossing His Lordshit it's Theo, so he never expected anyone else to risk it…'

'But *you* risked it, Louis,' said Abi proudly.

'And now we're all risking it,' added Jess, 'including you, Lysander, so back at you – stop beating yourself up.'

'Thank you.' Lysander smiled gratefully at Jess then continued his clean-up operation, spying a couple of abandoned champagne glasses on the windowsill. 'Ah,' he said, his smile fading as he peered out of the window, 'I think the repercussions have just started.'

'What do you mean, Dad?' asked Louis, joining Lysander by the window. 'Ooh, crap.'

Rushing over to the window, The White Lion's occupants crowded round Lysander and Louis, looking out into the street where Alan, Dex and Matilda were being confronted by a bloody-faced Dyer and the other thugs.

'Where is he, you little slut? Where's Lord Theodore?'

'Don't you *dare* call my daughter a slut,' yelled Alan, furiously trying to escape from Dex's restraining grip and run at Dyer.

'Who's going to stop me, faggot? Gonna slap me with your handbag, are you?'

'Looks like someone's already given you a slap, you disgusting creep. I'm going to find out who and shake their hand!'

'You'll get another kicking, you fucking queer, and we'll finish the job properly this time. Shame we didn't drown you last summer.'

'You fucking stay away from Al!' Dex took a threatening step towards Dyer, all pretence at holding back forgotten.

'And you're not going to get your filthy hands on Theo,' added Matilda, 'ever again!'

'Yeah?' Dyer was so angry he was virtually shrieking. 'Who's going to stop me?'

'We are,' said Louis, his level voice strong enough to silence both his friends and enemies.

Sneering, Dyer was about to argue until he saw whom Louis meant. The White Lion had emptied, its occupants now standing in solidarity behind Alan, Dex and Matilda, and all the while more and more Unsponsored were appearing in the street to add their support.

'It looks like your group is outnumbered, Dyer,' Louis continued, still speaking in a quietly menacing voice. 'You're not welcome here, Sponsors, so I suggest you leave – now. Blenthwaite protects its own, and by God that's what we intend to do.'

Chapter 22 – Trapped

Lord Bassenford was waiting in his office as his most trusted Sponsors arrived the following morning.

'No need to be shy, people,' he snarled, raising bloodshot eyes from his computer screen and slamming the morning papers on to his desk one by one, every front page headlining the story of Theo's disappearance. 'I know you'll all have seen what my apology of a son has done now...'

Pausing to draw a deep breath, Lord Bassenford continued.

'I haven't called you here today to discuss Theodore. He is *nothing* to me now. There are far more pressing issues we need to address.

'I'll begin with the subject of Lysander Trevelyan, who continues to be conspicuous by his absence. As you all know, I attended a wedding in the troublesome little village of Blenthwaite over the weekend. My brother-in-law's wedding. I'm not interested in discussing the ceremony, though. I'm interested in the fact Blenthwaite has become a hotbed of unsponsored activity, and Trevelyan appears to be heavily involved in this activity.'

Lord Bassenford drummed his fingers on his desk.

'I've had a look at recent records of Leisure and Fitness since I've been home, and they do not make happy reading. I won't bore you with the details – suffice to say Trevelyan has lost sight of the Scheme's aims.'

Mortimer O'Reilly looked as though he would be anything but bored by details of Lysander Trevelyan's failure to do his job, but Lord Bassenford addressed his head of household before the money man could summon the courage to speak up.

'Mooreland, show Ms Maloney in.' Unsmiling as ever, Mooreland left his place beside the office door and dutifully obeyed, returning a minute or two later with an attractive woman sporting an impressive mane of dark curls.

'Ladies and gentlemen,' said Lord Bassenford, 'I present to you Faye Maloney, the new Director of the Leisure and Fitness Sponsorship Group.'

This time, Mortimer found his voice without hesitation.

'Your Lordship, what about Trevelyan?'

'We'll come to that, Mortimer, but let's get through business first.' Addressing David and Julia Foster, Lord Bassenford said, 'From Trevelyan the elder to Trevelyan the younger. Your Adam seems to have struck up quite a friendship with Lysander's son. He told me you gave him the go-ahead to watch – what's his name? – training. Well, there's no need. The

Trevelyan boy will not be competing at the Olympics this summer.'

The Fosters looked horrified.

'David,' said Lord Bassenford, 'would you like to speak?'

'Yes, Your Lordship,' replied David Foster. 'Louis Trevelyan is, quite simply, the best British gymnast since... well, since Gideon Wallis. Wallis himself was the best British gymnast the world has ever seen. If you want the British gymnastics team to win gold medals...'

'I want the *sponsored* gymnastics team to win gold medals, David, not some unsponsored *scum.*'

David wisely shut up, despite knowing that no sponsored gymnast came close to Louis Trevelyan's talent.

'I've let you down, my friends,' said Lord Bassenford unexpectedly. 'I've been so caught up in the sense of occasion, with the Olympic Games being held here in the heart of the Sponsor-endorsed UK, that for a while I lost sight of the bigger picture. I promise you from now on my only priority will be the Scheme. I will expect the same level of commitment from all of you, and anyone delivering less than a hundred per cent will go the same way as Trevelyan.

'Julia, I now require you to contact your son. He can serve a useful purpose by providing a means of communication between us and that bloody village. Tell him that I need to speak with Lysander Trevelyan and his son.'

Establishing a visual link with Adam's laptop a few minutes later, Lord Bassenford immediately recognised the bar of The White Lion Inn.

'Ah, the unsponsored public house,' he said for the benefit of his inner circle, 'with all the good-for-nothing Unsponsored drinking their lives away. Good morning, Adam, have you carried out my orders?'

'Lysander is behind the bar, Louis is on his way,' replied Adam shortly, his failure to say 'Your Lordship' not going unnoticed.

'I see you're fast sinking into the deplorable way of life of the Unsponsored, Adam. Hanging around in pubs getting drunk all day, not showing respect to your superiors…'

Adam pulled a face. 'We're not getting drunk,' he said, 'we're cleaning.'

'Adam, I couldn't be less interested,' snapped Lord Bassenford. 'Put Lysander Trevelyan on.'

As Adam carried his laptop across the pub, Lysander came into view on His Lordship's big screen, casually dressed and wiping the bar with a wet cloth.

'Trevelyan,' roared Lord Bassenford, 'what the *hell* are you doing working behind an unsponsored bar?'

'Helping out, Your Lordship,' said Lysander, smiling pleasantly.

'So this is what you've been doing while Leisure and Fitness has been going to the dogs, is it?'

'Hardly going to the dogs,' replied Lysander, wringing out his cloth under a running tap then setting to work on another part of the bar. 'Last time I checked, and I do check regularly, Leisure and Fitness Sponsorship was more popular than it has ever been before.'

'Probably because you've gone soft, Trevelyan,' snapped Lord Bassenford. 'Letting people decide where and when to exercise, allowing your clubs to serve unlimited alcohol, ignoring blatant flouting of curfews. You've lost sight of the Scheme's basic aims – we make the decisions, the Sponsored reap the benefits…'

'With respect,' said Lysander, putting his cloth down and finally giving Lord Bassenford his full attention, 'leisure and fitness are lifestyle choices – *choices* being the operative word here.'

'You think we should go back to allowing those we sponsor to make mistakes and mess their lives up once more, like they used to before they had the Scheme to guide them?'

'You don't guide them,' retorted Lysander, 'you dictate to them…'

'Trevelyan, shut up. Your opinion is of no interest to me whatsoever as you're fired.'

A delighted Mortimer O'Reilly moved into a prime spot to view Lysander's reaction. To his dismay, far from being upset, Lysander gave an enormous snort of laughter.

'Trevelyan,' screamed Lord Bassenford as his former employee clutched on to the bar, tears streaming from his eyes, 'what is so damned funny?'

'I was under the impression I resigned at Christmas,' said Lysander, still chuckling. 'Have you finally accepted that resignation, then?'

'No, I never accepted your resignation. You were, until a moment ago, my employee. Now you're not. You're fired.'

'Very well then.' Scanning his former colleagues via the computers' visual connection, Lysander locked eyes with his replacement. 'Ahh, Faye Maloney,' he said with a grin. 'I might have known you'd be waiting in the wings to jump in my grave.'

'I have the aims of the Scheme at heart, unlike you, Lysander,' replied Faye, smiling smugly at her predecessor. 'You dug your own grave.'

'Enough,' snapped Lord Bassenford. 'I now need to speak to your son, Trevelyan. Where is he?'

'I'm here, Your Lordshit,' said Louis, appearing at Lysander's side. 'Is this going to take long? Only Gideon and I were working on a new floor routine…'

'Is Wallis with you? I want him to hear what I've got to say.'

Louis looked over his shoulder and called, 'Gideon, His Lordshit wants to talk to you too.'

As Gideon wheeled himself over to join the Trevelyans, Lord Bassenford regarded the three of them with narrowed eyes.

'Now you're here, Wallis,' he snarled, 'I'll keep this brief. I've had all I can take of you Unsponsored. Unless you, Trevelyan,' Lord Bassenford nodded at Louis, 'accept sponsorship, you will not be competing at the Olympics.'

'I will never accept sponsorship,' replied Louis.

'Then you will not compete at the Olympics. Simple as that.' Smiling grimly, His Lordship added, 'Oh, and one more thing – you may think you're very clever driving my men out of your little backwater, but you will soon find you are wrong. I'm going to crush the Unsponsored. I'm going to crush you once and for all.'

Clenching his hand into a fist to illustrate his point, Lord Bassenford cut off the connection with Blenthwaite and turned to his Sponsors.

'Later today, Faye, Mortimer and David will accompany Lady Marina and myself to Blenthwaite. Julia, I need you to stay here and oversee preparations for the Olympics, and Lady Rosanna will coordinate the little surprise I have in store for the London Unsponsored.' Lord Bassenford's eyes gleamed at mention of the little surprise, but he didn't elaborate beyond saying, 'I have no doubt that her desire to crush the Unsponsored matches my own.'

Sitting to the right of her father's desk, facing the occupants of the room, Rosanna nodded and smiled at Lord Bassenford's words, but her smile was unable to mask the sadness in her eyes. Never having believed herself to be sentimental, she had been taken by surprise to wake up that morning, fully recovered from her hangover, and discover she loved Adam so much that the pain of losing him was threatening to tear her apart.

Oblivious to his daughter's pain, Lord Bassenford leapt to his feet and concluded his speech.

'Those of you nominated to come to Blenthwaite have two hours to pack your essentials and be back here ready to go. So move!'

The Sponsors obeyed. One or two may even have bleated.

***

Following Lord Bassenford's abrupt goodbye, Lysander, Louis and Gideon continued to stare at the blank screen of Adam's laptop, unmoving and open-mouthed. Finally Adam walked over, shut the laptop down and turned to the trio.

'Well,' was all he could think of to say.

'Well what, Foster?' Gideon snapped.

'Well, what now?' said Louis, finding his voice at last. 'That kind of screws up our plans.'

'Well, I think an emergency meeting of Dory's Avengers is called for,' said Alan, who had been listening with interest to the conversation with Lord Bassenford.

'Is anyone capable of making a statement that doesn't start with "well"?' grumbled Gideon.

'Well, I think you're right, Al,' said Louis, grinning at Gideon. 'All of the Avengers, though?'

'Well, why not?' replied Alan.

Gideon roared that the joke had run its course.

'Sorry, Gideon,' said Alan with a chuckle. 'I think we need to get everyone together, and I mean everyone. Matilda's anxious to see Theo again, and I'd rather they were both here than out in the wilds.'

'Theo's in my cottage, Alan, hardly the wilds,' said Gideon. 'But I do see your point. After last night we've kind of declared war on the Sponsors, what with driving Dyer and the rest out of Blenthwaite. I can't see them staying away for ever, though, and you heard His Lordshit's parting shot. I think it's safety in numbers from now on.'

'I agree,' said Matilda, grinning sidelong at Alan. 'It's about time the lovely Theo became a permanent fixture in my bed.'

Unexpectedly, Alan grinned back at his daughter. 'Instead of tormenting me with yet more details of your sex life, Matilda,' he said, 'why don't you phone Faye and congratulate her on her new job?'

'I didn't realise you knew Faye, Al,' said Lysander.

'Yeah,' replied Alan, a little awkwardly. 'We... um... used to be in a band together.'

'Oh yes, I forgot she grew up round here. Keswick, wasn't it? So Faye was in a band?'

'She was, and a damn fine saxophonist too. Shame she sold out to greed and power.'

'Were you close then?'

'They were *very* close at least once.' Matilda's grin was back. 'She's my mother.'

Lysander's mouth dropped open and Matilda burst out laughing.

'Not a good look, Lysander, unless you're trying to catch flies. Cast your mind back to 1990: Dad, eighteen years old and totally beautiful, was trying to get out of a shitty relationship with some loser called Freddy – bit handy with his fists, by all accounts – and Faye offered him sanctuary in her flat. And her bed. Nine months later, Faye had a big round belly, and Dad had met and fallen in love with Dex. As soon as she'd popped me out, Faye disappeared down south in search of the goose that lays the golden sponsorship, and the rest is history. It was Dad and Dex who brought me up, so there's no reason why you would have known who my mam was. Faye and I have never been close.'

Thinking of Faye sitting in Lord Bassenford's office, newly appointed Director of Leisure and Fitness and keen advocate of the Scheme, Lysander didn't need to ask why.

'So, you're a Sponsor's daughter,' said Louis, playfully nudging Matilda in the ribs.

'Laugh it up, Lou-Lou,' retorted Matilda, nudging him right back. 'You've been son of Sponsor for long enough.' Sobering a little, Matilda turned to Louis's father. 'Talking of which, Lysander, now you're officially an ex-Sponsor, don't you think you'd better go and fetch Jenny from that sponsored school?'

'Hell, you're right,' he replied.

'And someone needs to fetch Theo and Izzy.'

'I'll go,' said Philip. 'I can take the Land Rover, and I'm probably the one person the thugs won't stop and search if they return. At least, I hope so.'

'Are we adopting a siege mentality then?' asked Abi.

'I think it would be an idea, until we know what the thugs' next move is going to be, for us all to stay together here in The Lion, yes.'

'In that case, I'm going to get Mam from the surgery, then nip home and pack some spare clothes. Come on, Cam, leave Chlo in peace for five minutes. You can give me a hand.'

'Good idea,' said Sarah, turning to Louis. 'We'll do the same.'

Georgia was already on the phone to Chris's veterinary practice. The poorly inhabitants of Blenthwaite, both human and animal, were going to have to fend for themselves for a while.

'Would you mind chucking some stuff in a bag for me, Phil?' asked Gideon as Philip returned from his room at the inn, car keys in hand. 'I don't have many clothes, so you may as well bring the lot.'

'No worries,' he replied. 'What about food?'

'Matty and I did a massive groceries shop this morning, and we've got plenty of champagne left over from the wedding in case we need cheering up,' said Dex. 'We should have enough food in the freezers to last us all at least a month. I must have had a premonition.'

'Who are you, Mortimer O'Reilly?'

'Oh God, I hope not,' said Lysander with feeling.

'Not missing your old sparring partner then, Lysander?' Philip said with a laugh as he headed for the door. 'Right, soonest begun, soonest done, I'll catch you all later.'

And with that, Philip, followed by Louis, Sarah, Abi and her brother, left the relative safety of the pub to prepare for whatever Lord Bassenford was planning to throw at them next.

***

An hour or so later, a rather unwieldy cartoon ghost clambered out of Philip's Land Rover and disappeared into the pub. Once Philip had returned from parking his vehicle, he followed the spectre inside, glanced around the room to make sure everyone had returned safely, then locked and bolted the door behind him.

As soon as the bolts were in place, the 'ghost' gave a wriggle and shrugged off its white shroud, it's haunting at an end. While Theo folded the large sheet that had protected his and his mother's anonymity on the way back from Gideon's cottage, Isabelle held out her arms to family and friends she'd missed so much over the last ten years, delighted to see each and every one of them again. If she could have enveloped them all in her embrace at once, she would have done so.

Once the emotional reunion had calmed down a little, Gideon called for order, impatient to discuss the eventful morning.

'Now everyone's here,' he said, 'shall we get down to business?'

There was a general murmuring of assent as everyone turned their attention to Gideon.

'Do you want me to leave?' asked Adam. 'Only my parents are Sponsors.'

'Don't be daft, Adam!' replied Matilda. 'No one's going to hold you responsible for what your parents do. If that were the case I'd have to leave too, given Faye's latest career move.'

'Yeah, so would I if Dad hadn't been sacked this morning,' added Louis.

'And I *definitely* shouldn't be here,' said Theo, grinning.

Laughing, Adam held up his hands.

'OK, OK, point taken. Thank you!'

'Wonderful,' said Gideon, his voice heavy with sarcasm. 'If everyone has finally finished beating themselves up for their unfortunate parentage, can we *please* get down to business?' He waited for everyone to settle down, then continued, 'The most pressing concern I have is that His Lordshit has withdrawn Louis's

Olympic entry. I don't mind saying I'm devastated…'

'How do you think I feel?' interrupted Louis.

'Devastated too, I should imagine,' said Gideon. Addressing everyone in the room, he added, 'Louis has put so much work into his training since Christmas.'

'So have you, Gid…'

'Being devastated does *not* give you the right to call me Gid, Trevelyan!'

'Yes, Trevelyan,' said Theo, chuckling. 'Learn some respect.'

'Button it, St Benedict!' retorted Louis.

'Excuse me, less of the St Benedict…'

'Oh, I do beg your pardon, Lord Theodore.' Louis sank into a deep bow. 'Has this wretched oik offended your aristocratic sensibilities?'

Grabbing every cushion within arm's reach, Theo launched an energetic attack on Louis, who dodged the blows with an agility only a gymnast could possess. Everyone else in the room cheered and whistled in support of the impromptu entertainment, with the exception of an exasperated Gideon.

'Will you two young idiots please *calm down?*' he roared.

Laughing, Theo flung the cushions back in the general direction of their seats then snuggled

503

up next to Matilda, while Louis crossed over to the bar and held up a lager glass.

'May I, Dex?' he asked, pouring himself a pint as soon as Dex nodded his approval. 'Don't look at me like that, Gideon,' Louis added, glancing up at his mentor. 'I'm not competing at the Olympics, so why can't I have a beer?'

'Why aren't you competing at the Olympics?' asked Brains.

'Oh come on!' Louis set his pint down and leant on the bar, looking in disbelief at Brains. 'You're supposed to be the clever one round here. His Lordshit said, "No sponsorship, no entry"...'

'And you're going to do as His Lordshit says?' Brains interrupted. 'Without question? You might as well get sponsorship if you're going to let him dictate to you like that.'

'Brains is right you know, Lou,' said Matilda.

'Of course he's right,' replied Chloe. 'But don't just blame Louis. We all gave up on the Olympics the second His Lordshit said no.'

'So what do you suggest I do then?' asked Louis, a little stung by the implication that he'd unquestioningly do whatever His Lordship commanded. 'Just waltz in and say: "Hi, I'm Louis and I'm a gymnast. Watch this..."?'

'I may have a little influence there,' said Philip. 'I can at least work on ways to gain you entry to the Olympic arena, Louis…'

'Er, hold on a minute, Philip,' snapped Lysander. 'I don't actually like the idea of you sending my son into what is potentially a very dangerous situation.'

'Louis wouldn't be alone,' said Abi, turning to Lysander. 'I'd be there right behind him.'

'Count me in, Abi,' said Matilda without hesitation.

'I knew you'd say that, baby,' said Alan, then he pulled himself together and added, 'I'll be there too, Louis.'

'And me, of course,' added Dex.

'You see, Lysander?' said Matilda. 'No one's sending Louis into a dangerous situation alone. We're all in this together.'

'All the same, Matty,' said Louis, 'even if Philip can organise some way of getting a bunch of Unsponsored into the Olympics – and please don't think I'm ungrateful, Philip – I can't just go out in front of the judges and leap on the parallel bars. I'd have to qualify, and it's way too late for that now.'

Before anyone could respond to Louis's statement, the peace and tranquillity of Blenthwaite was shattered as a convoy of people carriers roared along the main street, screeching to a halt outside The White Lion. Watching from the window, the Unsponsored looked on in dismay as Stephen Dyer got out of the lead vehicle and stood facing the inn, a self-satisfied smirk on his face. Behind him, a legion of sponsored thugs leapt from the other cars and assembled ready for combat.

'Still think you can make us leave, unsponsored scum?' yelled Dyer. 'Let's be 'avin' yer, then.'

Before Dyer had finished speaking, Matilda was heading for the door. Louis darted out from behind the bar and was at her side in an instant, their fathers and friends, including a balaclava-clad Isabelle, hot on their heels as they rose to the challenge of the hated Dyer.

'Well, Matty,' Louis said, 'it seems we're going into that dangerous situation a little sooner than expected.'

'Aye, Lou,' replied Matilda, looking as though she was thoroughly enjoying the experience, 'and like I said, we're all in it together.'

***

Anxious to return to Cumbria as quickly as possible, Lord Bassenford had hired a helicopter and top quality pilot to make the journey, and there was quite a reception committee waiting for him as he emerged on to the wide street in front of the sponsored Blenthwaite Hotel. Thugs were standing in formation on the forecourt looking immensely pleased with themselves, none more so than Stephen Dyer. Lord Bassenford didn't even need to ask – he knew from past experience that Dyer only ever looked happy when he'd inflicted a large amount of pain somewhere – but he asked nonetheless.

'It went well, Stephen?'

'All according to plan, Your Lordship. The Unsponsored didn't stand a chance. We must have outnumbered them four to one.'

'Did they actually think they could keep us out of the village?'

'They tried, Your Lordship.' Dyer sniggered. 'We taught them otherwise.'

'Excellent. Where are they now?'

'White Lion, Your Lordship.'

'All of them?'

'Yes, Your Lordship.'

'Theodore? And his unsponsored tart?'

'Yes, Your Lordship.'

'Trevelyan? Barrington? Montfiore?'

'All of them, Your Lordship.'

'Is that blood on your shirt, Stephen?'

Lord Bassenford's eyes gleamed with amusement and Dyer's smirk widened.

'It certainly is, Your Lordship. Lysander Trevelyan's, to be precise.'

Lord Bassenford grunted his approval.

'Top quality work, Stephen. I...' His Lordship's smile vanished abruptly. 'What the... where... where the devil is she going?'

His younger daughter, holdall in hand, was sauntering nonchalantly past the confused looking thugs who'd been commissioned with guarding The White Lion.

'Marina!' yelled Lord Bassenford. 'Stop! Stop her, you fools!'

Too late. As the brain-dead guards finally reacted, the pub door opened momentarily and a hand yanked Marina inside. For a few seconds the stunned silence was broken only by the clunk-click of the bolts once again securing The White Lion from the inside, then it was shattered completely by an ear-splitting scream of rage from the Head of the Sponsorship Scheme.

**

Marina stumbled into The White Lion, beaming around at the Unsponsored while whoever had pulled her through the door locked and bolted it again.

'Hello, everyone,' she said as her father's howl of anguish echoed around the village street.

'Hello, darling.' Behind Marina, a figure stepped into a patch of sunlight shining through the window and pulled a balaclava from its head.

'Eh?' Marina looked questioningly at her brother, who raised his eyebrows and made a circular 'Why don't you turn round?' gesture with his finger. Doing just that, Marina gasped, stammered a couple of incoherent words, then felt joy such as she'd never experienced before when her mother wrapped loving arms round her and held her close for the first time in ten years.

As Marina clung on to Isabelle and her heart-rate gradually returned to normal, Theo filled her in on everything that had happened in the short time since she'd returned to London. Meanwhile, all around them the Unsponsored tended to each other's wounds.

'What do you think His Lordshit has in store for us next?' Jess asked, holding a hastily improvised icepack, also known as a bag of frozen peas, to Lysander's swollen face.

'Dunno,' replied Dex, wincing as Alan cleaned the blood from a nasty cut on his ear, 'but we're probably not going to like it much.'

'If I were to hazard a guess, he's cutting us off from the rest of the Unsponsored.'

'I think you're right, Jess,' said Max. 'His Lordshit knows we've got a network, and you don't have to be Brains to work out that it runs from Blenthwaite.'

'And we've just seen what happens when we try to leave the inn.'

'What about Philip, though?' asked Alan.

'Good point, Al,' said Chloe. 'His Lordshit can hardly hold Philip prisoner in Blenthwaite, if that is his intention, nor Simone and Cathie for that matter…'

'And I can get word back to the Unsponsored in London,' said Philip. 'In fact, what am I thinking? I'll phone them right now…'

'What is it, Phil?' asked Simone, first to notice dismay clouding her husband's face.

'No network available,' Philip replied, looking up from his mobile phone.

Alan crossed over to The White Lion's phone. 'No tone whatsoever,' he said after listening to the silent handset for a few moments. 'Seems we've already been cut off.'

'What about the computers?' asked Louis, but Chris shook his head.

'The Wi-Fi's supplied by the telephone company. If the phone's cut off, we've got no Internet connection either.' Frowning, Chris looked at his own mobile phone and added, 'His Lordshit's been thorough. I've got no network either. I wouldn't even bother trying, Adam.'

'You're right,' said Adam, staring at his laptop. 'No connection available.'

'And the bastards have us surrounded,' added Matilda, having checked every entrance and found sponsored thugs guarding each one.

'Oh wonderful!' snarled Gideon. 'How on earth is Louis supposed to continue with his training if we're stuck in here?'

'Surely they'll let us go over to the studio,' said Louis. 'There are enough of them to keep an eye on us, make sure we're not making a break for it.'

'Oh yes, like I'm the ideal candidate to make a break for it…' began Gideon, but he was interrupted abruptly by Lysander.

'Louis, there is no way I'm letting you go to that studio. No bloody way.'

'But, Dad, like Brains said, we can't just give up on the Olympics…'

'I don't give a fuck about the Olympics,' yelled the normally even-tempered Lysander, taking everyone by surprise. 'You're far more important to me than the Olympics, Louis. The thugs will be delighted if you and Gideon voluntarily separate yourselves from the rest of us…'

'Divide and conquer,' said Marina, still snuggling up to her mother on one of the pub's fat sofas. 'It's a favourite concept of Father's. That's why he kept me separate from Theo for so many years.'

'Listen to Marina, Louis!' begged Lysander. 'You're my son, and I want you here where I can protect you.'

'I am an adult now, Dad, in case you hadn't noticed…'

'We could *all* go to the studio,' suggested Abi.

'That's just crazy talk, Sis,' snapped Cameron. 'Why would we go from The Lion, which has bedrooms, provisions, plenty of room, more than one shower, and beer, beer, beer, to maroon ourselves in Gideon's studio instead?'

Louis threw his head back in frustration.

'Why don't you train in Dex's gym?' asked Jenny, pulling on her brother's sleeve and looking up at him with serious blue eyes.

'What's that, poppet?'

'Dex's gym. In the cellar.'

Louis looked enquiringly at Dex.

'Yeah, Jenny's right,' said Dex, ruffling the child's hair. 'I got the cellar converted last year. After Al met with that spot of bother while he was out running, we decided we'd rather keep fit in the Sponsor-free safety of our own home. We've got so much space down there I had plenty of room to store all your original apparatus too, Louis – you know, when His Lordshit so generously kitted you guys out last December.'

Louis grinned at the memory. Following his decision to include Louis in Team GB, Lord Bassenford had indeed kitted the Blenthwaite studio out with brand new state-of-the-art gymnastic apparatus, even delighting the eternally cynical Gideon.

'Do you want to come look?'

'You bet!' Louis was on his feet in an instant, following Dex down to the cellar where his familiar old apparatus was waiting to be set up.

'Dexter Montfiore, you're a genius!' he said, hugging Dex in delight then thundering back up the cellar stairs to tell Gideon all about it. 'Dex has got everything we need, Gid. There's loads of space too, even for the rings…'

'And how am I supposed to get down to the cellar, you moron?' growled Gideon, his bad mood compounded by Louis once again calling him Gid.

'I'll carry you…'

'You'll do no such thing.'

'OK,' snapped Louis, losing his temper all of a sudden. 'I'll go and train on my own while you sit up here sulking. While you sit up here *giving up*. Whatever you decide, Gideon, *I'm* going to train.'

Gideon didn't speak for a moment, and when he did he addressed Dex rather than Louis.

'You seem to be able to achieve a lot without sponsorship, Dexter.'

'I've got money,' replied Dex, meeting Gideon's gaze. 'Money can still open the odd closed door, even in Sponsorsville. Besides that, Georgia and I are kind of exempt from sponsorship…'

'Rubbish! The Sponsors have been after you for years to get The Lion endorsed.'

'I don't mean The Lion, I mean us personally,' said Dex patiently. 'The Sponsors only force their control on the British, and we're American. If I can't buy what I want here, I can buy it from the country of my birth, and there's nothing the Sponsors can do about it.'

'So, Gideon, if you've finished insinuating that my Dex has sold out to the Sponsors,' snapped Alan, 'an apology wouldn't go amiss.'

'It's OK, Al,' said Dex, but Gideon apologised anyway.

'Alan's right, Dex. I'm sorry for being so rude. I suppose we're all a little overwrought at the moment, but I had no right to take it out on you. It's essential that we remain strong and united, now more than ever.'

'Dory's Avengers!' said Jenny, balancing on the wheel of Gideon's chair and giving him a hug.

'Dory's Avengers indeed, young lady, and what a clever idea you had to use Dex's gym.' Grinning at his protégé, Gideon added, 'By hook or by crook, Louis Trevelyan, you *will* compete for Great Britain in this summer's Olympic

Games. It's finally time for the Unsponsored to come out of the shadows.'

Part Four – London Calling

Chapter 23 – Oh What A Birthday Surprise

A few days after Louis's training for the Olympics resumed in the cellar of The White Lion, Lord Bassenford was sitting in the bar of the Blenthwaite Hotel, deep in thought following a phone call from his London-based daughter.

'Father, I hate to disturb you when you're so busy,' Rosanna had said, 'but we've been receiving a number of phone calls from the UK branch of Euro Logistics. They can't contact Philip Lorimer…'

'Obviously,' sneered Lord Bassenford. 'We can hardly have anyone in that wretched inn at liberty to phone round the country. You know that, Rosanna.'

'But Father, Euro Logistics UK can't, um, they can't…'

'Spit it out, Rosanna!'

Rosanna's sigh carried clearly from London to Cumbria.

'As you know, Father, the Olympic organisers have been working with Euro Logistics, but the operation's rather ground to a halt.'

'Nonsense. How can it grind to a halt?'

'It's not nonsense, I'm afraid, Father. Apparently the equipment in transit is so important, um, well, it can't be transported without Philip's go ahead…'

'Oh, damn!'

Lord Bassenford was furious with himself. He'd promised his Sponsors that he wouldn't get distracted by sentimentality any more, and instead he'd become distracted by his overwhelming desire to crush the Unsponsored. Of course, any opposition to the Scheme must be stamped out, but to imprison the head of Euro Logistics UK with the Olympics coming up? That was just careless.

Deciding there wasn't a moment to lose, Lord Bassenford summoned an unhappy Mortimer O'Reilly from his afternoon nap and barked out a set of instructions.

***

Sitting chatting to Isabelle on the window seat of The White Lion, Jess was astonished to notice the Director of Financial Sponsorship approaching the pub, trembling visibly.

'Mr O'Reilly,' she called, crossing over to the door as a timorous knock sounded, 'what do you want?'

'I have a m-m-message,' stammered Mortimer, 'c-concerning Philip…'

'Are you alone?' asked Jess.

'I am.'

Turning to the assembled company, Jess shrugged helplessly. It was Lysander who suggested they let Mortimer in.

'He's a coward, he won't try anything silly. I for one would like to hear what he's got to say…'

'And so would I,' interrupted Philip, 'being as it concerns me.'

Nodding, Jess waited until Isabelle had disappeared into the back room and Theo had descended into the cellar to inform Louis and Gideon of the surprise visitor, then let Mortimer into the pub.

'Morti!' said Lysander, squeezing the money man's chubby cheeks as Jess bolted the door behind him. 'I've missed you, you big, fat charlatan…'

'Dad, don't bully him,' said Louis as he and Theo emerged from the cellar and plonked Gideon and his wheelchair down.

'What, not even a tiny bit?'

'*No*, Dad. Seems you still have a bit of the Sponsor left in your soul even after all this time.'

Suitably admonished, Lysander went back behind the bar and showed off his prowess with a cocktail-shaker.

'Don't be scared, Mr O'Reilly,' Louis said, walking over to the money man. 'We won't hurt you.'

Mortimer looked apprehensively at the bolted door blocking his path to freedom.

'You're free to go as soon as you've passed on your message. The locked door's our insurance policy against them.' Louis gestured out of the window at the ever-present gang of thugs.

'Here you are, Mortimer, drink this,' Theo said, offering a cocktail to the money man. 'It'll steady your nerves a bit.'

Unconvinced, Mortimer said, 'Trevelyan mixed it, didn't he?'

'Yes,' called Lysander from the bar. 'It's a heady mix of arsenic and cyanide. Sup it down, Morti old bean.'

'*Dad!*' yelled Louis, while Gideon and one or two others in the bar stifled laughs. Turning back to Mortimer, Louis added, 'Theo's right, Mr O'Reilly, and I promise you it's perfectly safe.'

Feeling rather backed into a corner, Mortimer took the cocktail in trembling hands and sipped it. It turned out to be delicious, and did indeed calm his nerves.

'Now,' said Louis, watching with some amusement as Mortimer drained his glass and smacked his lips in appreciation, 'I'm sure

Philip's dying to know what this is all about, and I think I can speak for everyone when I say the rest of us are curious too.'

'Ah yes. Mr Lorimer, His Lordship wishes to extend his sincere apologies to you. We didn't realise you were here with the Unsponsored until your colleagues at Euro Logistics UK made us aware that you were missing, and His Lordship put two and two together. Of course, you and your family are free to return to London any time you wish.'

'Odd that my mobile phone was cut off, being as His Lordshit didn't know I was here,' said Philip, noticing Mortimer wince at the offensive name the Unsponsored used for his boss. 'However, I will play the game and pretend it was all just a big misunderstanding. I realise that you are simply the messenger here, Mr O'Reilly, for which I thank you.'

'His Lordship…'

'Excuse me,' Chloe said, 'don't you mean His Lord*shit*?'

'No I do not, young lady,' said Mortimer. 'Lord Bassenford is my boss, and that's how I'd like it to stay. I'm in enough trouble as it is…'

Mortimer shut up abruptly, but it was too late. Lysander immediately pounced on his loose words.

'I wondered why you were exiled up here, Morti old chum. Been a naughty boy, have you?'

Mortimer looked hopefully at Louis, expecting the young man to pull his father up again, but he was to be disappointed. Louis simply stared back at him, eyebrows raised in anticipation.

With a sigh, Mortimer addressed his reply to Louis. 'Actually, the reason I'm in Blenthwaite has something to do with you, young man. His Lordshit… er, Lordship…' Ignoring the titters of the Unsponsored at his slip of the tongue, Mortimer ploughed on. 'His Lord*ship* thinks you're the subject of a prediction I made many years ago…'

'Yeah, I know,' said Louis with a chuckle.

'You're not. I've never had the gift of sight…'

'No shit, Sherlock,' sneered Lysander.

'Oh, for God's sake, Trevelyan, shut up!' shouted Mortimer unexpectedly, prompting an 'Ooooh!' from his unrepentant nemesis. Doing his best to ignore Lysander's contemptuous laughter, Mortimer continued, 'Unfortunately, His Lordship still seems to believe the prediction is true and insists I have to stay here to witness the destruction of everything you and your friends hold dear…'

'That sounds fun,' said Louis, wrinkling his nose.

'So why is Faye here?' asked Matilda. 'And Adam's dad?'

'At our last Sponsors' meeting in London, His Lordship reminded us how harshly he used to deal with Lord Theodore whenever he disagreed with the Scheme…'

Theo drew a sharp intake of breath, and Matilda slipped a reassuring arm around him.

'…and he remarked he'd not hesitate to deal even more harshly with Louis here.'

Behind the bar, Lysander's mockery stopped abruptly.

'Over my dead body,' he growled.

'Aye, and mine,' said Abi.

'And ours,' added Sarah, laying a hand on Gideon's shoulder as he nodded in agreement.

'Yes, but what's that got to do with Faye?' asked Matilda.

'She's here because you're *here*,' Mortimer replied, looking at Matilda and waving a hand around the room. 'His Lordship wants David and Faye to remember at all times that he'll deal just as harshly with their son or daughter…'

There was a screech of feedback as Alan dumped Theo's Les Paul unceremoniously on the stage.

'Ditto Lysander's comment,' he snapped.

Turning towards the stage to address Alan, Mortimer said, 'You're an amazing guitarist. I often hear you playing as I walk past – not dissimilar to Gary Moore's style, if I may say so.'

'You certainly may,' said a very flattered Alan.

'I'm guessing you must be Alan Santiago.'

'Yes, I am, but I wasn't aware I was famous.'

'Oh yes – *infamous* even,' said Mortimer with a chuckle. 'It would seem that Faye's still got quite a hefty crush on you. She talks about you a lot – I don't think she realises she's doing it half the time, especially when His Lordship's around. It seems a little tactless to fantasise about one man while sharing the bed of another…'

'*What?*' said Matilda.

'Oh, don't you know? Your mother's relationship with His Lordship has gone, um, well, rather beyond platonic.'

Matilda shook her head and smiled wryly.

'Actually, that doesn't surprise me much when I think about it, Mr O'Reilly. Faye has a habit of getting on in life by spreading her legs – I'll wager that's how she won promotion to Leisure and Fitness Director.'

'I'll wager,' said Mortimer, smirking sidelong at Lysander, 'it's not the first time a Leisure and Fitness Director has won promotion that way.'

Lysander slammed the glass he'd been drying on to the bar.

'Come over here and say that, O'Reilly…'

Mortimer actually laughed out loud for a second, then composed himself and addressed Philip.

'Mr Lorimer, Lord Bassenford suggests you leave as soon as possible…'

'I'm reluctant to take orders from your tyrannical boss, Mr O'Reilly, but I will do as he wishes. Only because it coincides with my own wishes, though.'

'Thank you.' Clearing his throat, Mortimer returned his gaze to Alan and said, 'She's bound to quiz me, so I'd better ask – do you have a message for Faye?'

Alan picked up Theo's Les Paul and played a guitar riff that the music-loving Mortimer recognised as being from a song called *Get Over It*.

'Um, er, right then,' spluttered Mortimer, his brief flirtation with a sense of humour clearly at an end. 'I'll, um, tell her that. Perhaps…'

'Come on, Mr O'Reilly,' said Jess gently, patting the nervous money man on the arm. 'I'll see you out.'

Nodding around the room as Jess unbolted the door, Mortimer allowed himself a second or two to savour the relaxed camaraderie of the Unsponsored, then stooped his shoulders and left The White Lion to return to the tension and aggression of his sponsored world.

***

The moment Mortimer left the inn, Philip followed the money man outside and backed his Land Rover up to the door. He and his family then gathered their things together to make their journey home, returning to the bar when their packing was complete to say their farewells.

As a forlorn Max took Catherine's hands, Simone and Philip looked at each other, a silent message passing between them. Then Simone turned to the young journalist.

'Do you want to come with us, Max?'

Punching the air in delight, Max sprang across the room and engulfed Simone in a bear hug.

'That'll be a yes, then!' she said, laughing.

'It makes perfect sense, Simone,' Max said. 'Then I can resurrect the *Unsponsored Newsletter*...'

'Yes, I'm sure that's all you've got on your mind,' said Simone with a knowing grin at her daughter.

'But I doubt the thugs will let you leave, Max,' said Dex.

'They've not got a brain cell between them, Dex,' replied Theo. 'As long as all they see is the Land Rover leaving with Philip, Simone and Cathie in it, they'll consider His Lordshit's orders to have been carried out.'

'But it *won't* just have Philip, Simone and Cathie in it,' wailed Max.

'Listen to me, Max!' said Theo. 'I said as long as that's all they *see*. Philip has lots of space to conceal you until you're well clear of Blenthwaite.'

'Of course!' Max's beaming smile reappeared. 'Sorry to be leaving Dory's Avengers without a drummer,' he said, 'but I'm sure Ads can fill in for me.'

'I probably won't be very good…'

'You should have heard Max's drumming when the band first started,' Abi said with a grin. 'You can't be any worse, Ads.'

'I'll let that one go, Abilene,' said Max, 'being as I'm terrified of you. She broke my nose once, Ads.'

'You deserved it back then,' replied Abi, laughing. It was hard to believe that Abi had once loathed Max; over time, since his rejection of sponsorship, they'd become firm friends. Hugging him warmly, she added, 'Take care, Max, I'm going to miss you.'

As Max disappeared upstairs to pack, Simone said, 'Does anyone else want to come with us? I think we can probably manage one more stowaway.'

'Sarah?' asked Lysander. 'Do you want to go and check your brother's OK?'

Sarah looked undecided for a moment, then came to a decision.

'No,' she said. 'Much as I love Rick, Lisa and the kids, my heart is here with Louis and Jenny. Oh, and Gideon…'

'*Me?*'

'Yes you, you silly man. I thought you'd guessed by now…'

'Urgency, everyone,' said Philip. 'The thugs will get suspicious if it takes us much longer to load up the car, then no one will be coming with us.'

Reappearing in the bar with his hastily packed holdall, Max wished everyone luck then dived into the back of Philip's Land Rover, concealing himself under the Lorimers' coats.

'Looks like Max can't wait to get away from us,' said Louis with a laugh. 'Anyone else? Theo? Not missing Kensington, are you?'

'Piss off!'

'Obviously not.' Louis grinned at Theo then scanned the room, his gaze coming to rest on the London Unsponsored. 'It's between you guys, I think. Everyone else has too much of a reason to stay.'

'I'll go, if that's OK?' said Jim, the man who had unceremoniously hauled Louis into the London warehouse the previous summer. 'Brains, take care of my stuff, will ya, please? Don't want to hold the Lorimers up with my packing.'

As soon as Jim had concealed himself alongside Max, the Lorimers climbed into their Land Rover to begin their long journey home. The Unsponsored left behind in The White Lion packed into the doorway to wave them off, then locked and bolted the door and turned their attention to Sarah.

'Right,' said Louis, 'you and Gideon, eh?'

'First I've heard of it,' said Gideon, the gleam in his eyes belying his trademark growl.

Blushing slightly, Sarah repeated, 'I thought you'd guessed, Gideon.'

'Guessed what?'

'That I'm crazy about you.'

Gideon gaped, for once rendered speechless.

'Gideon,' said Sarah, looking a little apprehensive, 'say something.'

'You can wipe that frown off your lovely face,' he replied, dimples in his cheeks heralding a smile of pure joy, 'because, my dear Sarah, the feeling's mutual…'

He didn't manage to say any more before Sarah engulfed him in her arms and kissed him soundly, their friends cheering in delight at the unexpected romantic turn of events. As the band, with its newly appointed drummer, launched into a spontaneous rendition of *Love Is in the Air*, Gideon whispered to Sarah that his legs might be useless, but the rest of his body was still in full working order, and with that they disappeared into his temporary bedroom on the ground floor of the inn. Meanwhile, the thugs continued to mill around outside, listening to the happy sounds coming from The White Lion and wondering if the Unsponsored had finally gone mad.

***

The euphoria following the Lorimers' escape and Sarah's declaration of love carried the Unsponsored in The White Lion through the next couple of days, but like all good things, it couldn't last for ever. As boredom started to set in, Theo in particular found it increasingly hard to bear being a prisoner for the second time in his young life. In a bid to ward off uncharacteristic feelings of hopelessness, he clung desperately to his one connection with the outside world, becoming addicted to radio as he'd once been addicted to television.

'I like the music,' he insisted, ignoring his companions' moans about the endless stream of Sponsor propaganda and tweaking the dial to find a clearer signal.

It was via the radio that news of Lord Bassenford's surprise for the London Unsponsored came through on the evening of Theo's birthday at the end of June. As Gideon and Louis emerged from the cellar after their day's training, Theo was listening intently to Faye Maloney extolling the virtues of a new leisure and fitness complex planned for South London.

'Yes, it's wonderful,' she chirped. 'It's an area we've neglected for too long, as anyone looking at the awful high-rise slums we cleared today to make way for the first phase of the project will have realised...'

'She's out there in the street,' said Matilda in disgust, glowering through the window at Faye, 'bold as brass, the old tart.'

Faye gave Matilda a cheery wave. Matilda gave Faye the finger.

'Faye Maloney there,' said the radio presenter, 'Director of Leisure and Fitness, speaking from Blenthwaite in Cumbria. As Ms Maloney hinted, the first wave of the extensive slum demolitions planned for South London took place today in Walworth...'

'Turn that up,' said Sarah sharply.

'...make way for a fitness and hotel complex to benefit the Sponsored. The Unsponsored previously living in the slums had a very generous two weeks to find alternative dwellings...'

'Words straight out of His Lordshit's mouth,' murmured Theo.

'...many have gone to ground. The Sponsored remain baffled as to the attitude of the Unsponsored, none of whom were available for comment...'

'None were *invited* to comment, you mean, you brainwashed cretin,' snarled Sarah.

'...His Lordship, in his benevolence, has done them a favour. The slums weren't fit for human habitation...'

'Turn that off, Theo,' said Sarah, her eyes brimming with tears. 'I can't listen to any more. For God's sake, when will that bastard stop trying to destroy us?'

'When he's succeeded,' said Gideon, wheeling himself over to take her in his arms. 'Do you wish you'd gone home with Philip now?'

'I'm already home,' she mumbled into his chest.

'That's rather killed the party spirit,' said Theo. 'I'm so sorry, Sarah. Your brother lives in Walworth, doesn't he?'

Sarah raised her head.

'Well, he did. I don't believe for one moment that His Lordshit choosing to start this crap in Walworth is a coincidence.'

'No,' agreed Theo. 'And I don't believe him choosing to start it today is a coincidence either.'

'His Lordshit's outside with Faye and the radio guys,' Matilda reported from the window seat. 'Shall we go and kick some Sponsor arse, Sarah?'

'We'll do better that that, Matty,' Sarah replied, the sparkle back in her eyes. 'We'll celebrate Theo's birthday like there's no tomorrow and show that inhuman bastard it'll take more than his dirty tricks to crush us. How are we doing for champagne, Dex?'

Dex and Alan were already behind the bar, a bottle of champagne in each hand and big grins on their faces.

***

Lord Bassenford was indeed outside The White Lion, confident that news of his birthday surprise for Theo would have filtered through to the Unsponsored by now. As the evening sunlight reflected back at him from the long white frontage of the inn, he waited eagerly for some kind of reaction, but was disappointed to hear the unmistakable sounds of partying from within rather than the weeping and wailing he'd been anticipating. Exasperated, he was on the verge of ordering his companions back to the Blenthwaite Hotel when the door opened and Alan appeared briefly, shooting a champagne cork into the street and offering a cheeky salute to the Sponsors. Despite the fact the man was camper than camp, Faye's tongue appeared between her lips as she gazed longingly in his direction, and Lord Bassenford's temper snapped.

'Faye,' he roared, 'come with me. Now!'

Grabbing her by the arm, he frogmarched her back to the Blenthwaite Hotel and up to their luxurious room, letting loose a furious tirade the moment he'd slammed the door shut behind them.

'I've had enough of your disrespect, Maloney. You are sharing my bed – *my* bed. You are *mine!* What the hell do you think you're doing, lusting after that unsponsored poof? He's never going to fancy you unless you grow a cock and balls, you stupid woman.'

When Faye didn't reply, Lord Bassenford landed a vicious punch in her face, grabbing her shirt to prevent her from falling then slamming her violently against the wall.

'I am going to crush that scum in The White Lion, Maloney, starting with the poof you're so hot for. I'm going to hurt him. Hurt him badly. I'm fucking going to hurt him!'

Every time Lord Bassenford said the word 'hurt' he slapped Faye hard across the mouth, and as he threw her on to the bed and tore her clothes off, she could already feel her lips swelling painfully. Faye had always enjoyed sex in the past, usually the kinkier, the better, but as Lord Bassenford forced himself roughly inside her and pounded his way to a one-sided climax, she discovered that rape held no enjoyment whatsoever.

Chapter 24 – Dex's Avengers

The London Unsponsored were furious. For decades they'd accepted all that Lord Bassenford had thrown at them, preferring to remain under the radar and enjoy as peaceful a life as possible, but this time he'd gone too far. He had stolen their rights, their livelihoods, their homes – everything he could possibly take, he'd taken from them, and there are few adversaries more formidable than those with nothing left to lose. Max Barrington made sure word spread around the country like wildfire, working feverishly to release up-to-the-minute newsletters as blocks of flats were systematically destroyed, and in an unprecedented show of solidarity, more and more Unsponsored were arriving in London every day to offer their support.

Max was also using the medium of television to full advantage whenever the opportunity presented itself. 'As you can see,' he said, grabbing a microphone from an unwitting sponsored reporter and gesturing towards the huge crowd behind him, 'the Unsponsored have nowhere left to go. Men, women and children displaced in their thousands, living on the streets, cast adrift to make way for a sponsored playground. With the Olympic Games coming up, I don't think Lord Bassenford has thought this one through very carefully…'

Chucking the microphone back at the reporter, Max disappeared rapidly into the crowd, and Lord Bassenford, watching the news bulletin in The Blenthwaite Hotel, was dismayed to catch sight of Simone and Catherine Lorimer fleeing with him.

'My sincere apologies for any offence caused by that young man,' said the shaken reporter, walking briskly away in an attempt to draw the camera's focus from baton-wielding sponsored thugs charging after the unarmed Unsponsored.

The next night, Max again popped up on the evening news.

'Your Lordship, I'm sure you're listening. Stop destroying lives. Stop oppressing the Sponsored. Stop imprisoning my friends in Blenthwaite…'

With a growl, Lord Bassenford muted the television, snapped his laptop open and established a visual link with Rosanna.

'What the hell is going on?' he yelled at her. 'Why are the streets of London swarming with Unsponsored? Are you going to allow an all-out revolution before you'll do something about it, you useless little bitch?'

Rosanna didn't even flinch. Lord Bassenford raised the decibel level.

'You are pathetic, Rosanna! Call yourself my daughter? I'm ashamed – *ashamed*, do you hear me?'

'I can hardly fail to hear you, Father. I should think they can hear you in Timbuktu.'

'Don't give me your lip, girl, you're worse than Theodore! God, what have I done to deserve such embarrassments as children?' Lord Bassenford slammed his fists on to the table, a deep red flush creeping up his neck as another thought struck him. 'And furthermore, how the hell did Maxwell Barrington turn up in London? He's supposed to be in The White Lion with the rest of Theodore's worthless friends…'

His Lordship's rant trailed off as an image of Simone and Catherine Lorimer running with the Unsponsored flashed across his mind. Of course! *That* was how Maxwell Barrington had turned up in London.

'Philip bloody Lorimer!' he muttered. 'Foe, it would seem, not friend.' Snarling at his indifferent daughter again, Lord Bassenford added, 'Not only have you failed to subdue the underclass, Rosanna, you can't even manage something as simple as keeping the Lorimers onside. That's it, I've had enough. I'm returning to London, and you, madam, can get your useless carcass up to Blenthwaite.'

Rosanna simply shrugged and continued to paint her nails while her father took three attempts to cut off the visual link with a furiously jabbing finger.

On his way back to London in his luxury limousine, Lord Bassenford made another call, this time to Stephen Dyer.

'Yes, Stephen, Dexter Montfiore. You know which one he is?… That's right. It's about time he faced the consequences of housing my fugitive son in that hovel he calls an inn.'

That'll teach his boyfriend to make a play for my woman, too, he added in his head, totally missing the point that the play-making had all been on Faye's part.

'When? Tomorrow. Not a moment to lose, eh?'

Lord Bassenford chuckled nastily at Dyer's response.

'Of course you can rough him up a bit, Stephen. In fact, please do, but I want him conscious. And coherent.'

Now for some fun, His Lordship thought, ending this call in a much happier state of mind than he'd ended his conversation with his daughter.

***

Dex didn't stand a chance. One minute he was carrying a sack of rubbish out to The White Lion's bins, the next a van had screeched to a halt beside him and he was flung bodily into the back. So startled was Dex that he continued singing *My Old Man's a Dustman* for a few seconds until Stephen Dyer's fist slammed into his face, sending him sprawling against the thugs waiting in the shadows to wrench his arms behind his back and secure them with handcuffs.

'You're in trouble, faggot,' sneered Dyer. 'Big trouble.'

By the time the van arrived in Kensington hours later, Dex was battered, bloody-nosed and in a lot of pain, but as requested, he was still coherent when Dyer forced him to his knees in front of His Lordship.

'Excellent work, Stephen.' His Lordship rose from his chair and walked round to lean against the front of his desk. 'The unsponsored scum in its rightful place, kneeling in supplication before the Head of the Sponsorship Scheme.'

'I don't have a great deal of choice in the matter,' said Dex, his voice unusually nasal, 'being as your hired thug is leaning on my shoulder.'

Dyer slapped Dex across the face, his sovereign ring reopening a stinging cut on Dex's lip.

'Show His Lordship the respect he deserves!'

Drawing in a deep breath and blinking back tears of pain, Dex replied, 'I already am. He doesn't deserve any.'

Dex's breath left his lungs abruptly as Dyer kicked him in the stomach.

'Enough, Stephen,' said His Lordship. 'You can have some more fun soon, but first I need to make sure this pitiful creature understands exactly what's going on. Right, Montfiore, do you know why you're here?'

'No idea,' gasped Dex, still somewhat winded. 'Do I have any lifelines? Fifty-fifty? Phone a friend?'

'Silence! Sarcasm is not an attractive trait, Montfiore.'

'Oh, and kidnapping is?'

'So you do know why you're here,' said Lord Bassenford, smiling grimly. 'Chuck him in Theodore's old room, Stephen. It's about time it was occupied again.'

***

Alan, unsurprisingly, was absolutely devastated. As the hours turned into days with no word of Dex's fate, he teetered closer and closer to the edge of blind panic, constant activity becoming his only hope of staying sane.

'Dad, that doesn't need to be done now,' said Matilda, watching in concern as a wild-eyed Alan threw himself into a frenzy of cleaning the day after Dex's abduction. He ignored her and continued removing the band's gear from the stage.

'Dad, that *really* doesn't need…'

'I heard you the first time, darling. The stage may not need cleaning, but I need to clean it.'

'Yes, but you can't move Dex's... I mean, the keyboard on your own...'

'You can mention Dex's name, you know,' said Alan. 'I won't fall apart. When – *when*, not if – Dex walks back through that door, I don't want him to find me falling apart.'

In the evenings, Alan would spend hours playing the most heart-breaking tunes, Theo's Les Paul rejected in favour of a much-loved Epiphone Dex had bought him years earlier. Lord Bassenford would have been gratified, had he been in Blenthwaite, to hear the music pouring from The White Lion, Alan's pain reflected in every note, but instead he was in his London townhouse, goading a prisoner who resolutely refused to show any emotion whatsoever.

'Still no word from your boyfriend,' His Lordship sneered, wrenching open the door to the infamous fourth-floor bedroom and disturbing Dex's attempts to entice a tune out of Theo's old guitar. 'Seems he's no more worried about you than you are about him.'

Dex continued strumming a series of C, D and G chords and singing *When The Saints Go Marching In*, not even bothering to look up.

His blood pressure rising, Lord Bassenford snapped, 'Doesn't it bother you? You've been here for a week now. Seven days...'

'Thank you, Your Lordship, I do know how long a week is.'

'Don't interrupt me, faggot! Seven days gone, and your boyfriend can't even be bothered to get in touch.'

'Nice try, Your Lordship, but as you and I both know, Al's cut off from the rest of the country, which kinda handicaps him a little.'

'Nonsense. I reckon he's moved on to pastures new – no doubt Faye was more than willing to jump into the space you left in his bed…'

'What, is she no longer jumping into your bed?' said Dex with a grin.

Seething, Lord Bassenford snatched the guitar from Dex, hit him with it then smashed it on to the floor, stamping on it for good measure.

'Ouch,' said Dex blandly, his calm demeanour belying the pain the guitar had inflicted on his already battered body. Kicking the remains of the guitar to one side, Lord Bassenford stormed from the room, slamming and locking the door behind him.

The next day, His Lordship was back.

'What happened to that guitar, faggot?' he said suspiciously, eying the clean floor where the ruined instrument had been.

'Annie cleared it away for me.'

'Who the bloody hell is Annie?'

'One of your staff,' said Dex. 'Don't you know the names of your employees, Your Lordship?'

'I have better things to do with my time than fraternise with servants, and I'm not sure I like the idea of you getting friendly with them either. I need to arrange for this Annie to stay away from your room.'

Me and my big mouth, thought Dex ruefully. *I enjoyed her company.*

'Yes. From now on, your only companions will be Mr Dyer and my good self.'

'Wonderful,' said Dex, forcing a smile.

Ten days after abducting Dex, frustrated by his prisoner's apparent indifference to his plight, Lord Bassenford decided to focus his attention on Blenthwaite once again. Dex might be able to maintain a laid back appearance, but would the same be true for the more highly-strung Alan? Anticipating a satisfactory conversation with a broken man, Lord Bassenford switched on his computer and established a connection with Rosanna.

It was time to make contact with The White Lion.

***

Following her father's instructions, Rosanna, accompanied by Faye, walked the short distance from the Blenthwaite Hotel to The White Lion and rapped on the door.

'What do you want?' called Theo from within.

'Father wishes to make contact, Theodore, about, er…' Rosanna had a quick look at the licensees' names above the door '…Dexter Montfiore.'

Unbolting the door, Theo ushered Rosanna and Faye into the bar. Rosanna looked around until her gaze fell on her ex-boyfriend, and remained on him.

'Hello, Adam,' she said almost shyly. 'How are you?'

'Fine, Rose, thank you,' he replied. 'Would you like a drink? Faye?'

'I'd love a glass of dry white wine please, Adam,' said Faye, watching Rosanna's reaction with interest.

'Same for me, thank you, Adam,' said Rosanna. 'Your mother is very well, by the way, although she misses you.'

Astounded at Rosanna's uncharacteristic thoughtfulness, Adam thanked her warmly and went off to fetch their drinks.

Matilda wasn't so welcoming.

'What the fuck do you want, Faye?'

'His Lordship asked me to accompany Lady Rosanna…'

'Oh yeah, and you wouldn't have the guts to say no. This is partly your fault, you know. If you hadn't been drooling over Dad all the time, His Lordshit wouldn't have singled Dex out.'

'You're not saying anything I haven't thought myself, Matilda,' said Faye, watching Theo wrap comforting arms around her daughter. The affection he clearly felt for Matilda contrasted so starkly with his father's brutal treatment of Faye herself.

Snorting with derision, Matilda said, 'I know you have trouble keeping your legs together, but I still can't quite believe you'd sink so low as to let His Lordshit knob you…'

'Matilda! Please don't disrespect your mother.'

Faye had to blink as Alan entered the bar, so different did he look to his normal self. Gone were the bright clothes, sparkling hair grips and eyeliner. Instead he was dressed in a plain shirt and jeans, a pair of black-framed glasses replacing his usual contact lenses.

'Good afternoon, Mr Santiago,' said Rosanna. 'Forgive me for putting you through this, but my father wants to speak to you about Dexter Montfiore. I'm sorry I can't give you a heads-up concerning Mr Montfiore's state of health, but I'm not exactly flavour of the month…'

'I understand,' interrupted Alan, intrigued by Rosanna's apparent new humility. 'But why are you being so… er… nice?'

'Because I recognise your pain, Mr Santiago. I now know what a broken heart feels like.'

Looking at her feet, Rosanna could feel everyone staring at her in amazement, and she didn't dare glance up for fear of catching Adam's eye.

'Oh. Sorry about that, Your… er… Ladyship,' said Alan, taken aback. 'Please feel free to call me Alan.'

'OK, Alan.' Raising her head, Rosanna realised there was no hostility in her companions' expressions, not even Theo's, and a slight gleam appeared in her eyes. 'Please feel free to call me Lady Bitch.'

'Oops!' Alan clapped a hand over his mouth, and Rosanna smiled kindly at him.

'It's all right, I deserved it. Shall I call Father and let him know we're ready to proceed?'

Ignoring the nervous lurch in his stomach, Alan nodded, and Rosanna switched on her laptop. Establishing a visual link between The White Lion and Lord Bassenford's office, she then stood back as her father came into view.

'Er… are you Alan Santiago?' said His Lordship. When Alan nodded, he continued with his usual lack of tact, 'Good grief, you almost look like a man…'

'With respect, Lord Bassenford, I'd rather talk about Dex.'

'Oh yes, I imagine you would. Lord Bassenford now, is it? Not Your Lordshit? It's amazing what a leveller the loss of one's bed partner can be.' Turning to the loathsome Dyer, who was skulking behind his boss's chair, His Lordship said, 'Stephen, go and fetch Montfiore for me. Gently now, I don't think there's any part of him that's not already black and blue.'

Sniggering, Dyer left the room. A few minutes later, Dex stumbled into view as Dyer shoved him roughly into a chair next to Lord Bassenford then stood back to admire his handiwork. Dex's eyes were both bruised, the left one so swollen he could barely open it, and his split lip was twice its normal size, but his easy-going humour remained unharmed.

'Yeah?' he joked as Alan gasped in dismay. 'OK, I've looked better, but you've not exactly made much of an effort yourself, Al. Why are you wearing my clothes?'

'They make me feel closer to you, sweetie.'

'And your glasses?'

'All the better to see you with, my dear,' replied Alan with the ghost of a smile.

'Well, I don't want you letting yourself go in my absence.' Smiling back at Alan, Dex added, 'I'm kidding, darling. You're a sight for sore eyes, and boy! Do I have sore eyes…'

'Oh, for God's sake, pass the sick bucket,' interrupted Lord Bassenford, wrinkling his nose. 'As you can see, Santiago, your… er… friend…'

'Boyfriend,' corrected Dex.

'Shut up, Montfiore. Santiago, your… thingy… is at my mercy. As you can also see, my mercy is in short supply. I'll be blunt here: I don't want any more trouble from you Unsponsored. I've got the Games coming up and there's more than enough on my plate here in London, so Rosanna and the Sponsors still in Blenthwaite will keep an eye on you lot. If I hear of *any* insubordination, then Mr Dyer may have to teach Montfiore an even harsher lesson than…'

'I wouldn't do that, Your Lordship,' interrupted Alan, taking his friends by surprise as much as Lord Bassenford. Pulling something from the pocket of Dex's shirt, he waved it at the laptop's camera. 'Do you know what this is?'

'It's a passport…'

'Yes, Lord Bassenford. An American passport, to be specific. Dex's American passport, to be even more specific. Dex is an American citizen, and I'm sure the American Embassy will take a very dim view of you holding him prisoner.'

Lord Bassenford recovered his composure quickly, but not quickly enough. Alan was gratified to see the flash of horror in his eyes.

'If you continue to harm Dex in any way, I will be contacting the American Embassy, and your Scheme won't be able to bail you out then…'

'And how exactly do you intend to get in touch with the Embassy?' snarled Lord Bassenford.

'If you hurt Dex any more, I'll find a way.'

'You won't know…'

'I *will* know.' Hoping he was doing the right thing, Alan made eye contact with Dex via Rosanna's laptop and saw him smile encouragingly before a scowling Lord Bassenford cut off the visual link.

'I'm sure Mr Montfiore will be fine,' said Rosanna, shutting down her laptop and patting Alan on the arm as she prepared to leave. 'You made a very valid point there – even my father will be reluctant to take on the American Embassy.'

'Well if anyone's arrogant enough to try, it'd be His Lordshit… er, I mean your father.'

'My father may be arrogant, but he's not stupid.' Smiling sadly, Rosanna added, 'I wish you the very best of luck, Alan, and I hope you're reunited with Mr Montfiore soon.'

Thanking Rosanna for her kind words and dodging Faye's attempt to land a juicy kiss on his lips, Alan bolted the door behind the two women then turned to the others in the bar.

'Well,' he said, 'who was that and what has she done with the real Lady Bitch?'

'She does have her good side,' said Adam thoughtfully as Izzy emerged from the back room where she'd been hiding throughout the interview.

'Adam's right,' she said. 'Deep down, my Rose is a good girl.'

Theo looked as though he was about to argue that point, but caught his mother's eye and decided against it. Instead, he said to Alan, 'What a masterstroke, waving Dex's American passport in His Lordshit's face like that. Al, you're a genius. When did you think of it?'

'Couple of days ago, Theo sweetie,' replied Alan, sounding a little more like his usual self, 'when I was cleaning the gym.'

Louis exchanged a grin with Gideon at the memory of Alan's frenzied scrubbing and sweeping around them as they worked on floor routines.

'Why then?' he asked.

'It put me in mind of that little altercation with Gideon, Lou. You remember? The day Dex first showed you the gym…'

'When Dex pointed out that we're American, and therefore beyond the control of the Sponsors,' finished Georgie. 'Alan Santiago, you clever, clever man!'

'Steady on, Mrs Farrell, I am spoken for,' said Alan, laughing as Georgie engulfed him in a bear hug. Looking around the room, he added, 'I don't know about you, my friends, but the time has come for me to make a break for it. Tomorrow, I'm setting off for London.'

'How?'

'Well, if I can just get away from Blenthwaite, I'll contact Philip – I'm sure he can arrange some sort of transport south. One way or another, I'm going to get Dex away from that awful man.'

'*How* though, Alan?'

'Stamp my feet a bit? Throw a tantrum? Seduce Stephen Dyer? No, scrub that last idea. Yuk! I really don't know. Everything we've achieved so far we've pretty much done by accident, so I thought I'd carry on the great Dory's Avengers tradition of not bothering with plans…'

'I'm with you, Al.'

'I'm right behind you, Dad.' Theo and Matilda spoke at the same time, prompting a wave of support from the rest of Dory's Avengers, including Izzy.

'Do you think that's wise, Mum?' asked Marina in concern.

'Well, I'm not prepared to get left behind, darling,' replied Izzy, smiling. 'What would I do while you're having all the fun in London, knit a scarf? No, I think it's high time Isabelle Farrell came out of hiding.'

'I'm not sure it's safe for Gideon, though…' began Sarah.

'*Sarah!* I'd go out of my mind if you left me here. Besides, the Olympics begin in less than two weeks' time. I'm not missing Louis's big performance…'

'And I'm not big performing without Gideon,' added Louis.

'That's settled then,' said Theo. 'Tomorrow we'll make a break for it and descend on London, so may I suggest we let our hair down tonight, enjoy one final Dory's Avengers gig, and polish off that champagne sitting in the fridge?'

'Sound's good,' said Alan, leaping on stage and selecting Theo's Les Paul. 'But for tonight we're Dex's Avengers.'

Chapter 25 – Too Late

'Why didn't you tell me you're American?' Lord Bassenford asked the following morning, facing Dex over the breakfast table.

'The accent usually gives it away, Your Lordship,' replied Dex, eying with amusement the household cook's attempt to serve him an American-style breakfast. Prodding the rather unappetising-looking pancakes with his fork, he then enquired as to whether he could have a bacon sandwich instead.

'Mooreland,' snapped Lord Bassenford to the tall, miserable-looking man standing by the door, 'bacon sandwich for our guest, please.'

With very bad grace, Mooreland snatched the plate of pancakes from Dex, muttering something that sounded suspiciously like 'Ungrateful fuck', and stalked out of the room.

'Coffee, Dexter?' asked His Lordship. Dex nodded and grinned; the vast improvement in his treatment since Alan had produced his passport hadn't gone unnoticed. This morning, for the first time, Dex had been invited to join His Lordship for breakfast in the dining room, his status in the household suddenly having been elevated from prisoner to guest.

'If I'm a guest, Your Lordship, am I free to leave any time I wish?'

'Not sure, Dexter. I've invited you to stay in my home indefinitely, so it would be churlish, don't you think, to leave at the first opportunity? Perhaps you're not yet *au fait* with British etiquette…'

'I'm *au fait* enough to know that guests are usually permitted to have some say in the length of their stay. However, I appreciate the effort you've made to ensure my comfort since yesterday.'

'Make no mistake, I can ensure your discomfort any time I wish. Your… er… friend…'

'Boyfriend.'

'Don't split hairs, Dexter! Your friend may hold proof of your nationality, but while he and your passport are in the north of England, your country's embassy remains blissfully unaware of your situation.'

'So why are you treating me like a guest all of a sudden? And when did you realise my name's Dexter? I was convinced you thought it was really "Faggot".'

'Why all the questions, Dexter? I'm not an unreasonable man, I like to treat my guests with respect.'

'What, in case your guest's boyfriend happens to drop in on the American Embassy?'

'Which is highly unlikely, is it not? I suggest you don't antagonise me, Dexter. I may have to instruct Mr Dyer to teach you some more manners, as you seem to be a very slow learner…'

The conversation was interrupted by the ring of Lord Bassenford's mobile phone. Concern crossed his face as he looked at the caller ID, and in his anxiety he inadvertently switched his phone on to loudspeaker mode.

'Fellows, why are you calling? Where's Lady Rosanna?' Lord Bassenford had left strict instructions that security in Blenthwaite was to concentrate on guarding the occupants of The White Lion, while any contact with London could be dealt with by his daughter.

'Your Lordship,' replied Lee Fellows, his nervous voice clearly audible to Dex as well as Lord Bassenford, 'I'm sorry to say that… the Unsponsored in The White Lion… well, they've gone.'

'*What?*' roared His Lordship. 'Where have they gone? And tell me, where's my daughter?'

'We don't know, Your Lordship.' Lee Fellows sounded on the verge of tears. 'They simply vanished in the night, and they've taken Lady Rosanna with them…'

Lord Bassenford stared across the table at Dex, his numb mind trying desperately to grasp the implications of Fellows's words. Arms folded, Dex leaned back in his chair and winked cheekily back at him.

'Listen to me, Fellows,' His Lordship snapped, galvanised into action by the smug expression on Dex's face. 'I want you to leave for London *immediately*, and bring those goons Maloney and O'Reilly with you.'

Cutting off the call abruptly, Lord Bassenford glowered at his guest.

'Well,' said Dex, grinning, 'that kinda changes everything, doesn't it, Your Lord*shit*.'

***

It had been Theo who'd come up with the idea that Rosanna's change of attitude could be used to the advantage of Dex's Avengers. Putting his guitar down to enjoy a champagne break with the rest of the band after an hour and a half of nonstop playing, the music enjoyed from the street by Mortimer O'Reilly, Theo couldn't help but notice that the money man wasn't the only one hanging around outside. Standing in the middle of the road, staring blankly into space, was his heartbroken elder sister.

Joining his mother on her favourite sofa, Theo looked at her thoughtfully for a moment, then said, 'What do you think to inviting Rosanna in, Mum?'

'What, now? With me here?'

'Why not?'

'Well, er... isn't she on His Lordshit's side?'

'After today, I'm not so sure. I've never known her to be so... nice.'

'I have no objection, darling,' said Izzy. 'But I am biased, she's my daughter. I realise the rest of you don't share my affection for her...'

'I admit my motives aren't entirely unselfish, Mum,' replied Theo, grinning around the room and going on to address everyone. 'These are the facts as I see them: His Lordshit's left Rosanna in charge here in Blenthwaite. We need to get out of Blenthwaite. Rosanna's still in love with Adam, which appears to be the only thing she can concentrate on at the moment...'

'I'm not prepared to use her, Theo,' Adam interrupted. 'I still care about her too.'

'I wasn't asking you to use her, Ads,' replied Theo. 'I realise you're not a cad like me...'

'Ah, Theo, you're not a cad either,' said Matilda, laughing. 'No one could have expected you to resist someone as gorgeous as me.'

'Or as vain,' murmured Alan.

'Rich coming from you, Dad! Someone's got to carry on the Santiago tradition of being hopelessly vain while you're out of action.'

Alan's only reply was a loud and discordant twang on Theo's guitar.

'Shall we get back to the point, Theo?' asked Marina impatiently.

'Yes, Mari, of course. It's quite simple. Let's get Rosanna in here, reunite her with Mum…'

'Yes please,' said Izzy.

'And – I never thought I'd say this – appeal to her better nature.'

There were a few derisive snorts around the room, but Louis nodded his head in agreement.

'It is a risk,' he said, 'but so is everything we do.'

'I say do it now,' added Alan, 'before she walks off and the moment's lost.'

Without waiting for any more feedback, Theo unbolted the door and called to the sister he'd despised for his whole life, relieved when she came over without hesitation.

'Hello, Theodore. What can I do for you?'

'Will you come in? For a drink, I mean,' asked Theo, rubbing the back of his head awkwardly as Rosanna's eyebrows shot up in surprise.

'You're inviting *me* for a drink?'

'Er, yes… well, I haven't had much chance in the past.'

'All right then, thank you,' said Rosanna. 'I'd love a drink, so you can stop scratching your head now, you flea-bitten little scrote…'

Laughing at Theo's horrified expression, Rosanna assured him she was only joking.

'God knows, Theodore, I've given you enough shit in the past. I'll not be giving you any more today.'

'Why?'

'Like I said to Alan earlier, I've learned a sharp lesson from having my heart broken. All the money, all the power of the Scheme would never make me as happy as Ads did…' Rosanna broke off briefly and cleared her throat. 'Anyway, that drink. Is the offer still on?'

'Absolutely, Rosanna,' said Theo with a smile, opening the gate and offering his arm to his sister. Alarmed, the security guards in the street rushed over, thinking that Lady Rosanna was being kidnapped.

'What the hell do you want, Fellows?' demanded Rosanna.

'Your Ladyship, er, is it wise? Going into the unsponsored hole?'

'Fellows, are you questioning me?'

'Of course not, Your Ladyship. Should I ring His Lordship?'

Letting go of Theo's arm, Rosanna rounded on Lord Bassenford's head of security. 'My father's instructions were quite specific, Fellows: you guard, I communicate. Now, if you'll excuse me, I have business to transact with my brother.'

Taking Theo's arm again, Rosanna whispered to him that Lady Bitch had made her final appearance.

'Welcome, Rosanna,' called Lysander from behind the bar as she and Theo entered the room. 'Another white wine?'

'Yes please, Lysander. Theodore's buying. Hello, Marina.'

Looking uncertainly at her older sister for a second, Marina then hugged Rosanna and was delighted when the hug was returned.

'Hi, Rosanna,' said Alan, coming over with his hand outstretched. 'Thank you for your compassion earlier…'

'Ditto,' said Adam, kissing Rosanna on the cheek and making her go weak at the knees. 'It meant a lot to me to know Mum's OK. Talking of which, why don't you look behind you?'

Intrigued, Rosanna turned round, and this time her knees did buckle.

'Mummy,' was all she managed to gasp before falling, sobbing, into her mother's embrace.

***

Ten minutes later, Rosanna finally calmed down and collected her thoughts. Taking a fortifying sip of her wine, she turned to Theo.

'Did you invite me in here to be reunited with Mum, or did you have another motive?'

'Why do you always think I have an ulterior motive?' snapped Theo, but Alan hastily interrupted before the siblings could forget their truce and start squabbling again.

'There is another motive, Lady Rosanna, although it was my idea...'

'It was mine, Al,' argued Theo.

'It was my idea to leave tonight...'

'And you want me to help?' Rosanna asked.

'Well, yes,' said Alan. 'We thought, maybe, you'd be sympathetic to our... my... need to go...'

'OK, Alan, let me get this right,' Rosanna interrupted again, taking another sip of her wine. 'Because I was concerned about Mr Montfiore, because I'm hurting too, and because my mother's suddenly returned from God knows where, you thought I'd be prepared to betray my father and the Scheme?'

'Oh, here we go,' said Theo in disgust. 'I should have known better. Appeal to your better nature? You don't have one...'

'Oh, get lost, Theodore!'

'You get lost, Rosanna! You get your kicks out of watching your brother whipped unconscious – whatever made me think you'd changed? Lady Bitch has put in her final appearance, my arse.'

'Shut up for a moment...'

'I suppose you're going to give Mum up to His Lordshit now. Like father, like daughter…'

'Shut the fuck up, Theodore! I never said I wouldn't help you.'

'I thought you did…'

'You didn't give me a chance to say anything, you prick! Of course I'm not going to give Mum up. Also, I will help you. I don't agree with you being incarcerated in here.'

'Really?'

'Yes, Theodore, really.'

'Why don't you come with us, darling?' said Izzy, unexpectedly. 'I don't think it's going to be safe for you to remain here, not when His Lordshit finds out we've disappeared from under your nose.'

'You call Father "His Lordshit" too, do you, Mum?' asked Rosanna.

'Damn right! I despise the man. I regret leaving you all at his mercy every minute of every day, especially now I know how he treated your brother. I'd worry sick if I thought I was abandoning you to a similar fate.'

Looking at Theo, Rosanna realised the truth of her mother's words.

'I'm sorry, Theodore,' she said simply. Realising his sister was apologising for far more than their most recent spat, Theo nodded and smiled.

'Thank you,' he said.

'OK,' said Rosanna, addressing the whole room, 'I have a plan. Get your stuff together tonight. What time do you want to leave in the morning? If it's all right with you, make it as early as possible. The security guys are getting complacent, they tend to assume they don't have to be too diligent overnight. Try your utmost not to give any indication you're up and about. I'll send, I don't know...' Glancing out into the street, Rosanna noticed Mortimer O'Reilly in conversation with Lee Fellows. 'O'Reilly – yes, he'll do. I'll send O'Reilly to round up the security in the street, tell them we're having an emergency meeting while all is quiet. You use the opportunity to get away...'

'And leave Mr O'Reilly to take the flack?' asked Louis.

'Couldn't be better!' replied Lysander, grinning as his son snorted with disapproval.

'What about my dad?' said Adam. 'Sorry, but I'm not leaving him to face the wrath of His Lordshit.'

'It's OK, Ads,' replied Rosanna, her voice softening. 'David was recalled to London a few days ago. Sorry, I should have told you. His Lordshit – aha, I'm learning – His Lordshit wants him onsite with the Olympics so close.'

'What about your mum, though?' Theo asked Matilda. 'She's still here.'

'Sod her!'

'Matilda…'

'No, Dad! She's never brought us anything but grief. I'm sure she can shag her way out of this tight spot – it wouldn't be the first time.'

Before Alan could admonish Matilda again, Abi said, 'That tactic won't help poor Mr O'Reilly, though.'

'He looked so terrified when His Lordshit sent him in here,' added Louis. 'This will destroy him.'

'Should have a glance at his crystal ball then,' sneered Lysander. 'He's the reason we've had to cocoon you all your life, Louis, him and his stupid false prediction.'

'Well,' snapped Rosanna, her characteristic St Benedict impatience coming to the fore, 'unless anyone can come up with an alternative plan which covers *everyone*'s needs, we're wasting time now.'

'I agree,' said Alan. 'Sorry, Mr O'Reilly, sorry, Faye, but my only concern is getting to Dex.'

'And mine is to get Louis… er… nowhere…'

'It's OK, Mr Wallis, you don't have to tell me your plans,' said Rosanna, her temper fading as she smiled at the man in the wheelchair. 'Shall I go on with my idea?'

Everyone nodded, and Rosanna continued.

'Right. I'll have a meeting, early tomorrow morning, with the guards. All the guards. Don't worry, I'll think of something, but you mustn't waste any time. Get out of here quickly, get away.'

'Can't promise to sprint, Lady Rosanna,' growled Gideon, and Rosanna frowned at the obvious flaw in her plan.

'If only we could get in touch with Philip,' said Chloe wistfully.

'But you can,' said Rosanna, her face relaxing into a smile. 'Philip Lorimer, you mean? I don't know your name, sorry, but you're perfectly welcome to use this.'

Holding out her mobile phone, Rosanna was rewarded with a smile from Chloe in return.

'My name's Chloe. Thanks.'

Speaking to Philip, who was overjoyed at word from Blenthwaite, Chloe outlined Rosanna's plan.

'I wondered why Lady Rosanna's name came up on caller ID,' he said. 'What time do you want to leave?'

Consulting with Rosanna, Chloe replied that between 5.30 and 6am would be ideal.

'Better make it earlier rather than later,' said Philip. 'Give me a few minutes, then I'll get back to you.'

True to his word, Philip phoned back within ten minutes.

'Three vans will pick you up from the village boundary at 5.30am. One will be kitted out to carry Gideon's chair securely, and one can transport your luggage. I'll make sure there are cushions and refreshments for you all, but it would be best if you don't have to make any stops on the way. I'm sure you don't want to draw unnecessary attention to yourselves...'

Chloe grunted her agreement.

'And I have no wish to put my drivers at risk. Now, is Rosanna sure she can keep the thugs out of the way?'

'Yes,' replied Chloe. 'She'll keep them all in the hotel while we get clear of the village – they'll not realise we've gone for hours as they'll assume us to be asleep. Thank you so much, Philip, from all of us.'

'Don't mention it, Chloe,' said Philip. 'Good luck. I'll see you in London, tomorrow!'

Cutting off the call, Chloe handed the phone back to Rosanna with a warm smile then jumped around the room, clapping her hands.

'We're going home, we're going home, we're going, we are going home!' she sang repeatedly to the tune of *Three Lions* until Izzy voiced a sobering thought.

'I'm not leaving here tomorrow without Rosanna,' she said. 'How is she going to get away while she's distracting the thugs?'

'I'll make some excuse and slip away…'

'How, darling? You'll be chairing the meeting.'

'OK, how about this – I'll spout some rubbish about how I tried to negotiate a truce with you this evening, but to no avail. And,' Rosanna started to laugh, 'I'll appeal to the guards' violent natures by suggesting maybe we should single out some of you for punishment, set the ball rolling towards defeating you. That's the sort of thing they'll *love* to talk about, so I'll tell them to take half an hour to discuss ideas before they return to the street for their day of thuggery. I'll claim to be going back to bed for a couple of hours' sleep, but instead I'll grab my stuff and leg it.'

'Genius!' said Abi, looking in newfound awe at her cousin.

'It'd better work,' said Izzy grimly, 'because I'm not getting in any of those vans until all three of my children are safely with me.'

'It will work, Auntie Izzy,' said Abi, gesturing towards the thugs flexing their muscles in the street outside. 'Look at those cavemen. They'll love an opportunity to chat about beating us up – I can't think of anything they'd rather talk about. Meanwhile, Rose strolls up the road and joins us. Cuz, you're a genius!'

Rosanna, it turned out, was a genius. Her plan was as good as anything Chloe or Brains could have come up with and worked like a dream. By the time Lord Bassenford's guards realised that The White Lion was actually deserted rather than unusually quiet, the anonymous vans carrying Dory's Avengers, their luggage including an assortment of guitars and Max's drum kit, were well on their way south.

***

Lord Bassenford was livid. Picking the coffee pot up from the table, he hurled it against the far wall before rounding, unreasonably, on the head of household staff who had just returned with Dex's bacon sandwich.

'Clean that mess up, Mooreland, now!'

'Temper, temper, Your Lordshit,' commented Dex, looking longingly at the coffee pooling on the floor.

'Get out of my sight,' snarled Lord Bassenford, '*faggot!*'

Maintaining his unruffled demeanour, Dex took his sandwich from Mooreland with a smile of thanks then made for the kitchen, seeking fresh coffee and the friendly company of the cook, Mrs White. Meanwhile, Lord Bassenford headed upstairs to his third-floor office and called his London-based Sponsors, demanding their presence at an emergency meeting. Still fuming as they gathered in his office an hour or so later, His Lordship set up a visual link with Faye's tablet and left them to piece the events of the previous night together as he launched a stinging verbal attack on her and Mortimer.

'Never in my *life* have I had to tolerate such incompetence. *Never!* How could you let them go from underneath your noses? How could you let them take Lady Rosanna?'

Mortimer, sitting next to Faye in the back of Lee Fellows's car, looked terrified, so as usual it was Faye who responded to her boss's tirade.

'With respect, Your Lordship, it would seem that Lady Rosanna was in on the Unsponsored's plan to escape…'

'Lady Rosanna would *never* side with the Unsponsored, Maloney. Explain yourself!'

'It was Lady Rosanna who called a meeting with security first thing this morning. Really early, just after five o'clock. She sent Mortimer to gather in all the guards, saying she wanted to take advantage of The White Lion being quiet…'

'That's ridiculous! Rosanna knows we never call all security off the streets, not even for a second. What was the purpose of this meeting?'

'To discuss ways to subdue the Unsponsored, Your Lordship. Lady Rosanna said she wanted to start dishing out beatings in an endeavour to break them and asked the guards for feedback. We haven't seen her since.'

'Didn't anyone question where she was going?'

'She said she was going back to bed. We had no reason to disbelieve her.'

'So you just stood by and let the Unsponsored kidnap her! Oh, for God's sake, what do *you* want?'

Lord Bassenford turned in fury as Dex entered the room, cup of coffee in hand.

'That's no way to talk to a guest, Your Lordshit,' replied Dex, grinning at Faye via the computer's camera. 'Especially one from across the Pond. I can hear every word from upstairs, so thought I may as well join you. Hi, Faye – bad day, huh?'

'Hi, Dex, you could say that. You're looking a bit better today.'

'I am better, thanks. His Lordshit's kindly invited me to enjoy the comforts of his home, and the coffee's good…'

'Will you shut up!' roared Lord Bassenford. 'I'm trying to conduct a meeting here.'

'As you can see, His Lordshit treats his guests *real* nice,' said Dex to Faye, exaggerating his American accent as he settled himself in the armchair previously favoured by Theo. Doing his best to ignore Dex, Lord Bassenford continued to berate the Sponsors travelling back from Blenthwaite until the doorbell sounded three floors below.

'Aha,' he said, 'here comes another troublemaker.'

A couple of minutes later, Mooreland ushered Philip Lorimer into the room. Looking around him, Philip noticed that there wasn't a chair for him to sit on, and Lord Bassenford's hostility was palpable.

'Lorimer,' said Lord Bassenford, 'your unsponsored friends in Blenthwaite made a break for it last night, but I'm sure I'm not telling you anything you didn't already know. What part did you play?'

Recognising that the diplomacy between himself and the Head of the Sponsorship Scheme was at an end, Philip perched on the arm of Dex's chair and stared defiantly at His Lordship before replying.

'My friends needed transport. I supplied it.'

'What form of transport?'

'Do you really expect me to answer that, Your Lordship?'

'You do realise that the unsponsored *scum* you call friends have kidnapped my daughter, don't you, Lorimer?' snarled Lord Bassenford, his anger reaching fever pitch as Philip laughed.

'How unfortunate.'

'Lorimer! How would you feel if your daughter were to be kidnapped?'

'Devastated. But unlike you, I care about my daughter.'

The grandfather clock ticked away the seconds as the Sponsors waited tensely for Lord Bassenford's response.

'What,' he said, enunciating every syllable, 'makes you think I care any less for my children than you do for Catherine?'

'The answer is behind me, Lord Bassenford,' replied Philip, gesturing towards the iron rings set in the wall. 'I would die before I allowed anyone to treat my daughter the way you treated your son. Oh yes, Your Lordship, Theodore's told me all about it.' Continuing in a voice heavy with sarcasm, Philip added, 'It's probably a silly question – I'm sure a *loving* father like yourself will already have thought of this – but have you tried phoning Rosanna?'

Glaring at Philip, wondering how he'd allowed his brain to switch off to such an extent that he didn't think of something so obvious, Lord Bassenford dialled his daughter's number, this time deliberately leaving the phone on loudspeaker mode.

'Father,' said Rosanna cheerfully on answering, 'we've been expecting you to call.'

'Rosanna! Where are you? Are you hurt?'

'Not at all, Father. I'm currently nice and comfortable, becoming reacquainted with my brother and sister…'

'Shh! Don't tell him any more,' said Theo's voice in the background.

'It's all right, Theodore, I'm not as dumb as you.'

'Could have fooled me, Rosanna.'

'Oh, piss off, you little prick!' Speaking into the phone once more, Rosanna continued, 'Sorry about that, Father. As you can hear, Theodore and I still have some ground to make up. Yes, I'm fine. Please don't haul Faye and Mortimer over the coals, none of this was their doing.'

'Are you telling me you were in on this?' hissed His Lordship.

'Afraid so, Father.'

Lord Bassenford was silent for a couple of seconds as the implications of Rosanna's words sank into his brain: all three of his children had deserted him. When he did speak, he could only manage one word, and that came out as a pathetic whimper.

'Why?'

'Because I've had something of an epiphany recently. Being hurt isn't fun. Hurting people isn't fun. Your Scheme is based on fear and intimidation – Mummy was right all along. You don't help people, you dictate to them, rob them of basic freedoms. I no longer want to be a part of it…'

'Rosanna,' interrupted Lord Bassenford, 'is your mother with you?'

Rosanna was silent.

'Rosanna?'

'Yes, William, I am,' replied Isabelle.

Lord Bassenford closed his eyes and shook his head. Never had the Sponsors seen him so shocked.

'Shit!' he muttered, pushing his chair back and almost running from the room.

'William? Are you still there?'

Crossing over to Lord Bassenford's desk, Dex sat in the seat vacated by His Lordship and spoke to Isabelle.

'He's just left the room, Izzy. Think you took him by surprise there.'

'Dex! How are you?'

'I'm good, Izzy. I've still got one of those security tag things on my arm, though. Can't leave the house.'

'God, Dex,' said Theo's voice, 'sorry to hear that.'

'Hey, Theo, it's not all bad. I've been treated OK since Al made His Lordshit aware the American Embassy's likely to kick his ass. He's stopped Dyer kicking my ass, anyway.' Laughing, Dex added, 'Is Al with you?'

'No, sorry, Dex. He's… um… travelling independently of us.'

'I'm here though, Dex darling,' said Matilda. 'Love you loads!'

'Love you right back, Matty honey,' replied Dex, beaming.

'Get off my seat, faggot!' said Lord Bassenford, re-entering the room and shoving Dex out of the way. Speaking into his phone again, he hissed at his estranged wife, 'Isabelle, I told you, I warned you, not to come back…'

A merry laugh came from the other end of the line.

'What makes you think I'm going to dance to your tune, William? I never did when you had me under your control, so I'm certainly not about to…'

'Oh, don't be so sure,' said Lord Bassenford with a nasty smile. 'You'll soon learn the extent of my control.'

'You'll have to find me first.'

'Simple. I'll put a trace on Rosanna's phone.'

Lord Bassenford's smile widened as he listened to the frantic whispering on the other end of the phone. Then Rosanna spoke again.

'Thanks for the heads up, Your Lordshit.' Lord Bassenford winced. Apparently he was no longer 'Father' to Rosanna now. 'I'm about to lob my phone out of the window, so your thugs can pick it up from the side of the road for me.'

With that, Rosanna cut off the phone call.

'Your Lordship…' began Philip.

'Lorimer, get out of my house!'

'Lord Bassenford,' Philip wasn't going to give up that easily, 'might I suggest that you allow Dex to leave with me?'

'You're not in a position to make suggestions, Lorimer.'

'You can't keep Dex here for ever, Your Lordship. Sooner or later, Alan's going to arrive in London along with Dex's passport, and the American Embassy will get involved. Do you really need that on top of everything else?'

'What do you mean by that?'

'Well, surely you've noticed the streets of the city are rapidly degenerating into anarchy…'

'You mean your unsponsored rabble is running amok, Lorimer. I can soon quell a few underclass.'

'So why haven't you already done so?' asked Philip, unwittingly voicing the nagging concern of His Lordship's inner circle. One or two in the room had to check themselves before they inadvertently nodded in agreement.

'Get out, Lorimer.'

With an apologetic glance at Dex, Philip left the St Benedict residence. Still watching via the link on her tablet, Faye had heard every word of the exchange between Philip and Lord Bassenford, and as usual she couldn't resist offering her opinion.

'Philip's right, Your Lordship,' she said, Mortimer audibly whimpering as her words turned Lord Bassenford's attention back on them. 'About Dex, I mean.'

'If I needed your opinion, I'd ask for it, Maloney…'

'But you do need it. I watch the news like everyone else, I can see what's happening in London. The Unsponsored are starting to take control of the streets.'

'If that's so,' snarled Lord Bassenford, 'why has no one pointed it out to me?'

'Why do you think, Your Lordship? Now I've pointed it out to you, how are you going to react?'

'You, Maloney, are going to pay dearly for your insubordination…'

'There you go, Your Lordship. I've acquainted you with the facts, and your response is to have me punished. Does that answer your question?'

Mortimer's bottom lip began to tremble, but surprisingly Lord Bassenford didn't give the roar of rage that everyone was expecting. When he finally did speak, he addressed his question to the Sponsors in his London office rather than Faye.

'How many of you agree with Faye? Who has been seeing what's happening but not telling me?'

Looking round the room, Lord Bassenford found no one would meet his eyes.

'Well, that answers that question. Thank you, Faye, I'm glad at least one of my Sponsors has some backbone.'

Addressing Mooreland, who had returned to the room having seen Philip Lorimer out of the house, Lord Bassenford said, 'Ask Stephen Dyer to pop upstairs, Mooreland. Our guest is ready to leave.'

Five minutes later, a sulky Dyer received an unwelcome set of instructions from Lord Bassenford. His Lordship's enjoyment at holding a prisoner in his house once again had been nothing compared to Dyer's pleasure at having a member of the Unsponsored on hand to beat up whenever he felt the urge (which was often), but now it would seem the fun was over.

'You're no longer welcome here, Montfiore,' he snarled as he stomped down to the ground floor, shoving Dex before him.

'I wasn't aware you'd ever made me welcome,' replied Dex, smiling as Mrs White emerged from the kitchen.

'You off now, Dex?' she said, returning his smile. 'It's been a pleasure having you around the place.'

'It's been a pleasure meeting you, Mrs White,' replied Dex.

'Come here, give me a hug.' Checking Dyer was looking the other way, Mrs White slipped a compact London *A to Z* into Dex's back pocket. 'Annie found this hidden in Lord Theodore's mattress when she made the bed up for you,' she whispered. 'Head south of the river…'

'Thank you, and please give my love to Annie,' Dex whispered back, dropping a quick kiss on Mrs White's head.

'Get in here, faggot,' snapped an impatient Dyer.

'Hey,' Dex said, following Dyer into the security room and grinning at the huge screen on the wall, 'is this where you used to wank over Theo?'

Uttering a string of expletives, Dyer unlocked the tag on Dex's wrist then bundled him out of the front door. Shoving him hard in the back, Dyer watched in satisfaction as he staggered down the steps before falling flat on his face on the pavement.

**

The vans carrying Dory's Avengers arrived in South London late that morning, shortly after His Lordship had discovered that his estranged wife was back in the country. A very high-spirited Max was waiting with Catherine, Jim and a number of other London Unsponsored to help unload the vans as quickly as possible, then he led everyone into the huge old building that now housed the Unsponsored Network HQ.

'Wow,' said Theo, looking around. 'Don't the Sponsored realise you're here, Max?'

'They don't come looking, Dory me old mate. We've kind of made this part of South London an unsponsored stronghold, so they prefer to stay in their comfortable mansions north of the river and wait for us to go and convert them to the unsponsored way – which we do on a daily basis.'

Grinning, Theo put the pair of amplifiers he'd been carrying on the HQ's floor and unstrapped his guitar from his back. 'Sounds jolly good fun,' he said. 'Will we be going out today?'

'Could be, Dory, could be, but we're waiting for Philip to return first. Cathie told me he received a summons from His Lordshit earlier – a none-too-friendly summons.'

'Oh, *Cathie* told you, did she? So, are you and Cathie…'

'Mind your own, Dory, eh?' said Max, tapping the side of his nose.

The moment Philip joined the rest of the Unsponsored, an unrepentant smile on his face and his wife at his side, Alan pounced.

'Philip,' he said, waving Dex's passport, 'when do you think we should contact the American Embassy?'

'Let's have a breather first, shall we, Alan?'

'We spoke to Dex, Dad,' said Matilda jubilantly. 'He's fine. His Lordshit's realised he's got to treat him well…'

'Whoa there, Matty! What's this? You spoke to Dex? How?'

Realising that Alan and his travelling companions didn't know anything about Rosanna's phone call from Lord Bassenford, Philip suggested that he start from the beginning.

'His Lordshit's livid,' he told the assembled company as everyone settled down. 'He had Faye Maloney and Mortimer O'Reilly up on his screen, and I got the impression he'd been hauling them over the coals a bit. He hauled me over the coals a bit too…'

'Why, Daddy? Doesn't he have to keep you onside?'

'He does, Cathie, but that seems to be the least of his concerns at the moment.'

Between them, Philip, Isabelle and Rosanna filled their audience in on the morning's escape from Blenthwaite, the meeting and the phone conversation with Lord Bassenford.

'So His Lordshit now officially knows Isabelle's back,' said Max, scribbling notes in his reporter's pad as usual. 'How did he react to that news?'

'It certainly got him disconcerted,' said Philip with a grin. 'He even stomped out of the room for a while. Coming on top of the realisation that he's managed to alienate all three of his children, I did wonder for a moment if it had actually broken him.'

'Is that when Dex got to talk to Matty?' Alan asked eagerly.

'Yes, Alan,' replied Philip. 'Dex looks very relaxed, by the way…'

'But he's still trapped, I'm afraid, Al,' said Theo. 'He's got one of those awful security bracelets locked to his wrist, probably the same one I used to wear.'

'Hmm,' said Alan, sighing. 'Well, at least he isn't getting kicked about any more, which is a weight off my mind. I am going to give that Dyer such a slap when I get my hands on him…'

'You won't be alone there, Al,' said Jess.

'I suggested to His Lordshit that he let Dex go without getting the American Embassy involved,' Philip told Alan, 'but as I was being rather unceremoniously ejected from his house at that point I'm not sure he took any notice.'

'Hmm,' said Alan again, 'looks like it'll have to be the Embassy then.'

Philip persuaded Alan that it would be prudent to phone ahead, commenting that the American Embassy might not look too kindly on a rather highly-strung Englishman arriving unannounced on the doorstep. So far reaching was Philip's influence that it didn't take him long to get through to Charlie Rollins, an embassy official and a casual acquaintance of his. Although sceptical about the allegations that Lord Bassenford was holding an American citizen prisoner, Rollins had enough respect for Philip's standing in the UK to agree to meet without further ado and discuss the situation.

Facing Philip Lorimer, Alan Santiago and Georgia Farrell across his desk, Rollins finished his phone call.

'OK,' he said, 'Lord Bassenford will see us in half an hour.'

'How did he seem?' asked Alan anxiously.

'Relaxed,' replied Rollins, looking dubiously at Alan's flamboyant attire. 'You are the one who made the allegations initially, right?'

'They're not allegations. It's the truth…'

'We will see, Mr Santiago. Might I suggest that only you and I attend this interview with Lord Bassenford? We at the embassy have a good relationship with the Sponsors, and I have no wish to antagonise His Lordship by turning up mob handed.'

As arranged, half an hour later Rollins and Alan were shown into Lord Bassenford's office by Mooreland. Surrounded by a number of high-ranking Sponsors, Rollins found the whole episode a little embarrassing, and his embarrassment only increased as the interview progressed.

'William St Benedict,' said His Lordship unnecessarily by way of introduction, shaking Charlie Rollins by the hand. Alan ignored His Lordship's outstretched hand, instead sitting down without waiting to be asked.

'Please be seated,' said Lord Bassenford, smiling pointedly at Alan. 'Now, gentlemen, what can I do for you?'

'I've had a report from this... gentleman... here,' Rollins gestured at Alan, not sure 'gentleman' was the right word, 'that his, er, partner, Dexter Montfiore, an American citizen, is being held against his will in your house...'

Charlie Rollins's voice tailed off as Lord Bassenford bellowed with laughter. Looking scathingly at Alan, who was beginning to wish he'd put slightly less eyeliner on that morning, His Lordship said, 'I think your companion has rather a vivid imagination. Or perhaps a taste for hallucinogenic drugs – God only knows what these Unsponsored get up to. Mr Rollins, feel free to search my house from top to bottom. Feel free to question my colleagues here, who spend a large amount of time in my house and I'm sure would have noticed a random American incarcerated herein. All are *respectable* people.' Lord Bassenford again looked pointedly at Alan, who was surreptitiously trying to remove a pink grip from his hair and sneak it into his pocket. 'All are of high standing in the Sponsorship Scheme, and are therefore regarded with the utmost respect here in the UK. Ladies and gentlemen,' Lord Bassenford continued, addressing his Sponsors, 'have you noticed an American being held captive in my house?'

The Sponsors all obediently replied that they hadn't, some laughing incredulously at the notion that the benevolent Lord Bassenford would hold a fellow human captive. The household staff had also been warned to deny ever having seen Dexter Montfiore, so Lord Bassenford was confident in inviting Charlie Rollins to ask as many questions as he needed. Rollins, however, had heard enough. Ushering Alan hurriedly out of the office, he didn't even wait until they were free of the St Benedict residence before he gave vent to his anger, instead letting fly on their way down the stairs, his words carrying back to a highly amused Lord Bassenford.

'Well, that was embarrassing. I realise that you Unsponsored have some sort of grudge against the Scheme, but *how dare* you try to get the American Embassy involved! Don't you think we've got far more important issues than your little rebellion? What the hell's your problem anyway? Why can't you accept sponsorship? To my mind it offers so many benefits.'

'With respect…'

'Shut the fuck up, fag!' roared Rollins, his anger causing latent homophobia to come to the fore. 'I'm not interested in another word from you. How dare you accuse a respectable man like Lord Bassenford of kidnapping. If it were down to me, I'd have you horsewhipped for wasting my time.'

Sneering triumphantly, Stephen Dyer saw the furious Charlie Rollins and the crestfallen Alan Santiago out, but as he opened the door, his taunts died on his lips. Of all the rotten timing, why did they have to be leaving at the exact moment Faye Maloney and Mortimer O'Reilly arrived back from Blenthwaite?

'Alan,' called Faye, climbing out of Lee Fellows's car, 'you missed Dex by a couple of hours…'

'Excuse me?' said Rollins. 'And you are?'

'Faye Maloney, Director of Leisure and Fitness,' replied Faye with a smile, holding out her Gold Sponsor Card. 'Are you looking for Dexter Montfiore? His Lordship let him go earlier, hoping not to get the American Embassy involved.'

Charlie Rollins examined Faye's card, beginning to feel a little nonplussed.

'What do you mean, let him go?'

'Well, His Lordship's interested in bringing the hostilities between the Sponsors and the Unsponsored to a close before the Olympics. He was holding Dex as a negotiating tool, until Alan here pointed out that it might not be wise to hold an American captive.'

'Your colleagues upstairs said there'd been no sign of a prisoner in His Lordship's home, American or otherwise.'

'They're lying. His Lordship can be very persuasive when he wants to be.'

Charlie Rollins turned to Mortimer O'Reilly. 'Is this true?' he asked, although his instincts were already telling him to believe Faye rather than the stilted, rehearsed words of her colleagues in Lord Bassenford's office.

'Er, yes,' said Mortimer reluctantly, figuring that he was in so much trouble already, a little more was hardly going to hurt. Examining Mortimer's Gold Card, Rollins knew enough about the history of the Scheme to realise that he wasn't merely a high-ranking Sponsor, he was a founder member.

'Well,' said Alan, grinning at Rollins, 'best you put that horsewhip away, sweetie.'

At that moment, Lord Bassenford burst out of his house. How stupid he'd been, yet again!

He'd instructed the Sponsors in his office to lie for him, he'd primed his staff to do the same, but he'd failed to extend his orders to the outspoken Faye Maloney. Was he too late?

'Lord Bassenford,' said Charlie Rollins, 'it appears that you have in actual fact been holding an American citizen prisoner. I will be investigating this further.'

Lord Bassenford was too late.

Chapter 26 – Sport Wins

As the Olympic Games drew ever closer, Louis and Gideon spent their days going through routine after routine in their pursuit of the perfect ten. Since the exodus from The White Lion Inn, Lord Bassenford had withdrawn all his people from Blenthwaite and ordered them to return to London, so Philip had had no problem liberating Louis's essential apparatus from Gideon's studio and having it transported south. Usually Gideon coached Louis in a deserted HQ, the Unsponsored spending most of their time out on the streets of London canvassing the media, Unsponsored from other areas and also the Sponsored, more and more of whom were becoming disillusioned with their stifled lives as they finally recognised there was a viable alternative, but occasionally Abi or Theo would stop by to watch.

'Lou, that was amazing,' said Theo a few days before the Olympics began, watching wide-eyed as his friend completed a seemingly impossible routine on the parallel bars and landed with perfect balance.

'That's the one,' agreed Gideon. 'Perform like that, Louis, and no one will be able to deny you a place in the finals.'

'That's all very well,' said Louis, 'but is anyone really going to watch?'

'We just have to live in hope,' replied Gideon, doing his best to sound optimistic.

'Hope. Yeah, right.'

It turned out, though, that Louis's scepticism was misplaced. Hope arrived in the nick of time, and it came from a most unexpected source.

***

'Do you reckon we should go out canvassing tomorrow?' Matilda asked the night before the Olympic opening ceremony.

'I don't see why not,' replied Max. 'After all, we're only exercising our right to free speech.'

'I'm just worried that the sponsored media will twist it round to make us look like the bad guys,' Matilda persisted. 'You know how economical they are with the truth.'

'Shouldn't matter. We're getting more and more coverage from the international media over for the Olympics. Obviously they're not restricted by sponsorship…'

'But the point is, Max, essentially they're over for the Olympics, not to give us publicity. I'm worried that the Sponsors will make it look as though we're trying to sabotage the tournament while the news crews from other countries are covering the opening ceremony.'

'Point taken, Matty. Perhaps we could go out, but maybe only a few of us to distribute newsletters. Any sign of sponsored grief, we leg it back here.'

'Agreed,' said Matilda. 'The last thing we want is to get on the wrong side of the Olympic authorities and jeopardise any chance Louis and Gideon have…'

'Where is Gideon, by the way?' asked Louis, realising he hadn't seen his mentor all evening.

'He went out with Adam and Philip,' replied Jenny absently, distracted by the task of plaiting ribbons into Alan's hair.

'Why didn't you tell me earlier, Jen?'

'Louis! I've been busy, silly, making Alan look pretty.'

'Good luck with that, Jenny,' said Matilda, grinning at the child. 'It's not like Gideon to sneak off without telling anyone, though. Do you know what it's all about, Sarah?'

'No, Matty love,' said Sarah, trying not to feel put out that Gideon hadn't even told her. 'I'm sure it's nothing to worry about, though. Adam and Philip are hardly likely to lead him into danger…'

'And they didn't,' said Gideon, wheeling himself over to kiss Sarah, an extremely self-satisfied look on his face.

'Where have you been?' grumbled Louis. 'It's the night before the Olympics begin and you're gallivanting off God knows where…'

'I don't think you need me to hold your hand, Louis,' replied Gideon with a grin. 'Not when you've got Abi to do the job.'

'Don't change the subject, Gideon. Where have you been?'

'I've been to see a man – well men, actually, and women – about an unsponsored gymnast. Cinderella, you *shall* go to the ball.'

'Stop talking in riddles and tell me where you've been!' demanded Louis, his irritation growing relative to Gideon's smugness.

'He's been talking to my parents,' said Adam, approaching with Philip, 'and some people from the Olympics.'

'Adam! I wanted it to be a surprise.'

'Shut up, *Gid*,' snapped Louis, mildly satisfied to see the smirk vanish from Gideon's face. 'Go on, Ads.'

'Well,' said Adam as everyone turned to look at him, 'you know Rose is staying with my parents at the moment.'

Everyone nodded, smiling wryly. For a while Rosanna had been living alongside the Unsponsored, but quite a few of them had been uneasy about the situation, unable to forget the Lady Bitch of the past. To make matters worse, it had soon become apparent that Rosanna and Theo still couldn't spend more than a few minutes in each other's company without fighting, and when Her Ladyship had had a few choice words to say about the lack of amenities in the HQ it had been the last straw for many. Adam had hastily stepped in to rectify the situation, getting in touch with his parents to ask if they'd mind having a house guest for a while.

'When I took Rose to Mum and Dad's,' he continued, 'I was hardly going to turn round and leave straight away. I know they're both Sponsors, but they're my parents and I've missed them. Don't worry,' he added, 'I didn't give anything away. It was Dad who was giving stuff away to me, actually – stuff about Louis.'

Louis looked startled and Gideon started smirking again.

'Dad told his side of the story, from the moment His Lordshit decided last December to include Louis in Team GB. Mum and Dad are far more in touch with the real world than His Lordshit…'

'Who lives in his own exclusive cloud-cuckoo-land,' murmured Theo.

'Well, quite,' said Adam. 'As soon as Dad got back from Blenthwaite, His Lordshit was on at him to arrange for Louis to compete. Dad knew there'd be no point even trying to explain the rules of Olympic qualification. Instead, he had to find a way of getting Louis into the British team, and as a result he's been liaising with the Gymnastic Federation and Olympic officials since December. He was on the verge of a breakthrough when, lo and behold, His

Lordshit had a hissy fit and decided he didn't want Louis in the team after all.'

'Oh yes, the day I was sacked,' said Lysander, grinning. 'No wonder David looked so pissed off…'

'Oh, he was. So was Mum.' Suddenly Adam's face broke into a huge grin. 'I'm delighted to say, my parents have rebelled. They decided that they'd continue with the negotiations behind His Lordshit's back, and that's what led to tonight. Obviously, the Gymnastic Federation representatives had all heard of Gideon…'

Gideon inclined his head, looking immensely pleased with himself.

'And they wanted to meet with him, hear his opinion and learn more about his mysterious protégé.'

'I was the last piece of the jigsaw as far as the officials were concerned,' said Gideon. 'David and Julia had done all the groundwork. I haven't always seen eye to eye with your father, Adam…'

'No,' said Jess, 'neither did Elliot.'

'But he's redeemed himself just when we needed him most. I know your views, Jess, but I think even Elliot would agree that David Foster's finally come good. All I had to do was confirm that Louis is by far the best gymnast this country has ever produced…'

'Since you, Gideon…'

'No, Louis, the best *ever*. Thanks to David, the Olympic officials were already aware that you weren't able to compete in any qualifiers due to your lack of sponsorship. The recent media attention the Unsponsored have been getting has helped to underline the oppression going on in this country, and coupled with my guarantee that Louis's talent is well worth displaying to the world, that swung things totally in our favour.'

'So, no pressure, then,' said Louis nervously.

'None at all, Louis,' said Gideon, wheeling his chair over to the young man. 'None whatsoever, because you *are* the best.'

'If you say so,' said Louis, still not fully convinced. 'What next?'

'The qualifiers are on Saturday. You turn up. You show the judges what you can do. You qualify for the medal events. Simple enough for you, numb-nuts?'

'Which events?'

'The ones you bloody qualify for, you moron!'

'Gideon, don't talk to Louis like that!' snapped Sarah. 'He's not stupid.'

'It's OK, Sarah, I like Gideon yelling at me. It has a cosy familiarity about it. Right, Gideon,' continued Louis, turning to his mentor, 'I do actually know how this qualifying thing works…'

'I don't,' said Theo with a chuckle. 'Could you explain a bit more please, Gideon? Loudly. Calling Louis lots of nasty names as you go.'

'Dickhead,' said Louis, aiming a playful kick at Theo. Laughing as he was upended on to a beanbag by Matilda, he added, 'Careful, Matty, I think Gideon may just skin you alive if you injure me now.'

'He wouldn't dare,' said Matilda cheerfully.

'I wouldn't dare,' agreed Gideon.

'I wouldn't recommend you dare,' added Alan, his eyes widening in dismay when the assembled Unsponsored took one look at him and dissolved into raucous laughter.

'If I ever take advice from a man with a headful of pink ribbons,' said Gideon, his eyes streaming, 'my credibility won't survive the shame.'

'I think Alan looks very pretty,' said Jenny, looking as put out as her model.

'Glad someone's got taste,' grumbled Alan, narrowing his eyes at Dex who was on his back, clutching his sides. 'If you'd all like to stop giggling like schoolgirls, I for one am interested in learning more about how our fab unsponsored gymnast is going to qualify for the Olympic finals.'

'Quite simple,' said Gideon, trying hard to control his laughter. 'Louis does his stuff. The judges award him points for each event. If he scores enough points in total, he'll go through to the all-round medal event, and he'll also qualify for any individual event in which he achieves a high score. I'd expect to see Louis qualify for the parallel bars and possibly the horizontal bar, as well as the all-round…'

'So no pressure, then,' interrupted Louis again, nerves kicking in with a vengeance.

'None at all, Lou,' said Abi, squeezing his hand. 'If Gideon believes in you, then you're good enough.'

'We're all behind you, son,' added Lysander.

'Yeah, knock the Sponsored for six, Bleachy,' said Max, his pen flying across the page of his notepad as he recorded the conversation for posterity.

'Man up, Lou,' said Theo, starting to laugh again, 'or I'm sure Jenny can find a nice stash of pink ribbons for your hair.'

'OK, OK,' said Louis, holding up his hands, 'I believe!'

***

While Julia Foster was sitting in Lord Bassenford's office the day after the Olympic Games opening ceremony, dwelling on comments such as 'well organised' and 'cleverly planned' to describe a Sponsor-endorsed show that to her mind had been completely lacking in spontaneity or originality, her husband was watching an extremely talented unsponsored gymnast wow the Olympic judges. The sponsored British gymnasts had at first been suspicious and resentful about Louis Trevelyan's last-minute inclusion, glowering at him as they whispered among themselves, but as the day wore on they could only watch in awe as he performed, his confidence growing with every familiar flex of his muscles. Word soon went round that Gideon Wallis was back on the scene for the first time since his horrific accident, and that his protégé was, if anything, even more gifted than the great man himself. Before long, anyone who could blag a last-minute ticket to watch the men's gymnastics qualifiers had done so, and by the time the results were announced, the venue was packed to the rafters with excited spectators. And all anyone could talk about was the young man with albinism who'd appeared from obscurity to take the world of gymnastics by storm.

Glowing with pride, Gideon wheeled himself over to Louis and for once was at a loss for words.

'Come on, Gid,' said Louis. 'It's not like you to have nothing to say.'

'Don't call me Gid,' was all the older man could manage in a curiously choked voice.

David Foster was a lot more eloquent. 'You were brilliant, Louis. Absolutely stunning display. I knew you were good last winter, but you've surpassed my expectations. Amazing. Simply amazing. Gideon, you're a genius.'

Gideon's ability to speak returned. 'Louis is the genius, Foster. I'm just lucky enough to work with the best.'

'All the same, no one could have trained Louis better than you. Everyone knows that. You're amazing, both of you.'

'Do stop gushing, Foster,' said Gideon, beaming. 'I hope this doesn't bring you too much grief from His Lordshit.'

'Oh, it will. And do you know what? I couldn't care less! Sport won the day today, Gideon. Sport won.'

Gideon shook hands warmly with David Foster, a man he used to despise. 'Noble sentiments, David,' he said. 'Sport won, couldn't agree more.'

***

As Louis's inclusion in the qualifying round had come so late, only Gideon had been permitted to accompany him to the arena, much to the dismay of Dory's Avengers. Abi, Sarah and Lysander in particular had a highly frustrating day, biting their nails and watching the clock, radios pressed against their ears. Theo wasn't much better, driving everyone mad with his constant fidgeting until Matilda grabbed him by the hand and ran with him, whooping and screaming, around the perimeter of Unsponsored HQ. Even Jenny, although too young to have any memories of previous Olympic Games, had picked up on the fact that something important was happening and it involved her brother. She chose to deal with her surplus energy by back-flipping round and round her companions, demonstrating that Nicola had passed on her talent to her daughter as well as her son.

Inspired by Jenny's natural ability, Theo decided to try his luck as a gymnast too, declaring that the assembled company should 'Watch this' as he posed, arms held aloft, in front of his favourite cushion. After a number of failed attempts to execute a balanced headstand on the cushion, and a lot of piss taking from his friends, he was finally forced to admit that he was not the 'new Louis Trevelyan' and suggested finding a pub in which to pass the time instead.

'There's a good boozer up on Kennington Lane,' suggested Jim with the benefit of local knowledge. 'Unsponsored, of course…'

Jim's voice trailed off as Theo, Abi and Matilda were already heading for the door, the rest of Dory's Avengers hot on their heels. 'I'll stay here, shall I?' he said as Lysander took Jenny's hand to follow the others. 'Let Louis and Gideon know where you've gone.'

'Thanks, Jim,' replied Lysander. 'Sorry to desert you like this…'

'No problem, Lysander mate.' Laughing, Jim added, 'I'd never have believed it if anyone had told me a year ago I'd one day call Lysander Trevelyan "mate"! Go on, see you later.'

'Come on,' said Jess, grabbing Lysander's other hand and leading him out of the HQ. 'If in doubt, get drunk.'

'Ah, sound advice, Dr Donatelli,' said Lysander, realising as his fingers entwined around hers how much he'd missed a woman's touch.

Jim had recommended wisely. The Kennington Lane pub was run by Mary, a warm and hospitable Irishwoman who was delighted to have her bar full of visitors from Blenthwaite. By the time Jess, Lysander and Jenny arrived, Theo had already introduced his companions to Mary and the pub's unsponsored regulars, and Max was basking in their praise for keeping them so well informed with his newsletter.

'And to think you used to work for the Sponsors,' said Mary. 'Did you ever meet His Lordshit?'

'Once or twice,' replied Max with a shudder, 'but not as much as poor Theo here.'

'My God,' said Mary, realisation dawning as she turned to Theo. 'You're…'

'Afraid so,' said Theo with a grin. 'His Lordshit's son, to my eternal shame.'

As Dory's Avengers and Mary's regulars bonded and got to know each other, Lysander and Jess were facing a good-natured grilling from Abi and Cameron, thanks to Jenny spilling the beans as soon as she'd arrived in the pub.

'Daddy held Jess's hand all the way here.'

'Oh aye, Mam? Lysander?'

'I held your hand all the way too, young lady…'

'Yes, Daddy, but you held Jess's hand in a *boyfriendy* way.'

'Really?' said Alan, grinning over Abi's shoulder.

'Oh no, *numero uno* gossip has heard the rumour.' Jess rolled her eyes in mock exasperation, secretly having found Lysander's touch as pleasant as he had found hers. 'Might as well print it on a billboard.'

'No need now I'm on the case. Hey, everyone, Lysander and Jess are getting it on…'

'Subtle isn't your strong point, is it, Al.'

'Subtle is *sooo* overrated, Jessica sweetie,' said Alan, laughing. 'Oh look! The Olympics!'

The rumours concerning who had been holding hands on the way to the pub were forgotten as the huge domed arena loomed large on the pub's television screen.

'I'm joined now by David Foster, Director of the Sports Sponsorship Group…'

A number of Mary's regulars booed loudly at the mention of David's name. Adam glared at them, but Lysander hushed everyone before he had a chance to defend his father.

'…as we look at the results of the men's gymnastics qualifying round,' continued the television reporter. 'Of course, the main talking point has to be the last-minute decision to include an unsponsored gymnast in qualifying…'

'Just tell us if he's qualified!'

'Shh, Theo!'

'Yes,' David was saying on the screen, 'Louis Trevelyan, trained by none other than Gideon Wallis. Of course, being unsponsored, Louis had no chance to qualify for the Olympics through the usual channels…'

'Here comes the Sponsor propaganda,' moaned one of the regulars.

'Will you give my dad a break and listen to what he's saying!' snapped Adam.

'In the interests of sport, and of putting forward the strongest British team possible, we were able to come to an agreement with the Olympic Authorities and the Gymnastic Federation whereby Louis could compete in the qualifiers today. After all, lack of sponsorship shouldn't stand in the way of someone as talented as Louis Trevelyan…'

'Am I to believe what I'm hearing?' asked Mary incredulously as Adam smiled proudly at his father's words. On the television, the reporter was asking the question all of Dory's Avengers wanted answering.

'Did Louis Trevelyan qualify?'

'If I were to say that Louis is probably even more talented than Gideon Wallis in his heyday, I think you can guess the answer to that question,' replied David, beaming at the surprised sponsored television reporter. 'Sport won the day today. Louis qualified handsomely for the individual all-round final, and he will also represent Great Britain on the floor, horizontal bar and parallel bars…'

'YEEEEEEEAAARGH!'

David continued speaking, but his words were drowned out by an incoherent scream of triumph as Lysander launched himself from his bar stool and punched the air. As one, the Unsponsored in the pub broke into a jubilant dance of celebration, the jukebox deciding randomly, but highly appropriately, to accompany the dance with the strains of Tina Turner's *Simply the Best*.

'I was saving these for my daughter's wedding,' Mary said, returning from her large refrigerator with a crate of champagne bottles and popping the corks one by one, 'but I can always get some more. I've got a great team of unsponsored suppliers who never let me down when it comes to sourcing drinks for my regulars.'

Georgie, the only person in the pub close enough to hear Mary's words over the general hubbub, grinned conspiratorially.

'My brother and I run a pub up in Cumbria,' she said, 'so I know exactly what you mean.'

'So, an unsponsored gymnast in the Olympic finals. Just how good is he?'

'See for yourself,' replied Georgie, nodding at the television screen.

'Sweet Jesus, that's impressive,' said Mary, watching the footage of Louis's breathtaking qualifying performance on the parallel bars as she poured the champagne into glasses. When Louis landed on his feet at the end of his routine, arms held aloft and a huge smile on his face, the noise in the pub went through the roof and Mary had to resort to using the quizmaster's microphone to make herself heard.

'Help yourselves!' she announced, gesturing towards the glasses of bubbly sparkling on the bar. As the Unsponsored crowded round, all eager to raise a glass to their new hero, Mary cast her eyes over the pub and noticed a lone man standing empty handed, his attention glued to the Olympic Games footage.

Squeezing through the crowd, she passed him a glass of champagne. 'Here you go, Lysander, don't miss out.' Looking at the television screen, where Louis was racing over to his coach, his face wreathed in smiles, she added, 'He's quite amazing, isn't he? I take it you're related?'

'Oh yes,' Lysander replied huskily, turning gleaming eyes in Mary's direction as he savoured the proudest moment of his life. 'He's my son.'

Chapter 27 – Gold!

'Louis Trevelyan has done *what*?' asked Lord Bassenford in an ominously quiet voice, standing up slowly to face his head of household in the drawing room of his grand old London townhouse.

'He's qualified for the Olympic finals, Your Lordship,' replied Mooreland, his trademark sombre voice masking his apprehension at having to be the one to break the news to his boss. 'I caught the servants listening to the report on the kitchen radio.'

'Turn the television on, Mooreland.'

Lord Bassenford was just in time to hear David Foster's ecstatic pronouncement that sport had won the day.

'No, stay,' said His Lordship as Mooreland turned to leave the room. 'I want you to bear witness to this.'

'Does that mean,' the television reporter's voice blared as Lord Bassenford increased the volume, 'that an unsponsored gymnast is competing with the blessing, of the Sports Sponsorship Group?'

'While Julia and I head the Sports Group, yes,' replied David. 'But I think our days may be numbered.'

'So, Louis Trevelyan has qualified with the full knowledge and blessing of the Sports Group, but not necessarily of Lord Bassenford and the overall Sponsorship Scheme?'

'I should imagine His Lordship has full knowledge by now,' said David, laughing heartily. 'I think the blessing of the Sponsorship Scheme may be a little more difficult to come by.'

'Do you realise this could cost you and your wife your jobs?'

'Jobs, sponsorship – yes, I'm guessing we've lost the lot. Do I feel like a loser? Not at all! Sport won today, and I'm proud to have been a part of it…'

'Mooreland,' said Lord Bassenford, muting his television, 'fetch my laptop.'

***

The following morning, Lord Bassenford's inner circle, with the notable exception of the Fosters, arrived for probably their most tense meeting since the dawn of the Scheme. No one was in any doubt as to why they had been summoned: it had been impossible to turn on the television the previous night without being confronted with discussions about Louis Trevelyan's qualification and Gideon Wallis's emergence from obscurity for the first time since his accident.

'Mortimer,' barked His Lordship, sweeping into the room, 'may I congratulate you on the accuracy of your prediction all those years ago. It would seem that Trevelyan's son has indeed come back to haunt us in a most unexpected manner. It is a shame, is it not, Mortimer, that you couldn't also have predicted the *treachery* of some of the people I used to call friends?'

As Mortimer trembled in his chair, Lord Bassenford glared around the room.

'First, Lysander Trevelyan,' he growled. 'Lysander, my Leisure and Fitness expert, betrayed me. Then David and Julia Foster – I gave them the world of sport at their feet. I never expected gratitude, but I also never expected them to betray me too. My wife, my children – everywhere I turn, people are waiting in the wings to stab me in the back. Do any of you have plans to do the same? Faye?'

'No, Your Lordship,' replied Faye, her voice as steady as ever. 'I joined the Scheme as a keen advocate of its benefits and methods, and I remain so.'

'Thank you, Faye. Mortimer?'

'S-s-still with you, Your Lordship.'

'Good. Fiona?'

'Indeed, Your Lordship,' replied Dr Fiona Turnbull, the woman responsible for curbing Nicola Trevelyan's rebellious spirit by sinking her into a long-term drug-induced stupor. 'That will never be in doubt.'

'Excellent. Stephanie?'

Lord Bassenford asked each Sponsor in turn to pledge their allegiance to the Scheme. Mollified a little by their assurances, he then sat back in his chair, fingers steepled under his chin.

'Good,' he said finally. 'Thank you, my friends. Your support is invaluable to me. The Scheme is not – I repeat, *not* in crisis. The defectors will be dealt with severely, and Louis Trevelyan will not be competing in the Olympics. I'll get some of my best security men on the case, and once they find young Trevelyan, gymnastics will be a thing of the past for him.' Laughing nastily, Lord Bassenford added, '*Walking* will be a thing of the past for him!'

'Your Lordship, is that wise?'

'Faye?'

'Well, the world knows about Louis Trevelyan now, like it or not. The world knows that David condoned Louis's inclusion in qualifying. We don't have control over the world's media, Your Lordship, and I fear that to… er… punish either David or Louis at this time would be detrimental to the Scheme's reputation…'

'Louis? David? First-name terms, Faye? Anyone would believe you had some affection for these wretched people.'

Lord Bassenford was silent for a while, his expression unreadable.

'Unfortunately, I fear you might be right. Once again, it's down to Faye to point out unpalatable truths to me. Am I really such an evil tyrant that nobody dares disagree with me?' Smiling all of a sudden, Lord Bassenford waved a hand at his Sponsors and said, 'On second thoughts, don't answer that. I think I'd rather not know.'

'So, what's next, Your Lordship?' asked Mortimer tentatively.

'Ah, it speaks,' jeered Lord Bassenford. 'Can't you get your crystal ball out and tell me, Mortimer?'

'I'd rather you told me, Your Lordship,' said Mortimer, summoning up what little courage he had, 'being as everything I say seems to be wrong.'

To the surprise of all the Sponsors, not least Mortimer, Lord Bassenford roared with laughter.

'Goodness me, Mortimer, when did you get so cheeky? You almost sound like Lysander! That was a compliment, by the way.' Wiping his eyes, Lord Bassenford addressed the whole room. 'Well, I've got to hand it to Mortimer here, I wasn't expecting anyone to make me laugh today. Right, this is what happens next: Trevelyan is going to compete. Faye's right, we've not got much choice there. I suggest we celebrate the fact that a British gymnast looks set to win gold...'

'Shall we go one step further, Your Lordship?' Faye suggested. 'We could take the Unsponsored by surprise and actually give Trevelyan our support – officially, I mean.'

'Interesting, Faye. Yes, why not? We'll give our official backing to Trevelyan, turn up in numbers to cheer him on in the... what's he competing in again?'

'G-gymnastics?' ventured Mortimer. Lord Bassenford threw him a withering look.

'I *know* the man's a gymnast, Mortimer. I meant, which gymnastics *event* is he competing in?'

'Men's all-round final,' replied Faye, consulting her phone.

'That's the one. We'll cheer him on in the all-round final – I'll reserve a block of seats as soon as this meeting's closed – and rubbish the claims that he wasn't allowed to compete because he's Unsponsored, then break every bone in his lily-white body once the world's press has left the country.'

Faye raised her eyebrows slightly, thinking back to some stiff questioning she'd recently had to endure from Charlie Rollins concerning

Dexter Montfiore's abduction, followed by an even more intense grilling from government officials regarding Lord Bassenford's increasingly dubious methods of control. Faye, being Faye, had been amused by the fact that the government had lost no time in stabbing its former bedfellow in the back as soon as the American Embassy started asking embarrassing questions, but many of her colleagues had found their own interrogations a lot more traumatic. Noticing the expression on Faye's face, the supremely traumatised Mortimer O'Reilly frowned across the room at her, a clear warning to keep her mouth closed on the subject, but he could have saved himself the trouble.

Not even the outspoken Director of Leisure and Fitness wanted to be the one to tell Lord Bassenford he probably wouldn't get the opportunity to carry out his threat.

***

Three days later, Lord Bassenford arrived with a select few of his Sponsors to watch the men's all-round gymnastics final, and he took his seat with beaming looks. He felt completely relaxed, sure that he could use Louis Trevelyan's inclusion in the Olympics to the advantage of the Scheme – if Louis were to fail, Lord Bassenford would lament the young man's lack of Sports Sponsorship-endorsed training, emphasising the superb facilities and coaches he had spurned. If Louis were to succeed, Lord Bassenford would be the first to register his delight, rubbishing recent public claims of sponsorship oppression and discrimination against the Unsponsored and magnanimously offering to sponsor Louis's future training personally.

What could possibly go wrong?

Lord Bassenford wasn't the only one who had secured tickets for the final. Louis himself had managed to get a few for his nearest and dearest, so Lysander, Sarah, Abi and Jenny were able to accompany him and Gideon to the arena. Theo was initially a little put out that Louis had only been offered four tickets and there wasn't one for him, but on seeing him so despondent, Sarah kindly told him that he could have her ticket for the parallel and horizontal bars finals. Delighted that he would be able to cheer his friend on in person the following Tuesday, Theo hugged Sarah in gratitude then joined Matilda and the rest of Dory's Avengers in the Kennington Lane pub, his characteristic high spirits fully restored.

Now that Louis had arrived at the finals, he was far less nervous than he had been for the qualifiers. He had already come further than he ever dreamed possible, still not accepting that he was as good as everyone made him out to be, so whatever he achieved today would be a bonus.

'For God's sake, Louis,' Gideon yelled just before his first performance, thoroughly fed up with his persistent refusal to believe in himself, 'you're at the bloody Olympics! You're competing for a medal! When will you finally understand how talented you are – when you're on the podium accepting gold?'

Immensely reassured by his mentor's familiar bad temper, Louis grinned at Gideon then racked up a highly respectable score on the vault.

Throughout the day, the medal places were contested fiercely between Louis and gymnasts from the USA, China and Japan. Going into the final event – for Louis, the parallel bars – he was in the bronze medal position, conscious that a Brazilian gymnast had just scored an exceptional points tally on pommel and was making a late bid for a medal spot. His supporters in the arena looked on nervously as the tension mounted, but in the Kennington Lane pub, the atmosphere was a lot more relaxed. Fuelled by beer, the Unsponsored cheered Louis on raucously every time it was his turn to perform, whooping loudly (and a tad unsportingly) when one of his rivals for the medals came off the parallel bars halfway through his routine and incurred a costly points deduction.

Knowing that parallel bars was Louis's forté and deciding he had pretty much bagged himself a place on the podium, Matilda, glass of prosecco held aloft, leapt off Theo's lap, pulled him to his feet and started a conga around the bar.

'He's gonna get a med-al, he's gonna get a med-al, la-la lah-lah, la-la lah-lah!'

The conga ground to a halt as the pub fell silent for the first time that afternoon, no one daring to blink while Louis made a technically demanding routine on his favourite apparatus look like a stroll in the park. During the tense pause that followed while the judges deliberated over his score, the television cameras focused on the gymnast and his coach, who in turn were staring at the scoreboard. Then Gideon's eyes widened and his trademark dimples appeared either side of a huge smile. As the colossal score that had shot Louis to the top of the leader board appeared on the television screen, chaotic celebrating broke out in Mary's pub, the conga starting up again with a revised set of lyrics.

'He's gonna get a go-old, he's gonna get a go-old…'

And the conga was right. As the event drew to a close and the medal places were confirmed, the television cameras panned round to an astonished Louis at the exact moment he clearly said, 'Fuck me!' Then the implications of the scores sank in and pandemonium broke loose. The crowd of spectators in the arena leapt to their feet as one and raised the roof, cheering and screaming themselves hoarse; the usually lucid commentators were reduced to gabbling wrecks; Gideon punched the air so hard he nearly toppled out of his wheelchair. In Kennington Lane, Theo and Matilda ran up and down the pavement outside Mary's pub, a huge British flag held aloft between them and passing drivers saluting them with a chorus of car horns, while across the entire Sponsor-oppressed country, the collective amazement of the Unsponsored gave way to scenes of unbridled joy.

Louis Trevelyan, the unknown gymnast from the defiantly unsponsored village in Cumbria, had not only beaten the best in the world, he'd totally, utterly and completely annihilated them.

Chapter 28 – As Mortimer Foretold

Louis accepted his gold medal with an expression on his face that suggested he would wake up from this crazy dream any moment. Abi, Lysander and Sarah were all moved to tears as he stood proud on the podium while the National Anthem rang around the arena, Jenny turning to them in exasperation to ask why they were all crying when they should be happy. Lord Bassenford too stood for the National Anthem, smiling and applauding as the music ended, and when confronted by a host of journalists as he made for his car, he was able to tell them he was genuinely very impressed with Louis Trevelyan. Not so genuine, though, was his response when asked why the Sponsors hadn't put Louis forward to compete before the Olympics actually began.

'Unfortunately, the Unsponsored tend to keep themselves to themselves. They congregate in ghettos, don't look kindly upon outsiders, don't live to the high standards expected by the Sponsored in this country. Therefore, we had no idea that they were harbouring such a gifted gymnast. Even Louis's own father, Lysander Trevelyan, knew nothing of his son's talent while still in my employ. It only came to light when the son of David and Julia Foster, my

Sports Group Directors, struck up a friendship with young Trevelyan, and the rest is history.'

Listening to His Lordship's interview on a transistor radio with Gideon and Louis, Lysander shook his head in disbelief.

'Even Lysander knew nothing of his son's talent? Does His Lordshit think I can't speak for myself?'

'Time to put the record straight,' said Gideon, pointing at an approaching crowd of reporters, headed by Max. The reporters made straight for Louis, but found the young man still far too dazed by the enormity of what he had achieved to give a coherent interview.

'Oh, hello, Max. Who let you in here?' was all he could manage.

'Came in with these guys, Bleachy,' Max replied, gesturing towards a group of American journalists. 'They love anyone unsponsored, we've really caught their imagination. Oh, and well done, mate. You were ace today.'

'Cheers, Max. Looks like Gideon's talking, don't miss out.'

Sitting quietly with his father, Louis watched Gideon holding the world's press rapt as he told the unsponsored version of events.

'I understand Lord Bassenford has intimated that Louis didn't qualify through the usual channels because the Unsponsored were unwilling to share him with the world. I'm sure you'll make up your own minds whether or not His Lordship is speaking the truth, but from our point of view he is talking rubbish. It was Lord Bassenford himself who said only sponsored athletes would compete for Britain in these Olympics.'

'Gideon's right,' said Julia Foster, joining the interview. 'The Unsponsored always wanted Louis to compete, which is why Gideon has trained him to such a high standard. David and I have spent months negotiating a means by which Louis could bypass the qualifiers…'

'So,' said Max, 'let me get this straight. Louis was forbidden to qualify for the Olympics simply because he's unsponsored, and it was Lord Bassenford who forbade it?'

'You know full well it was, Max,' snapped Gideon.

'Work with me here, Gideon,' whispered Max, jerking his head towards the multitude of television cameras pointing their way.

'Oh yes, of course.' Gideon grinned conspiratorially. 'Yes, Lord Bassenford, William St Benedict, Head of the Sponsorship Scheme in the UK, whatever you wish to call him,' the expression on Gideon's face made it clear that he could offer a few suggestions, none of them complimentary, 'made it impossible for Louis Trevelyan to compete in the Olympic qualifiers simply because he exercised his right to reject sponsorship. Had Lord Bassenford had his way, no one would ever have heard of the young man who so comprehensively won gold here today.'

***

The following Sunday, Louis was once again competing in front of a capacity crowd and a massive television audience, this time in the men's floor final. The unsponsored revolution and Louis's unorthodox entry into the Olympic Games had caught the interest of people in free countries everywhere, and viewing figures for the gymnastics had shot to unprecedented highs. Regardless of the world's scrutiny, both Louis and Gideon arrived feeling relaxed and confident, Louis because he still didn't believe he was all that good, Gideon because he knew full well Louis *was* that good.

Enjoying another fiercely contested competition between the best gymnasts in the world, the crowd was wowed by the talent of a Chinese gymnast who took gold with ease, while Louis and a Russian competitor vied for silver. Louis performed his routine with a grin on his face, the leaping and tumbling feeling more like playtime than work, but to Gideon's dismay, he finished with a stumble that cost him execution points. As a result, although his execution and difficulty points together equalled the points scored by the Russian gymnast, he had to make do with bronze.

Louis was rather more coherent following the floor competition than he had been after the all-round final and was happy to face the barrage of questions from the assembled journalists.

'Louis! Louis! How do you feel about missing out on the silver?'

'I was beaten by the better gymnast, simple as.'

'Weren't you expecting to win gold, though?'

Looking mildly surprised at this question, Louis shook his head. 'I wasn't even expecting to qualify,' he replied. Gideon harrumphed loudly and Louis grinned sidelong at him.

'So you're happy with bronze?'

'Delighted,' said Louis, holding his medal out. 'Have a feel. It's heavier than you'd expect...'

'But, Louis... Louis... LOUIS! Don't you think your lack of sponsorship cost you the gold medal today?' This question came from a journalist known to be fiercely pro-Sponsor.

'Losing my balance cost me gold,' replied Louis, laughing out loud as Gideon harrumphed again. 'Sponsorship, however, would cost me my freedom. Way too high a price to pay.'

'But...'

'I don't see any sponsored British gymnasts competing in the finals,' said Gideon before the Sponsor advocate could finish his next question. 'Do you?'

As he watched this interview in his mansion in Kensington, Lord Bassenford's ivory tower started to crumble around him. The Unsponsored were successfully using the Olympics as a publicity platform, and he needed to redress the balance with immediate effect. His fingers flying over his computer keyboard, he booked a block of the best seats in the arena for the gymnastics events due to take place in two days' time then trotted downstairs with a smirk on his face to address the television reporters currently camping out in front of his house.

'Ladies and gentlemen, please would you broadcast this message every half hour across the terrestrial television networks. I wish to make contact with Lysander Trevelyan and Theodore St Benedict. Obviously I appreciate this is a rather unorthodox method of communicating with one's son, but Theodore and his unsponsored friends do prefer to remain aloof. Anyone would think they've got something to hide.'

His Lordship paused for a chuckle.

'My message is simple: I have ten spare tickets for the men's parallel and horizontal bars finals, due to take place in the North Greenwich Arena on Tuesday. I ask for no money in return for these tickets…'

'Which you will have bullied out of someone anyway,' commented Theo, watching the broadcast in Mary's pub with the rest of Dory's Avengers the following afternoon.

'…I ask only that two of the tickets are taken by Theodore and Lysander. I am inviting you to join me to watch Louis Trevelyan compete for gold. Your joy in his success is my joy. Your pride is my pride…'

In the pub, Lysander shook his head in disbelief.

'I would also request that my estranged wife Isabelle and my daughter Marina join me. Lysander, Theodore, I leave you to decide who will benefit from the other six tickets. Please respond via Faye Maloney. Thank you.'

Muting the television, Mary asked what everyone made of the message.

'I think he's trying to put us to shame,' replied Theo. 'Make himself look all magnanimous, and us look churlish if we refuse.'

'What are you going to do?'

'I think there's only one thing for it – we accept. Is that all right with you, Lysander?'

'Absolutely, especially as it means Sarah won't have to miss out now. I take it everyone's happy for Sarah to have one of the remaining tickets?'

When everyone nodded, Sarah smiled her thanks and flicked a jubilant thumbs-up at Gideon.

'Abi and Jenny must go, too,' she said.

'Well, don't forget we've also got the four tickets from Louis,' replied Theo. 'But I agree – if you and Lysander are going to be in the posh seats, it follows that Jenny should be there too. Abi qualifies as she's shagging our favourite gymnast…'

'So crude, Cuz,' murmured Abi.

'I'd like Jess to be there,' said Lysander, blushing slightly.

'Ah, you old devil.' Theo grinned at Lysander, then turned to his mother. 'What about you, Mum? Are you going to take His Lordshit up on his kind invitation?'

'Damn right!' replied Izzy with a laugh. 'Your pride is my pride? I've got to be there to see His Lordshit's face when Louis smashes all records to take gold.'

'I might not get gold,' grumbled Louis, nursing a glass of water while his friends enjoyed beers. Theo didn't even grace Louis's pessimism with a response, instead counting up the people confirmed for tickets on his fingers.

'Right, so that's me, Mum, Abi. Mari?'

'Yes please, Theo.'

'Mari, Lysander, Lysander's fancy piece…'

'Do you want a slap, Theodore?'

'Ooh, yes please, Jess!' Theo winked at Jess then continued to organise the seating plan.

'Jenny, Sarah – so we've got two more tickets, am I right? Plus four in the cheap seats.'

'I think they're quite good seats, actually,' commented Louis.

'Does anyone mind Matty having one of His Lordshit's seats? No? Thank you, everyone.' Dropping a quick kiss on his girlfriend's head, Theo then turned to Max and Catherine.

'How are you two fixed for tickets?'

'I'll be there in an official capacity, Dory me old mate. Managed to blag one of these little beauties.' Max grinned and held up his brand new press pass.

'Cathie?'

'Dad's got us tickets through his company,' replied Catherine shortly, still a bit cool every time she had to speak to Theo.

'One more ticket with His Lordshit then. Alan?'

'Yes, please…'

'What about me?' asked Dex.

'We're cheering on a Brit, sweetie, not one of your mob. Americans can go in the cheap seats.'

'Aw,' said Dex, turning big eyes in Alan's direction, 'don't leave me all alone…'

Finally the seating arrangement was decided. Chris and Georgie would join Alan and Dex in the seats secured by Louis, while Adam, Chloe and Cameron drew lots for the last of those with Lord Bassenford. Adam won the draw, which Gideon reckoned was only fair as he and his parents had done so much to ensure Louis could compete in the first place, but it did leave Cameron a little put out at being the only one of the Blenthwaite Unsponsored not to get a ticket.

'You come and enjoy the day with us, Cameron,' Mary announced, patting his shoulder and handing him a bottle of cold lager. 'This is where the party to end all parties will be tomorrow – even His Lordshit won't be able to accuse us of hiding away then.'

***

The men's parallel and horizontal bars finals took place on the most perfect English summer's day, and Lord Bassenford's welcome as his guests entered the arena was as warm as the sunshine outside. Playing the part of the benevolent host to perfection, he smiled effusively at the Unsponsored as they took their seats while the press photographers circled around, waiting to capture every moment of his reunion with Isabelle.

'William,' she said coolly, pulling away as he leant forward to kiss her. 'You're looking well.'

'And you're looking beautiful, Isabelle.'

'Incredible, really – you'd think the strain of being exiled from my children would have taken its toll. You'd think the pain of finding that my estranged husband had imprisoned and tortured our son would have shown around the eyes. No, William, I won't sit next to you. I think it would be prudent for me to sit as far away from you as possible, actually.'

Stung by Isabelle's words, Lord Bassenford watched her join Marina and Theo at the far end of his row of seats, surprised to find himself feeling a little envious of the loving relationship the three of them clearly shared.

'Pull yourself together, man,' he muttered as Faye sat down beside him.

'Everything OK, Your Lordship?' she asked.

'Couldn't be better,' he replied with a beaming smile, regaining his composure and looking appreciatively at Faye's long, slim legs clad in tight jeans. Lord Bassenford decided there and then to launch a charm offensive on her as the day progressed – hot weather always made him feel frisky, and her thigh pressing against his was causing his sap to rise higher than ever.

'Hi, Faye,' said Matilda on her way past, her skirt barely covering the essentials, and Lord Bassenford's thoughts descended into some positively lascivious mother and daughter fantasies.

'Hi, Matilda,' replied Faye. 'Where's your father?'

'He's over there.' Matilda pointed to where Alan and Dex were people-watching and laughing together. 'Why, do you want to swap places with Dex? Because you can't.'

'Thank you, Matilda, I know where I stand in your father's affections.'

'Dexter looks well,' boomed Lord Bassenford unexpectedly.

'Yes, Your Lordshit,' said Matilda. 'It's amazing the difference a couple of weeks without being beaten up can make. Now, if you'll both excuse me, I'm off to join people I actually like.'

'Your daughter's very outspoken, Faye,' commented Lord Bassenford, watching as Matilda straddled Theo's lap and kissed him hungrily. 'And a bit of a man-eater too, by the looks of it.'

'Can't think where she gets either trait from,' replied Faye with a flirtatious grin, running her fingers up the inside of His Lordship's thigh.

Oh yes, he thought, *today's shaping up to be most satisfactory.*

***

By the time the parallel bars final came around, Gideon was thoroughly fed up with Louis's nerves. Realising that his friends expected him to win gold, probably breaking the world record score he'd set less than a week earlier, the gymnast had spent the entire day jittering and biting his nails, paying so little regard to the horizontal bar final going on at the same time that he almost jumped out of his skin when he heard his name echo around the arena.

'Competing for Great Britain and Northern Ireland – Louis Trevelyan!'

'Go on,' hissed Gideon, shoving the dazed Louis in the back. Stumbling forward, almost losing his balance, wasn't the best way to start an artistic gymnastics final in the Olympic Games, Louis thought wryly as he fixed a smile on his face and acknowledged the judges. It didn't do him any harm, though; having had no time to get nervous about this event, he executed his routine flawlessly and landed with perfect balance – no rogue wobble to spoil the day this time.

Taking his seat next to Gideon again, Louis was happy to accept a drink of water and his mentor's feedback, all of which was positive for once. When the judges' score came through, putting Louis firmly at the top of the leader board, the crowd roared its approval, and even Gideon couldn't resist giving Louis a round of applause. The final contestant on the horizontal bar, a superb Dutch gymnast, gave them a moment of concern, his routine being by far the most complex of the day – so impressive that Louis caught Gideon making notes – but in the end it didn't matter. In a reversal of the contest for silver in the floor event, it was Louis who came out on top, his perfect execution of his routine more than making up for the lesser complexity.

Thinking this triumph would be enough to settle Louis's nerves, Gideon was dismayed to see the young man gnawing at his fingernails once again as the parallel bars final progressed.

'What the hell is wrong with you, Louis? You've already nailed one gold today, and this is your strongest discipline by far. What makes you think you're going to screw it up?'

'It's the Olympics, that's what,' snapped Louis. 'Slightly different to your studio in Blenthwaite.'

'Well, pretend you're there…'

'Bit difficult when I've got to wear these stupid tinted goggles because the flipping lights are on full beam.'

'Oh, stop moaning. You're up next. You can do it, Louis. For your mother, for Abi, for everyone who loves you. Including me…'

'For God's sake, don't get all sentimental on me now, Gid.'

'Get out there, show me the performance of your life, and…'

'*Don't call me Gid!*' mocked Louis, grinning at his mentor then stepping forward to tumultuous applause as his name was announced.

Louis did exactly as Gideon had asked. Not only did he break his own world record, he smashed it to smithereens. When he sprang from the bars at the end of his routine, a deafening cheer exploded all around the arena, the spectators leaping to their feet as one just as they had done after his all-round triumph. Punching the air in delight as he turned towards Lord Bassenford's seats, where his nearest and dearest were leaning over the barriers and screaming their appreciation, Louis knew exactly what he had achieved – the ridiculously high score, when it was finally announced, was almost superfluous as Gideon had already given his verdict.

'That was a perfect ten!' he yelled in delight, wheeling himself over to celebrate with the ecstatic Louis, his chair already bedecked with a huge British flag. 'Never mind these new-fangled scores – that was a perfect ten if ever there was one.'

As Louis raised the flag above his head and soaked up the rapturous applause of the predominantly British crowd, Lysander and Abi pushed their way down to engulf him and Gideon in hugs.

'Amazing,' said Lysander breathlessly, holding on to his son's shoulders, his voice hoarse. 'You are… amazing, Louis. I am… so proud… of you.'

'And I'm pretty damn proud of you too, Dad,' Louis replied, close to tears. 'I just wish Mam could have been here with us today.'

Before Lysander could reply, Abi slipped her arms around Louis's waist and said, 'She'll know, Lou. Somehow, she'll know.'

'And your father will know too, Abi,' added Gideon. 'He'd have suspected, all those years ago when he introduced a gifted little boy to a bitter and crippled gymnast, that one day it would lead to this. Sport *always* won with Elliot.'

***

Returning to the seats to watch his son presented with gold – twice – Lysander was a little dismayed to find the only spare place was next to Lord Bassenford, Faye having decided to join her daughter to celebrate Louis's triumph.

'You must be a very happy man, Lysander,' observed His Lordship as the last notes of the National Anthem died away for the second time and a beaming Louis turned a full circle on the podium to acknowledge the adulation of his fans. 'I have to hand it to your unsponsored son, he's a genius on those parallel bars.'

Lysander, his attention fixed on his son, didn't reply, but His Lordship carried on regardless.

'His mother was quite a talented gymnast in her day, I believe. What a shame Nicola couldn't be here to share this moment…'

'You, Your Lordshit, are the last person I'd want to talk to about Nikki,' snapped Lysander, turning to Lord Bassenford in contempt. 'Actually, you're the last person I'd want to talk to about anything.'

Lysander stood to make his way from Lord Bassenford's seats, pausing in front of his former boss and looking him straight in the eye.

'It's over, Your Lordshit. It's finished, this Sponsorship regime of yours, and I for one am glad. Leaving your employ was the best move I ever made. Earlier on, that breathtakingly talented gymnast who is also my son told me he's proud of me. A year ago, when I was a Sponsor, he didn't want to know me. Tell me, Your Lordshit – when was the last time *your* son said that he's proud of you?'

Watching Lysander walk away, Lord Bassenford found himself dwelling on the parting shot about Theo. When *was* the last time Theo had declared himself proud of his father? Had he *ever* declared himself proud of his father?

'Theodore,' called His Lordship, suddenly anxious to have a word with his son. Seeing Theo and Matilda making for the exit with their friends, he hurried after them.

'Theodore. Theodore, wait…'

As Theo turned in response to his name being called, Lord Bassenford was dismayed to find his path blocked by a number of official-looking people, one of whom he recognised as Charlie Rollins.

'Get out of my way!' he snapped. 'I'm trying to speak to my son…'

'William St Benedict?'

'You know full well who I am!'

'William St Benedict, you are under arrest for serious violations of human rights, for kidnapping, for false imprisonment, for torture…'

The government man continued to list the charges against Lord Bassenford, advising him of his rights as other officials snapped handcuffs on his wrists and bundled him past a legion of journalists, television cameras and the crowds exiting the arena. Helping him into a waiting seven-seater car surrounded by several police motorcyclists, his guards then got in all around him, cutting off any escape routes he may have been contemplating. Dazed by the unexpected downturn in his fortunes, Lord Bassenford raised his eyes from the shackles around his wrists and looked hopelessly through the car window at his last sight of freedom, his stricken gaze meeting his son's incredulous one.

'Theodore,' he mouthed, 'help me.'

It was then that the significance of the moment impacted on Theo's brain. Head held high, a triumphant smile spreading over his face, he mouthed, 'No' and compounded Lord Bassenford's misery with a cheeky wink.

'Earth to Dory,' said Matilda, slipping an arm round Theo's waist and grinning up at him. 'Are you still with us?'

'It's all right, darling,' added Izzy. 'It's over.'

'In quite spectacular fashion,' said Abi, pointing towards the huge crowd of journalists, Max very much in evidence, surging around as the government vehicles gradually moved away. 'Shall we get to our transport before that lot turn their attention to us?'

'Good idea, young lady,' said Faye, still tagging along behind her daughter and the Blenthwaite Unsponsored.

'You're coming with us, are you, Faye?' asked Dex with a laugh. 'I guess your job's a goner now.'

'I guess it is, Dex,' said Faye, laughing too. 'Matilda tells me the band's doing a gig in Louis's honour tonight. Would anyone object to me coming along?'

'Fine with us,' replied Lysander. 'It's the unsponsored way to give everyone a fair chance. The gig's in an unsponsored pub though, Faye.'

'Not a problem,' said Faye. 'As Dex so rightly pointed out, I'm probably an unsponsored Sponsor now. Are you sure you're all right, Theodore?'

'Absolutely,' replied Theo, finally tearing his eyes away from the government vehicles and grinning at Faye. 'Did that really just happen?'

'What, did Father really get arrested and bundled into a car in handcuffs?' said Marina. 'Yes, that happened, Theo. Poor Father...'

'I don't believe you said that, Mari! At least he's going to get a fair trial before he's locked away. Personally, I hope he rots.'

'I thought it was the unsponsored way to give everyone a fair chance...'

'He's the exception to the rule, Faye,' replied Theo. 'There aren't enough days between now and the end of time for him to redeem himself. Come on, let's get into the minibus.'

As everyone climbed into the transport, provided yet again by the super-supportive Philip Lorimer, his wife Simone drew up alongside, the roof of her Range Rover down and Gideon by her side.

'We would have left earlier,' said Gideon, laughing as Sarah squeezed in beside him, 'but Louis took for ever to cream up.'

'Sun block,' said Louis, waving a tube of the precious ointment from beneath his huge sunhat, 'is my friend.'

Following Sarah's lead, Abi left the minibus and leapt into the back of Simone's Range Rover with Louis.

'Anyone else?' Simone asked, chuckling.

'Wait for us!' called Theo, grabbing Matilda's hand. 'Better go now, Simone,' he added, squeezing into the back of her car, 'world's media approaching fast…'

Philip drove the minibus away slowly and Simone followed, the press photographers snapping away frantically as the Range Rover moved through the crowds. Louis and Theo climbed on to the backs of their seats and turned to face the media, ignoring Simone mumbling half-heartedly about safety and seatbelts.

'Lord Theodore! Louis!' yelled the journalists, running after the Range Rover. 'Lord Theodore, how do you feel about your father's arrest? What do you think is the future of the Scheme? What's next for you, Louis?'

'I think His Lordship is finally reaping what he sowed,' replied Theo, laughing as Matilda sang, 'No future,' Sex Pistols-style in response to the journalist's question about the Scheme.

'Champagne is next for me,' Louis told the journalists, turning to his mentor and adding, 'If you'll allow me that luxury, Gideon?'

'I'd allow you to call me Gid tonight, Louis,' replied Gideon, his face wreathed in smiles, 'I'm that proud of you.'

'I will be milking that, *Gid*,' said Louis. 'I keep on thinking I'll wake up in a minute back in your studio…'

'With Gideon yelling at you for sleeping when you should be training,' added Theo, chuckling. 'I keep thinking I'm going to wake up in a minute still locked in His Lordshit's house.'

'Well, you won't,' said Matilda, smiling up at Theo. 'Ever again. Things really couldn't get any better, Dory babes. His Lordshit's regime is over, the sun's shining…'

'That's a good thing?' asked Louis, pulling his sunhat over his eyes.

'We're off to see an amazing band…'

'With a hot lead singer,' said Theo, winking at Matilda.

'And celebrate these babies,' added Gideon, turning round to dangle Louis's two gold medals in front of the youngsters.

'Do you reckon pole-dancing will ever be an Olympic sport, Lou?' asked Matilda. 'I quite fancy winning one of those medals.'

'And I would seriously love to see Gideon training you,' replied Louis, almost falling off his perch with laughter.

'So, shall we call this the best day ever?' Theo asked.

'Aye,' replied Matilda, reaching up to high-five him, 'it most definitely is.'

The mood around the UK became increasingly jubilant as the weight of the Sponsors' oppression lifted, strangers everywhere putting aside their inhibitions and hugging each other spontaneously, their joy compounded by news bulletins showing footage of Lord Bassenford's thugs being rounded up and arrested, the loathsome Stephen Dyer sobbing like a baby as he was led away in handcuffs. Even the weather joined in with the celebrations, the sun continuing to shine down on the newly liberated country and the fair-haired young man who had always been destined to play a leading role in the downfall of the Sponsorship Scheme.

'Well, it wasn't *just* me, was it?' said Louis suddenly.

'Wasn't just you what?' asked Abi.

'It wasn't just me who defeated the Sponsors, like Mr O'Reilly predicted. It was Dory's Avengers and all the Unsponsored...'

'True,' said Abi, grabbing one of the gold medals from Gideon and hanging it round Louis's neck, 'but no one can deny that you're the star of the day.'

Simone parked up outside Mary's pub and a deliriously happy crowd surged out, chanting Louis's name and soaking the Range Rover passengers with champagne. Hands reached out and a protesting Louis was hoisted on to the crowd's shoulders, Sarah only just managing to prevent the exuberant Unsponsored from doing the same with Gideon. As Theo helped Sarah manoeuvre Gideon into the safety of his wheelchair, Louis resigned himself to his fate, smiling and shaking eager hands as he was borne aloft into the pub, the popping of an indecent number of champagne corks and a raucous chorus of *Louie Louie*, almost as incoherent as the original, greeting his arrival.

'Come on, Matty,' said Abi, grinning at Matilda. 'Let's get some of that bubbly before Louis ends up wearing it all.'

The pub was in absolute chaos. A noisy mass of people thronged around, packing themselves in even more tightly to make room for Gideon's wheelchair to pass, their feet sticking to the tacky champagne- and confetti-covered floor. Party popper streamers were draped everywhere – over the drinkers; the band's equipment; the television screen which was currently showing a rerun of Lord Bassenford's arrest – but of Louis there was no sign.

'Where the heck is he?' Theo yelled in Abi's ear.

'No idea,' she yelled back, shrugging. 'I hope that bunch of pissheads didn't drop him.'

A clearly drunk Cameron squeezed himself through the revellers, bare chested, a large British flag tied round his waist.

'Abzlene,' he slurred, hugging his sister. 'Sh-just fabuloush.'

'I'm guessing Mary was right about you lot having the party to end all parties here today,' Abi said, laughing.

'Sh-brilliant,' replied Cameron, staggering backwards and clapping an arm round Theo's shoulders. 'Theo, Cuz, Hish Lordshit not gonna hurt you any more.' Wagging a finger in Theo's face for added emphasis, Cameron repeated, 'Not any more. He bin arreshted.'

'I know,' said Theo with a grin, extracting himself from his cousin's drunken embrace. 'I saw it. Live.'

Cameron staggered again, an equally drunk Chloe weaving into his path just in time to stop him from collapsing on Gideon's lap.

'Gideon,' she chirped, swaying precariously and clutching on to his wheelchair for support. 'Olympic world gold record, shamazing. Louis'shamazing.'

'Absolutely,' agreed Gideon, his relief palpable when Sarah manoeuvred his chair out of the drunken youngsters' way to join Isabelle and Jenny in a relatively quiet corner of the pub.

'So where is Louis?' asked Abi. 'Cameron? Chloe? Anyone know?'

'Shover there.' Cameron waved a hand vaguely in the direction of the pub's stage then pulled Chloe towards him and landed a kiss on her forehead. 'Chlo, you're beautiful. Fanshy a fuck?'

'Mmm,' replied Chloe, lifting her face for a drunken snog before she and Cameron staggered off and disappeared into the crowd.

Theo and Abi roared with laughter.

'If he can raise anything more than a smile tonight,' Theo said as Matilda, bearing two bottles of champagne, rejoined them, 'he's a better man than I am.'

'Oh, I seriously doubt that,' replied Matilda with a wink.

'Come on,' said Abi, relieving Matilda of one of the bottles, 'let's find Louis.'

Astonishingly, Cameron had been right. Abi, Theo and Matilda found a soaking wet Louis sitting next to his father on the stage in front of Max's bass drum. Plonking herself down on his other side, Abi wrapped her arms around him and attempted to pull him close.

'I'm a bit sticky,' he warned, resisting. 'God knows how much champagne I've had tipped over me in the last ten minutes or so.' Lifting a bottle still containing some of the precious liquid to his lips, he drank it down appreciatively then added, 'Tastes mighty fine after all these weeks of abstinence.'

'I don't care how sticky you are,' insisted Abi, redoubling her efforts to pull Louis into a cuddle. 'You're the man I love and I want to hold you.'

This time Louis didn't resist, instead wrapping his arms around Abi and burying his face in her hair.

'What are you doing hiding away in the corner, Lou?' asked Matilda, perching with Theo on the edge of the stage. 'You're the hero of the day...'

As if to illustrate her point, the pub television blared out the sport headlines.

'Top story from the Olympics,' it boomed, 'British gymnast Louis Trevelyan completely obliterates his own world record score to take his second gold of the day on the parallel bars...'

The Unsponsored in the pub roared their approval as Louis's performance was replayed. The gymnast himself buried his face further into his girlfriend's hair.

'He's a bit overwhelmed,' said Lysander, rubbing his son's back. 'This time last year, he'd never been further from home than Kendal...'

'Until a certain voice from the past called out to him for help,' said Theo, taking a good gulp of champagne then tapping Louis lightly with the bottle. 'Here you go, Lou. I always find champers helps when you're a bit overwhelmed.'

Louis looked up at his friend. 'Cheers, Dory,' he said with a slight smile, taking the bottle and swigging it back. 'Talking of overwhelmed, are you OK? I'm not the one whose father was arrested earlier.'

'He's not my father, Lou. He forfeited that right many years ago.'

'You really feel nothing for him? Nothing about his arrest?'

'Only relief that it's all over.' Sighing, Theo took the bottle of champagne Louis was handing back to him and drank deeply before continuing. 'After he shut me away, I spent – oh, it must have been the first two years waiting for him to come up to my room, tell me it had all been a mistake, tell me he loved me. But he never did. So I gave up. Quite frankly, I feel like my father died when I was a child and some vile imposter called William St Benedict took his place. I did my grieving long ago, so now I'm feeling nothing but relief, happiness and pride. Today's all about you, Louis.'

'That it is,' said Abi, turning Louis's face to hers and kissing him.

'Sod this!' said Matilda, never one to have much patience with sombre moments. 'Are you ready to rock, Lou?'

'Hell yeah, Matty, more than ready,' Louis replied, his face breaking into a huge grin. Fishing a pound coin from her bag, Matilda trotted over to the jukebox, typed in a search then flicked a triumphant thumbs-up at her friends. As the first bars of *Rockin' in the Free World* rang out across the pub, Mary muted the television, which had been showing a potted history of the Sponsorship Scheme to a soundtrack of boos and hisses, and the Unsponsored responded to Matilda's choice by singing along raucously, another batch of party poppers sending colourful streamers sailing over them. Rejoining Theo, Louis and Abi on the stage, Matilda pulled them to their feet for an enthusiastic rendition of the song's chorus, Lysander electing to remain sitting in the shadows, clicking his fingers and soaking up a moment of uninhibited joy he'd never have believed possible in his Sponsor days.

'Come on, guys, jump!' yelled Max, pushing his way with Adam to the front of the floor and holding his hands up to his friends on the stage.

'Jump! Jump!' agreed the Unsponsored all around, following Max's lead.

'Jump, guys,' called Dex, struggling through the crowd with the rest of Dory's Avengers, the opportunist Faye taking advantage of the mass of people to sidle over and press herself against Alan.

Sliding off the stage, Lysander added his encouragement. 'Jump, Lou,' he shouted, raising both hands in readiness then lowering one to sneak an arm round Jess's waist as she appeared at his side.

'Shall we?' said Louis, looking at Theo, Abi and Matilda.

'Try stopping me!' replied Matilda, taking a rock 'n' roll leap of faith and crowd surfing across the room.

'I'm so glad she put knickers on this morning,' murmured Theo as the people below him enjoyed an unrestricted view up his girlfriend's skirt.

'C'mon,' she yelled, reaching the bar and sitting on top of it, a full bottle of champagne held aloft. 'Come to Matty, Theo – you know you want to!'

'Shall we?' asked Louis again, taking Abi's hand.

'Try stopping me,' replied Theo, echoing Matilda's words as he grinned over at her. 'On a count of three – one… two… three…'

With a rebel yell, the young man who had suffered more than anyone at the hands of Lord Bassenford grabbed hold of his cousin and his best friend – the man who had first brought hope back into his life a year earlier – and dived into the welcoming arms of the Unsponsored.

About the Author

 Following a lengthy spell of full-time employment with a Cambridge based publishing company, Alison Jack took a year off in 2012 to write her debut novel, *Dory's Avengers*. While working with her editor on the first edition, she discovered a love and natural aptitude for editing, which led to the launch of her business Alison's Editing Service in January 2014. Once her contract with her original publisher had come to an end, Alison decided to use the skills she'd amassed and give her own novel an extensive structural edit with a view to self-publishing a much improved second edition of *Dory's Avengers* in 2016.

Alison enjoys a number of hobbies and interests when not reading, writing or editing, including fell walking, wakeboarding, playing guitar (badly), listening to music (played well) and watching football, golf and horse racing. She currently lives in a beautiful village on the outskirts of Cambridge with her partner Andy and two cats.

Author photograph taken by Bruce Felstead

Printed in Great Britain
by Amazon

61576655R00385